T0367523

Cracks in the Wall

J. MORRIS LAVALLEE

authorHOUSE®

AuthorHouse™
1663 Liberty Drive
Bloomington, IN 47403
www.authorhouse.com
Phone: 1-800-839-8640

Published by AuthorHouse 01/22/2015

ISBN: 978-1-4969-5698-9 (sc)
ISBN: 978-1-4969-5697-2 (e)

Contents

Chapter One

The early morning sun rose over the Washington Monument, bringing to life a city engulfed in its crime, politicians, diplomats and statues to its heroes, leaders and legends. It's very hard to believe that the average person still plays a part in any of it anymore.

But today will be different. A man standing alone at the Viet Nam Veteran's Memorial Wall will change that for himself and another man, who doesn't know he even exists.

Two security guards were making their rounds and had logged the same man standing in the same place for hours. After 9/11, everybody in that city was a suspect. Having been there for most of the night, they would have to look into it. Evans, a security guard with the Parks & Recreation Department for thirty-five years -- having gone to work himself after returning from Viet Nam -- was used to talking to vets at the Wall.

Just another one of us, can't get that damn war out of his head.

Evans drove up to the stranger in his golf cart to see if there was any need to watch this guy.

"Excuse me, are you all right?"

The stranger just stood staring at the Wall like Evans wasn't even there. He was dressed only in a sweatshirt, jeans, field jacket and jump boots, hair to his shoulders and a 4-5 days' growth on his face. For some reason, Evans didn't get the feeling this guy was dangerous, and after all the years he'd been doing this, he hoped today he wasn't wrong. Evans pulled his tazer from its pouch in case anything happened. Again he asked,

"Are you okay?"

Just then the stranger slowly turned his head towards Evans.

"Do you have any idea which one it is?"

"What?"

"What is the name? I can't find it, it's not here."

"Are you a vet?"

"No. I am dead."

With that, Evans called for backup. The stranger turned his head back to the Wall and continued to mumble. A few minutes later, three more guards arrive to assist. Evans knew the guy needed some help. Whenever they got somebody like this, you never know how it was going to turn out. Evans told the others what was going on, that he tried to talk to the stranger and got no answer, except that *he was looking for something and that he was dead.*

"He didn't break any law, and if he doesn't want to go, we can't force him."

Evans's sergeant said he would call the Metro to stand by just in case there was a problem. Evans asked the sergeant if that was necessary.

"Look, Evans, I *know* you've got a soft spot for these nuts, but get him off the site and do it *now*."

"Sarge, let me talk to him…"

"*No*, he's been standing there for hours - that we know of."

"…the guy hasn't done anything to haul him off."

"Look, I don't *need* a reason; Homeland Security gives me all the reasons I need."

"Sarge?"

"Look Evans, we got a group of visiting dignitaries from Israel coming through at ten, and I don't want anything going wrong, do you understand? Now get it *done*."

"Sarge…"

"You have your orders!"

With that, the sergeant left just as the Metro showed up. Evans briefed the two officers and they took over. Evans figured he'd stay to see how it would turn out. He'd seen his sergeant deal with vets like this before. He didn't like it, but there wasn't much he could do. His retirement was coming up. The fact was, the sergeant was a prick that didn't care about Viet Nam vets that were still having a hard time after all these years.

Well, the Metro boys did their job, just like they always do.

The stranger was taken away handcuffed and headed for the psych ward downtown. Evans sat in his golf cart, hoping the stranger would be all right. As he rode off, he mumbled under his breath, *"Fucking war."*

As they pulled into the emergency entrance of the VA Hospital, Peter came alive and violent.

"You bastards aren't going to put me back in there again, I'll kill you. Oh, no, not again! I'm not going back, not this time!"

He kicked the separation screen and began screaming. The officers pulled to a stop and tried to calm him down. One officer ran inside to get help with him. The officer told the desk attendant he had a hot one and needed some help to put him out before they had to tazer him. The officer ran back out to assist his partner. Peter had managed to break out the side window, and being a big man, six two and weighing two sixty or more, there was blood all over the window and on the side of the car and on Peter. The ER attendant came running out and screamed at the officer holding Peter down against the side of the car,

"HOLD HIM UNTIL I CAN HIT HIM WITH A SLEEPER OF HALDOL!"

Both officers managed to hold him down.

"God *damn*, this guy is tough!"

In a few minutes after that the Haldol was kicking in. The officers could ease up while the attendants got him on a stretcher. By now he was limp, drooling and manageable. One officer radioed in to say they had made the transfer then and they would be down for a cleanup. The ER doctor had Peter in full restraints to make sure he stayed calm.

"With all the Haldol in him he should be out for days."

They checked his vitals and cleaned up his minor cuts and shipped him upstairs to psych.

Three days later Peter woke up, not being able to move, with a hangover from hell and no idea how he got there.

As he opened his eyes all the fear, rage and anger spilled out in a scream and lunge that would bend the bars on the bed and wake the entire ward. As he exhaled he fell back, and again three more times till he was out of breath. Nurse Webster came running in to see if he was all right she knew he could not break the straps that were holding him. She had seen patrons coming off a long period of sedation come out this way, but this was as primal as she'd heard in a very long time.

"Mr. Davies, can you hear me? I'm Nurse Webster, my first name is Carol. Can you hear me? You're going to be all right, you're going to be all right. You had a rough time the last two or three days, but you're safe now. I know the restraints are not comfortable; it was for your safety. We'll get them off as soon as we can."

Peter opened his eyes slowly and saw her standing over him; he whispered hoarsely: "I'm thirsty, I'm thirsty."

Carol Webster gave him a few sips and a few seconds later she gave him some more. He was starting to wake up.

After a few sips of water he could speak, so the nurse could hear him. She was a woman in her forties with blond shoulder length hair with too much eye shadow and perfume from some clearance sale; not hard to look at, but she seemed a little hard edged. Although his thoughts were scrambled and the last thing he thought he remembered was seeing John Jacobs' name on the Wall, and that couldn't, it just couldn't...

Could it be the same guy? God, he hoped not.

He knew he wasn't going to tell anyone, anyway.

"Could you tell me how I got here?"

"You were brought in three days ago after a run-in with the law."

"The law...what are you talking about?"

"Doctor Brown will let you know when he comes later."

Peter was getting a little agitated but knew he'd better not let the nurse know.

"OK, so where am I?"

"In the VA Hospital, in downtown DC."

"Would it be possible to take these straps off?"

5

"All right, but remember, they can go back on just as quick."

She was OK with taking off the hand straps, but for now she would keep the legs and feet the way they were.

"Nurse, I *need* to use the bathroom."

"I'll have the orderly come in and help you with that."

"Look, I need to see the doctor as soon as I can."

"He'll be here when he gets here. Besides, you're not going anywhere, anyhow."

Peter thought to himself, *what a bitch*, as the door closed and she was gone. His mind was racing almost out of control. *Now* what could he have done, did anyone know about Jacobs…*if the fucking orderly doesn't get in here quick I'm going to piss myself, Jesus, where's my van, my clothes, my money, what the hell did I do this time…*

He hadn't had a blackout since he quit drinking twelve years ago…

God damn, I'm going to piss myself…

He started to holler just as the orderly came in, just in time to hear Peter swearing.

"Hang on, buddy, we'll get you hooked up."

He had a urine bottle that he passed to Peter. Seeing his hands were not strapped down, he could relieve himself without any help from the orderly.

"God damn, that feels better."

But it would be a lot better if he could get out of this bed and get out of here.

What shit did I get into this time; I thought that shit was all behind me.

He had long since put that time in the mountains of Laos behind him, and Jacobs…no one could ever know. He would take it to his grave. He was starting to get agitated and it seemed like days had gone by, but he knew it was just anxiety. By now he got to move around enough to be able to sit up in bed, even though his legs were still strapped down. The thought entered his mind, *could he get the leg straps off and get out of here without anyone knowing?* Managing to reach over with his left hand, he found the clasp and started to try to get it off the bar, just as the door opened.

"Hi, I'm Dr. Brown, and you must be Houdini. You're wasting your time. They hook from the bottom, so what you're trying to do will just frustrate you more."

"Ok, my turn. What the fuck am I doing strapped to this bed with a hangover from hell and you making jokes?"

Dr. Brown walked over and got a chair and sat down. Prescott Brown was a man in his fifties, about the same age as Peter, with thinning blond hair. He had a slight build with pale blue eyes, and seemed to dress out of a Brook's Brothers catalogue.

"OK, fair enough, I'll take off the straps."

Peter sat up, trying to get some feeling in his legs.

"Where are my clothes and my van keys?"

"Your clothes are in the closet and your keys are with the Metro police."

With that, Peter took a deep breath and looked at Dr. Brown for a long time before asking, "*What happened?*"

"I don't know. I was hoping you could tell me."

"Doc, the last thing I remember was stopping at the Wall to get an etching for a friend back home whose brother got killed in the Tet Offensive. The next thing I'm in here."

7

"OK, look, let's start over. The Metro brought you in three days ago after the Parks people had noticed you standing there talking to yourself."

"So, talking to myself is a crime?"

"No, I don't know if talking to yourself is a crime, but when you do it for thirty-six hours in the same place and in public, there might be something wrong with you. All they were trying to do was help."

"OK, I'm good with that, why do the police have my keys?"

"They brought you from downtown."

"Could you get me something for this headache, my body feels like it got run over by a *truck*."

"Let me finish telling you how you got here, and then I'll get you something for your headache. You gave them no trouble until you got into the parking lot of the hospital, and then for some reason, you decided to trash the back of their car. It took three of us and two of them to put you to sleep. That's where the hangover comes from, and the cuts and bruises come from you trashing the back of the car. They pumped enough Haldol into you to knock out three horses."

"Look, doc, I have an idea what might have happened. It could have been too much coffee or too much stress."

"Have you been doing any drugs, drinking?"

"Don't you people ever *look* at your records? I've been clean and sober for twelve years. It's all in your files, the answer is *no*, I have not been doing any drugs or drinking."

"Your files show you had some drug problems while you were in the Navy, and you spent some time with the Marine Corps."

"Yeah, they needed somebody to polish the brass there. Big on that, you know."

"Well, this is getting us nowhere. I would ask you to stay so we can help you with these blackouts but I can't keep you here more than seventy-two hours, and you've already passed that. I'll get the nurse to do up the paperwork to hand you over to the Metro."

"Metro?"

"Yes, the Metro police. You did about three thousand dollars worth of damage to their car, as well as tearing their uniforms. If they had their way, they'd have you right now. The only way you're not going to jail is if you stay here and let us try to help you get to the bottom of what's going on with you."

"If that's the only option I've got, I guess I'll stay here."

"I think you're doing the right thing. Look, I'll be back tomorrow and we'll talk some more. In the meantime, the nurse will have some forms for you to sign."

"Yeah, what are they?"

"Some for the police to say you're here voluntarily for treatment and the others are to allow us to treat you. Look, if there's anything you might need, see Nurse Webster. Her bark is worse than her bite. She's a good nurse and a real pro, she's seen it all. See you tomorrow."

With that the doctor left.

A few minutes later, Peter tried to stand up and fell over. Nurse Webster walked in just in time to see him picking himself up off the floor.

"Are you all right?"

"Yeah. A few days in bed will do that to ya."

"Are you sure you're all right?"

"If being locked up in this place is the right thing, yeah, I'm all right."

He sat back on the edge of the bed.

"Did Doctor Brown tell you about some paperwork you need to sign?"

"Yeah."

A few minutes later Nurse Webster came back with the paperwork for him to sign. He scribbled his name on them and passed them back to her.

Then she asked, "Would you like to get cleaned up?"

"Yeah. I need a shower and maybe something to eat. I'm starving."

"I'll have Travis get you hooked up with a shower and something to eat."

"Would it be all right if I sat by the window?"

"I don't see why not. Well, there *is* a small problem. You need help to get there."

"I guess my legs aren't working yet."

"Not a problem, that's what we're here for."

She helped him to the window and he sat down.

"Look, keep working your legs back and forth and the strength will come back. I'll send in Travis."

With that, she left.

The view from the window was not the best; a few buildings, a huge parking lot and the highway. The sun was just going down, a time of day that had always made him feel alone and being alone was something he knew well. So very well.

Some time later Travis came in with clothes, towels and some bathroom supplies.

"Hey, bro, are you ready to get cleaned up?"

"Yeah."

"Look, I've got some things I thought you might need, toilet things, you know, and some clean clothes. Those have to be getting pretty ripe by now."

"Yeah, ripe is the word."

"After you get cleaned up they're sending in some supper for you. I told the kitchen you were a big guy and hadn't had anything for days, so they're going to send two trays. Look, I've got to go with you while you get cleaned up. It's not my rules, it's Doc Brown's order. He just wants to keep an eye on you, and I'm it. I've been doing this so long that you won't even know I'm here."

Peter just kind of smiled.

"That's the way to go. Keep doing that and you'll be out of here in no time. Look, if there's anything I can do for you that will make your stay with us easier, let me know."

"OK."

"Hell, you might even get to like me. My wife would disagree with that, but she's not here, thank God."

Peter just shook his head and smiled.

"Come on, bro, let's get you hooked up."

They left the room and entered the hall. There were people all over the place - nurses, doctors, patients. For some reason he could not look anyone in the eyes, so he put his head down and his new friend led the way. When they got to the shower, Travis turned one on.

"Let it run for a while, it will be easier to regulate the heat that way."

Peter took his time, seeing he had not been out of that room in what seemed like years. It was good to just move around a bit. His legs were still sore, but at least he could feel them again.

Though the washroom wasn't that big, Travis held to his word -- it was like he wasn't even there. Peter thought maybe he sat on one of the commodes and read the paper or something.

After getting out of the shower and drying off, he was looking in the mirror combing his hair. He was thinking to himself, *they can't know, they just can't know.*

"What's that?" Travis asked.

"What?" Peter asked.

"You said something to me."

"No, no, just thinking out loud."

"Better be careful about that around here, with talking to yourself. When I first got here I did that and they wanted to give me a bed, just kidding. The shower help ya?"

"Sure, yeah, sure."

He wondered if Travis had heard him.

"No big deal. I didn't say anything that meant anything. Besides, I'm crazy, and crazy people talk to themselves all the time. I think I could use that food now."

"Sounds good to me. Let's go."

The clean clothes felt good, and being clean helped, too.

If I've got to be here, God knows how long, I might as well try to make the best of it. Beats jail.

Walking past the nurse's station, Nurse Webster told Peter she had some meds for him.

"What is it?"

"It's just something to help you sleep and calm you down."

"Yeah, sure."

She handed the meds to Travis.

"Make sure he gets these after he eats."

"Ten-four, young lady."

Peter was getting to like Travis. He had a good sense of humor and didn't take himself too seriously.

Back in the room, Peter saw the food and realized how hungry he was. Even hospital food looked good. He sat on the bed and ate everything on both trays. Travis had left.

When Peter was done he went back and sat in the chair, looking out the window.

A few minutes later, Travis returned. Peter asked if there was any way he could get a smoke. Travis got very serious this time.

"That could be tough. Look, I'll try, but don't get your hopes up. I'll be back later."

Travis left.

Peter took his meds and continued looking out the window. While he was getting showered they had changed not only the linen, they changed the whole bed. This one was a lot easier to deal with. No straps.

He fell asleep for a while. When Travis came back he said, "Look, dog, if I help you get a smoke and you skip on me, it's my job and my pension, so give me your word."

They shook hands.

"I've got to take you down to the x-ray department."

"X-rays?"

"No big deal. They're gonna run you though a whole series of tests."

As they walked down the hall to the elevator Peter noticed how quiet it was.

"Where is everyone?"

"Shift change," Travis replied. "That's how we'll get you a smoke, they're all in meetings. Just follow me and don't ask questions, OK?"

"OK."

When they got off the elevator in what seemed to be the cellar, they headed down a long corridor to the morgue.

"The morgue?"

"Yeah, the morgue. It's quiet in there and nobody talks and it's got the best ventilation in the whole place."

Travis turned the lights on and closed the door

I don't have any smokes, they took all my things when I got here.

"Dog, you must be looking for these," and with that, Travis passed Peter his cigarettes and lighter. "When we're done, I'll take those back, 'til next time."

He got Peter an ashtray, and with that they both lit one up. Peter was glad there were no bodies out. He wasn't real good with that sort of thing, never was.

They sat on a stainless steel table and didn't say anything for a few minutes, when Peter broke the silence: "Man, you take a lot of risks. You've only known me for a short time. I'm locked up in a nut ward and as far as you know, I could be a serial killer."

"No, you're not. I've been working here for a lot of years. You've lost something and you're looking for it.

"Yeah, I've lost something all right. Yeah, that's it, you got it. Travis, has anyone ever told you that you look like Ice T?"

"Ice T?"

"You know the guy that plays on that cop show, what is it, criminal intent, SVU?"

"No, and besides the only one I pay attention to on that show is the girl."

"Good call."

"Come on, Pilgrim, we better get to the lab and back down to the ward before they think you killed me or something really fucked up." Travis shook his head and laughed.

After Peter got his blood drawn and gave a urine sample, they headed back. Neither one said anything to the other. Travis broke the silence: "So, tomorrows the big day."

"What the hell are you talking about?"

"Oh, they didn't tell you? Doc Brown will try to get into your head." Travis got very serious. "Doctor Brown is the best we got. He really cares about what happens to his patients. Work with him. If anyone can help you, he can, with the demons in your head."

"Where did you get all this knowledge about demons in my head?"

"Khe Sanh, 1968."

As they got to the ward they stopped at the nurse's station to sign Peter in.

"Good, you're back, it's time for meds."

The nurse looked very familiar. He noticed her name tag, "Webster." Then it all came back -- the day he woke up in his room, tied to his bed. He felt like he was going to faint and started to fall back when Travis caught him, as Webster got a chair for him to sit in.

"What happened? I was standing there, and now I'm sitting here."

"Pilgrim, I think you fainted."

Nurse Webster got him some water and checked his vital signs. Everything was fine.

Peter said, "Maybe all the walking after being in a bed so long had something to do with it."

"Maybe. Let's get you your meds and get you to bed." Travis helped him to his room.

Peter sat on the side of the bed.

"Sleep well, Pilgrim."

"Hey, Travis?"

"Yeah?"

"*What* is going on with me? That never happened to me before."

"Let Doc Brown help, it'll be OK. Get some sleep."

Travis went back to the nurse's station to see what was next. Nurse Webster was waiting for him.

"Did you take him down to have his smoke in the morgue, like all the others?"

"OK, nurse, you're not playing fair."

"Hey, Travis, do you think this one knows that you're Brown's psych P.A.?"

"You know Webster, you need to find a hobby, maybe take up knitting or crossword puzzles…and besides, I don't think he cares. Have a nice night."

With that Travis headed out.

Peter sat there on his bed for a moment, then he decided to go sit in a chair. Looking out the window, he thought to himself, *what a fucking view, a parking lot.* The meds started to kick in and he fell asleep in the chair.

Webster came in some time later and woke him up, and told him to get into his bed, that he'd get a better night's sleep that way. He wasn't in bed too long before he went to sleep.

He woke up the next morning with a headache. He was getting used to them from the meds.

This is no worse than a hangover from drinking for two days.

Just as he sat up, Travis came walking in.

"Hey, Pilgrim, how'd you sleep last night?"

"OK."

"I don't have to follow you around this morning, getting cleaned up and getting around here."

"Let me guess, I can go anywhere except off this floor."

"You got it. Sounds like you've been here before."

"Yeah, you might say that."

"Doctor Brown will be in this morning to see you. I don't know exactly what time, but he'll be in."

"When do you think they'll let me go anywhere I want to go?"

"Well, I guess that really depends on you, now, doesn't it? Look, when the Doc clears you to go around the complex, I'll show you around here. We've got a lounge on this floor with a TV, we've got some books and magazines in there. If there's anything you'd like to read, let me know, and I'll get it from the library."

"Yeah, I know."

"Hell Pilgrim, you *have* been around these places before."

Travis turned and left. Peter got cleaned up, had something to eat and went to sit in the lounge for a while. One TV for ten vets, typical VA. They all want to watch something different, and nobody gives in.

To hell with this, I'll go back to my room.

He went back to the chair and continued staring out the window at the million dollar view. The morning went by and still the doctor hadn't shown up, so after lunch it was back to the window, sitting there. When Doc Brown had come in, Peter saw his reflection in the window and made no notice of him being there. The doctor asked if he would like to talk.

Peter looked over his shoulder and said, "Do I have a choice?"

"Davies, how hard are you going to make this on yourself? OK, if you don't want to talk you have that right, and I have the right to give you back to the Metro. You have to make up your mind. There are lots of patients in here that need help and *won't* fight me every step of the way."

With that the doctor walked out. Peter turned back to the window. A few minutes later Travis came in.

"I was outside the door and heard what Doc Brown said. Look, Pilgrim, if you think the doc is calling your bluff you're wrong. I was across the hall, and overheard what was going on; for Christ's sakes, Davies, give it a try. It beats jail or would that be the easier, softer way out for you?"

"Get the fuck out of here you fucking *arrogant* spic!"

"Have it your way," Travis said, and left.

Peter put his head in his hand, and started to cry.

He felt a hand on his shoulder.

"Give it a try," said the voice, and the hand squeezed. It was Travis.

Peter looked up and said "I'm sorry for what I said to you. My head is so *fucked up*, I can't make sense of anything anymore. I need help and I'm afraid to get it."

"Look Pilgrim, a lot of us have gone through the *same* shit. Before they gave me the job here, I was a patient, and I fought tooth and nail to hold onto those demons we talked about."

"OK, Travis, I'll talk to the doc."

"OK, I'll go get him."

"Again, Travis, I'm sorry for what I said to you."

"Hell, don't let it bother you; my mother-in-law's been calling me things ten times worse for years. I don't listen to her, either." And he left the room.

Peter sat looking out the window, still sobbing. Doctor Brown came walking back into the room.

"Peter, I think you made the right decision. Now, let's see if we can get to the bottom of this."

"Doc, I really don't even know how to start. This is a fucking mess."

"Just start from the beginning, it's usually the best place to start."

"What do you mean, like *childhood*? Is that where you want to start?"

"OK, look. What I like to do sometimes Peter, is just let the patient talk about whatever he wants. There's no right or wrong, there are no tests and no graduation. Just talk to me about what's going on inside your head."

"I've been through all this so many times."

"Well, maybe this will be the last time."

"Maybe you're right."

Peter sat there for a few minutes.

The doctor said, "Why don't you tell me about growing up?"

"I thought after all the work I've done in A.A. it would be behind me by now, but here goes. I come from a large family, there were seven of us, but two have died."

"When they were children?"

"No, they were adults."

"Oh, I see."

"Isn't this the place where you ask me if I was molested as a child?"

"Were you?"

"No, I was ignored."

"Where do you fall in the seven?"

"At the end."

"Tell me about them."

"Who?"

"About your siblings, and where you fit in, I'm interested."

"Well, my older brother is old enough to be my father."

"Does your brother have children?"

"Yeah, five of them. Then brother number two, he's old enough to be my father as well."

"Does that brother have children also?"

"Yeah, five. Brother number three--five kids, sister number four--six kids, sister number five--three kids, sister number six-- four kids, and I have two children."

"Are you close to any of them?"

"Now, that's funny," Peter snickered.

"What do you mean by that?"

"Are you *listening* to me or *what*?"

"Yes."

"I *told* you, they *ignored* me."

"That can mean a lot of things."

"Fuck this. Look, my mother was fucking nuts. My father was either drunk or working. I was born when my folks were in their forties. Hell, my brother and sisters were grown up. I had two sisters living at home, my sister Louise and sister Carmen."

"How did you get along with them?"

"I told you, my mother was crazy. My mother was fucking crazy. If it wasn't for my two sisters at home, I would have had nothing but a mother who was out of her mind, and a father who was not there."

"So they took care of you."

"Yeah, you might say that."

"How were you in school?"

"I sucked. You see, I got up in the morning, if there wasn't anything to eat before school, or there was bad weather coming in, my mother would keep me home."

"Did you go without food a lot?"

Peter just shook his head. "*Yeah, did you?*"

"That seems to make you angry."

"Oh, here we go. *Look*, when I was a kid we would eat good on Friday and Saturday, and maybe Sunday."

"You told me your father worked all the time."

"Yeah, that's right. I keep telling you, my mother was fucking *crazy*."

"But you didn't tell me how."

"My father didn't make a lot of money, and my mother would blow it on junk food and God knows what else. My father would just give in, and maybe he'd had enough of the screaming. He was OK with coming home on Friday and staying drunk 'til Sunday, and sleeping it off all day so he could go back to work on Monday."

"How long did that last? Did it ever change?"

"Yeah, it sure did. It got *worse!*"

"Worse?"

"Yeah, I *said* worse, did I fucking *stutter*?"

"Talking about this seems to be getting you upset. Maybe we should stop for today."

"Look, this was your idea to bring all this bullshit back up, so the least you could give me is the dignity to fucking *listen*."

"OK, let me cancel my other things for this afternoon."

The doctor left for about five minutes and came back.

"OK, you have undivided attention. Let's continue. You said it got worse."

"Yeah. My older brother came to live with us."

"Which one?"

"The third brother and his three kids."

"How did that make it worse?"

"Now we had *two* drunks in the house, one good drunk and one mean one."

"What do you mean, violent?"

"Sometimes. The brother that came to live with us, at times was my hero."

"Why was he your hero?"

"I remember, before he came to live with us, my mother used to talk about how smart he was, and a good fighter and a lady's man, and that he didn't take shit from anyone. I'd never had a male figure in my life to show me things like how to throw a football, or hit a baseball. Oh, yeah, did I also tell you he was a *great* athlete?"

"Well, did he show you these things?"

"No, no, he told me I would never be anywhere near as good as my nephew Charlie."

"Charlie's my older brother's son, who's a few months older then I am. And the reality of it was he was a very good athlete. I was referred to by my brothers as a momma's boy."

"Were you a momma's boy?"

"Well, my older brothers seemed to think so. You know, doc, I don't totally blame them. There were times when my brothers wanted to take me to do things. The problem was, I never knew if my mother would let me go, or not."

"What kind of things?"

"My older brother used to take his kids swimming on hot summer nights down to the local pond. A lot of times they would ask me to go. I never knew 'til the last minute if my mother was going to let me go, or not. A lot of times we'd come right up to the point where they'd come to pick me up, and she would just say, "No, no you can't go, you might drown, you might drown." So, an entire day of hoping to do something fun, and it's all bullshit again."

"How would you react to that?"

Peter got very quiet for a few seconds.

"I'd go climb in my box in the back yard and cry."

"Box? What do you mean, box?"

"There was a marina across the street. The guys used to give me boxes that the outboard motors came in, and some tape, and I'd build forts out of them in the back yard. I'd climb in the box and go off into my own little world."

"Didn't your brother stand up to your mother? For God's sake, he was just taking his kids swimming."

"Doctor, how long have you been a psychiatrist?"

"About thirty years."

23

"I keep *telling* you *over* and *over*, the poor woman was *crazy*. Can you reason with someone who's totally crazy? Besides, my brother knew what kind of hell there'd be to pay, if he did try to argue with her. They gave up, and I went to my box."

"Did you have any idea when these things were going to happen?"

"*Heh, heh.* Ah, do you have any idea when it's going to rain?"

"So, let me get this right, now. So, they're nine people living in your house, and before they got there, there was barely enough food for who was there. Did your brother work?"

"I remember the first winter he was with us. I think he was on unemployment or something."

"It must have been pretty rough, then."

"Yeah, it was rough all right. But thanks to the church and the Salvation Army, we somehow managed to get through. We sold everything in the house that wasn't nailed down. That wasn't a bad thing though, because it made more room."

"What exactly does that mean?"

"Well doc, you see, there were nine people living in two bedrooms. The kids tripled up in beds, some people slept in the living room and on the floor."

"Seems like a pretty rough way to grow up."

"Yeah."

"You spoke of your older brother who used to take you places. Did he help any?"

"No, he didn't. Look, doc, I don't know why, maybe he wasn't making enough, I don't know. This is like...this is like forty years ago, you know? Some of it's vague. Some of it I'd just as soon *forget*."

"So how was school at this time? I mean, were you going to school regularly?"

"I was until I got my neck broken. Well, it wasn't really broken, I just cracked a couple vertebrae in my neck."

"How did that happen? Were you in a car accident?"

"Nah, the brother that was living with us threw me headfirst into a snow bank, after I white-washed one of his kids."

"That sounds pretty drastic."

"Yeah, I think so."

"How long did you spend in the hospital?"

"A couple weeks, they fitted me with a body cast and sent me home."

"Was it a full body cast, or a partial body cast?"

"Partial, just from the waist up. Yeah, it went all the way over my head and my face was sticking out. Kind of like an astronaut, I guess."

"How long were you in the cast?"

"Two or three months, I think."

"It must have been incredibly uncomfortable, considering the environment you were in."

"Yeah, you might say that."

"Was there any reprisal from your parents over your brother's actions?"

"Nope, none whatsoever. He told them it was an accident, and that was good enough, I guess. To tell you the truth, I don't know if it was, or it wasn't. You know doc, I've had pretty much enough of this for the day. I will leave you with one more detail. While in that cast, I caught

25

lice from one of his kids, and had to live with the constant *itching* inside that cast. For how long, I really don't know. I remember hitting my head against the back of the door jamb, screaming because I itched so badly."

"Since you've been talking about these things, you don't seem to display a lot of emotion. You get agitated, but it doesn't seem to…to *affect* you that much."

"Just like the fucking Brady Bunch, huh, doc?"

"OK, well, let's end this for today. I'll see you tomorrow sometime. I've got you scheduled for an MRI and a CAT scan tomorrow morning. Maybe some of this loss of time is physical. I just want to cover all the bases. Are the meds I'm prescribing, are they helping any with your sleep?"

"Yeah, so-so."

"I'll make sure tonight that they give you something to help you sleep."

"How 'bout the hangover tomorrow morning?"

"I'll add something with it that will take care of the hangover for you."

"When do you think I'll be able to get out of this room and walk around, other than the lounge?"

"If we continue doing what we did today, it'll be a couple of days."

"OK, I guess that works."

"OK, well, I'll see you tomorrow sometime, more than likely in the afternoon."

As the doctor stood up, Peter looked at him and said, "V.A. must be paying good money these days…imported Italian loafers, hmm."

Doctor Brown looked down at his feet as Peter turned back towards the window. He left Peter's room, and felt it odd that Peter would comment on his shoes.

Well, he was right, they were Armani.

Brown just shook his head, and went to work on Peter's chart. Again, he looked down at his shoes.

Doctor Brown finished all his reports and headed out for the day. He told one of the nurses to page him if anything serious came up.

"Other than that, see you tomorrow."

With that he headed down the hall. Travis met him going out. Brown stopped to talk with him about Peter.

"Travis, what's your take on him?"

"You know doc, I don't know. He's guarded at times, and other times it's like this is all a big joke."

"Did you notice Travis that at times, when he's looking out the window, it's like he's gone?"

"I have noticed, there are no facial expressions, no movement, nothing. He just stares out into nowhere."

"I don't think so. He's somewhere else."

"Yeah, but where?"

"Travis, keep working on him. Maybe we can help. See you tomorrow."

"Oh, one last thing…as I was leaving his room he commented on my shoes, and laughed, then turned back to the window."

"Who knows doc, maybe he's a fashion critic."

"Yes, *that's* it! Good night."

Travis headed to the ward and Doctor Brown headed home. Walking across the parking lot, he had the feeling that someone was watching him. He thought to himself, *this is D.C., not the lowest crime rate in the country.* He looked all around, but there was no one in sight, so then he headed to his car.

Just as he got in he looked up; he could see Peter standing in the window on the fourth floor, looking down. They made eye contact. Peter just nodded, then turned around.

It almost gave Brown the willies. Brown started his car and headed home, once more looking up. Again, Peter was watching.

Prescott drove off. When he got on the highway he decided to listen to some music for the ride home, so he turned on his favorite classical radio station for the ride. It always helped with the stress of the day, but not that night. Flight of the Valkyrie by Wagner was not coming in, so he put in a CD of Chopin for the ride instead. Leaving the compound he thought to himself that before 9/11 it was easier to get around this city. The hospital was in a high crime area. But he had never had any trouble coming and going.

Driving past the projects, he thought about how many kids would have to grow up the same way Davies did. Not that his story was worse than some he'd heard over the time he had been in the V.A. system. It was not that he often thought about patients after work; in his work, he had to detach or he could not be objective. It was just part of the job.

As he came to a stop light there were kids standing on the corner. Their stereo was blasting so loud that it drowned out the music in his car. They couldn't have been anymore then twelve or thirteen, hustling for God knows what. At the next light was the Outpatient bar. Over the years many of the staff he had worked with would go there after work to unwind. The hospital had a large host of interns and residents. In the nineteen years he'd been at the hospital he'd never stopped for a drink.

The light turned green. He turned left to get onto the beltway and home to Alexandria and the gated community he lived in. It would usually take about thirty minutes to get home if the traffic was on his side.

The traffic was on his side, for a change. When he got to the driveway of his house there were cars everywhere.

What charity is she giving money to tonight?

He passed the cars and drove around the back to the garage. The door opened up and he drove in. Getting out of the car, he noticed that the cover was half off one of the cars he had collected over the years. It started when his grandfather left him the 1934 Bentley when he died. Prescott had always been fascinated with fine machines, but felt that he never had enough time to appreciate them, with everything that seemed to take up his time. He walked over to the antique car and pulled the cover down over the front. Heading to the door that led into the kitchen, he stopped to look at the cars once more. All six had covers, and other than seeing the front of his Cobra, it had been months since he drove any of them.

Going in, he closed the door behind him. Lauren the housekeeper and maid had been with the family as long as he could remember.

Her mother had been with us all the time I was growing up; they were like family. Being an only child, and with my folks traveling as much as they did, Lauren and I were very close, like brother and sister. In our world, there was nothing we wouldn't talk about. When I moved down here, her mother had died, and Boston wasn't home anymore for her. She'd never married, and the offer I made was three times what she could make up North. Besides, I knew that I could trust her to tell me what was going on in the house when I wasn't there.

"Good evening, Dr. Brown."

"Good evening, Lauren. What's going on in there?"

"The misses is having a committee."

"What is it this time, 'Save the Endangered Hula Hoops'?"

"You'll have to ask her." With that Lauren just smiled and shook her head.

"Well, I'd better get out my check book."

"Dr. Brown, can I get you something to eat?"

"That would be good. Something that isn't good for me. I'll eat in my study."

"Remember your diet the misses wants you on!"

He laughed. "It's just between you and me."

"Yes, sir."

"Oh, Lauren, was T.J. over today to work on cars?"

"No, he wasn't."

"That's odd, one of the cars had its cover half off. Did you see anyone out there?"

"Dr. Brown, you'll have to ask the misses. I don't have any idea."

"Lauren, *nothing* slips by you."

"You'd better ask the misses."

"OK, bring me my food when it's ready."

"Yes, sir."

"I am going to be in my study."

"I put the mail on your desk."

"Good, thanks. Oh, hey, do you have some of those chips I like?"

"Yes, I do, but if the misses finds out I'm getting them for you she's going to fire me. Remember the last time I got you things not on her list?"

"Don't worry, you're not going to be fired. It's just not going to happen."

"Doctor, would you like me to tell the misses you're home?"

"No, I'll go in later."

His study was on the back side of the house. It was quiet and he could unwind after work without being interrupted. He closed the door to his study. He sat at his desk and started to open his mail when Lauren came in with his meal: tuna melts, chips and a large glass of whole milk.

"Thank you for supper."

With that, she left. Closing the door behind her, she thought to herself, *he's the only one in this house that knows how to say "thank you". Well, back to work.*

After he finished his meal, he started going through his mail. Lauren came back in to get the plate and his glass.

"Lauren, are you sure there wasn't anybody in the garage this afternoon?"

"I'm not sure if they were in the garage, but Anna and some of her friends were hanging around outside the garage after school."

"OK, that's all I need. I'll ask my wife what the story is about that."

"Well, if you're not going to need anything else, I'm going to finish cleaning up after the guests leave, and I'll be done for the night."

"No, I'll be all set, Lauren. Have a good night."

After she left the room, he opened up the bottom drawer of his desk and pulled out his favorite bottle of Jack Daniels. He kept the whiskey in there because his wife didn't approve of his drinking such bottom-shelf booze, but he'd been drinking it since college, enjoyed it, and he was going to *continue* drinking it. He poured himself two fingers and put the bottle back in the drawer.

He sat there for a few minutes, finishing the rest of the mail, and decided he'd see what was going on in the house. Walking into the living room, he spotted Patsy, walked over and gave her a kiss on the cheek, and asked what was going on this evening. She told him that the people who were there were forming a committee to help disadvantaged children in the inner city.

"How much of this project do you know about, at this point?"

"It's been around for about a year, year and a half."

"Well, exactly what do they do?"

"They choose children from the inner city schools and try to set them up with families in the country for a few weeks in the summer."

"Then what, send them back to the ghetto after that?"

"Well, it's an opportunity to show them that there's something more than living in projects."

"Well, then, maybe we should try to do something about the projects."

"Prescott, you're blowing this out of proportion again."

"Yeah, maybe so."

She walked him around, introducing him to some of the people who were going to be on the committee. He'd never seen any of them, didn't know who any of them were. He was quite cordial, and when he was done he decided to turn in for the evening.

With that, he excused himself, went upstairs to take a shower, and went to bed. He read for a while and fell off to sleep. He never did hear Patsy come in or go to bed.

The alarm went off at six-thirty. He showered and got dressed for work. Downstairs, Lauren had breakfast waiting for him. He never ate much for breakfast: grapefruit, some orange juice and two cups of coffee. While he was going through the newspaper, Anna came in, getting ready for school.

"Mom said it would be all right if I went to the mall after school."

"Well, that's OK with me."

"Well, could I have a credit card?"

"What if I give you twenty dollars, would that be enough?"

"All my friends have plastic."

"OK, I'll give you one of the credit cards, if you tell me who was in the garage yesterday afternoon."

"Yeah, T.J. was over. He was doing something with the cars...I don't know what he was doing."

"No, Anna, that's the wrong answer. T.J. was not over here yesterday. So, which one of you or your friends were in there? I just want the truth."

"I don't *know* who was in there."

"Yeah, you do. It was you and your friends."

"Whatever."

"You know your mother's going to give you a credit card when I leave for work, so why are you asking me? If I find out that you or your friends are playing with my cars, you'll be a very old lady before you go back to the mall."

Anna stormed out of the room. Lauren picked up the plate from the table and said to Prescott, "Kids these days."

"Lauren, have Patsy give me a call sometime this morning, when she gets up and around."

"Yes, Doctor, I'll do that."

"Have a good day."

"You too."

"Good-bye."

He grabbed his briefcase and his coat, and headed to his car.

Traffic wasn't with him this morning, so he had time to think on the way into work. *Anna's sixteen years old, going on twenty-five, and thinks everything just drops out of the sky for her when she demands it. I'm a psychiatrist, and I can't figure out what's going on with my daughter, or should I say, 'stepdaughter'?*

Chapter Two

Travis came into Peter's room at about 7:00 the next morning. Peter was already up sitting in the chair, looking out the window.

"Hey Pilgrim, is there anything exciting out there this morning?"

"Nah, just people coming and going."

"Well, you ready for your CAT scan and MRI?"

"Yeah, I guess so."

"When we get those things done we'll get you back, and get you something to eat."

"Hey Travis, what's the chance of getting a smoke this morning?"

"Let's see how long it takes, I can get you hooked up. I'm not sure, no promises. It's harder to pull it off during the day, there's more people around."

"Man, having to sneak around for a cigarette."

"Remember Pilgrim, we've got to be politically correct today." Travis just kind of laughed. "Pilgrim you ready man?"

"Hey Travis, you want my opinion?"

"Do I have a choice, Pilgrim?"

"Political correctness is intellectual fascism, as far as I'm concerned."

"Damn, I got to get me a bumper sticker with that on it! Don't worry Pilgrim we'll find a way to get you a smoke."

"Hey Travis, you don't suppose I could get into some regular clothes today, do you?"

"Why don't you ask Doctor Brown when he comes in? He's still kind of concerned with you maybe skipping country, you know? Why, you don't like the pajamas I gave you?"

"Nah, it ain't that. They used too much soap, and my balls are irritated."

"That isn't good. Look, we'll hook you up. Let's go down and get your MRI and CAT scan and we'll see what we can do. We'll figure it out, one way or another. You chafed real bad? I mean, you need some powder, or something?"

"Nah, it's OK for now, I can deal with it."

"Remember Pilgrim, everybody who works in here is a government worker. One time, they put so much bleach in my scrubs, I was walking out of the building and they fell off me."

"Travis, you've got more bullshit then ten people."

"Oh, that's just wrong, that's just wrong."

On their way over to radiology Travis said, "Ah, I know where I can get you a smoke. On the way back, we'll stop in the maintenance department. There's a back door there, you can have a smoke. If you run off on me, I will hunt you down."

"Nah, I'll be good. I just want a smoke man."

"Let's get these tests done and on the way back, let's see what we can do. You know Pilgrim, I don't do this for everybody."

"You know, it's funny, a girl in high school told me the same thing in the back of my Chevelle."

"I think I know her."

"You pay her alimony too?"

"No, you got me on that one."

The MRI and CAT scans took about an hour, hour and a half. Peter told Travis that he wanted another CAT scan.

"The tech had some good music for me to listen to while they were doing the test; some tape with all sixties stuff. It's been years since I've heard the whole Sergeant Pepper album. What kind of music did you listen to growing up?"

"I grew up listening to country."

"Country?"

"That's right."

"Damn, a Mexican who looks like a rapper that listens to country. And they think I'm nuts."

"Come on Pilgrim, we'll stop by the maintenance department to have a smoke and a real cup of coffee."

The maintenance guy Charlie, nice guy, didn't say much. *All the time we were there, he was whistling "Dixie", "Dixie", wow!*

As Peter and Travis were standing outside by the maintenance department, Travis asked Peter how the sleep was going.

"Oh, not too bad."

"Any bad dreams, any flashback shit going down?"

"No, not really."

"How'd you feel about that conversation you had with Doc Brown yesterday?"

"Whaddaya mean, how did I feel?"

"I mean, do you feel like you got anything out of it?"

"Yeah Travis, here's what I got out of it. A white trash drunk baring his soul to a guy in fifteen hundred dollar loafers!"

"Pilgrim, you got a problem with his shoes?"

"Yeah, I got a problem with anybody who wears fifteen hundred dollar shoes, Travis."

"Well, I guess I'm okay, I get mine at Wal-Mart."

"Personally, I'm partial to K-Mart's blue light special."

"Damn Peter, I love your sarcasm! Well, let's get headed back, I'll get you something to eat. See if I can do something about those pajamas of yours, see if the Doc will let you get back into some regular pants today."

"Seriously, Travis, I've dumped that shit with more people over the years."

"So, you've gone through this before, then?"

"Yeah, oh yeah."

"Did these lapses in time…is that something new, or has this happened to you before?"

"You know, for a guy who empties bedpans, you ask a lot of questions Travis. Yeah Travis, they've happened before."

"Well, all I can tell you Pilgrim, is work with the Doc. He's really good, like I keep telling you. And who knows, maybe you'll convince him that fifteen hundred dollar loafers are just wrong!"

"Yeah, right."

As they walked past the nurse's station, Webster told Peter he had some meds to take. Travis told Peter he would get him breakfast and get it to his room.

"No, never mind, I'm not hungry. I'll wait 'til noon."

"Are you sure of that?"

"I'm sure."

Peter took his meds and headed for his room. Sitting there looking out the window, he noticed a young man getting out of a pickup that reminded him of his son. Seeing the young man, he started to think about all the times when his kids were growing up, when he was either emotionally or physically absent. He told his daughter he was coming down to visit a week ago, and he knew that he would have to call her to let her and her brother know where he was, and that he'd be there when he could.

Man, those kids have been through a lot of shit.

Travis came to get him for another blood test. Peter must have dozed off sitting in the chair.

"Come on Pilgrim, let's go. We got to get some blood drawn. Pilgrim, wake up, wake up."

Peter didn't respond. Travis knew that it was not a good idea to try to wake up someone with the shit Peter had going on, by shaking him.

Again: "Peter, Peter, Peter! Wake up!"

Travis got close to him. "Peter! Peter!"

Peter jumped out of the chair and pinned Travis against the wall.

"Pilgrim, Pilgrim, it's Travis, it's Travis."

Peter let go just as another orderly came running in.

"Is everything OK in here?"

"Yeah," Travis told him. "It's OK, just some bad dreams."

"Travis, I am sorry, I don't know what happened. I was sitting there thinking about my kids and dozed off."

"Has that happened before?"

"Yeah, a lot."

"Well, I'll try to find another way to get you up, if I have to do this again."

"I am real sorry about that."

"No big deal, Pilgrim."

"You were saying I've got more tests."

"Yeah, they need more blood."

"OK, let's go."

Walking down the hall, Peter asked, "Travis, do you have any kids?"

"Kids? I'm Mexican, and Catholic. What do you think?"

"How many?"

"Five. Just one still at home. She just started high school, and the others, I've got two boys in the Navy and a daughter that's a nurse that works in here."

"On this ward?"

"No, in another part of the hospital."

"What about the other one? That's only four."

"He's in jail."

"I'm sorry about that."

"He's a good kid, just made some bad choices."

"I know what you mean. My son did some time for drugs."

"How is he now?"

"He's doing good."

"Let me guess, it's all your fault?"

"Yeah. Oh, yeah."

"I went through the same thing with mine. Remember Peter, we all have choices. Sometimes it's easier to blame others than to look at ourselves."

"Yeah Travis, but it still hurts."

"Yeah, it does."

"Is Dr. Brown coming in this afternoon?"

"Yeah, that's why they had me get you down here before lunch."

"Do you think I could call my daughter to let her know what's going on?"

"Where is she?"

"Both my kids live in North Carolina. I was on my way down to see them when all this shit happened."

"How do you think she'll react to you being here?"

"It's not the first time I've ended up in places like this."

"Ask the doctor what he thinks. I know he'll let you call. She's probably worried by now."

"Well, I don't know about that. Sometimes I don't think they care if I am alive or dead."

"Pilgrim, you might be right, but my gut tells me you're wrong."

"Maybe."

After they were done Peter went back to his room and ate lunch. When he was done he brought his tray out to the lunch cart and decided to watch some TV in the lounge. All that was on TV was the news, more chatter about the election year; more promises, more lies, the same results, and just different faces.

After seeing that for a while he decided to go back in his room. Coming out of the lounge he almost ran into Dr. Brown.

"Davies, how are you doing today?"

"All right, I guess."

"Let's talk some more, are you up to it today?"

"What if I say 'no'?"

"Then I would say that's up to you, and it's also up to you how long you're going to be here."

"Then in that case, I'm all yours. I'll be in my room waiting with the giddy anticipation of a virgin on her wedding night."

"I've never had anyone quite put a talk session in those terms. Very good, see you in a few minutes."

Peter just shook his head and went to his room. Standing looking out the window he thought to himself, *Brown's as sarcastic as I am.* He laughed and shook his head. Peter knew that Brown would be in soon to talk, and he was starting to realize if he worked with them, maybe he could get off the charge he had hanging over his head with the police, and get out of this fucking hospital without getting into the shit that happened when I was in the service. It was a long time ago, and thanks to a fire in some vault in the Midwest most of my records had been burned or blacked out. The VA had tried to get my records opened before, but with all the kids coming back from Iraq and Afghanistan they had bigger and better things to hide than some old grunt that they long ago written off as some kind of nut with a bad drinking and drug problem.

That thought made him feel better. He'd been through this all before with the VA and the PTSD program. The long stays, the meds, the testing. There was no way they were going to find out now.

Dr. Brown walked in and startled him out of his ruminations.

Peter said from the chair, "Oh, it's you. You startled me."

"Do you always get jumpy like that?"

"No, I think I was dozing off. I'm a very light sleeper."

"That would make sense, with your background and the PTSD. I am sorry I startled you. I'll try to make more noise before I come the next time."

"Yeah, thanks."

"Are you getting enough to eat? And how have you been sleeping?"

"Yeah."

"How are the headaches?"

"They're getting better. Did you get the results back from all the testing you've been doing?"

"Some. Some aren't back yet. This is all a process."

"Yeah, I know."

"Do you mind if I call you Peter?"

Peter broke out laughing. "Look, Doc, we both know that you have all my records, both service and all the times I've been hospitalized. Hell, you probably know more about me than I do. Besides, I've never had anyone who could afford shoes like yours ask my permission for anything, so, yeah, it's all right, you can call me Peter."

"Why do you have a problem with my shoes?"

Peter leaned forward in his chair and looked Brown straight in the eyes. "You're the doc, you figure it out."

Peter had never looked Brown in the eyes since he'd been admitted. The look was cold and intense; it seemed like some sort of challenge.

"All right, I will. Would you like to start where we left off the last time?"

"Yeah, why not."

There was silence for a few minutes. Peter sat back in his chair.

Dr. Brown broke the silence.

"You told me about your two sisters who were there at home, looking after you."

"Yeah, I can't even imagine how it would have been if they weren't there. I could count on them to make sure I had the things I needed. Especially Louise. I remember when she got married to a guy who was in the Navy. I was a ring bearer in her wedding."

"Was that before your brother moved in?"

"Yeah, I used to hope that she would move far away with her husband and take me with her."

"Did that happen?"

"No."

"Did she ever leave?"

"Oh, that's another story."

"Tell me about it."

"After they got married they moved into a place down the street from us."

"Was your brother living with you at that time?"

"No, he moved in later."

"Let's see if I've got this right: sister out with her husband. Who was left home?"

"My mother, father, other sister and me."

"How were things at home then?"

"At that time as long as my sister Louise was close to me I felt safe from my mother's fits."

"Was she ever violent or abusive?"

"Knowing what I know now, I would say 'yes'."

"How so?"

"I could go into all kinds of shit about that, but not now."

"Who knows, maybe now is the best time."

"No, it's not."

"Peter, you've got something going on, to bring on the episode that happened to you. That's why you're here. The state you were in when they brought you in is either trauma of some kind, or something physical. I'm having tests done to get to the bottom of it. We have to look at everything if we're going to help get you out of here, and stop these lapses in time from happening again."

"OK, I'll give you an example. I remember when I was probably seven or eight, just before my brother moved in with us. My mother used to clean houses for rich people. She used to take me with her on a couple of jobs. One in particular, I'll always remember. Mrs. Feldman. Ah, yes, Mrs. Feldman. Her husband was a professor at a local college, I don't know for sure. I'll never forget that old bitch. I used to have to sit in the kitchen on a stool, basically in the corner, while my mother cleaned the house. The old lady would give me a piece of biscotti and a glass of water. You know, to this day, Doc, I still hate fucking biscotti."

"OK, so, where is this going, Peter?"

"OK. I was sitting there after she gave me the biscotti one day, and now I thought a glass of milk would probably make it go down easier than the water. I got up and walked towards the window. The old lady was in the garden, tending to her flowers. I snuck into the refrigerator to see if they had any milk. So, I took the carton out, opened it up, and started drinking out of it, just as the old bitch came in and caught me. She screamed at the top of her lungs like it was a million dollar quart of milk, scolded me for drinking milk out of her refrigerator without asking, threatened me that if I ever touched anything else in her house my mother would never work there again. My mother was coming downstairs, and the old bitch went right up to her and started to scolding her about how I wasn't brought up right, I was stealing her milk, and how I needed to be taught some manners."

Well, I went back and sat in the corner, and waited for my mother to finish. My mother got done, she paid her and we headed home."

"What happened when you got home?"

45

"Oh, it wasn't when I got home that was the fucking problem. It was on the way home that was the fucking problem."

Doctor Brown leaned forward in his chair and said, "Peter, it's OK, tell me, what happened?"

"She grabbed me by the arm and dragged me down the road with her. She dug my arm all the way home to where it was bleeding, screaming all the way, telling me I was no good, I was going to make her lose her job, and I was just like my brother, I was nothing but trouble. She said, "If you steal things from rich people, you'll go to reform school."

"You see, Doc, that's why I have a problem with fifteen hundred dollar loafers."

"What did you do when you got home?"

"I don't remember."

"Was that an isolated situation?"

"No, not really."

"Did you tell anybody about that situation?"

"No, why bother?"

"Would you like to take a break for a little bit, Peter?"

"No, no. I want to get back to the situation with my sister I was telling you about earlier. She and her husband were living down the road. She got pregnant, and I found out that he was going on deployment, was going someplace else. I guess he got stationed somewhere else. So, my sister moved back in with us while she was having her baby. My niece was about six or eight months old when he left.

I remember there was an argument between my mother and my sister, about her going with her husband. I think he might have been in Florida. That arguing went back and forth for three or four months. I remember my mother saying that if she took my niece away, that she'd kill herself. I was still hoping my sister would go, and take me with her."

"Did she go?"

"No. One day they had a big argument. My mother said she was going to jump off a bridge and take my niece with her. It was quiet for a few days, and then I went to the store with my sister to get a few things. We hadn't been gone too awfully long. When we got back, my mother and my niece were both gone. My sister never really said anything to me about it, and it took me a few years to figure out what it was all about. We lived right in town, so we went all over town seeing if we could find her and my niece. We walked down towards the bridge, which was where my mother always said she was going to jump. We ended up going to my aunt's house, that's where my mother and niece were."

"What happened after that?"

"After that no one really talked about it. I know my sister didn't go with her husband, and sooner or later they got divorced, after a few years."

"I've asked you this before: did anyone else notice this insanity?"

"If they did, it was a well-kept secret. You know, Doctor Brown, if you didn't have me imprisoned in here, you and I wouldn't be talking about these things. I realize I'm here because I made the choice to stay here instead of going back downtown to face the charges of disorderly conduct, or who knows what. You know, I put most of these things to bed a very long time ago."

"Well, having been in a Twelve-Step program, did you do any step work around any of these things?"

"Yeah, I've done some, but nowhere near this detailed."

"Well, from what I understand of a Twelve Step program, honesty and dealing with those demons are what keep a person sober and off drugs."

"Some days, Doc, you just hang on by the tips of your fingers. You know, I don't think about this shit all the time anymore."

"Well, there's obviously something there, considering the catatonic state you end up in periodically."

"Doc, maybe I've got a brain tumor the size of a basketball, how about that?"

"No, I don't think so, you're pretty high functioning for having one that big. OK, let's get back to growing up. How long did the insanity last? I mean, did the intensity of the insanity last? How long?"

"It continued, but it changed. We moved into a bigger apartment just around the corner from where we lived."

"Were your brother and his children still with you at that time?"

"Oh, yeah."

"Well, how was it different for you, then?"

"I was about eleven years old, and it was the first time I'd ever had a bedroom of my own."

"How was school going at that time for you?"

"It basically sucked. I was about two and a half years behind everybody else. I was taken out of parochial school and put into public school. I don't know why, nobody ever talked to me about it. It didn't bother me any, the parochial school I went to had quite a caste system: the haves and have not's. We certainly weren't at the top of the parish's Who's-Who list. Oh, wait a minute, Doctor, I'll tell you something. For some reason, the nun that was teaching the class that I was in decided to put my desk in front of the whole classroom. You know, I really don't know why, but I do remember her making an example of me, about either not behaving, or not being able to do the work, I'm not sure. But I know that I hated the bitch, and I hated all the kids in the class, too."

"So then, you were glad to go to public school?"

"Yeah, for a short time."

"Oh, what happened there?"

"I remember them giving me lots of different tests: playing with little blocks, little figures and pieces of paper with weird ink blots."

"So they were evaluating your potential? Well, did they have the records from the parochial school?"

"I really don't know, I really have no idea, but I can tell you this: I didn't feel like I fit in there, either. But I remember one day I got a reprieve."

"A reprieve? In what from, what kind of reprieve?"

"I saw the Beatles on Ed Sullivan, and knew that I was going to be a musician, one way or another."

"OK, so what did you do about it?"

"I hounded everybody who existed to get me a guitar."

"Had you been interested in music prior to that?"

"I've always been interested in music. It always seemed to be so private."

"Did you ever get the guitar?"

"I did get an acoustic guitar, I think I'd just turned eleven or twelve."

"Did your folks get it for you?"

"No, actually, the other sister that was living with us, Carmen, her boyfriend bought it for me, and based on what

I know about instruments today, it was a pathetic guitar. But I'll always be grateful for him doing that."

"Was there anyone in the house that played guitar who could help you learn how to play? Did you learn how to play, eventually?"

"Yeah, I was doing pretty good, actually."

"Well, did anyone in the household give you encouragement?"

"Heh, heh, you are so funny, Doctor Brown. Yeah, yeah, I got some encouragement, Doc, yeah. There was a big party one weekend, and when I got up the next morning, Sunday morning I believe, yeah it was Sunday morning because there were still bottles lying around and people hung over, my encouragement was sitting in the corner of the hallway. Someone decided to show their appreciation for my musical genius by stomping on it with their foot."

"Did anyone take responsibility?"

"Ha, ha, ha, ha, ha. Now what do you *really* think, Doc? Come on! Come on! I'm sitting here baring some of the shit that's bothered me forever and you have to ask that question?"

"No, I guess not. Did you ever get another guitar?"

"Yeah, a few years later."

"Did you buy that one?"

"No, my folks did. You see, a couple of years later, we moved to a town over from us, it was about eight or ten miles away. We lived in a low-income housing project. It was good, it was real good. Lots of kids to play with, but the best part was, it was just my mother and I, my father and my sister who were living there at the time. My older sister lived next door with her kids. One of my brothers lived across the street, and another one lived up the road."

"Getting back to school again, how did you fare with the new school system?"

"About the same. The transition was difficult because I was the new kid on the block, and I learned how to fight that way. Rough neighborhood, either you'd get the shit kicked out of you one day, or kick the shit out of somebody, the next day. Either way, somebody's going to get the shit kicked out of them."

"It seems like things changed quite a bit in that period of time."

"Well there was less partying going on. More like a normal household, whatever that was, with my mother's rants and my father's inaccessibility. His drinking had slowed down a lot."

"Now, let's see, you were twelve or thirteen at this time? And what grade were you in?"

"The fifth grade. Thirteen years old, in the fifth grade. Even then, I knew that I had missed some really important basics of education that would hound me for a very long time."

"Hey, Doc, did I ever tell you about how I learned to read?"

"No, I'm curious, how did you learn to read?"

"I was four or five, and I used to hide in a storage closet in the attic of this little apartment we lived in. It was before my brother came to live with us. There was a set of books stored up there that belonged to somebody, my brother, my brother in law, somebody. They were like home improvement books, little projects to do around the house. There were thirteen of them. Good number, huh, Doc? I turned the light on, thumbed through these books, and I would associate the pictures with the words. Good by-product, though, I learned how to build many things, that way."

"You were four or five!"

"Why, is that too far out of the realm of your psychological profile, Doc?"

"Why would you say that?"

"It seemed like the right thing to say."

"Have you always read a lot?"

"I have. Now, let's get back to me, and school, and growing up. I've got some wonderful things to tell you."

Dr. Brown jotted in his notes, *the patient seems to become irritated and sarcastic when the mere thought of his intelligence is questioned.*

"Oh, yeah, at the end of the fifth grade year, just before school let out, now remember, I'd only been in that system since February of that year, the teacher sent home a letter saying that I was not going to be put into the sixth grade, that I would have to stay back, again. So, again, another series of tests. Gotta love those tests. At which time they determined that there was a special education class at the local junior high school that would probably be very helpful to me. I jumped at it, because the thought of repeating the fifth grade at thirteen, fourteen years old was just unbearable. So, I spent the summer playing, mowing lawns, trying to make a buck wherever I could."

"How was the guitar playing coming?"

"I became bored with it, because I couldn't get the instruction that I needed. So, I decided that I was going to be a rock star anyway, but I would have to find another instrument."

"And did you?"

"Yeah, I did, I started playing drums."

"And how did you do at that?"

"Good. I've been playing ever since. Hell, I can even teach."

"So you gave up the guitar?"

"No, years later I picked it up again, and piano as well."

When Peter talked about music he became more animated. There seemed to be real joy there.

"Peter, when you talk about music you light up. It's very important to you, isn't it?"

Peter just shook his head sat up very straight, ran his hands through his hair and said to Doctor Brown, "It's the only thing they can't take away."

"Who are 'they'?"

"Everybody."

"Do you want to talk about that?"

"No.

"Could we get back to where we were?"

"Ok."

"Can we get back to the music later?"

"Maybe."

"How did the special education class go for you when school started?"

"A joy beyond words."

"Tell me more about this class."

"There were six of us in the class. We had one teacher, Miss Clough. Let's see now, there was a girl who was obviously very retarded, one that used to drool, a couple of disciplinary problems, and me and my buddy Ralph."

"Well, of course you know too, at that time you were growing up, the educational system was just coming into its own, helping students with special needs."

"Oh, doctor, spare me the fucking platitudes, will you? It really gets back to what I said earlier: it's all about the haves and have-nots. If I'd have been a rich boy from the right side of town, the school system would have made sure that I got the help that I needed after my neck was broken."

"You seem to be very bitter about these things."

"Bitter's not the word, fucking *pissed*, how's *that*? Does *that* work?"

"How long were you in the class?"

"Two years."

"Do you think it helped you at all?"

"Yeah, it did. I'll tell you what it taught me: it taught me that, if you take a beating long enough, you're gonna fight back."

"So you fought a lot in school?"

"Yeah, I got tired of being called a 'retard', and a 'freak'. I made a decision at that point that I was not going to let anyone put me down, or physically fucking abuse me, because I didn't fit into their little mold."

"Peter, I'm going to have to end it for today. There's something I would like to run by you before I leave. I'd like to have you have a series of tests tomorrow, or the next day."

"Yeah, what kind of tests?"

"Ah, aptitude, motor skills, cognitive reasoning."

"Oh, oh, you mean problem-solving, motor response, logical reasoning, eye-hand coordination?"

"Yeah, yeah, those are the things I would like to have you tested on."

"Well, doc, I'm all yours, how's that? The last two times I had those done, one in a private psychiatric ward, and one in the VA system, although they were a few points separated from each other, I was listed as 'high functioning, reason and problem solving skills, excellent control of language" and I figured out how to put the round pegs in the square holes. If the round peg you use has a smaller circumference than the overall dimension of the square, the peg will slide into a square hole. But then again, there's that nasty space left over that no one really knows what to do with. To make a long story short, doc, both tests put me in a category of 156 to 158 IQ."

Peter stood up and stretched.

Doctor Brown said, "I'll see you tomorrow. Have a good evening. If you need anything, let me know."

"Do you have any sanity in that bag of tricks of yours?"

"Excuse me?"

"Nothing."

Peter turned towards the window as Doctor Brown was leaving. Peter looked back over his shoulder at the doctor and said, "Have you checked yours lately?" and looked back towards the window.

Doctor Brown headed out towards the desk. Travis was walking up the corridor. Doctor Brown stopped Travis for a second, and asked him if he would spend some time with Peter in the afternoon to show him around the complex.

"I think it's about time we let him see the rest of the complex. Keep a close eye on his reactions, if he thinks he's going to be going off on his own."

"You know, Doctor Brown, this guy's got more going on than he's even letting us know about."

"I'm aware of that, and we're going to find out what it is."

"I don't know, I really don't know about that. Remember what old Doc Evans would say, "He's really just another patient."

"Yeah, maybe so."

Travis looked at him and raised his eyebrow. Yeah, that's right, just another patient."

Doctor Brown headed off to do some paperwork.

Travis headed in to see Peter, to see what was going on with him. Travis stuck his head in Peter's door. Peter was still looking out the window.

"Pilgrim, you want to get off the ward this afternoon for a while?"

Peter looked at Travis and said, "Travis, you're a life saver, you're a fucking *life*-saver."

"I'll be back in about a half hour or so, I've got some things to do. I'll take you around the complex, show you where the PX is, the recreation room, occupational therapy, and the smoking room?"

"Will I be able to go there alone?"

"You gettin' sick of my company already? I'm not sure, that's Doctor Brown's call. But I guess it would be soon. He must be pleased with the work you guys are doing. OK, I'll be back in a bit."

Travis left. Peter looked towards the window.

Peter could see just a whisper of the top of the Washington Monument from the window. He felt a strange sense of irony, that in his fifties he would end up in a VA hospital in Washington D.C., a place where lives are changed, made, destroyed; great wealth amassed, decisions made by politicians affecting the lives of faceless people. Maybe he just loathed authority, or as far as he viewed it, insanity. Part of Peter still wanted to believe that there was a reason why so few have so much control over so many. Bills that will never be passed, wars that can never be won: *I wonder if this is what the Founding Fathers wanted?*

He ran his hands through his hair, and thought to himself, *Is there anyone still left out there who remembers the missions they sent us on, high in the mountains, to clean up the wreckage of their bureaucracy? Fuck, we're all on the edge of insanity.*

Looking back to the parking lot, he noticed a woman and a young girl getting out of a car, walking towards the hospital entrance.

"Goddamn, they wear good clothes in this fucking city!"

"What's that, Pilgrim?"

"Ah, I was just muttering."

"Sounded like you were saying something about clothes. Pilgrim, you're fucking obsessed with clothes!"

"Nah, it's just been a long time since I've been able to read Cosmo to find out what the fashion trends are for this year."

"Dude, you're a trip!"

"Well, Travis, where are we headed today?"

"Couple things changed, Pilgrim. We gotta do another MRI."

"Why's that?"

"I have no idea."

"All right, if that's what they want."

"Travis reached down in his pocket and threw Peter a pack of smokes.

"Travis, you know I don't have any money."

"Yeah, well, you'll get some soon. Don't worry about it. Hey, Peter, let's get you hooked up with a service rep who can help you out with stuff like that. They can get you some money if you don't have any."

"I've got an ATM card in my personal belongings, but I don't know where the hell they are."

"Oh, I can get that for you. There's an ATM machine down by the PX, we can get you hooked up down there. Ready? Let's go. I'll round that up while you're getting your MRI done. Pilgrim, while we're out and about, is there anything else you think you might need, or anything else you need to do?"

"Yeah, while you're getting my wallet, I'd really like to get my cell phone. I need to make a call to my kids, let them know that I'm not dead."

"I don't know if I can get your phone, because of the restrictions you've got on because of the stuff between you and the Metro. I'll give it a shot. If that doesn't work, I'll find you a phone before the night's out. Besides, cell phones don't work in here real good, Peter. Let's go."

Walking past the desk, Peter said to Travis, "Does Webster ever smile?"

"Occasionally."

"I think she needs to be ridden hard and put away wet, personally."

"Yeah, we had one guy in here who used to refer to her as a combination of Nurse Ratched and Hot Lips."

Peter said, "Ratched, Ratched…oh, *One Flew Over the Cuckoo's Nest!* Oh, Travis, that's just wrong!"

"Well, I got you to laugh, even if it was at Webster's expense."

They finally made their way down to the MRI again. He checked in at the desk and then went and sat down in the waiting area. The technician came out and called his name.

"Weren't you here the day before yesterday?"

"I was. Hey, tell me something, how many times can they slice and dice you before you no longer exist?"

"Oh, you're safe, you've got three or four more times to go before that happens."

"Oh, joy."

The MRI took about 35 minutes. Peter went back out and sat down. Travis was waiting, and he had his wallet.

"Come on, Pilgrim, we've gotta hurry up because the PX closes at five, and it's almost four-thirty now."

When they got to the PX, Peter drew forty bucks out of his ATM card, and bought some razors and shaving cream. He got a couple of sodas, and gave Travis back his four bucks for the cigarettes. He asked Travis if he thought he could buy a lighter, and Travis told him no, the smoking room had an external lighter on the side of the wall and that patients in the psychiatric ward weren't allowed to have lighters. "Travis, I know that I was seeing if I could get one by you."

"Nice try, Pilgrim."

"Isn't that a little radical, Travis?"

"Yeah, I agree with you. I think things like that should be dealt with by the individual, but there are a lot of people in a whole lot worse condition than you are."

They walked out of the PX and headed down to the smoking room. It was a small room, maybe ten by fifteen. There were a couple of guys sitting in there, not saying much. Travis and Peter had a smoke, and Peter decided he was going to ask Travis about Doctor Brown's background.

"What do you mean, "background", Pilgrim? You mean his medical background, psychiatric background?"

"Look, Travis, the guy wears fifteen hundred dollar loafers. He drives a top of the line SUV Land Rover."

"Why would that make a difference to you, Pilgrim?"

"I'll tell you why, Travis. He's about my age, your age, right?"

"Yeah."

"I sometimes have a problem sharing my shit with people who don't understand it. Remember the protesters, Travis? The bags of piss? Getting spit on? Remember all that, Travis? Did you experience any of that coming back from the land of good and plenty?"

"I didn't, but I have some friends that did. I've known Doctor Brown for a long time. It would be hard for me to believe that he could have been involved with anything like that."

"No, Travis, that's not what I'm saying. How many guys did you know that got deferments because they knew somebody? Ok, Travis, are you a Mexican-American?"

"Yeah, I'm also half French."

"Damn, that's a combination. I come from white trash."

"Why are you shitting on yourself like that, Pilgrim?"

"OK, let me put it this way. I come from the wrong side of the tracks, growing up I had my share of surplus food, and everything that went along with it."

Peter got very serious and looked Travis straight in the eye.

"Do you agree that our war was made up of minorities and white trash?"

"Yeah, Pilgrim, you're right. I'm going to tell you what, and I'm being very serious, like you are right now, Pilgrim. Prescott Brown is not that kind of man. I'll tell you that, Pilgrim, if you want to know about Doc Brown, you're going to have to ask him yourself."

"Travis, I'm just trying to make sense of all this, you know?"

"Ask him, you might be surprised what you get for an answer."

"No, I don't think so."

They finished their cigarette and headed back upstairs. The woman and the girl that Peter had seen in the parking lot were walking towards them. She stopped Travis and asked him if he knew where Prescott was. Travis told her he believed he was still going rounds.

"Well, there were some files that he had left at home, he wanted me to drop by."

Peter just stood back against the wall and couldn't help but notice the rock on her left hand. The young girl with her was probably sixteen, seventeen. She looked totally annoyed with everything, and very impatient. Even though the woman and Travis only spoke for a second, Peter figured out it must be Doctor Brown's wife and daughter. They went on their way, and Travis and Peter headed back upstairs.

In the elevator, Travis said, "I know you're going to ask, so you might as well."

"Is that his wife and daughter?"

"Yeah, that's his wife and daughter."

"Jesus, Travis, is that kid ill, or something? *Jesus Christ*, is that kid skinny!"

"Look, Pilgrim, between you and I, and just between you and I, I believe she has a real serious eating disorder."

"Hmm. The curse of the affluent. Makes all kinds of sense to me."

Travis just shook his head. When they stepped out of the elevator, Doctor Brown was waiting for them.

"Doctor Brown, your wife's looking for you. Something about records."

"Thanks, Travis, I'll talk to you later."

The elevator door closed behind Brown. Peter mumbled under his breath, "It's the fucking Brady Bunch." Travis didn't hear him that time. Peter told Travis, "I'm headed down to my room."

Peter walked off.

"Pilgrim! I can get you hooked up with a phone at eight o' clock tonight. OK, is that going to work for you? And another thing, Pilgrim, I've gotta have your wallet back."

"What the *fuck*? Travis, it's a good thing I like you."

"Why, thank you so much, Pilgrim. If it was just up to me, you could keep your wallet. But it's not up to me, so we've just gotta go with the drill for a while."

"Yeah, I guess I'll just have to fucking deal with it, Travis."

Walking past the nurses' station, one of the nurses told Peter she had something for him the doctor had prescribed him.

"Yeah, what is it?"

"It's something for your agitation."

"No, thanks, I *like* my agitation."

"No, seriously, Davies, Doctor Brown wants you to take this medication."

"No, seriously, I *like my agitation.*"

"I'll have to report this to the doctor, you know."

"Good, you do that." With that Peter headed back to his room.

The young nurse was sort of taken aback. She'd only been working at the hospital for a few weeks, and had only worked two shifts in the psych ward. She spoke to Nurse Webster to see how to deal with it.

Webster told her not to worry about it, and that in time she'd be able to roll with the punches. A few minutes later Webster went into Peter's room with the medication.

"Peter, you really need to take this medication."

"OK, Webster, tell me what it's going to do, just what is it going to do? Put me into a more placid, lucid state? More pliable? More agreeable, less sarcastic? No, Webster I'm not taking that heavy a dose of Klonopin for anyone. Been there, done that, and I've got the ripped t-shirt to prove it."

"All right, have it your way. I'll report it to Doctor Brown, and maybe you can come up with another alternative."

"Webster, you're such a credit to your profession."

As she left, Peter pulled up his chair, put his feet on the window sill, and chuckled to himself.

Peter's afternoon went by pretty quickly. He sat in the lounge for a while and watched the news. Luckily enough, the lounge was fairly empty, except for Dave. Dave was another patient who, one day would speak in a language all his own. The next day, he would be completely understandable. Peter liked him quite a bit, and thought Dave seemed like he had accepted the fact that he was going to be there for a very, very long time.

Peter had graduated to the point where he could take his dinner tray from the cart and eat in either the lounge or his room. Today Peter took his tray to his room. The good thing was, he was getting his appetite back. The bad thing was, it was institutional food, and there was never enough of it.

Hell, looks like there's enough food there to feed Brown's kid for a month.

When he was done, Peter brought his tray back to the cart, and returned to his room. A while later, the young nurse came in with a med tray. Peter could see the poor kid was terrified, so he figured he'd let her off the hook. Just a little tiny thing, frumpy, reddish-blonde hair. You could tell by the way she stood she was probably a very shy person, a very timid kid.

I don't need to screw with her, she's just trying to do her job just like so many other people.

"What's your name, anyways, cutie?"

She looked up and said, "Beth Anne."

"Look, I'm sorry about giving you a hard time at the desk, I really am. I took Klonopin once before, and it just didn't work for me."

She shook her head and said, "I understand."

"Now, you're sure there's no Klonopin in there, right?"

"I'm sure."

He laughed and said, "It's OK, don't worry about it, it's no big deal."

As she was leaving, Peter said, "Good luck, Beth Anne, in your new profession."

"Thank you Mr. Davies. I really appreciate that."

"Yeah, just call me Peter. I feel old enough as it is."

She sort of hesitated, and said, "Have a good evening, Peter," and left.

Peter then went back to looking out the window. He knew Travis would stop by later to let him use the telephone. He was trying to think of what he would tell his daughter. This had happened before, and he knew that both his children must be getting tired of it. He had never had the courage or the strength to tell them some of the things that he had gone through, experienced as a child. Part of him didn't think they would believe him, another part thought it might only drive them further away.

God, when is this going to end?

He felt his eyes water up, and a tear fell down his cheek. He knew in his heart that his kids didn't deserve his inability to be there, but he was beginning to realize that he didn't deserve having to go through what he did, either. It was times like that he knew the sarcasm wouldn't work. Deep down inside, he hoped and prayed that maybe this cat Brown would be able to help him, that this time, it would be different. He also knew it depended on how willing he was to share it all. His fears told him that could never be, he could never tell it all. So, he decided that he was just going to tell her for now that he threw his back out, and he was going to be in the V.A. hospital for a few weeks for therapy. Not to worry, that he'd call back as soon as he could.

Just then, Travis walked through the door.

"Want to go for a walk? You all right, Pilgrim? You look pretty upset. What's going on, man?"

"I'm just thinking about what I'm going to tell my kids, you know?"

"You could try telling them the truth."

"Nah, they've heard this truth too many times."

Travis pulled up a chair.

"You know, Peter, as parents we really don't have any guidelines to go by. For a very long time, I didn't tell anybody about anything. It almost ruined me. My kids also bear a series of scars."

"How'd you deal with it?"

"Very much like you, Peter. I quit drinking and was forced to get some help. The help only started working when I was willing to let it work. Although, I think your sarcasm is very funny, it's keeping anybody from getting inside."

Peter looked Travis straight in the eyes, and said, "I can't do this again."

"Yes, you can, Peter, yes, you can. You wanna pass on that phone call for tonight? Maybe it's not the best time to make one."

"I need to make it, Travis."

Travis said, "Well, OK, come on then."

They headed down the ward, down to the second floor. Travis opened a room with a phone in it.

"Take all the time you need, Pilgrim, I'll be back in a little bit."

"You mean, you're going to leave me alone?"

"Is there a reason why I shouldn't?"

Peter wanted to say something sarcastic, but instead said, "No, no reason."

He sat staring at the telephone trying to remember the number, and more importantly trying to quiet his nerves. After what seemed to be ten minutes, he started dialing.

The telephone was ringing, and it rang, and rang, and rang. Finally, the answering machine picked up. It was his daughter's voice telling him to leave a message, and she'd get back as soon as she could. He started to leave a quick message, then changed his mind and hung up. He sat there waiting a few more minutes. He knew he had to make the call and leave a message, but he dreaded it more than anything else that had happened since he walked through the door of the insane asylum. Peter's thoughts raced. Maybe it was time to let this whole thing go, just let it all out, finally, let things fall where they would. He felt too tired and too old to hang onto the truth and his pride anymore. *Those kids have suffered too much for my fear of the past.* With everything he had, he picked the phone up and dialed again. The phone rang, and this time the answering machine picked up sooner. He wanted to tell her the truth, but he couldn't. He hung the phone up again, without speaking.

He stood there for a moment, then dialed the phone once more. This time he hung up before the answering machine picked up. She had heard it all too many times before. He would have to wait and see where this all went.

He sat there for what seemed to be hours. Eventually Travis came back in and said, "Hey, Pilgrim, you want a smoke before you go back upstairs?"

"Yeah."

"What's the matter? How'd the phone call go?"

When Peter didn't respond Travis shrugged and moved on. He'd accepted that Peter was sometimes quiet and brooding and knew he'd come back around. It was always Peter who had to break the ice.

"Come on, let's go have a smoke. It's going to be all right, I'm telling you this is going to pass, it can all pass, if you work with us."

They sat in the smoking room and lit up a cigarette.

"How did you deal with all this, Travis? How did you deal with the insanity of all the *bullshit*, the death, and carnage, and the lies?

"Just like you, Peter, I didn't, for a long, long time. I ended up here when I was thirty. I'd been drinking for three weeks. My wife left and went back to New Mexico and took the kids with her. All I remember about it was, when they came and got me, I was getting ready to burn my house down."

"How long were you in here?"

"Six months. I was lucky, though Peter, it worked for me the first time. I guess I was desperate enough. I don't know, I really don't know. I finally tried some medication and some counseling and getting honest with myself; you know, that's the only thing that worked."

"Does it get easier?"

"It just becomes less important."

Peter looked at his cigarette, and then looked at Travis, and he was laughing.

"You know these things are going to kill us, you know that, don't you?"

"That's OK, the food they serve in here might kill us faster."

"No shit."

"So, how did you end up working in here, anyway? Were you a corpsman in the service, a medic? What's the story?"

"No, just a grunt, dog-faced grunt."

"Lemme guess, just another poor minority caught up in the draft."

"That's just about the size of it. You can spend a lifetime blaming, never getting the answers you want, then one day, you wake up a bitter, angry, resentful old man."

"You saying I'm old and bitter, Travis?"

"You're no older or more beat up than I am." Travis paused to take his last drag. "Are you ready to go back up, Pilgrim? I gotta go home and watch a basketball game."

"Who's playing?"

"Celts and Lakers."

"Playoff already?"

"Yeah, the first game."

"Where they at?"

"LA."

"Who's your team?"

"I'm from the west coast, what do you think?"

Peter laughed. "Hard call. Lakers?"

"Nope, Celts."

"Travis, are you still fucking with me?"

"Nope, I've been a Celts fan since the early eighties."

"Yeah, me too. Travis, stop for a minute. I want to talk to you about something before we go back upstairs."

"Yeah, what's up?"

Peter leaned against the wall of the empty corridor and turned away from Travis. "Do you think if I was to tell the doctor about something that happened while I was over there, something bad, he would turn me in?"

"Pilgrim, it doesn't matter. You have to tell him. We all did our share of fucked up shit. I can't help you with this. I only know that we have all suffered enough, from the war.

69

Pilgrim, let it go before it kills you, and it will. All the years I've been working in here, more die than don't. Many drink themselves to death. Others die because of drugs, suicide. Some end up in jail, and some just stare out windows for the rest of their lives. It's all up to you, Pilgrim. Go get some rest. Your window is waiting for you."

Peter turned to tell Travis to get fucked, but he was gone. *Where the hell did he go?*

Peter got back to his room and sat down on the bed and started to cry. He was sobbing so loud a nurse came in to see if he was all right. It was the new girl, Beth Anne.

"Mr. Davies, are you alright?"

"No, I'm not. Could you please see if I could see Dr. Brown? I would really like to talk to him. Please, could you do that for me?"

Beth Anne went back to the nurses' station and told Nurse Webster about Peter's request.

"Page Travis and have him call us."

A few minutes later Travis showed up to see what was going on.

"Davies wants to talk to Brown."

"Good, it's about time. I'll go talk to him for a few minutes and get a make on this."

Travis walked in. "Peter, what's going on with you tonight?"

"One minute I'm talking to you in the hall, and then you're gone. Where did you go?

"Nowhere, Peter, I walked up here to the ward with you. Peter, it's what we call sensory overload. You're caught between your subconscious and your conscious. Peter, I haven't been totally up front with you. I'm Doc Brown's psych P.A. Dr. Brown's been working with some new methods to help vets for the last ten or fifteen years. Not totally conventional, or congruent with the way the V.A. likes to work."

"Well, what is it, and how does it work?"

"I was the first one he ever tried this method on. The results were so good I decided to go into medicine. I was a medic in the Army, and Doc Brown all but paid for me to go to school. What the V.A. didn't pay, he did. What made you ask for help now, Peter?"

"When I walked in here I saw the window, and what you told me hit me like a ton of bricks. You think I can get a chance to talk to the Doc tonight?"

"Not tonight, Peter. Get some rest. We'll both be in tomorrow and tell you how we're going to start this."

"But what if…"

"No 'what ifs'. It's time, Pilgrim.

Peter hung his head and said, "Sorry for calling you back in Travis."

Travis put his hand on Peter's shoulder. "It's gonna be all right. Get some rest, stay away from the window, and don't worry maybe I'll see the last half of the game. Course, everybody knows the Celts are going to win anyway."

As the door clicked shut Peter had a sense of calm come over him, he felt like Travis was right, and it was going to be okay. That was new for him, Peter had never had much luck with trusting anybody on their word. He thought maybe Travis was different, a while later the young nurse came in to give Peter his nightly meds, and he was already fast asleep.

Beth Anne returned to the nurses' station and asked if she should wake him up to take his meds. Nurse Webster told her to wait and if he woke up later to give them to him, then let him sleep. "He needs the rest."

Chapter Three

Peter slept through the night, and when he woke up, he noticed it was the first time in days his head wasn't splitting from the meds. Lying there his thoughts started racing again. Did he tell Travis too much? If he played along with Brown, what was going to happen if that day in Cambodia came out? He knew how to work around all this psycho babble bullshit. He'd been doing it for years, but this time something seemed different somehow. He was beginning to trust Travis, that could be the difference. A cold thought came to him: that maybe it was time to let it go and let the chips fall where they would. The times he'd been hospitalized before he hadn't been facing jail time. If he left the hospital he would do some time, but if he told them the truth about Captain Jacobs, how much time would he do for that? Between the guilt and the fear, Peter had spent most of his life separated from any peace or anyone getting too close. He was getting too old and too tired to hang on to this lie anymore. The tears that had started last night started again and he couldn't stop them. Travis opened the door and saw Peter sitting on the bed with his head in his hands.

"Pilgrim, what's going on?"

Peter looked up at him and he said, "It's time, it has to be."

Travis sat on the bed next to him. "Pilgrim I'm sure that some gunny or top told you once that the anticipation of the kill was always worse than the act itself."

Peter snapped back with: "What the *fuck* are you talking about? Travis of course they did, but what does that have to do with this?"

"Pilgrim, I was talking about your anticipation of working with Doctor Brown."

"Look, Travis, I like you, but my head's fucked up enough as it is, without you trying to constantly get into it."

"Pilgrim, do you really thinks that's what I'm trying to do?"

"Oh, come on Travis, don't bullshit a bullshitter."

"OK, Pilgrim, point taken. Just trying to get a point across to you."

"That's better, Travis, now we're on the same page."

"Point taken. I just came in to see if you wanted to get a smoke before you saw Doc Brown?"

"Yeah."

"I would also like to talk to you about how Doc Brown is going to proceed with your therapy."

Peter leaned forward and nailed Travis with a look. "Proceed with my therapy? I feel a little like a lab rat!"

"You know, at times, Pilgrim, you can be a bit difficult."

"You know, Travis, they put initials after your name and you become something that I don't really understand. Are you the same guy that shared a smoke with me in the morgue on a slab, or am I dreaming here?"

"Touché, Peter, touché. Get cleaned up and we'll go have a smoke."

"Yeah, OK, give me a few minutes to get myself together."

About twenty minutes later Travis came back. "You ready, Pilgrim?"

"Yeah, I'm as ready as I'll ever be."

As they walked down the corridor Travis told Peter what the Doc likes to do is a combination of deep hypnotherapy and EMDR."

"What's that?"

"Done with lights along with the hypnosis, and here's the part that the VA doesn't like: no meds. Just talk therapy."

"How the fuck does he get away with that?"

"When you get to know him better you'll find out he's more than some rich trusty with imported Italian loafers."

"Yeah, if you say so."

Travis couldn't help but notice how distant and sarcastic Peter had become since he had asked Peter about the anticipation. Travis had a feeling that he may be getting too close to this patient. Travis had been working like that for about five years and he and Doc Brown were having good luck, although it was hard for Travis in the beginning not to get involved with patients. When Dr. Brown saw that happening he would have Travis back off or take him off the case altogether. Travis was beginning to think maybe this was happening with Peter. He and Brown would have to talk about it. He would have to get together with Dr. Brown, and soon, before Peter's first session.

In the smoking room Peter finally spoke.

"Travis, I'm sorry if I get a little testy with you. I've got lots on my mind."

"Not a problem, Pilgrim."

"So, how does this thing work with the doctor, anyways?"

There was nobody in the smoking room with them so they could talk.

"The first thing that's going to happen, and it's already started, your meds are being decreased. Did you notice that?"

"No, not really."

"Sometime this afternoon I'm gonna take you downstairs to a room that Doc Brown does his hypnotherapy in, and his EMDR. There are two large, very comfortable chairs, and suspended from the ceiling is a glass crystal with a low-level laser light that hits the crystal as it spins."

"How soon after that do we start cutting off the heads of chickens?"

Travis shook his head, chuckling, "Oh, Peter, you never give up!"

"I'm just fucking with you, Travis let's get back to what's going on here. So there's basically a mirrored disco ball."

"Yeah, but much smaller. This thing's only about two or three inches in diameter, about the size of a tennis ball."

"Oh, OK."

"Then he'll ask you a series of questions as he's putting you under, and from the questions, he'll have a specific point where he would like you to start speaking."

"You know, Travis, I've been told that not everybody can be hypnotized."

"Well, you're right, it may work, it may not."

"How long, ah, does this whole process last?"

"Most sessions are between an hour to two hours."

"How many of these sessions does it usually take?"

"Well, I guess that depends on you, doesn't it, Pilgrim?"

"No, really, come on, Travis, I'm really serious, I'd like to know how many sessions other people have had."

"I've seen some people take up to six months at one or two sessions a week, and some as little as three sessions."

"OK, are these sessions recorded?"

"Yes, Peter, they are."

"Who has access to these tapes?"

"Only Doctor Brown and myself."

"Oh, *really*. OK, Travis, I've been in the VA system for almost thirty years. I'm aware of its bureaucracy, and how fucked up the system can be. *You're* telling me that *no one* but *you* and *Doctor Brown* have access to this, right? Yeah, *right*, yeah, *OK*, I believe that like I believe in the *fuckin' Easter Bunny*! *No fuckin'* way! I'll go to *fuckin'* jail! I won't deal with this *bullshit anymore*!"

Travis walked up to Peter and said, "Look, I've been with you now for almost three weeks, and if you think for one minute Brown will turn you over, you're wrong."

Travis turned around, and locked the door of the smoking room.

"And if you think that I don't know that there's something there, something that happened in the fuckin' hills a long time ago, that you're afraid of…then you should believe in the fucking tooth fairy."

"*Horseshit*, I'm not afraid of *anything*, Travis!"

"OK, you want to give up, you want to go to jail, go to jail! That simple. You're 56 years old, you've been carrying this horseshit since you were probably 20, you know and I know it's going to kill ya. Period!"

"Yeah, what the fuck do you know about fuckin' keeping secrets, Travis?"

"Want to know what I know, Peter, here's what I know. You any good with history, you got your history down Peter?

All that fuckin' sarcasm, you got your history down? Mei Lai, Calley, those things mean anything to you? I was a private in that unit. I had to testify against my comrades about them cutting kids in half with their bayonets, and Calley sitting there laughing, thinking it was a fuckin' joke! Every fuckin' time we went on patrol I didn't know if I was going to get it from the back or front. I'd been out there six months and they called me to testify for a court martial. You know that bullshit they teach you about protecting your brothers, and leaving no one behind, all for one and one for all? I know the fuckin' deal, dude, I know the fuckin' deal. If it hadn't have been for Prescott Brown, and his voodoo ways, I'd have been dead on the street from fuckin' drinking and drugging, with no family, nothing except me and my fuckin' secrets!"

Travis turned and walked over to unlock the door.

Peter just stood there, didn't say a word, not a word.

Travis looked over his shoulder at Peter as he was going out the door. All he said was, "You're with this, or you're not. No more games. If you walk out of here with me now, you have a chance. If not, enjoy your jail time."

"OK, Travis, OK."

"Ok, *what*?"

"I'm with ya."

Travis walked back into the smoking room. Peter sat down on the bench. Both men sat for a moment, collecting themselves.

"You were asking about the recordings that Doctor Brown makes. They're to help you, first of all. They're to help him. Prescott Brown gets away with some stuff that the VA doesn't like it because he has more relatives in high public offices than you can imagine. Two years ago his uncle donated $5,000,000.00 to the wing on the other side of the building. He doesn't take a yearly salary, it goes to the American Legion, the DAV and other veteran's services. He's been called on the carpet before Congress on no less than five occasions for some of his methods. His success rate is about 80%, which is *twice* as much as the conventional VA method. *That's* how he gets away with it, that's why only he and I can access the recordings. You know, he didn't pick you for your warm, fuzzy personality. You fit the criteria."

Peter sat for a moment, trying to decide if he really trusted Travis. "This afternoon, huh?"

"Yeah, this afternoon, Pilgrim. Come on, let's go get a drink."

On the way to the vending machines Travis noticed that Peter did not say a word. When they got there Travis asked Peter what he wanted.

"I haven't got any money on me."

"*What do you want?*"

"Oh, I'll have a Diet Pepsi."

Travis passed the soda to Peter.

"Thanks, Travis."

"Don't thank me, thank Brown. It's his dime."

They didn't say anything. They walked back up to the ward. They got to Peter's room, and Travis said the doctor would be in around 1:30.

"I'll be in to get you at about 1:15."

"What time is it now?"

"Must be close to 11:30. I see the lunch trays are coming up."

Travis left.

At about quarter to noon, one of the orderlies stuck his head in and told Peter lunch was ready. Peter sat there for a few minutes, thinking about what was going to happen later this afternoon, and didn't have much of an appetite. He knew if he didn't eat something Webster would bitch, as usual. So, he went out, picked his tray up and sat in the day room. He thought to himself, *Institutional food has got to be one of the severest crimes against Nature possible.* He picked at it for a few minutes, ate the jello with the weird stuff in it. All the time his head was racing about what he was about to do; he didn't really know how to deal with it. He'd remembered reading one time that they couldn't hypnotize someone unless they chose to be hypnotized. He kept that in the back of his mind, just in case.

He returned the tray to the cart, and got in line for his meds. When it was his turn, Webster told him that his meds were on hold until later this afternoon, by order of Dr. Brown.

"Good, I don't like taking them, anyhow." Peter walked off.

Back in his room he swung the chair around and stared out the window. He couldn't help but think there was something very, very different about this time, being in the hospital. Of course, he'd never been facing jail time for an episode, either. Under his breath he asked, "How the fuck did I get into this shit? Maybe it's time for it to end. God*damn*, am I tired of this."

"Pilgrim, you ready?"

"Well, I suppose."

"Pilgrim, we're not going to start this again, are we?"

"No, Travis, I'm ready. Let's go." Peter said, sounding resigned.

They headed down the corridor into the elevator. They went down four floors to the basement. Once off the elevator, they walked down another corridor and went into a small office on the left hand side. In the room there were two chairs and a desk with some paperwork spread across it.

"I thought Brown was supposed to be here, Travis."

"He'll be here in a bit. I want to explain to you how this session is going to go, so they'll be no surprises. You good with that, brother?"

"OK, let's have it."

"In the next room there's a large, very comfortable recliner. The room is dimly lit, there are some sound effects, such as waterfalls..."

"Travis, are you shittin' me? Are we going to have a session of aromatherapy, as well?"

"No, it's just a way to help you relax. It's just a soothing sound, you know that."

"OK. Sounds a little New-Age-y to me, Travis."

"Just be open minded."

"Ok, Travis, yep. I'll dispense with the sarcasm."

"Yeah, sure you will."

"Travis, I read an article about this EMDR. Could you explain a little bit about it to me? I'm really curious."

"It's done with a series of lights that flash back and forth. Once you've pinpointed a trauma or an event that continues to trouble you, the motion of the lights helps you to focus in and face the trauma more easily with the help of the therapist."

"Is Dr. Brown going to be using that today?"

"He usually doesn't use it in first time sessions."

"So, is it like hypnosis?"

"No, no, not really. It's more like getting in touch with your subconscious."

"Oh, OK, I guess. Now, is he going to use all of these things at one time? I'm a little confused, I feel like a fucking guinea pig, Travis."

"You're not a guinea pig, Pilgrim." Travis said with a small chuckle. "Here's what's gonna happen in this session. You're gonna get real comfortable, we're going to place some electrodes on your forehead and on your chest so we can monitor your respiration."

"What about the ones on my head?"

"We'll monitor alpha waves in your brain."

"You're gonna *what*?"

"We're going to monitor the alpha waves in your brain."

"Oh, great. OK, alright, alright, I made a deal with you, OK."

"It's a way for Dr. Brown to monitor and record what happens to you, and your brain when you go into one of these states, or episodes that have caused you to be in here."

"Alright, here goes."

"OK, I'm going to explain this to you once more, Peter. We record you on video, we monitor your respiration and your brain activity. That way later we can look at it to see if there are any discrepancies."

"It makes more sense now. I've heard all I need to hear."

"Doctor Brown is going to ask you a series of questions, to help you relax even more. At that point, once you're relaxed, he's going to ask you to tell him about a certain situation."

"How does he know what to ask?"

"From the conversations that you've had with him, and Peter, from the conversations that we've had."

"I know you work for him, Travis, but are you telling me everything that you and I've talked about, you tell him?"

"No, only the essence of it, Pilgrim, only the basics."

"Oh, that's a good word, Travis, that is such a good word: the *essence*."

"Yeah, I thought you'd like that word 'essence'."

"It's poetic, like lilacs in the Spring."

Just then Dr. Brown walked in through the door.

"Well, how are we doing today?" Prescott said with a quiet smile.

"I don't know about 'we', but I'm a little suspicious of all this, Doc. We're not going to get to kill a chicken or something later, are we?"

"Would you like to kill a chicken later?"

Peter just laughed and shook his head saying, "You two are unbelievable. Well, Doc, if we're going to do this, let's do it."

"I'll be back to get you later, Pilgrim. Enjoy yourself. It's gonna help. Trust me."

"Trust, coming from a government worker. Now, that's a concept.

Travis just shook his head, laughed, and walked out, closing the door behind him.

Doctor Brown unlocked the next door. "Come on in, get comfortable. Sit here, Peter."

"A leather couch. Imagine that."

"I would like you to sit here, put your hands in your lap, lay your head back, and close your eyes. Can you hear the waterfall behind you? What does it remind you of?"

Peter sat silently for a moment and then said, "The wind through the trees on a warm summer day." There was none of his usual sarcasm.

"Is that a fond memory for you?"

"I'm not sure. Just sort of peaceful and...clean."

"Now I would like you to concentrate on the waterfall and the wind through the trees, and very slowly start counting backwards from 25."

A memory came through Peter's mind: it was a very peaceful setting. As a boy he used to sit in the woods by his house and listen for the wind through the trees.

"...Eighteen, seventeen, sixteen, fifteen, fourteen, thirteen, twelve..."

"Peter, can you hear me now?"

"Yeah. Do I know you?"

"We're old friends."

"Oh. Oh, OK."

"Do you feel like talking, Peter?"

"Yeah, I think I'd like that."

"Would you like to tell me about when you went into the service?"

Peter sighed.

"Did you enlist, or were you drafted?"

"Both."

"Both?"

"Yeah, I got a draft notice so I enlisted instead."

"How old were you?"

"Nineteen."

"You must have just graduated from high school."

"No, I dropped out long before that. I was working, actually. I had a good job."

"What were you doing?"

"Building things."

"You like building things?"

"Yeah, it makes me feel whole."

"Tell me more about you going into the military."

"Not much to tell, really. I don't think."

"I would like you to focus on the time just before."

"The night before I was taken to the airport, I was at my mother and father's house. Two of my brothers stopped by to visit, to say 'good bye and good luck'. A couple of other people I knew stopped by."

"Were they having a get-together for you?"

"No, not really. I remember about 9:30, 10:00, I went to bed. I didn't sleep all that well. I had to be in the induction center at 6:00 the next morning. It was a long trip to the induction center, or it seemed like one. No one in the car said anything to anybody, just kind of sat there. I got out of the car, my mother told me to be careful, that was pretty much it. I grabbed the small bag I had and headed into the induction center. I'd already been sworn in at that point. It was just a lot of waiting until the bus took us over to the airport. I remember I didn't like flying the first time. It made me uneasy." Briefly Peter paused as if on the plane again.

"We landed at O'Hare airport at about 11:00 that night. I finally got to Great Lakes Training Center at 1:15 in the morning. They assigned us a bunk and a barracks. I fell asleep, actually, sort of passed out, I guess. What seemed to be a few minutes later, I was being dragged out of bed by somebody screaming and throwing trash cans around. Screaming, *'Reveille, reveille, reveille'* over and over again. I remember asking myself 'What the fuck am I doing here?' Everything seemed so chaotic, people hollering and running around, it didn't make any sense. 'til I heard this one, booming voice above everybody else. I couldn't figure where it was coming from. Seemed like it was coming from everywhere. Everyone else quieted down other than the one voice. He informed us his name was Chief Hassle, and he would be our company commander, if we survived. I'll never forget him, He was about six foot four, as black as night, screaming in my left ear so loud the blood vessels in my head must have wanted to pop. He had everyone stand in front of the bed that they'd slept in the night before. We stood there for what seemed like hours. As your name was called, a tag with a number was given to you. We were told to put it on our coats with the barracks number on it. They told us we had fifteen minutes to get ready, we would be marching to another barracks which would be our home for the duration of our time at RTC. We all got outside and stood there as another Chief got us into some kind of formation. A few minutes later Chief hassle returned. He continued to scream at everyone. It was cold, was drizzling. To tell you the truth, I was scared as hell. As we arrived at the new barracks, bunks were assigned to us. Chief Hassle then ordered us to stand in front of our bunks at attention. As he walked up and down the barracks, he informed us he was not our babysitter, or our friends, and if we didn't do things his way we would make an enemy we would not soon forget. He stopped at one of the black recruits, got in his face, and asked him if he thought, for one fucking minute, that because he was black he was going to have it easy. He was the dumbest fucking nigger he'd ever met. Then the Chief said 'One thing you girls better remember, and remember good, is I don't wear gold, and I don't like honkies any more than I like niggers. You've got five minutes to get out on the grinder and get into formation, and if you don't do it right, you'll do so many fucking push-ups you'll wish you were dead.' We all made a good effort to get into formation, and apparently failed miserably. True to his word, he had us do push ups. More and more push ups, until the fucking asshole decided to tell us how to do it right. After more push ups than I can remember, he started to ease off. I don't know, I guess maybe we were starting to get it right, I'm not sure. He screamed for us to come to attention. The black devil asked if anyone had any marching experience. One kid spoke up and said he went to a military academy for high school. Hassle told him to get his ass up there and teach us how to march, or it would be his hide, if he didn't."

"Do you understand what I'm saying, General Patton? You fucking understand me?"

"Tamper, the kid who volunteered, would become our squad leader, or "Patton", as Chief Hassle called him, and he worked with us for the rest of the day. At about 5:00 we marched to the galley for supper. After the meal was over, we marched back to the barracks. Chief Hassle was waiting in all of his glory. He told us to stand by our bunks."

"I'm going to explain the very basics about the rules", he said. 'You had better learn them, and learn them good, 'cause I'm not gonna repeat them. One, you take a shower every day. I will not tolerate a dirty body from anyone. If you don't know how to stay clean, I will teach you, and that will be an experience you will not soon forget."

"As he walked back and forth giving the rest of the rules, he would stop now and then and get in someone's face for that seemed to be no apparent reason. As he walked by me, he stopped and got in my face."

"Where are you from?"

"Maine," I answered.

"Where the fuck is that? Oh, yeah, I heard about that place. It's where guys like you fuck moose and bear. God knows you're too ugly to fuck anything else."

"No," I replied.

"No, what?" he returned.

"No, I don't fuck moose."

"Wrong answer. Now give me fifty. And when you answer me, you answer me 'Yes, sir' and 'No sir'. Do you understand, asshole?"

"I guess I wasn't fast enough getting to the push ups. He grabbed me by the shirt and threw me to the floor." Peter paused, shifting around on the couch.

"Peter, are you comfortable?" prompted Prescott after a half minute or so.

"Yes."

"Would it be all right if I asked you a series of questions now? Would that be OK?"

"Yes."

"Did the company Commander's brutality remind you of any childhood incidents?"

Peter sat straight up from the couch, yanked the probes from his head and chest and threw them on the floor. Prescott was taken aback and sat back in his seat.

"I am so fucking tired of this fucking psycho-babble fucking *bullshit*! I'm intelligent enough to know that if a person doesn't want to be hypnotized, you *can't hypnotize him*, OK?"

"Peter, I thought we had an agreement that we'd try this process to help you with your catatonic states. I can't help you if you won't work with me, OK? If you're still playing us it needs to stop now, this has gone on too far."

"No, an agreement's an agreement, but we're gonna do it my way."

When the doctor said nothing Peter continued, "Travis, when this is done do you think we can go down to the morgue and grab a cigarette? That place is quiet."

"Travis isn't here with us." Prescott said with condescension.

Peter sighed loudly. "You've got an examination room here to hypnotize people in. It's comfortable, there's waterfalls. You're taking vital signs, and there's a mirror. There's somebody in there monitoring this. It's OK Doc, I watch cop movies, I know what these things are like."

Prescott slammed his notebook closed and threw it on the coffee table beside him.

"OK, OK, we'll try it your way, but this is the last time, the last goddamned time I'm playing this game with you."

"Alright, doc, I was beginning to think you didn't have any emotions other than deadpan. I like that, it's good." Then Peter leaned forward and said, "Who knows, doc, maybe you and I are more alike than one would like to think."

"Now explain to me how you want to do this, and if I'm not satisfied I'm leaving, and I'm calling Metro, and they can do with you what they please."

"Now that's the bedside manner I can understand. Here's what I'd like to do: hook me up with your monitors, run the tapes. I just want to tell you how I remember it, that's all. All of it. OK, that was the deal with me. I've been through this so many times, with the therapy, with the medication, with the talk therapy, and apparently it didn't work, obviously, 'cause I end up crazy in front of monuments talking to myself. I think I just need to be heard, does that make any sense to you?"

Doctor Brown didn't respond verbally; he just nodded.

"Travis, could you come in here and help me hook Mr. Davies up with the monitoring system again?"

Peter didn't say anything. Travis came in, kind of looked at Dr. Brown and did his thing. There were no words exchanged by anyone at this point.

Peter leaned back in his chair. Doctor Brown asked Travis if everything was hooked up in there, if he was ready. On the intercom system Travis said, "Yeah, I'm set."

"As I was doing my push-ups I could see him walk to another recruit and stop. He asked him the same thing.

"And where are you from, maggot?"

"New York" was his response.

"Where in New York? New York's a big fuckin' state."

"Brooklyn."

"Oh, so you must steal cars and sell drugs."

"No, sir."

"Bullshit, everybody in Brooklyn sells drugs and steals cars. What makes you different, maggot?"

"My folks taught me better than that, Sir."

The black devil just kind of shook his head and laughed.

"Your mommy and daddy taught you shit. I'm your mommy and daddy now, and you'll learn everything my way, or you'll wish you never laid eyes on me. Now go down and give me fifty just 'cause I don't like your fuckin' looks."

As he walked around the barracks he chose random recruits to abuse and humiliate. This went on for what seemed to be hours, and then out of the blue he said, "I'm leaving now. Reveille's at oh-six-hundred. You'd better sleep well because tomorrow, the fun and games start again."

Everyone helped each other. Those who had experience making up beds, or as they're called now 'racks' to Chief Hassle's specifications, helped those who didn't. The mood in the barracks was very tense. You could feel the fear and the anxiety about what was to come. I got a shower and got ready for bed. It was eleven o'clock when Tamper hollered "lights out". It was very quiet except for the muffled voices. I guess a lot of guys were praying about what could happen next. I know it didn't take long to drift off to sleep. It had been a long day.

"Peter, if we're going to do it this way I'm going to have to ask you questions, or we can stop right now."

"That's fair enough."

"Continue."

"Boot camp was like exercise in mental masturbation. One day you felt like you had it licked, the next day you wanted to crawl into a fetal position and give up."

"Did you ever do that?"

"Yeah. One night I was so tired of all the games that were played I huddled in a corner and cried like a baby."

"I've heard a lot about people going through boot camp. It all seems to be pretty redundant."

"Yeah, you might say that."

"Did you have any difficulties going through boot camp?"

"'Difficulties', hmm, let's see. I watched a kid have a massive coronary from doing six point push ups. 'Cause no one bothered to look at the medical hold tag he had on his shirt saying he had a heart condition."

"Wait a minute, you're telling me this young man had a heart condition, there was a medical hold tag on his shirt, and no one noticed?"

"No, no, you got it wrong. It's not that no one noticed, no one gave a fuck. The company commander in the holding company that I was in when I first got there…he didn't care, he just didn't care."

"So you witnessed this?"

"Yeah, I witnessed this. We were in a room with, like, forty people doing six count push ups. The company commander finally took notice when the kid grabbed his chest, screamed, fell on the floor and started going into convulsions. We were all told immediately to go outside, I never saw the company commander after that, and I never saw the kid, 'cause he was fucking dead."

"Did you have any problems with the academic portion of boot camp, or the physical portion?"

"No, not really. Oh, they did threaten to put me back and start all over again."

"Why was that?"

"I flunked qualifying on the rifle range. They sent me back a second time and I flunked that, too. They told me if

I flunked a third time I was going all the way back to the start of boot camp, and I'd been there eight weeks."

"So, on the third try the thought came to me that maybe I could convince the gunner's mate to let me shoot left handed, 'cause I am incredibly left handed. That's when the fun began."

"Did he let you shoot left handed?"

"He sure did, after a while of complaining to him, and begging him. He explained to me the mechanics of shooting, of the spent shell casing coming out and shooting very close to the side of my head."

"Did you pass this time?"

"I did. And, uh, the gunner's mate let me go four times, and to his amazement and mine as well, I got almost 100% each time. I was relieved because that portion of the insanity was over with, I wouldn't have to deal with that again, heh heh heh."

"Did the rest of the time you were there in boot camp go smoothly?"

"Yeah, other than the rape it was pretty smooth."

"Other than the *rape*?"

"Oh, yeah, I almost forgot about that. I was taking a shower one night, a buddy of mine and I, we witnessed a guy get raped."

Doctor Brown leaned forward in his chair and said, "You're going to have to be a little more specific about this situation."

"Sure, why not. I was in the shower and I heard a smash, it sounded like someone throwing a grapefruit against a wall. Over the water, I could hear it over the water. I looked over to see what was going on. A black kid named Michael had smashed this white kid's head against the shower wall and was proceeding to mount him. Blood was going everywhere, coming from the white kid."

"Mount him?"

"Oh, come on, doc, come on, you know what I'm talking about. OK, he was sodomizing him, that's a good word, OK, I'll go along with that. I ran out to get the company commander. He wasn't there. So I reported the incident to the head recruit of the company, who also happened to be black. There was a lot of commotion going on, finally the company commander showed up. The kid who got violated went off, I believe, to the hospital. Our company Casanova apparently went to the stockade."

"Was that the end of it?"

"Oh, no, no, no. That was just the tip of the iceberg. Almost immediately my friend Allen and I who witnessed the situation were getting requests to make sure we didn't see anything, so poor Michael didn't get ten years in Levenworth. It started out as suggestions, and became outright threats. I failed to tell you that that company of sixty eight, sixty nine men, were three quarters inner city from Detroit and Philadelphia. And there was a severe race issue going on in the military at that time.

"Did you experience any of that at Harvard or Yale or wherever you went to school? There probably wasn't a lot of that going on there, was there?"

"No, there probably wasn't. Did you report any of them?"

Peter laughed sardonically. "To who? The minute they found out that we had turned them in, or were willing to say what we saw, we'd have been pushed down the stairs, or woken up with our throats cut. That's the real deal.:

"How much longer were you going to be there after that incident?"

"I think about a month."

"Were they isolated threats?"

"Oh, no, they were constant. Every time someone walked by us, they'd make reference to "the brother ain't goin' down for no honky mother fucker.""

"Did you ever think to go to someone higher then your company commander?"

"How long have you been in this system? The first thing they teach is to follow the chain of command. We did get a break, though, we had a liberty coming up."

"You got 12 hours' liberty after eight weeks? How? Did that help?"

"My buddy and I got so drunk that we got thrown in jail, Cook County jail."

"For what? Just being drunk?"

"No, it had something to do with throwing TVs out the window of the tenth floor of a hotel in downtown Chicago. Someone could have been hurt or even killed. Luck was on our side. They fell on the awning instead of the ground."

"How many did you throw out?"

"I don't remember. We just kept throwing them out. I think I was in a black out or something."

"How did you get back to boot camp?"

"After ten days in Cook County the Navy brought us back to stand captain's mast and get our punishment."

"What happened at mast?

"We got 14 days in a unit called SID. That stood for special indiscretion division."

"How was that?"

"We got up at 4:30 and went to bed at 10. The entire day was breakfast, lunch and dinner, which we got a half hour on each of those, and the rest of the day was calisthenics and harassment. The thing that surprised me the most when I think about it is, it was like no big deal, it was just boys being boy, sailors on liberty. When the fourteen days were done at SID, they assigned us to a new company."

"Did you end up testifying on the assault case still?"

"They called us down to legal. My friend and I had to make a written statement to somebody, a lawyer or somebody, I don't know, somebody in the office. Never really heard anything else about it, actually."

"At that point, how many weeks did you have left in boot camp?"

"I think it was three, three or four. It was getting down to the wire."

"Was the rest of the time there uneventful?"

"Yeah, other that the race riot in the galley."

"Race riot in the galley?"

"Remember, this was 1970, and there were a lot of racial problems in the military."

"Would you like to elaborate on all of that?"

"Heh, heh, heh. Elaborate? Yeah, I guess I can elaborate. Here's what happened: we were just getting done eating, took our trays over to the scullery, when all hell broke loose. It was like a bar fight scene in the movies."

"What started it?"

"Okra."

"Okra?"

"Yeah, you've heard of okra, right? It's part of a soul food thing?"

"Yeah..."

"Apparently the okra was overdone."

"Do you view everything with cynicism?"

"No, only things that are cynical. On a serious note, it had something to do with the galley trying to have a soul food night, and it not being done right or something. I really don't know. There were, like 800 to 1000 people in this room, and all the doors were being plugged with people trying to get out. Lucky enough, the tables were bolted to the floor, so we hid under the table hoping it would all straighten itself out. I didn't want to get involved, and neither did the two guys I was with. We started to hear glass breaking, the windows were getting broken out by anything anybody could throw through them, so we figured we were going to crawl out through one of the windows as soon as things calmed down a bit. Then came the fire hoses."

We did manage to squeeze out through one of the windows that was broken out. There was screaming and water hoses and security, it was just a mess. There was a recruit lying outside on the pavement. He had been cut up. I think he got cut by the glass falling out the window. It looked like his legs were cut off, I'm not sure. He was screaming. All I wanted was to get out of there. The minute we got out, we double timed it back to the barracks. I didn't see anything, I didn't want to have nothing to do with *any* of it."

"Peter, coming from a small New England area, was that your first encounter with any kind of racism?"

"Yeah, pretty much."

"Did it leave you scarred?"

"Oh, Doc, are you trying to ask me if I'm a racist? No, I'm not a racist. I believe in equal opportunity. I don't care if you're black, white, red, green or yellow, if you're an asshole, you're an asshole."

"Well, you got through that. Yeah, the rest of the time was really uneventful. We waited for orders to find out where we were going, what schools we might be going to. I had been guaranteed an A school because my grades were high enough. I found out a week before we left boot camp that I had gotten an A school for aviation electrician's mate in Jacksonville, Florida."

"How'd you feel about that?"

"I thought the Navy had lost their mind. I didn't know anything about electricity, but it was a school, so I lived with it, tried to keep an open mind. I was pretty apprehensive, though, because I had dropped out of school, and felt really insecure about my abilities, at that point."

"So, the big day came…graduation. You get to stand at attention for two hours, while all the talking heads said what a great job you did, and what an opportunity we had, serving our country. Then awards were given out. They were giving out awards for achievement, oh, let me rephrase that, *outstanding* achievement. I was standing there hoping that this thing would get over quickly, when they called out my name. Front and center. I had no fucking idea what this was all about. Front and center to the company commander; he awarded me a marksmanship ribbon, oh, no, let me rephrase that, that's a *sharpshooter's* commendation for "excellence on the rifle range." I accepted the ribbon, saluted, made an about face and made it back to my position in the formation. A half hour, forty five minutes, and it was a done deal."

"We all headed back to the barracks, where we were going to be on liberty for the rest of the day. Back in the barracks I sat on my bunk and read the commendation; it said that I had achieved some of the highest scores on the rifle range in five years' time. It was signed by the company commander, the battalion commander, and the base C.O. The C.O. was the guy who gave me 14 days of SID less than a month earlier."

"Did you have any idea that was coming to you?"

"None whatsoever. The only thing I knew was when I convinced the gunner's mate to let me shoot left handed so I could qualify, that he sent out four or five different targets, which was different from the first time when they only sent two. I thought I did pretty good, but I really had no idea what that was all about, and I really didn't care."

"This time when I went on liberty, I stayed out of trouble. I just kinda walked around, got something to eat, and I actually went back to the base early. I knew that I'd be leaving there in a couple of days, and I had an opportunity to rest a little bit. It had been a zoo for the last fourteen weeks. I came away, though, with a different sense of self because of that experience."

"After all that, I thought that I'd pretty much be able to deal with pretty much anything. Boy, was I in for a let-down."

"How so?"

"We'll get to that later, Doc."

"Would you like to end this for today?"

"Yeah, I think that's a good idea. Well, where do we go from here, Doc?"

"If this doesn't work then we do it my way."

"Your way?"

Doctor Brown closed his book and leaned forward. ""Peter, if I think for one minute that your fucking with me, I'm going to have you out of here and in jail faster than you can come up with some sarcastic remark. Are we clear with that?"

"Yeah, I'm clear. Just let me tell my story."

"OK, tomorrow."

Doctor Brown got up and headed for the door.

"Doctor Brown I'm straight up with this. I need to tell someone, and you're it."

"Travis will see you back to the ward. Tomorrow."

Peter sat there for a few minutes until Travis came walking in.

"Come on, Pilgrim, let's go."

Peter turned to Travis as they were in the hallway.

"I don't know, Travis, what I'm scared of, but this stuff is so fucking deep. Has Doctor Brown ever dealt with any of his patients like this before?"

"Yeah, a couple of times, rare but, a couple times."

"It's the only way I can get this out. Everything is so bottled up, fear of the hypnotism, the lights and all, I've just got to suck it up and just let it go."

"If that's what you gotta do Pilgrim, that's how you gotta do it. The one thing I do know for sure, Pilgrim, there's only three ways to do this for you: the right way, the wrong way, and your way."

"I guess. Maybe I got a brain tumor or something that's making me this crazy."

"Well, if you do, Doc Brow and Art Perry will certainly get to the bottom of it. Or should I say the top of it, seeing it's in your head?"

"Real funny, Travis, real funny."

As they got to the elevator to go up to the third floor where the ward was, Travis said, "You're on your own from here, Pilgrim. I gotta go try to make heads or tails of the tapes I got from your session this afternoon."

"Jesus Christ, is it that bad?"

"No, actually not, it's just the part of my job I hate most. Get something to eat and some rest, I'll see you in the morning."

Peter got up to the ward where his room was. He happened to look at the clock. It had almost been five hours since he went down. That kind of took him aback.

Five hours? I couldn't have been down there five hours.

As he walked by the nurses' station, he asked Beth Anne what time he had gone downstairs.

"It was about one-thirty when Travis picked you up after lunch."

"What time is it now?"

"Don't you see the clock? It's six thirty."

"That's what I thought it said. Oh, well, just time slipped by, I guess."

"We've got a dinner tray here for you we kept warm. You can pick it up anytime you like."

"Now's as good a time as any, I guess. Besides, I'm hungry for a change."

She passed him the tray and he went to sit in the lounge. Two of the vets in the day room were arguing over television. One wanted 'Jeopardy', the other wanted 'Larry King'. They resolved it, they settled on 'Little House on the Prairie'.

Peter knew that he needed a good night's sleep. When he finished eating, he took a shower and got ready for bed. He was tired and was going to go to bed early. He had asked at the nurses' station if he could possible have his meds early so he could go to sleep.

"Not before nine."

"You mean I can't have the meds, or I can't go to sleep until nine?"

"No, you can go to sleep now, you just can't have your meds until nine. If you're asleep, we'll wake you up. Go take a nap."

"Yeah, I'll see if I can do that."

When he walked in his room he stood over by the window and looked out over the parking lot, just in time to see Travis and Dr. Brown walking across it. Peter wondered if he was getting anywhere. He watched as Dr. Brown and Travis just drove out of the parking lot. It seems as though, as he stood in the window looking out, he sort of went into a trance. A few seconds later he heard a voice from the other side of the room.

"Mr. Davies, are you done with this food tray? Mr. Davies, are you done with this food tray?"

"Excuse me, yeah, I'm done with it."

"You certainly didn't eat much this evening."

"I wasn't real hungry, Beth Anne. Besides, I'm watching my girlish figure."

She just kind of chuckled.

"You know, I hear there's a good movie on in the TV room this evening."

"Yeah, What is it?"

"Something about aliens."

"Yeah, maybe I'll check that out."

She left the room and he stood there again for a few minutes. He thought maybe he'd watch the movie, go check it out, see how that worked.

Once more, he looked out the window and wondered what Travis and Dr. Brown might be doing this evening. For a second, a thought flashed through his mind: Maybe I'm beginning to like them. *Yeah, right, more like tolerating. Anything to get the fuck out of here.*

He lucked out, there was a nice soft chair in the TV room. A repeat movie in a VA hospital, imagine that. Well, if things got too bad, he could always have some of that jello with the funny things in it.

He must have dozed off. One of the orderlies woke him up and told him it was time for bed, he might consider going to bed.

"Yeah, that's a good idea. Yeah, that works."

He stood in line and got his meds, then went to his room. Lying on his bed again, he couldn't help but wonder about the possible conversation between Travis and Dr. Brown, about the session that afternoon. *Oh, hell, maybe they weren't talking about me at all.*

He fell off to sleep.

Travis walked Dr. Brown to his car, and asked him if he was going to see the game that night.

"No, I don't think so, Travis. I've got a letter to write to an old friend I haven't heard from in years."

"Well, I think I'm going to stop down to the bar, have a cold soda water and maybe watch the game for a while before I head home."

"That sounds like a good idea. See you in the morning, Travis. Have a good evening."

"You too. Drive safe."

They both left the parking lot about the same time. A few minutes later Travis pulled into the Outpatient's parking lot. *Quiet* night, he thought to himself. The residents and interns must have had a hard day, called it an early night.

He walked in and headed over to the bar. His friend Gary had been a bartender for years.

"Hey buddy how you been? I haven't seen you in a long while."

"Seemed like you stopped coming up to the hospital to visit. Has working in this joint driven you off the wagon yet, Gary?"

"Nope. Twenty four years last month, Travis."

"Jesus, where the hell does the time go?"

"OK, let me see. Soda water with lime."

"Close. Lemon."

"Well, at least I was half right. Really, Travis, what brings you here tonight?"

"I really don't know."

"You're not thinking of giving it all up and acting like some of these nineteen year olds in here, are you Travis?"

"Nah, I just need a different scene. Between the patients and home, doesn't seem like I do much of anything else, anymore."

"You still going to meetings?"

"You know, Gary, it seems like it's been a long while since I have."

"Well, you know what works, Travis."

"Well, one thing for sure, Gary, some things never change."

"You must be coming on what, fifteen, sixteen, seventeen years clean?"

"Yeah, something like that."

"Well, keep up the good work. Here's your water. No charge, water's on the house for letting me preach to you."

Just then Gary was interrupted by someone wanting a drink.

"What's it going to be?"

"Captain Morgan's and coke."

"Comin' right up."

Travis was watching the basketball game, and out of the corner of his eye he saw Dr. Brown come in through the door.

He thought to himself, *Now that's odd. I don't think he's ever been in the Outpatient.*

Dr. Brown walked up to Travis and asked him what he was drinking.

He held his glass up and said, "sparkling water."

Travis called Gary over and asked him, "Have you ever met Dr. Brown from the hospital?"

"No, not officially, I've seen you around the halls in there."

"Dr. Brown, this is an old friend of mine, this is Gary Powell. Gary, Dr. Brown."

"Please, call me Prescott."

"Then Prescott it is. And what's your poison, Prescott? Let me guess. Grand Marnier."

"Good guess, but I'd just like a double shot of Jack Daniels."

"A man after my own heart."

"Tell me Gary, has Art Perry been in here this evening?"

"No, but you'll hear him long before you see him."

"So, about what time does he usually come in?"

"Ah, it's fairly early for Perry."

"You think he'll be in this evening?"

"Like clockwork. Trailing behind him two or three residents who don't look like they've slept since junior high school."

Prescott asked Travis who's playing tonight.

"Knicks and Bulls."

Travis realized that he was a little uncomfortable. In the fourteen or fifteen years he'd worked with Prescott Brown, he'd never known him in a social setting, only professional. It felt a bit awkward.

Gary broke the silence to ask Prescott if he was shrinking lots of heads up to the VA.

"I don't know if I'm shrinking theirs, sometimes I think I'm shrinking mine."

Prescott's drink was gone. Gary asked him if he'd like to have something else.

"Yeah, a beer."

"What kind?"

"Michelob Light."

"I just happen to have a cold one right here." He brought it up to the counter, flipped the cap off and handed him a glass.

"Oh, I don't need a glass."

Travis just kind of looked at him without him noticing. He thought to himself, *No glass? Hmmm.*

Travis finished off his water and told Gary he thought he'd head home.

"Gary, good seeing you again. I'll see you soon, hopefully. Well, if I can get on the other side of the Beltway in the next twenty minutes, I'll catch the last half of the game and get to bed."

Gary reached his hand out to shake Travis' hand, and hung on closely for a second, and said, "Maybe we should hook up some Saturday afternoon, there's a real good meeting in Alexandria."

"Yeah, let's do that Gary, I think that would be good. Let's do that soon, OK?"

"You got it."

"Dr. Brown, I'll see you in the morning. You have a good evening, Sir."

"You too, Travis. Drive safe."

As Travis was heading towards the door, it opened and Art Perry and his band of tired residents came rolling in.

Perry made eye contact with Travis and said, "Travis, what the hell are you doing here?"

"I brought a colleague." Travis turned to one side and pointed to the end of the bar.

"Prescott Brown in *this* dive? Oh, *this* is going to be interesting."

"Well, Art, happy hunting," Travis said as he went through the door.

"And who do we have here? Dear god, it's Prescott Brown! What brings you here? God know you're not slumming."

107

"I just wanted to see how the other half lived."

"You mean 90%. OK, let's get down to it. What really brings you here?"

"Just wanted to run a few things by you that's all."

"Let me guess-is it the patient you've requested three CAT scans for?"

"Yeah that's it."

"I told you the first time I found nothing. There's nothing to indicate why this patient goes catatonic, nothing physical that I can find."

"Could I get you to do it one more time?"

"Why are you even bothering?"

"This one intrigues me."

"Prescott, they all intrigue you. There isn't a day that goes by when I don't have to stop this process, Prescott. If it was just up to me he could come down one hundred times, two hundred times. It doesn't work that way, at least not in the real world."

"Well, that was a low blow, Art, real low."

"No it wasn't either. Look, Prescott, I know the good work you do up there, but every time I do a procedure I have to justify it."

"Just once more, Art. Do the CAT scan and MRI just once more, would you please?"

"Look. If I can find a deceased patient's name to put it under, recently deceased, I'll run him through once more, that's it. Unless he starts growing another head, there isn't anything else I can do, past this one."

"All right. I know you'll do the best you can."

"Now, really, Prescott, what makes this one different from the rest of them?"

"I don't know. The guy's my age, when he's on it, he's sharp as a tack. Way above normal intelligence. And bitter and angry as hell."

"Hell, he could be one of my relatives. Tell me, Prescott, when he goes into one of these things do you notice any physical changes? Rapid eye movement, rapid heart beat, raised blood pressure, perspiration...?"

"I haven't been able to induce one of these things since they brought him in here from the Metro."

"Have you tried your hypnotism, that system you use on them?"

"Yeah, this afternoon. Twenty minutes after I thought I'd had him hypnotized, he pulled the probes off and asked me how stupid I thought he was."

"Hell, maybe the guy's playing you. Hell, maybe it's easier to play you in here than to sit behind bars downtown. Did you bother seeing if the Metro might get his police records, if he has any, to see if this has happened before, this intensely? How 'bout meds, is he responding to them? I know you're trying everything, I'm just sitting here trying to be the devil's advocate, so to speak.

Prescott threw his hands in the air and said, "I'm baffled, with this one I'm baffled."

"So what you're telling me is that nothing's working."

"No, not really. The only thing that seems to work is me sitting there and letting him tell this story about his life. That's the only time that he responds to any of the questions, to anything. That's when he responds, when I allow him to tell his story his way, it flows out of him like he was in the moment, when he's telling me."

"OK, well, let him do it that way, then."

"Yeah, but…"

"Yeah, but *what*?"

"That's not the way we do things."

"He's bruising your ego."

"No, I don't think so."

"I think so."

"No, that can't be."

"Oh, yeah, that's right. Can't be. Look, Prescott, I don't know a lot about your field. To me, it's all voodoo and psychobabble. I know you've helped a lot of patients, you and Travis do some really good work. Hook him up with the electrodes, let him tell his story. While he's telling you his story, can you ask him questions?"

"Occasionally."

"Look, if anything, I know this. All of these guys have a story. Some of them are full of shit, some are real. But if that guy's got some deep, deep scars that he's afraid of, let him talk. He'll get to it. He may not realize he's getting to it, but he will, and you'll pick up on it. Maybe then you can help him."

"I think he's going to fight me all the way."

"Probably. But then again, Prescott, that's why you get the big bucks."

Prescott finished his beer and set it on the bar He thanked Gary for the beer and told Art he'd see him later on.

"Gimme a couple of days, I'll figure out a way to do this guy's CAT scan and MRI. This is the last time, though, no more. You could live in this bar and it's not going to happen again. You know, maybe you ought to just med this guy out. Guys have done it before. Make him nice and comfortable, let him stroll the halls doing the thorazine shuffle."

"Nah, this one's different."

"Ah, famous last words. I said that about my last three wives."

"Good night." Prescott headed out the door.

"What do you think about all that Gary? You've been listening to the conversation."

"I don't know. I think, you know, maybe the guy's just a garden variety drunk."

"Nah, there's got to be more going on than that, or Prescott wouldn't have gotten this far."

"Well, Art, it's all Greek to me, anyways. Would you like something to drink?"

"Yup, my usual."

"Lemon."

"Nope, lime tonight."

"Damn it! I've always got a fifty-fifty chance of getting that. How these kids doing this year, Art?"

"The second year class here, and out of the original twelve, four of them have washed out."

"Is that your average, normally?"

"Yeah, it's about average. At the end of the year, if I end up with about half of what I started with, I think I've done my job."

"You know, Art, you're a good man to watch after these kids through this process. I'm your bartender…why do you do this, Art?"

"'Cause I had somebody do it for me a long time ago."

"You're a wonderful human being, Art, I don't care what anyone else says about you."

"So, Gary, tell me, what did you think of Prescott Brown?"

"He seemed out of place, to me."

"Well, this isn't really his cup of tea, Gary."

"Yeah, that's what I figured. I'd heard rumors about him years ago. Lots of old money from up North, huh?"

"That's an understatement, Gary. I could never figure out what makes the guy tick. Best schools, best tutors; with his qualifications, he could have been teaching at any of the best schools in the country, or in the world, for that matter."

"Yeah, how so?"

"Well, let's see: he started off at Exeter Academy, top of his class, then Yale undergrad, magna cum laude and Harvard Medical School to top it all off. He had a choice of some of the best psychiatric hospitals in the country, and out of the blue he chooses Bellevue. How d'ya suppose that happened?"

"I think maybe he got hooked up with some of those screaming liberals at Harvard, and grew a conscience past his money."

"He could have gone into private practice anywhere, for any amount, and he ends up at a VA hospital."

"I don't know, don't you think you're being a little hard on him, Art?"

"Ahh, maybe a little. Don't get me wrong, he's an excellent doctor with a good reputation. He cares and he's willing to buck the system."

"Now, there, doesn't that make you feel better, Art? You said something nice about the guy."

"I'd like him a hell of a lot more if he didn't have such a stick shoved up his ass. Forget I said that."

"Forget you said *what*?"

"Yeah, you got it. Gimme a couple of dollars in quarters so I can shoot some pool with these kids before I go home and get a good night's sleep."

"Enjoy your game."

Gary went back to work, and Art went to shoot a couple of games of pool. There was a mix of music coming out of the juke box: rap, some old school Motown. One kid kept playing over and over 'Teen Spirit' by Nirvana.

Prescott noticed as he left the parking lot that it was a clear, clear night. He didn't very often get to see the stars, being so close to the city like that, but tonight you could see some.

He headed on to the Beltway and home to Alexandria. Traffic was very, very thin. The thought occurred to him, maybe he should leave the hospital late every night, he'd have less traffic to deal with.

As he pulled into his driveway he noticed it was quiet there tonight; no cars, no lights, no fundraisers, no kids. The garage door closed behind him as he got out of his car. He quickly looked at the other cars; they hadn't been touched. He was grateful for that. By the time he had gotten home, Lauren had gone home. There was a note on the counter from her saying his mail was on his desk, there was something in the fridge for him if he wanted to nuke it, and she hoped he'd had a good day, and would see him soon.

It was good; the house was quiet and his wife and daughter were probably in bed or in their rooms, either watching tv or on the net. For him, that was time to himself. He heated what Lauren made him for supper, that and a glass of milk, and went into his study to go through the day's mail. There wasn't much for mail. After he was done eating he decided to check his e-mail. It had been days since he'd done that. Scrolling through all the garbage, he got one from an old class mate he had not heard from in a few months Dan Jenson. What could he be up to?

"Dear Prescott, it's been too long since we talked. I am sorry about that. Life sometimes gets too busy. I was at a seminar in Boulder, Colorado last week, and I just happened to run into an old friend of ours from the summers we spent up in Maine when we were in prep school. I know that you remember Abby Westrom, the girl that was working at the resort while we were there. If I recall, you sort of had a thing for her, and how your mother almost lost her mind when she found out that she was working there and not a guest. Didn't she threaten to send you to Europe with your father if you didn't stop seeing her? Oh, she's doing well. I'll tell you more about that later. Just got a page from the hospital. One of my patients tried to hold up a McDonald's with a squirt gun. Time to lock him up for a tune up. Press, do you remember that you wanted to be a lobsterman and I wanted to be a rock star? Maybe we should have done that. Less pay, less stress. Well, maybe for you. I liked getting high too much to have become a rocker. I'll be in D.C. in a few weeks. Let's get together for dinner; no excuses will do. Your friend, Dan."

Prescott closed his e-mail, poured himself a good drink as he looked at the glass. Maybe Rod Stewart was right- the first cut is the deepest.

When the drink was gone he turned out the lights and went up to bed. The next morning came without anyone being up. Lauren asked if he wanted breakfast.

"No, just a glass of orange juice." As he left he stopped Lauren.

"Do you remember Dan Jenson who used to go on vacation with us when we were kids?"

"Was he the one that your father used to threaten to cut his hair?"

"That's him."

"Why?"

"I got an e-mail from him last night."

"How long has it been?"

"Ten, twelve years."

"That's too long for old friends."

"Yeah, you're right. See you this evening."

"You, too."

He got into his car and started to drive out and stopped. The thought ran through his head that, unlike Dan, he never rebelled. When his mother told him he would have to stop seeing Abby, he just stopped seeing her. When Dan ran off from his first year in college to follow the Grateful Dead, and after a year off, said that he was going to join the Peace Corps, hell I was a senior in college before he came back. I remember he was telling me about all his adventures and that going back to school now had some kind of meaning. Being the true rebel he was, he decided to go into medicine instead of law like his father and older brother. Always do the right thing, Prescott.

He started to leave when he stopped again. Pulling back into the garage, turning off the Land Rover and getting out, he looked over at the cars he had that he hardly ever drove, except on special occasions. He walked back and forth: six classic cars that never get driven. Not today.

He pulled the cover off the sixty three split window, because today he was taking that one to work. Climbing into the Corvette, he didn't know how long it had been since he'd even sat in it. Turning the key, the car came to life. His mechanic always kept them in good running condition. Pulling out of the driveway and onto the street, it occurred to him that doing things on impulse was very foreign…but not today. It did feel good to drive something that responded that well to the road. He turned on the radio and found an oldies station. He was hoping to hear some Beach Boys; it would certainly fit the ride.

Peter woke up at about 8:15. He got a shower and had a cup of coffee before breakfast. It was good to be able to get around, at least on the ward, without Travis behind him every time he turned around. Walking past the nurses' station, Nurse Webster asked him if he was OK.

"Why's that?"

"Well, you were up and down all night long."

"I don't remember that. What do you mean by 'up and down all night'? I'm not following you. I went to bed around 9:30, and as far as I know, I slept all night. I feel like I got enough rest, so, you know? Who knows. Well, as long as I didn't try to escape, or cause hate and discontent, I guess we'll just have to leave it at that."

"Would you fill in Travis and Doctor Brown on that when they come in this morning?"

"Fill them in on *what*? I slept through the night."

"In Beth Anne's report it shows that you stood by your window looking out for well over two hours. When she asked you if everything was OK, you just turned to her and shook your head up and down, and turned back toward the window."

"So it's a crime to look out a window?"

"No, it's not a crime to look out the window."

"So, then, what's the problem?"

"The problem is, you have *no* recollection of it. *That* is the problem."

"You've never had patients that sleepwalk before? You've never had patients who looked out the window because they couldn't sleep, and couldn't remember it, for whatever reason?"

"I'm not talking about them, I'm talking about you."

"Yeah, yeah, right, whatever." Peter headed back into his room. He stood by the window, looking out. The part they were all missing was he *liked looking out the fucking window!*

A few minutes later, Travis walked in.

"Morning, Pilgrim. What's going on?"

"Oh, Christ, here we go again. Yeah, they tell me I had a bad night, and I didn't have a bad night, and Nurse Webster seems to be making a big deal out of it."

"What in the hell are you talking about, Peter?"

"Oh, you mean you didn't talk to Nurse Ratched about my mental state?"

"No, I haven't spoken to Nurse Ratched, *I mean Nurse Webster.*"

"OK, Travis, I'll give you my version, because she's going to give you *her* version."

"This is too early in the morning, Peter. I haven't had a second cup of coffee yet. What in the hell is going on?"

"The night nurse said that I was up and down all night, stood by this window for a couple hours, didn't respond when they asked me questions other that shaking my head up and down."

"Did you sleep well?"

"Yeah, I actually woke up rested, for a change."

"Oh, maybe it's got something to do with some of the stuff you talked to Dr. Brown about yesterday. You didn't cause any hate and discontent, so I wouldn't worry about it too much."

"Finally, *someone* sane. Travis, are you familiar with the Shakespearian quote, 'That a sane man must appear insane in an insane world'?"

"I thought Spock said that."

Peter just laughed and shook his head.

"Look, we're going to do the session this morning instead of this afternoon, Peter. Doctor Brown's got a couple of other things he needs to do, we've got to do a couple of intakes this afternoon. I'll be coming back up to pick you up at about 10:00. In the meantime, try to avoid Nurse Webster, will ya?" Travis chuckled a little.

"Yeah, yeah. I tried ignoring a case of the clap one time, too."

Travis started to leave, and Peter broke out laughing hysterically.

"Pilgrim, what the hell's going on? What the hell's so funny?"

"Travis, c'mere, I gotta show you something."

Travis walked over to the window.

"Does that black, sixty three split window look familiar to you?"

"No, but I sure wish I had it."

"Do you know who just drove up in that?"

"How could I know that?"

"Because it's your boss."

"*What?*"

"Your boss."

"I knew he had a couple cars, I never knew what he had. Hey, it's good to see those old things still on the road."

"Hmmmmm." Peter started laughing again.

"What's so funny, anyways, Pilgrim?"

"I'm not sure, but I see some humor in all of this."

"When you figure it out, would you fill me in?"

"Absolutely, Travis. Absolutely."

As Travis left, Beth Anne stuck her head in the door and said that the breakfast trays were in. He thanked her. Walking out the door behind her, he asked, "Have you ever had a ride in a sixty three split coupe?"

"What's that?"

"Well, it's not the Metro."

She looked at him with a puzzled expression, like she had no clue what he was talking about.

"Oh, nothing, just rambling. Had a bad night, you know." He chuckled again, more to himself than to Beth Anne.

After breakfast he went down and washed his face, then strolled down to watch some television until Travis came up. Walking past the nurses' station, Webster informed him that he had some meds to take.

"Didn't you give these to me in the middle of the night?"

"No, I didn't give them to you in the middle of the night."

"I was just checking."

The natives were restless in the lounge that morning. Dave was walking back and forth aimlessly, mumbling. Rob was trying to convince everybody that he didn't belong there, that he was above all that. Charlie informed Peter that he was going to be leaving soon, and that he was going home for good. Apparently, no one informed Charlie that that was probably not going to happen; but if that's what he needed to hang onto to get through another day, Peter told him he'd be leaving soon, and good luck.

It dawned on him how much the news actually did affect him. There just never seemed to be anything good on it. *Maybe I ought to just stop watching the news*, he thought.

Peter went back into his room and looked out the window, still admiring the sixty three split window. He wondered if it was the 396 or the 427. He thought to himself, *it's quite a car. Not many left, not many made. Pure Detroit muscle. Pure muscle.*

Around 10:00 Travis came in and said, "Are you ready, Pilgrim?"

Walking back down to the therapy room that he was in the day before, Travis told him they were going to do something a little bit different, and hoped he'd go along with it.

"We're just going to turn the microphone on, as you and Doctor Brown talk, but we would like to place a heart and respiratory monitor on you, just to see how you react to things."

"Yep, Travis, I made a deal with Doctor Brown, and I'll keep the deal as long as he keeps it with me."

"Oh, he'll do that, Pilgrim, he'll do that."

Peter went in and sat down, and Travis hooked him up. They sat there and chit-chatted about basketball, a lot of nothing for about fifteen to twenty minutes.

"You suppose when this session's done you can sneak me out for a smoke, Travis?"

"Well, I'm under the impression that if this goes well, Doctor Brown's going to give you rights to go down to the smoking room."

"Smoking room?"

"Yeah, there's one down by the gym. We get through, everything goes well, I'll take you down and show you where it is."

"Oh. That sounds good. Aren't they worried that I'll run off?"

"I don't think so. I think you probably want this more than anybody."

Travis headed towards the door.

"Hey, Travis, why'd you lie to me? When I first met you, you told me you were at Keh Sahn. And then later on you told me you were at Mei Lai. Well, which one is it? One was the Marines, the other was Army. Why did you lie?"

"I didn't. I had to get your attention, and that was the only way to do it."

"OK."

"Peter. Mei Lai. Straight up, Mei Lai."

"You didn't have to lie to me, man."

"I did what I had to do to get you to start talking to me. And I'd do it again. Got that clear, Pilgrim?"

"Crystal."

Peter just sat there, thinking. He'd been there what seemed to be a couple of weeks, giving him the rights to go

121

down to the smoking room; *Jesus, I'll be glad when this shit is over with. Well, it beats the hell out of jail.*

Just then, Doctor Brown walked in.

"Morning, Peter. How are you today?"

"Is it a 375 horse 396, or a 450 horse 427?"

"What?"

"The 'vette."

"Oh, the car."

"Yeah, I saw you come in this morning. I got to admit, you look better driving that than you do that Land Rover."

"I think it's the 450/427."

"You what? You've got that car and you don't know what it has for a motor in it?"

"You'll forgive me for not being a motorhead, won't you?"

"Yeah, I just love those old cars, Doc, that's all, I just love those old cars."

"Well, I'm glad you appreciate it."

"You know, Doc, it's funny. In a way, I sometimes think I get along with machinery better than people. Sorry about the crack about not knowing what sized motor. I sometimes assume that, if I know it, everybody else must know it. I know; you're going to say that's a self-esteem issue."

"Yeah, I might say that."

"It's just what it is, Doc, it's just what it is."

"When I read the morning report, the nurses said you had a rough night."

Peter sighed loudly. "I don't know. I don't recall anything. I woke up rested; they tell me I was up, staring out the window half the night."

"Nurse Webster said you got irritated when she mentioned it to you."

"Look, Doc, I'm in here because of going into catatonic states. They tell me I stood by the window for a couple hours, not even making a peep, just staring out into nowhere. What the hell's going on with me? I don't get it. I mean, I believe 'em."

"If I was to make an educated guess, Peter, I would say there's something deep in your psyche that you just can't deal with."

Peter snorted. "Yeah. Yeah, I guess so. You know, I'm gonna tell you something, and if you tell anybody, I'll swear I didn't say it: the sarcasm's the only thing that I have that I feel safe with."

"Well, you're certainly good at it. What do you say we pick up where we left off yesterday?"

"How many of these things are we gonna do, anyway?"

"As many as it takes to find out what is going on."

"I hope you're a patient man."

"I am."

"Yes, Dr. Brown, I am."

"OK, Peter."

"With my orders for a school in Jacksonville, Florida, and ten days leave I was going home to do nothing. The flight to Boston from O'Hare was good. Had a couple drinks and got some sleep. I had a two hour wait at Logan for my flight to Portland. We landed at about eight thirty. My oldest brother was there to pick me up."

"He must have been happy to see you."

"Yeah, I'm sure he was."

"What do you mean by that?"

"My oldest brother is a good man, and I have a lot of respect for him, but he doesn't show a lot of emotion. It's just the way he is."

"Was there any welcome home celebration for you?"

"Not really. My folks were glad I was home. One of my sisters lived in the neighborhood and she was there, and my brother in law. All I really wanted to do was go to bed and sleep, knowing I didn't have to get up at five in the morning. But guess what?"

"You were up at five?"

"You got it."

"Did you go back to sleep?"

"Not really. I just laid there wondering if I was going to tell my folks about getting thrown in jail and the other things. After tossing that back and forth in my head for God knows how long, I decided to not say anything about any of it. I finally got up at about seven or so, showered and went down stairs."

"My father was just leaving for work and asked me what I was going to be doing today, if I had anything planned. I told him I really didn't know, I just wanted to rest, take it easy, see a few friends. I asked him if I could use his car, and he said yes, but I'd have to give him a ride to work. I did that. I dropped him off at work, told him I'd pick him up around five. He told me to be careful with his car and to make sure I put gas in it."

"I really didn't do much. I went down to the beach and took some pictures with a camera I had bought at boot camp. I like taking pictures. Saw a couple of guys I knew in town, and you know, Doc, actually, I got stoned for the first time. I really enjoyed it a lot, but I figured because of the whole Navy thing I wasn't going to do that again. Ha! That would soon change."

"You're home ten days from boot camp, getting ready to leave again, and you don't do a lot of anything?"

"Nah, I just drove around the back roads. I liked driving around the back roads, I used to do that all the time, by myself, it's quiet. I visited some of my family real briefly and let them know I was alive. Ten days were up, I got a ride to Portland, and headed down to Jacksonville, Florida."

"Got to NAS Jacksonville and checked in. Got my barracks assignment, it was Thursday and I wasn't going to be starting classes until Monday, So I had some time to check things out. Seemed like a booming place, there must have been forty bars outside the main gate."

"The barracks were more like a college dorm than barracks. There seemed to be a party going on twenty four seven. I found out that was because there were classes in shifts eight to three and four to ten."

"Did you make any friends?"

"A few. There were two guys in my room and we used to hang around on weekends. I didn't do a lot of partying when I was there. The school work was hard for me and I kept falling behind. Mid point through the school I was called in to the senior chief's office to get a pep talk. The chief wanted me to go to three extra classes at night to get some tutoring. If I didn't I was going to fail and would be sent to the fleet, and the way they said it, it sounded like the worst thing on earth. I said I thought it would help and when would it be starting?"

"Tonight."

"That works. Besides, I didn't have much of a social life. Anyway you know I was there six months and only got off the base four or five times. Remember all those bars I told you about? I went once and it was like being back in boot camp. There was too much race shit going on. I didn't need it. One guy in my room was a red neck from Alabama. Hated blacks and that. All we ever heard about it was sickening; he hated them and they hated him, and I didn't want anything to do with any of it."

"Look doc where I came from there was only one black family and no one that I know looked at them any different than anyone else."

"How did the rest of the time go?"

"I was doing OK. The extra classes helped. There were three weeks left when the barracks master at arms called me into his office."

"Davies, the battalion commander wants to see you in his office tomorrow at one hundred hours."

"What's that all about?"

"I don't have a clue, I just pass the word down."

"OK, thanks. Hey, what building is that in?"

"You've been here six months and you don't know where his office is? 425, second floor."

"Thanks." I kept looking at the piece of paper he gave me with the time on it. I had been around long enough to know when they call you up to battalion it had to be bad news or at least that's what other guys were saying. It was hard not to think about what the battalion commander wanted. I had a hard time getting to sleep. It kept going over and over in my head. The next morning I got up and went over for breakfast. I didn't go to class, I knew I would be excused because of having to see the commander at eight thirty. I got ready in dress uniform. I didn't much like the dress whites but in Florida, with the humidity the dress blues would kill you. Doc, did I tell you how much I hate humidity?"

"No."

"I guess not. I thought I knew what humidity was. Was I wrong. His office was about four blocks from the barracks. It was a nice day, but hot. When I got to his offices his yeoman asked if she could help. That was an understatement. This girl was maybe five ten, five eleven, blonde, very well built. Hell, she could have been a model. The thing that I noticed was her skirt was very short, not at all regulation. Oh, well, the old man had good taste."

"She said that I could go in. Entering his office I came to attention."

"At ease, Airman Davies. I would like to talk to you about an opportunity the Navy would like to make available to you."

"Sir?"

"Would you be interested in a program that the Navy and Marine Corps has?"

"What would that be, Sir?"

"Sniper scout school."

"Sniper school? What would they want me to do?"

"That you qualified so highly on the rifle range."

"Sir that was just luck. I couldn't hit the broad side of a barn. I was just lucky to talk the gunner's mate into letting me try left handed so I wouldn't have to go back through boot camp again."

"I would like you to think about it and get back to me in a couple of days."

"Sir, if I don't do this will it change anything that I'm doing now?"

"No, Davies, the Navy doesn't work that way. Nothing will change."

"Thank you," and I left.

"How did that make you feel?"

"You know, to tell the truth I was scared and excited at the same time."

"Were you thinking about doing it?"

"No I wasn't. Not 'til I called home that night."

"What happened?"

"I was going to tell my folks about the conversation I had with the commander and what they thought I should do. I never really asked them for much advice about anything, but this seemed important and I didn't really know what to do about anything but this seemed important and I didn't really know what to do with it. When my mother picked up and I asked how everybody was at home; that was the wrong thing to do. Off she went about her grandchildren and how Charlie just got a new job at the steel factory, and how she knew he'd go a long way seeing that's where my father and brothers worked."

"Did she ask you what you were doing?"

"Ha ha, don't you get it? They never asked me anything. Do you want to hear something funny? They used to tell me that when my mother was pregnant with me she thought I was a tumor until the doctor told her that she was going to have me."

"Who told you that?"

"Everybody."

"OK, aside from that, did you ever get the chance to tell her what was going on with you and the commander?"

"No, just something I had to keep to myself."

"Did you run the offer by anyone?"

"Nope. Besides if I would have told anyone my father would have just written it off as Peter trying to be a big shot."

"So you didn't have much interaction with your family?"

"To say the least. I just didn't matter."

"Did you take the offer?"

"Don't you know?"

"What do you mean by that?"

"Did you read my records?"

"Most of your records are blanked out."

"Does that tell you anything at all? Look, when you agreed to let me tell you this story, I told you I would work with you to get to the bottom of these blackout things or whatever they are."

"And I will."

"The next day I decided to go over to the commander again about the whole thing. I was on the fence. I had mixed feelings about it, but was curious enough to want to know more. At noon after lunch I walked over to find out if I could see the commander after class. I was out at three. His yeoman said he had time at four, and to come back then. I told her I would. As she turned around I took a good look at her and knew it was time to hit the beach for some fun. Walking back to class I ran into one of the guys in my class. I didn't really know him that well, but he was always talking about all the girls he was going out with that hung out at this bar he went to. I asked if I could go with him the next time."

"Sure I'll get you laid. Did you have a girlfriend at home?"

"No, not really. There were a couple of girls I was hanging out with the summer before I got drafted, but then I decided to join the Navy and they had to go back to school."

"Did you stay in contact with those two girls?"

"With one of them. The other one went back home."

"Back home, she wasn't from your area, then?"

"Nah, she worked at a resort area down on the water, down on the ocean."

"Where was she from?"

"Oh, upstate New York."

"Well, you could have stayed in touch with her there."

"No, no, I don't think so. You see, I had the misfortune of meeting her parents one weekend when they came up to visit her. Her mother was rude and obnoxious, and in my presence referred to me as 'that one'. So I told Lizzie it was nice knowing her, hope everything worked out for her."

"Was that the only explanation you gave?"

"Yeah, that was it. You see, doc, I had been treated like that most of my life, and I wasn't going to be treated like that by anyone anymore."

"So that must have hurt?"

"You know something, doc, you never get used to being judged before someone knows you."

"So that was it?"

"Yep, that was it. Have you ever been put into that situation? No, I'm sure you haven't."

"Well, getting back to the offer that was made to me. I decided to go with it. You know, when you're young and you have ideals and you think you're invincible, everybody wants to be good at something. I headed back to class, and at 3:30, 4:00 I headed over to the commander's office. It was easier this time, I wasn't distracted by his yeoman, his yeoman had been replaced by a very frumpy woman who was hoping she could stay in the service long enough for "don't ask, don't tell' to show up. She told me it would be a few minutes before I could go in and see the commander, so I just sat there. Well, she wasn't very friendly. I asked her where the bathroom was, she snapped at me and said, "In the Navy, it's called 'the head'. She told me it was down the passageway on the left."

I said 'thank you' and she mumbled something, I don't know what it was she said. When I returned it was time to go in and see the commander. I went in his office and snapped to attention, he told me 'at ease'. He asked if I had come to a decision. I told him not completely, I'd just like to have some more information, if that was possible. He told me he could give me some information, if that was possible. He told me he could give me some information, but the rest of it I'd be getting down the line if I decided to go with it."

"What I have here is, you'll finish here, have five days' leave, then you'll report to Quantico, Virginia."

"How long would I be there?"

"Twelve weeks."

"That's not a Navy base, is it?"

"No, it's a Marine base."

"Marine base? Sir, this is getting confusing."

"If you volunteer, you'll be TAD'd to the Marine Corps for training and assignment."

"Sir, I've always been under the impression that the Marines didn't like sailors so much."

"Old sea stories, airman, old sea stories. We're all one big team."

"Yeah, I'm going for it, yeah, I'm going for it."

"I hope you've had time to think about this and to talk with maybe your folks about it."

"Yeah, I've thought about it. Now that I've agreed, is there going to be any more information?"

"Someone will contact you here in the next week or two, and they'll have more information for you."

"He stood up, thanked me for being willing to volunteer for something, and that he hoped it all worked out, and said 'dismissed'."

"That was a pretty bold move with as little information you had."

Peter leaned forward and said, "No, doc, it was a dumb fucking decision I made."

"Then why did you make it?"

"You know, I didn't know then, but I know now. I just wanted to feel like I made a difference, that I counted for something. Oh, yeah, let's see: low self-esteem, poor nurturing, no affirmation, neglect, abuse, self-loathing, are those all the right clinical words for someone making a stupid fucking decision like that without information?"

"Well, the one thing I've got to say is that you're well-versed at the correct words."

"Hmmm."

"There are times when you talk about some of these things you become very agitated."

'Yeah, let's see: I'm nineteen years old, I just volunteered for something that you aren't even going to fucking believe when I tell you, hell, doc, I don't even believe half of it half the time. I call home to talk somebody about this thing, my mother's talking about her grandchildren and how fucking wonderful they're doing, I'm getting ready to fuck up the rest of my life, and she's telling me what a great job my fucking nephew just got. Yeah, probably some self-loathing. What do you think?"

"And I left the commander's office, went back to the barracks, got dressed in civilian clothes, and headed downtown to get laid. On the way out of the barracks I met up with the guy I spoke to earlier who was supposedly the cat that knew all the happening spots off the base. But he didn't know anymore than I did, he just like to talk about it."

"Well, if you were nineteen years old, how were you getting into bars, 'cause wasn't it 21 at the time?"

"Yeah, but there was a guy in the barracks that had an ID card factory going where he'd alter ID cards and make you 21."

"Wasn't that illegal?"

"Course it was."

"Didn't it worry you, you might get caught, get busted?"

"Three quarters of the people on the base had altered ID cards. Besides, the bars weren't going to turn people away, that's what they're there for, to get people drunk."

"Well, what happened? Did you find any companionship?"

Peter just broke out laughing. "No, I didn't find any companionship, nor did I get laid. But I did get drunk.

133

Luckily, it was Friday night, so I didn't have to worry too much about the next day. I went for it. You want to hear something really pathetic, Doc? I'm sitting at the bar, it's about 2:00 in the morning, I'm broke, drinking my last beer. A black hooker sat next to me and asked for a date. Told her I was flattered, but I was so broke I couldn't pay attention. I told her how lovely she was, and I wished I had some money. She said, 'Baby, 'cause you lie so well, I'm going to buy you a drink.' I told her no, I was serious, she was lovely. She just laughed, patted me on the shoulder and said, 'I'll see you at payday, boy.'"

"Did you see her again?"

"No, no, no," Peter chuckled. "I decided to head back over to the base. I passed out in my bunk, woke up the next afternoon some time. I remember waking up, I was thinking that the whole conversation I had with the commander was some kind of weird dream, you know? A little while later I realized no, it was the real deal."

"Sounds like you were having second thoughts?"

"I'm still having second thoughts. But I went through with it. I had about three weeks left to go at school, it went by pretty quick. I seemed to be drinking more, though."

"Was there a type of graduation?"

"No, you finished your course, then you went over and sat in the holding company for a few days, waiting for your orders to come in." "If I recall, didn't the commander say someone else was going to be getting a hold of you with some more information?"

"Yeah. In the holding company barracks there was a bulletin board. When your orders came in it would be assigned on the board, and then you'd have to go to personnel and pick up your orders to where you'd be going. I went over the personnel to pick up my orders and my travel voucher. The chief said I had to come back at 3:00 in the afternoon, there was someone there who needed to speak with me. When I asked if I could have my orders, he said, "You'll get them all at 3." Most of my things were all packed up, it didn't take me long, I was hoping I could catch a flight in the evening. I was going to go home for a few days, maybe meet up with some friends I hadn't seen the last time. I headed back over to personnel at 3:00, spoke with the chief, and he told me to wait a minute, there was somebody there who wanted to speak with me. I waited there for a few minutes. A young lieutenant came out and called me into his office. I was in civilian clothes, so there wasn't all of the attention-snapping and all that. I asked him what he would like to talk to me about."

"I have a set of orders for you for Pax River, Maryland. It's a six week school to primarily familiarize yourself with P-3 Orions."

"Lieutenant, I had a conversation with the commander about three weeks ago, I volunteered for a program at Quantico, Virginia. Is that still happening?"

"Yes, it is, but we have to do a security check on you."

"Excuse me?"

"A security check."

"I thought everyone in the military had security checks done on them."

"Yes, that's correct, but there are different levels of security checks."

For some reason, the hairs stood up on the back of my neck. "Could you tell me why?"

"All I'm going to tell you at this point is you may be dealing with some sensitive material, or sensitive information. And a higher level of background check is needed."

"I'm in trouble now."

"Excuse me?"

"Just a joke."

"High security clearance is no laughing matter."

"Yes, sir."

"When you complete Pax River, your orders will be cut for you to go to Quantico, and that solely depends on your background clearance."

"Yes, sir, I understand."

"Good luck, airman."

"Thank you, sir."

He handed me my orders and said, "Dismissed."

"They didn't seem to be giving you much information, were they?"

"No, not really. At that point I was getting probably more curious than apprehensive. Besides, I always wanted a 007 briefcase when I was a kid, and could never afford one."

"007 briefcase?"

"Just a joke, doc, just a joke. I didn't catch a plane that night, I caught one the next morning. I was kind of at ease because I knew that when they checked into my background, where I came from, they probably wouldn't give me the orders, anyways, and I'd go get my fingers all greasy on airplanes. I called my folks from the airport and told them I was coming in, I didn't know when, so I'd call them if I needed a ride from Portland. I lucked out, though, on the flight from Boston to Portland I met a guy who was heading up in that same direction, he said he'd give me a lift if I wanted it. I got to Bath at about 4:30, 5:00. Like usual, there wasn't much going on, it was just 'Oh, I'm glad you're home, how long are you going to be home?"

"Five days."

"Oh, good. Where are you going after that?"

"Pax River."

"What are you going to be doing there?"

"Working on airplanes."

"Oh, good. Oh, your brother just bought a new car. Wait 'til you see it, it's beautiful. He'll be over later."

"That's good."

"I took a shower and changed my clothes, and sure enough, my brother came over. He bought himself a new SS Monte Carlo, 1970 SS Monte Carlo. 'Course that's all we heard about, how he paid cash for it. Oh, yeah, he also gave me shit about being in the Navy."

"Why would he do that?"

"I tried ignoring it."

"You really seem to have a bit of a problem with your family, don't you?"

"No, I just don't understand them. I mean, hell, when I was a kid, he used to take me to little league games, he was a good guy, but he just constantly boasted about everything. He treated everybody that way. He left at about 9:00 and I went to bed. I remember it was late March, and it was a real nice day, so I decided I was going to hitchhike down to the beach, just to be alone, just to get away. I mean, you're in the middle of schools and boot camp and you're never much alone, you never really get a chance to think."

"I bought a new camera when I was leaving Jacksonville, a 35mm SLR. I liked taking pictures, I figured I'd try it out.

So, I hitchhiked down to the beach, got a couple of rides. One guy I knew when I used to work down at the bait dock. It was getting around, oh, 3:00, so I decided to hitchhike back. I hitched a ride with some people and got up to the main road. I was kind of walking along, and a car came screaming up behind me and slammed the brakes on, threw the car in reverse and came back, screaming again to a halt. It was an old buddy I used to play in a band with when I was in school. First thing he says was, "Where the fuck did your hair go?" Then he said, "You wanna get stoned?"

I hadn't seen Larry in about a year, year and a half. What the hell was I doing out there? I told him I was home on leave, and I was going down to the beach to take some pictures. "Somebody told me you had joined the Navy, I thought you were out of your fuckin' mind."

I told him I got a draft notice, and I was going to get drafted anyways. "Fuck that, I'd have went to Canada." So, we headed out, headed back into town. He said, "Reach under your seat."

"What am I looking for?"

"You'll find it."

"I pulled out a clear plastic bag, must have been two pounds of pot in it. He said, 'Pull out a real fat bud and roll a joint."

"I can't roll a joint, Larry, I never could."

He said, "Oh, well, there's a bowl in the glove compartment, use that instead."

"And we proceeded to get stoned. We drove around and around and around, listening to Iron Butterfly over and over on his tape player as loud as it would go. I have no idea how long we were there. We turned onto 'the basin'."

"Basin?"

"Yeah, it's a series of old wood paths, nobody bothers you out there. I told Larry I was getting wicked hungry, getting the munchies, so we stopped at a little center store. I bought some chips and a couple of beers. Larry didn't drink, he just smoked dope and did acid, too. That was going to come later for me."

"The afternoon melted into the evening, and the evening into the night. Next thing I know, I'm sitting on the beach, and I am so stoned, I don't know which end is up. A girl I knew when I was in school came over and sat next to me and asked how I was doing."

"I'm not really sure. Larry got me so stoned I can hardly think straight."

"Don't try. Just go with it."

"Go where with it?"

"You'll be all right."

"I will?"

"Yeah, you will."

"Well, Larry's like that. Larry likes…what he likes is to get people stoned. So you're in the service?"

"Was it the lack of hair?"

"No, Larry told me."

"Yeah, I'm in the Navy."

"Are you home on leave?"

"Yeah, I got five days leave. I'm going to fly back on Friday."

"Where are you going from here?"

"Pax River, Maryland."

"What will you do there?"

"Work on planes."

"That sounds like fun."

"Yeah, fun." I was coming down off the pot and I knew that I had enough. I could finally start to think straight. The fact that I could have a conversation with Cindy told me that."

"I said I would have to head home, that it was getting late and I needed to get a ride back to town. We got up and walked over to where Larry was, but he was gone and I had no idea where he had gone. At first I was pissed, but it didn't surprise me, as stoned as he was. God only knew where he could have gone."

"I told Cindy the thought of having to walk back into town at God knows what time it was didn't sound like much fun."

"Look, I have a girl friend that lives up the road about a mile. She might give you a ride back to town."

I asked where she lived.

"Just past my friend's house."

"I would sure like a ride."

"Come on let's go."

Walking to her friend's house, we talked about getting out of Maine and going somewhere else.

"You know, Doc, why is it when you're young things always look better somewhere else?"

"I don't think that only applies to young people."

"But it does sometimes seem that way."

"Did you get a ride home that night?"

"Yeah, Cindy and her friend gave me a ride."

"Did you see them again after that?"

"Yeah, Cindy told me to write her and let her know how I was doing."

"And did you?"

"Yeah. Oh, I didn't see Larry again 'til the next afternoon when he came over to bring my camera that was locked in the trunk of his car. My sister was pissed off because I came in so late the night before and I was going out with Larry again. As I was leaving she said, 'I hope you get home at a reasonable hour tonight."

I just laughed and said, "Don't wait up."

"Sounds more like what your mother would say then your sister."

"Yeah, she sometimes took on that role. She looked out for her little brother."

"Peter, when you said that you rolled your eyes and shook your head."

"Doc you'll hear more about that later."

"Did you stay out late?"

"No I was in early. The first thing I told Larry was that I was not getting stoned with him and that was all there was to it. He was good with that."

"What did you do?"

"We went over to a friend's house and jammed for a while."

"What kind of music did you play?"

"Some blues and lots of Black Sabbath. They were out at the time, and we were really into it. Still am, as a matter of fact. I got home about ten and everybody was happy, although I did get interrogated, but I was used to that. I just told them what they wanted to hear and everything was good. After that I took a shower and went to bed."

"The rest of my time home went by fast and Friday came. I got my brother to give me a ride to the airport."

"Which brother?"

"The one who used to give me so much shit about being in the Navy."

"Did he give you shit on the way?"

"No, he cried."

"He cried? About what?"

"Me going off alone. He kept telling me to be careful, just be careful."

"Let me see - he gave you shit when everyone was around, and when you're alone he tells you to be careful? That's textbook passive aggressive, wouldn't you say?"

Doctor Brown just shook his head and said, "Continue."

"The flight back to Pax River was uneventful. I wrote a letter to Cindy. It was short- I thanked her again for getting her friend to give me the ride and that I had a good time talking and hoped she would write back. I mailed it when we landed. I managed to hook a ride with a couple of other sailors that were going to Pax, so we all chipped in fifteen bucks and rented a car. It was about a three or four hour ride from the airport. It was kind of fucked up because I didn't really know where Pax was. I knew it was somewhere in Maryland. I was glad that they knew that I knew that I was going to VO 30 and it was in Pax. When we got there it was about ten p.m. and none of us had to check in 'til the next day so we decided to get a room at a motel off base for the night. After checking in we decided to get something to eat and check out all the titty bars around town. We had the car 'til the next day with no miles, so we made good use of it."

"I only had a few drinks. It was in the middle of the week so things seemed slow. One of the guys I was with got thrown out of this one place for being too drunk and grabbing one of the girls so we put him in the car and ended the night."

"I drove back. I was the most sober. We put our friend to bed and threatened to tie him to the bed if he got up."

"Did he?"

"Once he passed out, me and the other guy stayed up most of the night watching him so he wouldn't get sick or try to go out."

"Did you know them before you met them at the airport?"

"No, just a couple of sailors going to the same place. I was asleep when the wakeup call came at nine. I was glad that I got a few hours of sleep before I had to check in. It would be a while before I got anymore."

"What do you mean by that?"

"I'm coming to that. We all drove over to the base. They dropped me off at VP thirty hanger. We said goodbye and I hoped I would see them around. I walked in and asked someone where the personnel office was, and they told me to follow them and they would take me there. I walked in, told the yeoman I was checking in and here were my orders. I passed him my orders. He looked at them and went to talk to his chief. The chief came over and told me to follow him. We went into his office and he closed the doors."

"You're going to Quantico. You've been TAD'd to the corps."

"What they told me was I would be going there after I left here."

"It's still true, you're just leaving. Look I don't make the orders, I just post them out."

"OK, when am I supposed to be there?"

"0-800 tomorrow."

"I don't have time to get there by then."

"Look, I'll get you a hop out of here to Andrews and you can take the train to Quantico. They run all the time. Airman, if you don't mind, what are you going there for? You're not corpsmen."

"Chief, to tell you the truth I'm not quite sure myself."

"Oh well I've been in the Navy twenty-four years and nothing surprises me. Good luck. Go sit outside and when I hook you up with a flight I'll let you know."

"Chief, about how long?"

"Not long. Planes leaving all the time. Get a coffee."

"I'll get back soon." I got a coffee and sat down. No sooner than I took a sip the chief came out."

"Airman come in here. I got you a ride. It's leaving at noon from hanger 9. It'll get to Andrews. When you get there see the loading master on the flight line and give him this."

"It was a note from the chief. His name is Sergeant Roy. Sergeant Bill Roy. He'll hook you up and get you to Quantico." The chief was right. When I got off the plane I asked one of the ground crew if he knew Sergeant Roy. One airman told me to follow him into the hangar where he introduced me to Roy. I told him that a chief from VP thirty's personnel sent me."

"Yeah, Smithy called and said you needed a lift over to Quantico. Have you ever been on a Huey?"

All I could do was shake my head.

"I'll try to get you on it. It's headed right where you're going."

He told me to hang out and he'd see if he could get me on.

Peter leaned forward. "You know, I've flown a lot and I still don't care for it."

"Oh, was that the reason for your reaction when the sergeant told you about going on the Huey?"

"Yeah, you got it." Awhile later the sergeant came back. "You'll ride with them, but you have to put your uniform on."

"Why? I flew here on a C-130 and I didn't wear my uniform."

"Remember, we're Air Force, and they're Marines. They have different rules."

"Yeah, I've heard they're leaving in an hour. See the crew chief. He'll set you up. When you change I'll have the duty driver get you to the flight line."

"I told him thanks and went to change for the ride."

With my dress blues on, I went back to the duty sergeant and asked him if the duty driver could give me a ride to the flight line. I threw my stuff in the back, climbed in the front and we headed across the tarmac. It took us a few minutes to get there. I didn't realize how huge the base was. The duty driver asked me if I'd ever seen the President's plane, and I said no, no I hadn't, except on television.

"Well, we're gonna pass right by it here, in a minute or two."

A couple of hangers past the President's plane, there were three or four choppers sitting out front. The driver dropped me off and pointed to the office door, said "Go in there, they'll get you hooked up. You're all set, have a good day."

145

I thanked the airman for giving me the tour. I grabbed my bags and headed inside. There was a corporal standing at the desk who asked if he could help me. I told him what was going on. He said, "Yeah, we got a bird going out, but I didn't hear anything about taking any passengers."

"The personnel chief at the Air Force hanger said it was all set up. Do you know who I can talk to?"

He said, "Yeah, I'll ask the captain, the pilot, see if he knows anything. I haven't heard anything about it. Stay right here, I'll be right back."

A few minutes later he came back in with the captain.

"So, you're the guy who needs a ride up to the farm?"

"Yes, sir. The farm?"

"Yeah, that's what we call Quantico, 'the farm'."

"Alright." He pointed out the door to one of the choppers that was just sitting there. He said, "That's the one we're taking. So, go tell the crew chief you're hooking a ride with us."

"Who would I be asking for?"

"Don't worry about it, he'll find you."

"I got about 25 yards from the chopper and the biggest black man I've ever seen in my life came around the corner from the backside of the helicopter. He put his hands on his hips and just shook his head. I walked up to him and asked him if he was the crew chief.

"Yup, that would be me."

"Did they tell you I was hitching a ride with you guys over to Quantico?"

"Yeah, just a few minutes ago. You ever been in one of these things?"

"No, I can't say that I have."

"Get your stuff in there and strap yourself in. We're gonna be leaving in about five minutes."

He reached in his flight suit and pulled out two barf bags.

I thought to myself, *Now this is a hell of a way to start this off, isn't it?*

"Were you scared?"

"Not scared, apprehensive. Oh, along with the two barf bags he informed me that if I puked, I'd better get it all in the bags. If I got any on his bird, then I would be cleaning it up with my tongue. And I had no doubt in my mind that he was serious."

"He showed me how to fasten the seat belt that I was in, told me that it would be fun, that I'd really enjoy it. Doc, have you ever flown in a Huey?"

"No, I can't say that I have. I've flown in helicopters before."

"When the engine starts turning up the rotors, you would swear that it was going to vibrate itself apart. All the flight was the pilot, co-pilot, crew chief and myself. I was really hoping he would close the doors, but he didn't. We lifted off, and at about 40 or 50 feet off the ground we made a 180 degree turn, you could see the ground, looking down beneath you, and away we went. It was a short flight, only about 35 minutes, and it got a little more comfortable as we went on. When we landed, the crew chief told me there was a duty truck that would take me over to personnel, if that's where I was going."

"What the hell *are* you doing here?"

"I've been assigned here for sniper scout school."

"You've been *what*?"

"Yep."

"He just laughed and shook his head. The duty truck picked up the pilot and co-pilot. I climbed in the back of the pick-up truck and told the driver I needed to go over to personnel, if he could give me a lift over there. It was about a mile, mile and a half from the landing zone, and I noticed all the activity going around. It didn't seem like anybody walked anywhere, it seemed like everybody was either double-timing or marching."

"He dropped me out front of the administration office, told me the place I needed to go was around the corner and two doors in. I thanked him and walked in.

"I couldn't help but wonder what I had gotten myself into. Would there be another Chief Hassle, or someone worse? My brother was in the Marines, and told me horror stories about Marine training. I wondered if I could handle it or if I'd have to drop out. Thanks to the determination that Chief Hassle had taught me in boot camp, I was not ready to give up yet."

As I entered the building, I asked a Marine where to check in. He pointed to an office down the hall to the right. I walked in with my orders and handed them to a sergeant who was standing at a desk. He literally tore them out of my hands, opened them, looked them over and told me to wait 'til the gunny came back.

I sat around and tried to start a conversation with the sergeant, but he ignored me like I wasn't there. About a half hour later a sergeant came walking in. The sergeant behind the desk handed him my orders. As the gunny looked over them, every now and then he would look up at me and shake his head.

Then out of nowhere he said, "Airman, get your ass in my office."

As I walked past him to his office I couldn't help but notice how sharp the creases in his uniform were. He wasn't a big man, about 5'5", 5'6". He walked in behind me, threw my orders on his desk, then he turned to me and said, "So, the Navy thinks you're something pretty fucking special. Well, as far as I'm concerned, you're just another stupid fucking squid, and that's how you'll be treated. You now belong to the Corps, and that means you will do things our way. Do I make myself clear, asshole?"

"Yes, sir," I replied.

"Don't call me 'sir', fuckhead, I work for a living. You address me as Gunnery Sergeant Walker. Is that understandable?"

"Yes, Gunnery Sergeant Walker."

"We had another squid like you awhile back and he couldn't handle it. I don't think you're gonna either. We'll see how long you last."

Gunny Walker picked up the phone and called in a corporal, told him to get me a bunk and a new uniform because my Navy uniform stunk, and it was making him sick. The corporal took me to the barracks. He told me I should enjoy the walk, because after tomorrow everything would be double time, everywhere you go.

When we got to the barracks, the corporal whose name was Evans showed me where to sign in. Evans introduced me to two Marines standing by a Coke machine. They just looked at me and shook their heads, gave me a strange look, turned around and walked off. Evans then brought me over to the supply sergeant for my new uniforms. I got four sets of Marine green utilities, two sets of camos, four pairs of underwear, Marine green, two belts, two hats, one pair of tennis shoes, one pair of combat boots, six sets of socks, and one pair of jogging sweats, orange with a large Marine insignia on the sweatshirt.

After Evans was done showing me everything I needed to know about the base, I walked back over to the barracks, changed my clothes into the uniform of the day, which were green utilities. A lance corporal walked into the barracks and told me Gunny Walker was looking for me, and to go to his office on the double.

When I got back to his office the sergeant told me to sit down and wait. Gunny Walker came out of his office, pointed at me and said, 'Get in here now, maggot. Did you get all checked in?"

"Yes, Gunnery Sergeant Walker."

"OK, stand at attention when I talk to you. Tomorrow you start your training. The day begins at 0600 with a barracks and foot locker inspection. After that, an hour's worth of PT, the Corps way. After that, we go on a five mile run. The Corps way. You're going to have many different classes here, many different indoctrinations into weapons, map reading, intelligence, ordnance. Tomorrow after PT and the run, if there's anything left of you, you and four others will have a full day of indoctrination into what this training is about."

With that he left me in his office for what seemed like hours. In reality it was more like five or ten minutes. There was a corporal with him whose name he told me, was Rodriguez.

"The corporal will work with you. He will be with you every waking minute. He will show you the Corps way and you will learn it, and if you don't, before I send you back to the Navy, I will do everything in my power to make your life a living hell. Do you understand, asshole?"

Without thinking I said, "Yes, sir." That got me thrown against the wall where he tore the front out of my shirt and lifted me off the floor. His nose was about a quarter inch from mine. Screaming at the top of his lungs, "You are going to hate me more than anyone you've ever met before. I will drive you out of my Corps."

With that he let me down. He turned to the corporal. "As for you, if you don't teach him right, you'll wish that you were leaving with him. Now get the fuck out of my office."

Rod gave me the eye and we headed out. "The gunny didn't give me your name."

"It's Peter Davies."

"My full name is too long to bother with, so everyone calls me Rod, just Rod." We double timed it back to the barracks. I asked Rod if there was anywhere I could get something to eat.

"Yeah, the club has takeout, but you can't go over 'til the gunny lets you have those privileges."

"Privileges?"

"Yeah, when you go through indoctrination tomorrow, you'll see how this all works."

"Look, I'm hungry. I haven't had anything to eat since early this morning. When I left Pax River there were a few vending machines in the next barracks."

"Oh, great. Look, Davies, I shouldn't do this but I will this time. I'll see if one of the other guys would go over for me while I help you get your things in order for morning inspection."

I reached in my pocket and gave him ten dollars.

"What do you want?"

"What do they have?"

"Burgers, small pizzas, sandwiches."

"Just a couple of burgers."

"Will do." Rod left and a few minutes later he came back. "You're hooked up. Now let's get to work."

By then it was seven o'clock: Oh, oh, that's nineteen hundred hours the Corps way. Rod was a lot of help with everything. It was pretty much like Navy inspection, just more anal. It was ten minutes before lights out and I still hadn't eaten. I asked Rod when I would get the food.

"I asked Rioux to get it for me, and he will."

Just then this tall skinny kid with his glasses on the end of his nose asked, "Who ordered this shit? You, Rod, or is it the new guy?"

"No, it's mine."

"Bullshit." He passed me the bag. "Whatever you do, don't let the gunny catch you."

Rod asked Rioux if he had seen anyone heading back.

"No, but Walker sees all, all the time."

I just shook my head. "I guess I'll just throw it out."

"I wouldn't do that either." Rioux just shook his head. "Evidence. Look, seeing the beaner didn't introduce us, I'm Tommy Rioux."

"Peter Davies."

"I know that. Now this afternoon I was at my last day of brain washing, and when the chief left for coffee I looked at the new assignments on his desk. Look, when tight ass is done with you, I'll take you where you can eat and take a break. Oh, by the way, we refer to Rod here as the green monster. That cat is so gung-ho he'll only wipe his ass with green shit paper."

"Rioux, you're so full of shit."

"That's right, but remember, the next time I play sticky finger with the bar maid you've got the hots for at the club, I won't let you smell it for free."

As Rioux and I were walking away, Rod threw a pillow and missed us both. "Rioux, if he does that good on the range, it might take the heat off of you."

We went down to the laundry room. The table and chairs.

"We use this sometimes to play cards while our clothes are washing. Around here you wash your clothes all the time." We sat and talked about where we were from. I told him I was from Maine.

"Where in Maine?"

"About thirty miles from Portland."

"Yeah, so you must be close to Bath, right?"

"Have you ever been there?"

"Yeah, my father worked there in World War Two."

"What? So did mine."

"When we were kids we would go up in the summer for two weeks. A friend of his had a cottage on Damariscotta, nice lake. I got my first boat ride on that lake, and look at us now."

"And you're from where?"

"South Jersey. Ever been there?"

"Nope."

"After the war, the old man got a job in a small boat yard. Met my mother, had five kids and lived happily ever after. At least that's what they like to think. Nothing is ever what it is, Peter."

"No, I guess not."

"Well, we'd better be getting back. Lights will be going out any minute."

"Is this whole thing a mystery?"

"Hell, the entire base is shrouded in mystery. This place is split into three areas: to the north is where the CIA trains, to the south is where the FBI trains, and we have the rest. Stop thinking about it. You'll find out in time. Go get some sleep. The fun begins in less than seven hours."

"Did you say that when the *chief* let you look in the folder on his desk?"

"Yeah."

"You said, Navy chief?"

"Yeah, I said Navy chief."

"I didn't see any Navy personnel coming in here at all this afternoon."

"You've gotta look real closely at the insignia on their uniform, 'cause everybody on this base wears either utilities or camis."

"Oh, OK."

"You'll find there's every branch here in some kind of position. You'll learn that in today's indoctrination. Get it out of your head, get some sleep. You're going to need it."

Just before hitting the rack I asked the roving watch to get me up at four so I could work on my things before inspection. I was trying to be quiet so as not to wake anyone up. There were twelve of us in the squad and only two had even noticed I was there.

Someone came out of the head. It was Rod. He came right over and started helping. He worked with me for about an hour, then started on his own things. I kept watching what he was doing. Before I knew it, it was ten of six. I felt OK with things and I thought I would do OK for the first time in that environment. That was the wrong thing to do.

At 0600 sharp Gunny Walker came in. One Marine hollered, "Ten hut!" Everyone jumped to attention at the front of their racks. The corporal named Evans was with Gunny Walker. Evans was writing on a clipboard. As the Gunny walked around the barracks, he would stop at one bunk, open up a foot locker, pull out clothes and throw them on the floor.

"Do it over, Marine. Two hours of extra duty," he snapped.

The Gunny was giving out extra duty for everything he could find, and some things that he couldn't. When he got to me he stopped, got in my face, and said, "This asshole is Navy." Then he grabbed me by the ear and said, "Gentlemen, Airman Davies does not have a regulation Marine haircut. He will have one by this afternoon under your tutelage, will he not, gentlemen?"

Everyone replied, "Yes, Gunnery Sergeant Walker."

"It had better be high and tight, 'cause if it's not high and tight enough, I'm gonna pull your ears down to where it is."

As he was tugging on both earlobes, I thought they were going to detach. In my face he screamed, "Don't eyeball me, boy."

"Yes, Gunnery Sergeant Walker."

"Is it 'yes', you're eyeballing me, or 'no', you're not eyeballing me?"

"No, I am not eyeballing you, Gunnery Sergeant Walker."

"That's better."

He kind of made a circle and looked at the eleven other men in the barracks. "Davies, it's your lucky day. I'm not going to look at your locker or your bunk, because I know it's not done right. Eight hours of extra duty."

"Gentlemen, I'd like to introduce you formally to Airman Davies. Davies comes to us from the Navy. You Marines know the Navy, the ones who take and haul us to places where we fight, while they sit in their cozy ships ten miles offshore, reading comic books and drinking coffee? Back to business. Apparently, for some unknown reason, the Navy thinks he's a shooter."

And again he stepped back into my face.

"The only true marksmen I've ever known come out of Paris Island, and I know you didn't go there. But I guess we're going to give him a try. Now get ready for PT."

As we were all rushing out the door I could hear him scream, "Davies, I'm gonna be on you like white on rice. Now, hit it."

After we straightened out the things Gunny Walker wanted done, we assembled in the parking lot. Rod called out "Right face, double time to the count."

We double timed it to the PT course, which was about two miles from our barracks. When we got there Rod led us in an hour's worth of calisthenics. They were much harder than anything in the Navy boot camp. I thought to myself,

This isn't Marine boot camp. *What the fuck did I get myself into?* I kept going over and over in my head, *I'm not going to let him get to me, I'm not going to let him get to me.* I would do whatever I had to, to prove the son of a bitch wrong.

After the calisthenics, we were going on a five mile run. A ten minute break after calisthenics. Coming down over the hill you could see Gunny Walker running towards us. When he got up to the formation he informed us that he would be on the run with us today. From the start of the run, the Gunny ran beside me, screaming in my ear that I should quit and save the U.S. taxpayers money.

"Davies, I think you should go back to the Navy to a plush bed, and leave the fighting to real men."

About half way through the course, I fell down and started to puke. That just gave the son of a bitch more ammunition. He told me if I was going to puke on his obstacle course, I was going to eat it up with a spoon. I swallowed hard, got up and continued to run. He was in my ear for the entire run. I'm soaked clean through to my sneakers from sweat. I don't think the fucking guy ever broke a sweat. He'd say things like, 'The paperwork's all filled out, you come back to my office and sign it, you'll be on the bus out of here in less than an hour."

I kept saying, "No, sir, no, sir, no, sir."

He must have been taking it easy on me. "I may not break you now, but I am going to break you. And you are going to go back with your dick in the dirt."

We got back to the barracks and had fifteen minutes to change and head to the chow hall for breakfast. It wasn't like a Navy chow hall. You went through the line once, that's all once; so you'd better get what you wanted first time through. Stipulation was, anything that was on the tray that fell onto the deck was what you would be eating. The rest of your meal would be thrown out.

When breakfast was done, we got into formation outside the galley and ran back to the barracks in formation. Myself and one other guy were pulled out of formation, told to go to Building…I don't remember what the number of the building was. Everything was spread out so vastly. I guess I've just never been good at the running stuff. The thought did dawn on me that maybe everything on that base was spread out intentionally. My feet were starting to get sore. I was hoping that when we got to the indoctrination, I'd be able to get off my feet for a few minutes. Hopefully.

When we got to indoctrination we were met by Master Gunnery Sergeant Olson. He would be our instructor for the entire indoctrination period. He started with a lecture on the importance of advanced sniper scout teams. It's kinda funny, it's like it was the first time I ever heard that word. Growing up with World War II movies, even some World War I movies, it just never seemed to have the bite when you're looking at it. But, there I was, something I volunteered for. I don't think I'd ever been that lost in indecision. Part of me wanted to get away immediately. Another part was excited and curious. And another part almost felt sick to my stomach.

We were joined by two other people from another company who were being indoctrinated. Gunny Olson introduced us to each other, gave a brief background of where we'd come from. He didn't seem to have the malice that Gunny Walker had towards anybody in the Navy. The first morning, we got a brief history of sniper scout teams, that had just come about after World War II. I didn't realize that a lot of countries had criticized the United States and a few other countries for using snipers. I like the history and Gunny Olson made it interesting. After three hours I was getting a clue of why I was there. Oh, hell, I guess I knew from the time the commander called me to his office.

"You know, Doc I never had anyone tell me growing up that I was good at much of anything. Yeah, low self-esteem, I know."

"No, that's not what I was going to say. I was going to say the Navy must have thought so."

"Yeah, I guess you're right. To really feel that you're a fuck up and not able to do anything right, and then one day Uncle Sam tells you how good you are at something, and it's killing."

"And were you good at it?"

Peter leaned forward and all he said was, "Very", and then he went blank- with a lifeless look on his face. He just sat there, no movement, almost trance-like.

"I sat there for what had to be two or three minutes. Then he takes a deep breath sat back and said, "Kind of goes against all the things we were taught, huh, Doc?"

"Peter, would you like to end for today? Travis, we're going to stop for today. Do you have all the audio from today?"

"Yes, Doctor Brown."

"Tell me, why do you record everything we talk about, anyways?"

"Oh, I go over it and try to get a better idea of how to help you. You know, things like body language, movement. It's something I started years ago. It can't be used against you in court or in any other matter. It's protected by the doctor-patient privilege. Peter, I am going to let you get around the hospital on your own."

"Where can I go?"

"Anywhere in here, but not outside without Travis. I know that you are aware of the consequences if you don't follow directions."

"I'll be good. Besides, I'm getting used to the place. Kind of like home, just bigger."

He sat back and laughed. "Well, that's it for today?"

"Same time tomorrow. Try to get some good sleep tonight. I would like to double our session tomorrow, if you're up to it."

"Can I go now?"

"No, you'll go back with Travis."

"I thought you said I could go anywhere in the hospital?"

"You can, but you have to check out on the ward. There's a sheet. Travis will show you when you get back."

Peter sat back and shook his head.

"Travis will be right in to get you. I'll see you tomorrow."

As the Doctor opened the door to leave.

"…Doc, did you like Dante's *Inferno*?"

"The book?"

"Yeah, the book."

"Yes, I suppose."

"Oh, I was just curious."

He closed the door behind him. Travis was standing there.

"Did you hear what he just asked me?"

"Something about Dante's *Inferno*."

"I'd like to know where he comes up with these things. Sometimes I think he's just playing us."

"You know how you told me to put all the sensors under the chair he sat in so he wouldn't know about them? Would you take a look at them now?"

"No I'll do that tomorrow."

"No, doctor, you should look at them today, before you go home."

"What's the rush?"

"You know that I don't make requests like that very often. Please come back with me later and let me show you what I'm talking about."

"Could you just tell me now?"

"No, you'll have to see this for yourself."

"OK, get him back to the ward and I'll see you back here in two hours."

"Thank you, Dr. Brown."

"Thank you."

Travis went back to get Peter.

"Travis my old friend, come to take me home?"

"I hope you're not getting used to this place."

"No, I'm trying on institutional life."

"And how do you think it fits me?"

"I like the old you better, but remember, there are many sides to all of us, wouldn't you say?"

"Yeah, I would."

"So Dr. Brown is going to let me off without you."

"Is that what he told you?"

"It is."

"What do you think about that?"

"I'm as giddy as a school girl."

"When we get upstairs I'll show you the check out sheet. You'll have to write your time out, where you're going and the time you'll be back. There are some places you can't go that will be on the sheet."

Travis got the sheet from the nurses' station and showed it to Peter. As they walked into his room, Travis said, "One thing: if you leave without filling this out your privileges will be cancelled. Are you good with that?"

Peter just shook his head.

"Does that mean you are?"

"Yeah."

As Travis was leaving his room, Peter turned from where he was standing next to the window.

"Let's still go have a smoke sometimes, huh, Travis?"

"Yeah, you bet."

He turned back to the window and Travis left.

Chapter Four

Travis had some paperwork before he would meet with Dr. Brown. It was hard for him to concentrate on what he was doing. It had been ten years that he and Doctor Brown had been monitoring patients like Peter and he'd never seen anything quite like that. Oh, hell, it must be the gear. *I'll call maintenance and have them take a look at it before I show Doc Brown.*

What was going on with the read outs? He knew Peter was guarded and very cautious with what he said. Even his sarcasm was all directed out, never in. *If this is a game he's playing, he needs to win the gold ring.*

Just then the phone rang. It was maintenance calling back. They told him they had someone going down right then, and could he meet them there. He told them he'd be right down.

When he got there, the tech was already going over the equipment. The tech told him, the good thing about this gear was that Brown had bought it, and it was the best.

"What do you mean?"

"The VA would never buy gear this good, not for this kind of work. You see, the whole system has a central diagnostic port so I can hook my laptop into it and it will scan all the systems individually. Look: EKG, good, brain waves, good, pulse, good. The video, audio, all good. Hell, it even has the ability to continue running for thirty minutes after all the power in the hospital is off. What was going on, for you to call us down here?"

"I hope you don't think I'm nuts, but at one point in one of our sessions today, everything went flat and the video monitor went to snow."

"How long did that go on?"

"Two or three minutes? Oh, that's not a problem. Give me the back-up disk and I'll run it through mine. If I see it I'll have a better idea what's going on. Don't feel crazy, these things do all kinds of weird things. I've been working on computers for twenty years and nothing surprises me."

"Here it is. I'm sure it's something simple."

"Do you remember where you were in this session when it started? OK, fast forward it to that point and we'll have a look."

He asked if he would have to leave while he looked over video and audio, or would it be OK for him to stay?

"Of course, I have to ask because of the Privacy Act."

Travis said, "Oh, yeah, this is OK. Did you get to the glitch yet?" Travis looked up at the tech. "It's not here."

"What's not there?"

"That three or four minutes. It's not here."

"The only way that could be is if you turned it off, then turned it back on."

"I did *not* turn it off."

"Do you need to use this again today?"

"I wanted the doc to look at them today."

"When is he coming back?"

"In about an hour."

"OK, I'll hook it up to the mainframe upstairs. I'll do a complete scan."

"How long will that take?"

"About an hour."

"Thank you."

"I'll page you when I'm done."

Travis decided to go have a cup of coffee and wait for the call. He knew that Dr. Brown would page him as well, so he got his coffee and went back down to look over the tapes again.

As he was unlocking the door he was paged by the tech. Closing the door behind him, he called him back.

"Yeah, Travis here."

"Cool. I've got some bad news for you."

For a second Travis was relieved. "So the equipment was acting up?"

"No, not at all. Everything is working fine. There must be a mistake."

"Nope, I ran it through twice. It's not your gear. Hell, I wish all my systems ran that well. Sorry, Travis, if you have another thing come up, call Paul."

"Thanks."

"No problem, Travis. Talk to you soon."

Travis hung up. He was sitting there, not knowing what to think, when Dr. Brown opened the door. Travis snapped around to see who it was.

"Sorry, Travis. Didn't mean to startle you."

"No, that's OK."

"Now, what is it that's so important that wouldn't wait 'til tomorrow?"

"This afternoon, during the session with Davies, when you got to the part where you told him, 'The Navy must have thought so', then he goes, 'You must be right; to really feel that you're fucked up and not able to do anything right, then one day Uncle Sam tells you how good you are at something, and it's killing."

"OK, go to that part now."

"Watch, when he leans forward and says, '*Very*' the screen goes to snow and audio goes dead."

"How long does that last?"

"Two or three minutes."

"Can you remember what he was talking about at the time?"

"Nothing. He just sat there with that blank look for two or three minutes, and all of a sudden he takes a deep breath and sits back like nothing happened."

"What the *fuck...*?"

"Travis, what's wrong with you?"

"Watch this- the picture comes back at the same time he takes the breath."

"Travis, you're right. I'll be damned. Play it back again."

"And the techs say there's nothing wrong with the equipment?"

"No, nothing doctor."

"Is is possible that he's doing this?"

"I don't know how he could."

"...or that he'd want to."

"Something's not right here. Remember the first session, when you tried to hypnotize him and he pulled all the probes off?"

"Do you think he might be aware this is going on?"

"Then today when he asked if we were recording that didn't seem to bother him."

"But remember, he doesn't know about the probes in the chair."

"What do you think is going on with him?"

"I have no idea, but we're going to find out. Call Art Perry and order another full CAT scan."

"He's not going to be happy."

"Oh, tell him I'll buy all his kids at the bar a round of drinks, the good stuff."

"OK."

"And Travis, I don't care where you get it or how you get it, but I want everything on this guy you can get your hands on: service records, schools, jails, hospitals, anything. Call in favors if you have to; use my name, and get it as fast as you can for me, can't you?"

"Yeah, I can."

"Good. I'll see you tomorrow. Have a good night."

"Yeah, good night, doctor."

Going back upstairs, he remembered an old friend who worked at the Pentagon. Maybe he would know how to get more information on Peter. The stuff the VA had was limited. The police that first brought him in had his civilian records. Nothing drastic: a couple of arrests for simple assault, bar fights, three or four psych ward stays in his hometown hospitals. The VA had him in on five occasions for depression; one suicide attempt; he went through the Post Traumatic Program twice with no trouble there. He'd been getting an 80% service connected disability.

That's where to start. When Travis got to his office he called Veterans' Services and asked how to get all of Peter's service records. They told him the only way he could get them was if the vet signed a release from.

"We have him in here, and he's committed."

"That doesn't matter."

"What if the patient is incapable of signing the release form?"

"Then you'd better have a lot of patience."

"What do you mean?"

"You're looking at least six to nine months and three feet of paperwork."

"Is there any quicker way?"

"That *is* the quicker way."

"Well, thanks for all the help."

"Glad to be here."

As he hung up the phone, Travis sat there for a few minutes shaking his head.

No wonder this country is so fucked up. What the hell, I'll give it a try.

Travis went back to see Peter about getting the release forms signed. As guarded as Peter was, Travis didn't think he would have much luck.

When Travis walked into Peter's room he was standing looking out the window, the same place he was when Travis left.

"Pilgrim, do you ever do anything besides look out that window?"

"I like to watch people coming and going, wondering if they know how little control they have over their very existence."

"Does anyone?"

"No, probably not. And what brings you here this late in the day, Travis?"

"Dr. Brown would like to know if you would sign a release from."

Peter finished the words for Travis, "...so you can get my service records."

"How did you know that?"

"Been here before. OK, I'll sign them. I *will* tell you this: it's a lot of wasted paper."

"What do you mean by that?"

"You'll see."

"I'll get you the forms tomorrow. Hey, Pilgrim, thanks."

"You're welcome", he said as he was turning his head back to the window.

Travis headed back to his office to see if he could get the forms faxed over to him before he headed home. It was too late: Veteran's Services was already closed for the day. He thought out loud, 'Tomorrow's another day. Maybe there's a good movie on TV tonight,' and he headed home.

Walking through the parking lot, he knew Peter was watching him, and sure enough, he was. Just as Travis was getting into his car he made eye contact with Peter, and waved. Peter just nodded his head.

One the ride home, Travis was thinking about Brandon McKenny and how they used to play on softball leagues in D.C. ten years ago. Travis hadn't seen him since Brandon got transferred over to Langley. He wondered how he could get in contact with him. It had been at least five years since he'd last talked to him.

When he finally got home he was beat. The beltway traffic was always crazy that time of the day, and all he wanted to do was get something to eat, watch a movie and go to bed. Opening the back door to his house, went into the kitchen. His wife Ellen was getting her coat on.

"Hi, honey, how was your day?"

"Long and interesting."

"Look, I'm going shopping with some of the girls. Do you need anything while I'm out?"

"Yeah, a phone number."

"You need a what?"

"A phone number."

"What the hell are you talking about?"

"Do you remember Brandon McKenny and his wife?"

"Yeah, Donna. You used to play softball with him some years ago when they lived here. I've got their number."

"How do you have that?"

"They still send us Christmas cards every year."

"They do?"

"Yes, they do, and we send them one as well."

"How come I didn't know about this?"

"You know the wall in the living room that I put all the cards on at Christmas? *This* year, *look* at them; you'll be surprised. OK?"

"OK, I get the point. Do you have his number?"

"In the address book by the phone. Love you, baby boy. Oh, don't wait up, I could be late."

"OK, drive safe."

As she was closing the door, she said, "Oh, your supper's in the fridge, just nuke it."

While his supper was heating up, he got the address book and sat at the table opening it to the Ms. There it was: 'Brandon and Donna McKenny, 321 Highland Street, Buckroe Beach, Hampton, Virginia. Phone: 757-555-2113.'

Just then, the bell on the microwave went off.

After getting his meal he sat down to eat, thinking to himself, *this whole thing with Peter Davies was getting very strange.* How would he ask Brandon, who he hadn't spoken to in years, to find information about a patient? *Oh, hell I'll just call and tell him what's going on. Maybe he can lead me in the right direction, and besides, I need to thank him for all the cards at Christmas. Here goes.*

He dialed the phone and waited. It rang and rang, then a young girl answered.

"Hello?"

"Yes, is this Brandon McKenny's house?"

"Yes, it is."

"Is he home?"

"No, he's at work."

"Well, do you know when he'll be home?"

"At about eleven."

"Who am I talking to?"

"I'm his daughter."

"Is your mother at home?"

"Yes."

"Could I speak to her?"

"Yeah, sure." Just then she hollered out, "Mom, it's for you."

She was so loud the phone almost fell out of my hand.

"Yes?"

"Hello, who is this?"

"Donna, it's Travis from DC."

"It's so good to hear from you. How's Ellen?"

"She's doing good. The kids, they're all grown up and pretty much on their own. And yours?"

"Only one is left at home, that's Tammy who answered for you. I hope you're not dead from her phone manners. They need a little work. You know, Brandon was talking about you guys recently, how much fun we used to have at those softball games."

"Yeah, I miss everything but the hangovers."

'Brandon said the same. It was good catching up with an old friend. Look, he'll be home at about eleven, but you could call our shop. Tuesday is our slow night, and I know he would love to hear from you."

"Shop?"

"He's not at Langley anymore. They pensioned him off about six years ago, but I'll let him tell you about that. Do you have something to write on?"

"Yeah, hang on; OK, go."

"It's called 'Ribs, Ribs and More Ribs'.

"He's working in a rib shack?"

"We own it. Remember he used to say if he ever got out of intelligence, he would do something intelligent. It was his idea."

"Is it going good?"

"Very. Look, Travis, I don't want to tell you anymore. I want him to tell you. The number is 757-555-4869. Tell him I said to call."

"Ok. Good talking to you. Good night."

Now he dialed the number and it rang once.

"Good evening, and thank you for calling "Ribs, Ribs and More Ribs' Brandon speaking. Can I help you?"

"Do you have tacos to go?"

"Tacos at a rib shop? The only guy I could think of that would ask anything that dumb is the same guy that blew that inner city softball tournament game by tripping over his big feet on a third base infield pop fly. Travis, how the hell are you?"

"How did you know it was me?"

"Travis, I spent seventeen years listening to messages and deciphering communiques. Besides, you don't forget good friends that easy. You must have gotten the number from Donna."

"Yeah. Brandon, what the hell are you doing running a rib shop?"

"The government pensioned me off about six years ago."

"They did? For what?"

"I'm not really quite sure. I think they thought I was asking too many questions. After Bush came into office, then nine-eleven, it seemed like there were no rules anymore. Not that there were many before. Besides, you know the deal. Travis, what got you to call me anyways, after all this time? I'm glad you did, but I know you."

"Yeah, OK. I'd like to pick your brain about how to get some information on a patient I've got."

"Travis, if you want to know anything other than what's in barbecue sauce, it will have to be in person."

"OK, what's in your sauce?"

"I'm not telling. It's a secret. If I told you then I'd have to kill you."

"Ha, ha! Brandon, I don't need to talk to you about this. Look, I go up to Arlington every two weeks to visit my mother who lives in an assisted living home near my brother. Can you get some time on Thursday?"

"Yeah, I can."

"Give me your e-mail address at work. No, give me your home e-mail. I'll send you what time and where to meet. I'm looking forward to seeing you. Hey, Travis, do you still have that softball shirt?"

"Oh, you mean the one that has 'Slick Spic' on the back?"

"Yeah."

"Yeah. And do you still have yours?"

"I do."

"To one thick mick."

"To one slick spic."

"See you on Thursday."

"Good talking to you, Travis."

He hung up the phone and went to the fridge. He poured himself a big glass of milk and went in to watch TV. There wasn't much on, so he decided to take a shower and get some reading in before going to bed.

The next thing he remembered was getting up to go to the bathroom. His wife was already fast asleep and the clock said it was two am, so he went back to bed. The alarm went off at six. He got up, dressed and headed for work. He liked to go in early to beat the traffic.

He pulled into the parking lot at ten of seven. As he got out of his car he happened to see Dr. Perry pulling in. It was as good a time as any to ask about another CAT scan.

"Good morning, Dr. Perry. How are you today?"

"Alright now, but that could change at any time. Dr. Brown would like another CAT on Davies."

"What the hell is wrong with that guy?"

"Don't shoot me, I'm just the messenger."

"You know, Travis, in Roman times you'd already be dead."

"Dr. Brown said he'd buy a round of drinks at the bar for all your kids, and he said the good stuff."

"It had better be."

"I'll pass that on to him. You see, I didn't ruin your day that much, now, did I? Have a good day, doctor."

"You too, Travis."

Every morning he would stop off at the canteen to get a paper and coffee, then go to his office to check his messages and appointments for the day. Things were slow that morning: two intake interviews, a report on another patient of Dr. Brown's. He would have time to run down Peter's records before the session with him at two that afternoon, but the first thing he would have to do is get a release from Peter.

After looking at the sports page and having his coffee he went upstairs to Vet Services to get the right forms. Travis hated to deal with them. It seemed like everyone that worked in that office was about twelve years old, and everything they did had to be on either e-mailed or on the web. Travis was old school and liked talking to people face to face.

When he went into the office in the part of the hospital that he didn't really know that well, he always wore his name tag and ID on his shirt. Sometimes it helped to cut the bureaucracy, sometime it didn't.

Lets see how it works today. There was no one in the office when he got there except the clerk.

"Can I help you?"

"Yes, I called from the psych ward yesterday about some release forms for one of Dr. Brown's, that's Prescott Brown's patient."

"And those are his service records?"

"Yes, service records, would you have any others?"

"We have some of his med records."

"Is there any chance we don't have everything?"

"Oh, yes, the VA takes out everything except the summaries after ten. After that you have to request them if you want more detailed records."

"Why would they do that?"

"It saves on paper and time; we either scan the document and store it, rather than have multiple copies all over the hospital, or the country, for that matter."

"Thanks for the information."

"Give me a minute, I'll get those forms."

The clerk printed off the forms and handed them to Travis. Travis thanked him and then went over to see if Peter would sign them.

Travis stuck his head in Peter's door. He was surprised not to see him standing in the window. He wasn't in his room at all.

Travis looked in the lounge. Finally, after not finding Peter on the ward anywhere, he asked Beth Anne where he was.

"Dr. Brown gave him off-ward privileges."

"Oh, yeah, that's right. Did he happen to say where he was going?"

"'The canteen' is what he wrote on the checkout sheet."

Nurse Webster came over and was kind of laughing.

"What's up you guys?"

"Davies signed out and I asked what he was going to do with his new found freedom."

"With no exasperation at all on his face, he said he was going to find a cup of coffee that wasn't brewed from ground up boot soles of SS storm troopers and walked off. He has a way with words."

"Yeah, you might say that. Could you page me when he comes back?"

"Hold on, someone just buzzed to come in. It might be him. You're in luck, it's him."

With a coffee cup in his hand, Peter walked past the nurses' desk. He lifted his cup up, motioning *success,* and went to his room.

Travis walked into the room behind him.

"So, did you find a good cup of coffee in a VA hospital?"

"Just OK. Travis what brings you here this early?"

"Remember the release forms I asked you about yesterday?"

Peter took the forms from Travis, signed them and gave them back to him.

"Now the story unfolds. You think figuring me out before was hard? Wait 'til you see them."

"Why? Is there something in the records that might enlighten us to the black outs you have?"

"No, I don't think so."

"Then what is it, Peter?"

"Travis, I've had that same question asked of me before, so I'll tell you what it is: *bullshit,* that's what it is, *bullshit.*"

"What's bullshit, the records?"

"They'll send you all bullshit."

"Are you telling me that the records are *lie*?"

"That's for you and the guy that wears fifteen hundred dollar shoes to figure out. I'm tired of trying to justify my very existence. If you don't mind, I'd like to look out the window now."

"OK, Peter. Remember, you have a session with Dr. Brown this afternoon."

Peter just nodded. Travis stopped by the nurses' desk on the way out.

"Keep an eye on him for me."

"What are we looking for?"

"I don't know, but just check in with him more than usual."

"OK, we'll call if anything changes."

"Thank you, ladies." Travis left after dropping off the request for Peter's records. He headed to his office to do reports. After two hours of working on them, he decided to get lunch and check with Vet Services about the records. The same clerk told him that they should be on his fax anytime after one. He thanked the clerk and went to eat.

When lunch was over he caught Dr. Brown in the hall and asked if he could see him in his office before that afternoon's sessions.

"Sure, I'll be back there in about forty-five minutes. Will that work?"

"It will."

"OK, I'll see you then."

Travis was hoping that the faxes were there in time to look them over before he met with the doctor. Just as he sat down at his desk, the fax machine went off. He was hoping it was what he was looking for, and he thought to himself, 'I just better stop shitting on those kids at Vet Services.'

He was surprised to find out that there were only three pages. That didn't seem right, so he called down to Vet Services. He lucked out; he got to talk to the same clerk.

"Hey, this is Travis calling from psych. Do you remember this morning I requested some records on a Peter Davies?"

"Yeah, I just sent them up."

"Yeah, but there are only three pages. Does that seem right to you?"

"It's not the usual way, but we sometimes get them like that."

"There's *got* to be more."

"Look, I asked the Navy Department three times, and they said that was it."

"Hey, thanks again for all the help."

Travis hung up the phone and started to look over Peter's records. Looking over them he thought to himself, *What the hell is this, half is blacked out?* The other half looked like dates were scratched out and new ones added. All the time he had been working at the hospital he'd seen some records with things blacked out that were probably classified, but this made no sense. Looking at the clock, he knew he had to see Brown in ten minutes.

Picking up the phone, he called Vet Services again. The phone rang and rang. He hung up. *I'll run this by Dr. Brown and see what he says.*

Travis headed over to his office. He saw the doc coming down the hall.

"Travis, you're late. What's so important to get you here early?"

"I'd like to talk to you about Davies."

"You mean our problem child?"

"Yeah, him. It's going to take more than ten minutes to figure that cat out."

Prescott opened his office door and Travis walked in.

"Travis, there's some coffee if you'd like. I don't know how fresh it is, but you're welcome to it."

"No, thanks, I'm good. Remember you told me to get all the information I could on him? Well, here it is. Three pages."

"Three pages?"

"…and half is blacked out, and most of the dates don't work with what he's been telling us."

Prescott sat back and took off his glasses.

"Did you, did you look over his civilian inpatient hospital stays?"

"Yeah, I've been over them two or three times, and nothing stands out. There's nothing there to explain what happened yesterday."

"I get the same thing when I look at them. Remember I told you about my time at Belleview, when I was doing my internship? Have you ever been there?"

"No."

"Sometime you should go, but make sure it's during a full moon."

"Do you believe that sort of thing?"

"It doesn't matter if I do or I don't, it's proven that on a full moon there are more visits to the hospital than any other time of the month. I'm getting off track, here. Peter sort of reminds me of a young girl that used to get admitted every four to six months."

"How did she remind you of Peter?"

"Well, the police would bring her in from all over town. One time they found her in the library, talking to herself, staring at a statue. Another time she was standing right in the middle of the road in Times Square."

"The reason that I say she reminds me of him, that they're so similar, is that when she wasn't catatonic, she was intelligent, articulate and argumentative. We did the usual meds and observation. The big difference was that she was susceptible to hypnosis. She was my introduction to hypnosis; one of the other doctors had been using the procedure for three or four years, and I started to assist him on it."

"How many sessions did you hypnotize her before you got anywhere with her?"

"After the fourth or fifth session, it's not clear right now, Dr. Lutz asked her about her family, and her response was, 'They don't know me anymore.'

"Then he asked her why it was that they didn't know her. Her reply was, 'They don't like Claire.' When he asked her who was Claire, and why didn't they like her, she said, 'When I got in that car accident, Claire came to live with me."

Then Dr. Lutz asked her what she meant by that. She responded, "I'm not talking about this anymore, you wouldn't understand," and she pulled all the cords off, just like Peter did.

Travis looked frustrated. "What happened at that point?"

"She was talking to an orderly. Thanks to Dr. Lutz, you have the position you have today, because he was the first one to do that. He would plant student psych nurses on the ward to see what information they could get out of the patients, when doctors were too intimidating. *Exactly* like the situation we have here. The girl asked Wendy, who was studying to be a psych clinician like you, if she believed in spirits. Wendy told her no, but she believed in angels. She said to Wendy, "You see, that's why Dr. Lutz wouldn't understand, because she's an angel, and she lives with me, and she tells me what to do."

"Where did you go from there?"

"We medded her out as being schizophrenic. She had no history of violence, either toward herself or anyone else, and we put her back on the street. I never saw her again during my time there, I was rotating out of there in six months, anyway, and I never really stayed in contact with Dr. Lutz. But here's the interesting part: Wendy was sort of a new-age, holistic, crunchy type, and felt strongly that the girl was talking about a walk-in."

"Oh, I've read about that. At the moment of death, while your spirit is outside your body, a roaming spirit who hasn't crossed over occupies your body."

"Yeah, that's about it. That's how I read it."

"Hold it. We're all men of science; this is fucking voodoo, ya know?"

Prescott looked Travis directly in his eyes. "Travis, can you explain the three minutes of snow on your tape yesterday? His heart rate, breathing, everything, everything was gone, wasn't it? Can you explain any of that?"

"No, I can't."

"Here's what I'm beginning to think: A, he's just playing with us. Or B, the thing that he's hiding, to him is so terrible and so traumatic that if he speaks of it, he'll lose his mind. Or worse. Again, how do you explain the lost time?"

"I can't."

"We're going to have to continue going, and see what happens."

"Are you going to confront him about the three minutes yesterday?"

"No, not yet. But soon. Did that help you out at all, Travis? Did that answer any questions for you?"

"No, it *didn't*."

"Welcome to the world of psychiatry."

"Dr. Brown, there's an angle I'd like to try. I have a friend of mine who went to work for the Pentagon, later went to work over to Langley. He was an intelligence specialist, and he always prided himself on saying he could find out anything on anybody at any time. I'd like to take Thursday off, he's going to be in town, and it's been a while since I've seen him."

"What do you hope to find out?"

"When I was in the service, there were always rumors of black ops, clean up missions, and, hell, there were even rumors going around that the CIA was giving LSD to certain subjects to try to enhance the fighting machine."

"Travis, that rumor's been circulating since the 50's."

"I know that, but I'd still like to see what I can find out. You know, Brandon knows his stuff."

"You should be careful poking around with your friend's career. The boys at Langley don't like people snooping in their stuff."

"Well, he's retired now, and owns a rib joint over on Buckroe Beach on the peninsula."

"Oh, good."

"Another thing, doctor, when I asked Peter the other day to sign the release forms for his records, his comment was, "And now the fun begins." Are you going to mention that we've gotten his records back?"

"I wasn't going to mention it, but seeing that was his comment to you, I think we should look at it a little closer, don't you?"

"Yeah, I think that would be a good idea. Oh, yeah, doctor, one more thing. I'm going to hook you up with an ear monitor today, and a microphone. That way, if by some means when he's talking, and he goes into one of those states, I'll be able to know what's going on."

"Why don't you go up and bring him down here in a few minutes? It's time for his session, anyway. If he brings up the records, pick his brain. See what you can get out of it."

"Alright, Dr. Brown, I'll see you back here. I'll be back here in about a half hour."

Dr. Brown went back to finish off some paperwork, and Travis headed up to get Peter.

Travis walked by the nurses' desk and pointed to Peter's room. Nurse Webster just rolled her eyes and nodded, as if to say, "Yeah, he's in there."

He poked his head into the room. Peter was sitting on the edge of the bed, staring at the floor. Without lifting his head, he said, "How was the record hunting, Travis?"

"I think you know how it was, Peter."

He slowly lifted up his head and looked at Travis. "About this time, you and Dr. Brown should be trying to figure out if, A, I'm filling you with a line of bullshit, or B, I'm crazy, or C, it's all an illusion. Then, D maybe, it's all of the above."

"Well, Peter, you may have a point, but we're going to find out, aren't we?"

"You know, Travis, I really hope you can. I really, really do. Are you here to escort me to Dr. Prescott Brown's torture chamber?"

"Yeah, I'll walk down with you."

"I have one really, really important question to ask you, Travis. Could you possible fine out what those little things are they put in the jello?"

"Put in the jello?"

"They put something in the jello that I don't think is part of any of the known food groups."

Travis just shook his head and laughed.

"Pilgrim, you never cease to amaze me. Come on, let's go."

As they walked down to the session, Peter said, "You didn't have much luck with the records, did you Travis?"

"How do you know that?"

"Did you?"

"No, we didn't, but we will."

"Look, I've been trying to get the V.A. to believe me for thirty years: the fucked up dates, no mention of half of the training I got, my time in Laos and Cambodia, and God knows where else."

"When you were over there, you were in a unit, right?"

"Right."

"And you remember the friends you had? I'll bet that you even have pictures of some of them."

"Yes, I do."

"How about you?"

"I used to."

"What do you mean, 'used to'?"

"I had this house fire about twenty five years ago and all my things got burned."

"No, you're not hearing me. My things, pictures, addresses of old friends that I trained with, all gone. I tried getting a hold of some of them, but it was like they never existed."

"Yeah, I know what you mean, Pilgrim. Time has a way of doing that."

Peter stopped and grabbed Travis' arm.

"No, no, Travis, there was nobody that could verify that I was there. *Nobody*, not even the V.A. *Nobody*."

"Look, it will be alright. Just work with us and we'll find someone. Dr. Brown has a lot of connections in high places. He'll find something."

"No, he won't."

"Don't be so sure."

"I'm very sure."

"Then how can you find out about a person that isn't here?"

Travis just looked at him. "Talk to the doc about that."

"Oh, Travis, a little to delusional for you? No, a lot."

Dr. Brown was standing in the hall. When they got there, he said, "How are you today, Peter?"

"You'll have to ask Travis. I'm sure he has some thoughts on that."

Prescott just looked over at Travis. Travis just shrugged his shoulders and said nothing.

"Peter, would you like to start off today where we left off yesterday?"

"That's what I'm here for."

"OK, go in and get comfortable. I'll be right in."

Travis put a head set on the doctor, in case Peter had another episode like the day before. When he came into the room where Peter was, Prescott asked, "Well, how have you been sleeping?"

"OK." Peter replied.

"And the meds seem to be working?"

"Yeah."

"Well, then, do you have anything you'd like to talk to me about?"

"No, let's just get back to where we were yesterday."

"OK, then, it's all yours."

"Back to Quantico. The time there went by faster than I thought it would, and I was getting used to all the shit that Gunny Walker was passing out. And the friends I made there were different than the ones I made in the Navy."

"How so?"

"They were closer, tighter, more like a brotherhood."

"How did you do with the training?"

"A lot better than I thought I would when I got there." Peter leaned forward. "You know, doc, I would have gone into hell with those guys especially Rod, who covered my ass from Walker until I got things right."

"But how did you do with the training?"

"Oh, back to that. I did OK I was a good student."

"You told me that the Navy thought you were a good shot and that's why they approached you for that training."

"Yeah, that's it, doc. You're talking to a guy that when I was a kid, all I did was make model cars and read. I maybe shot a gun with my cousins on their farm two or three times. Not a big outdoorsman, would you say?"

"Would you?"

"A couple of days before we were to leave for advanced combat training at Pendleton, Gunny Walker called me into his office. On the way over I thought, 'What kind of shit was I in now?' When I got there I told the personnel man I was there to see the Gunny."

"Yeah, he's waiting. Go in."

I entered his office, snapped to attention.

"At ease, Davies. Well, you're almost done and you made it. Look, you're one of the best shots I've ever had come through here, and I put you in to try out with our shooting team, but the Corp kicked it back. I don't know why, but they did."

"Gunny?"

"Yeah?"

"Didn't you tell me that if they turned me down…"

"Oh, hell, I just wanted you to know that I think you're a good man, even though you are a squid, and I would be proud to have you in my Corp. You get it?"

"I think so."

"If you tell anyone that I said that, I will deny it. Now go on the beach with your team and have a good time."

"Thanks, Gunny."

"Now get the fuck out of here."

Leaving his office I felt like I had finally became part of something, and that I was glad that I had gone through with all the bullshit."

"Peter, what did you learn while you were there?"

"OK, OK, they taught me how to shoot. It was all about the mechanism of shooting long distance. It's quite a science."

"You know the Gunny told you that he put you in for the shooting team. What did he mean by that?"

"It's a big thing among the grunts. The Marine Corps shooting team, they rank second or third in the world, if my memory serves me."

"Did you ever find out why they turned you down?"

"You know, doc, if I had a fucking clue why they did half of what they did, I probably wouldn't be this fucked up."

"You're really pissed off at them, aren't you?"

"No, what would make you think that? OK, listen, and please listen good. Because of the records and all the other shit I think they pulled, I don't know if it's real or just some drug induced nightmare."

"Maybe we'll find out."

"Yeah, sure."

"Peter, what are you doing here if you don't think we can help you?"

"I don't know if there is any help for me, doc. I just want to tell my story without you thinking I'm crazy, or maybe telling it will prove that I am, and at this point it doesn't matter which it is."

"OK, Peter tell me your story."

"A couple of nights before we were all headed for San Diego for advanced combat training, Rod and a few of the other guys told me about a party that was going on, and asked if I wanted to go. It was the first time in six or seven weeks that I didn't have extra duty, and it was the first time anyone had asked me if I wanted to go on the beach with them, since I'd arrived.

Me, Rod, Rioux and Wilson got ready and headed for the gate. Just outside the base there was a package store, we all decided to get something to drink for the bus ride to town. We all got pints so we could hide them in our coats.

I got a bottle of Jack Daniels and a pack of smokes. It was a riot on the bus, we were all trying to hide our bottles from the driver. Everyone else on the bus could see what was going on, and they were laughing at the show we were putting on. When we got to town, Rod said the party was at the house of a couple of girls he'd met. It was a few blocks away, so we started walking down. When we got to the party there were about twenty people. Everyone was smoking dope and drinking. I had a pretty good buzz on from the Jack on the bus. As Rod introduced us to the people he knew, some girl came up and said, "Hi, I'm Liz, what's your name?"

"I told her 'Peter'."

The first thing out of her mouth was, "Wanna get stoned?"

I said, "Sure, why not?" She passed me a bowl and I took a long toke. It had been awhile since I'd been stoned, and it hit me like a ton of bricks. I was really getting stoned. After nine weeds of smelly barracks and body perspiration, Liz looked *real good*. It wasn't that I was doing real good with her; I had a feeling that this chick was so loose, and I really didn't care. Not a bad looking girl, about 20, dark brown hair, maybe 5'3", 5'4". She was wearing tight jeans and a tie-dyed halter, which really impressed me, considering the size of the girl's melons...no, boobs. That was good enough for me.

As we drank wine, smoked dope and listened to Led Zeppelin on the stereo, at this point I was *really* high, and feeling *really* good. She said to me, 'Would you like to drop some 'cid?"

I said 'what?'

"You know, windowpane."

"I knew what it was, I had never done it, so I said, 'Sure, why not?' Besides, Doc, I wasn't going to risk blowing a chance of getting laid, ya know?"

"Did you?"

"Hang on, I'm getting to that."

"OK, continue," Prescott said wryly.

"So I follow her into this place, it's dark, candles everywhere. She was playing with something on one of the bureaus in the bedroom, and I was sitting on the edge of the bed, enjoying the hell out of my Strawberry Hill wine."

She walked over and said, "Here, take this. It's the best windowpane in Virginia."

"I put the tab on my tongue, and sat there. She did the same thing. I knew it would take a while to start acting. I knew enough of my friends who had done it, to know what to do, but not what to expect. We sat there laughing and drinking wine. I don't know when I asked to see her boobs, and without batting an eye, she took her halter off. The next thing I knew, we were rolling around the bed, making out. After a while, the acid must have been kicking in; the flames on the candles started to grow, turning all different colors. Some even reminded me of rainbows, and it seemed like I could smell every one of them. The room was starting to breathe and my body was tingling all over. As we were rolling all over the bed, it felt like I was watching myself, like I was suspended from the ceiling from invisible ropes.

All this seemed to go on for hours. Then I heard the clock on the dresser. I couldn't help but think of how long it seemed between beats. One minute I thought I was having sex with her, the next minute I was looking at myself in the mirror. I seemed to get lost in my left eye. Just as quickly, I was drifting through space. I don't know how long it went on, but the last thing I remember was standing in a field with dead bodies all around. Some were even stacked like cords of wood for the winter chill. I wasn't scared or freaked out, I just felt incredibly alone. The next thing I knew, I started to wake up. It took awhile for me to clear my head. When it did, I found out that I was alone. The clock on the bureau said it was 10:30 in the morning.

I looked around the room for my clothes and got dressed. There was no sign of Liz and the candles had burned out. I half stumbled into the living room to find Rod sleeping on the floor, with an empty bottle of wine tucked under his arm. I woke him up and said, "We'd better get back to the base."

It took awhile for him to get his shit together. He asked if I'd ever had a hangover so bad that my hair hurt?

"No, we'll work on that the next time."

We didn't say much on the walk to the bus station. Between puking and gagging, and wishing for a pound of aspirin, there wasn't a whole hell of a lot to say.

We got on the bus, sat down. Right out of the blue, Rod goes, "You got laid, didn't ya?"

The mother and children sitting beside us were not impressed, by any means.

"I think so."

"You think so? What kind of fucking answer is that?"

"If you don't quiet down, we're going to get thrown off this bus."

"Fuck this bus. Did you get laid, or didn't you?"

"Tell the truth, Rod, I was so fucked up, I can't remember."

"Oh, just tell yourself you did, and that it was good."

"That works."

The bus ride back to the base seemed to take for*ever*. It was a good thing it was Sunday. We wouldn't have to deal with Gunny Walker. I decided not to tell Rod about the acid, but I knew I would try it again. It would be awhile before that happened.

Sunday was real laid back. Recuperate from the hangover and get ready to leave on Monday. We would get a flight out of Dulles to O'Hare in Chicago, then to San Diego. We had plenty of time to travel, didn't have to check in until the following Friday morning. When we got to Camp Pendleton for advanced combat and jungle training, things were about the same as they were at Quantico. It was good going to a new assignment with the squad; sort of made things more familiar. Rod, Jones, Lopez, Wilson, Rioux and the rest, and I got more shit from the new gunny because I was in the Navy. I was used to it by then, I knew I could take about anything they wanted to deal out to me. Two days a week we were in class, three days a week we were in the field, and the rifle range was open to anybody at any time you wanted to use it. I used to like to go out on the range after class alone to shoot. The command wanted us to go out in teams, but when the day was done they didn't really care as long as you brought them your scores; but if they went below of that with a spotter they would stop until they came back up."

"Did that ever happen to you?"

"No, it's hard to explain shooting. To me, it's kind of like a Zen rhythm, getting into a zone. If I can see the target, I can hit it. Shooting alone, there are no distractions. That's probably why I never had a permanent spotter when I was over there."

"Peter, tell me where over there is?"

"You know."

"Oh, you mean the records didn't tell you?"

"Look, Peter I'm tired of this cat and mouse game that you play. I'm trying to help, and you're not cooperating with me. Now, you're going to tell me, or this whole façade you've been playing is over, and Metro can have you right now."

"Whoa, I didn't think you had it in you, doc. OK, I'll tell you what I know. I was in Southeast Asia, and that's all I know; maybe Thailand, Viet Nam, Laos, Cambodia, I really don't know. This may come as a shock to you, but I've heard those things before from other vets. Has anyone ever told you that no they just right me off as being a nut. Dr. Brown just shook his head.

"Will you work with me and Travis so we can get to the bottom of this mess?

"Yeah."

"Now, let's get back to Pendleton."

"The training was going ok, but it was starting to get boring, my shooting was getting more consistent but some of the shit we were doing was, as far as I was concerned, was nuts."

"How so?"

"They would drop us in air and then come out and capture us, interrogate us, then tell us where we went wrong. It seemed like they were teaching us something, but it was nothing like the real thing."

"After about five weeks they told us to get ready for jump school at Fort Bragg, North Carolina. I know that at some point we would go to Bragg, but I had to laugh to myself about the fact that we were on the East Coast less than a month ago. We all knew how the government likes to throw money away."

"How was jump school for you?"

"OK, but I still think jumping out of a perfectly good airplane is nuts."

"So you didn't care for jumping?"

"No, not really."

"I know that it's all voluntary, so why didn't you quit?"

"Because everything that they threw at us was a challenge, and I wouldn't give anyone the opportunity to say that I quit."

"How long were you there?"

"Fourteen days. We did lose Rioux; he broke his leg landing the last time we jumped."

"Was it bad?"

"Bad enough. The bone was coming out through his thigh. Lucky bastard."

"What makes you say that?"

"He was going home and didn't have to deal with all that shit anymore."

"You told me that you had volunteered, but you seemed to have so much contempt for the military..."

"Not then I didn't. I thought that I was doing the right thing: my duty and all that; Mom, apple pie and the girl next door."

"Shit, Peter, you are so cynical!"

Peter just laughed. "It's a versatile tool, is it working?"

"We'll see, won't we?"

"Rioux headed home and the rest of us headed back to Pendleton. We had one week left, and that was called 'hell week'. We would have to stay up for five days and go around the clock putting up with whatever they asked you to do."

"How did you do?"

"I started to hallucinate after four days, I think it was."

"Four?"

"Yeah, it was four. When it was over they let us sleep for a day or two, then that training was over. Out of the twelve of us, Rioux and Wilson dropped out. There was a small graduation ceremony where we all got pins for finishing; two days' liberty to do whatever we wanted."

We knew that when we got back on Monday we'd have orders, and we all had a good idea where we were going. We all talked about it a little, but didn't want to think much about it to ruin our liberty, and that was that.

Rod told me that Lopez had relatives close by in La Mesa and we were going with him to party with his old friends.

"Do you remember being young and just doing things on the spur of the moment? Seems like two lifetimes ago."

Rod said, "Maybe we could get fucked up and laid and maybe this time you'll remember who fucked you."

"Rod you fucking grease ball."

"Oh, now, that hurt."

"Just shut up and get ready or we'll leave you here and not have your token squid to fuck with."

"Not likely."

About that time Lopez came into the barracks singing in Mexican and dressed like a pimp from T.J.

"Rod, who the fuck dressed you?"

"Hey, I got to look good for my people."

I said to Rod, "This should be fun."

"When we got there, there was a van waiting for us. Some of his friends or relatives got up and gave him hugs and at that moment it dawned on me that they were all speaking Mexican or Spanish, including Rod. One of the guys opened the side door and motioned for us to get in. The driver said, "There's some beer in the cooler, help yourself."

"I figured he was talking to me, seeing that was the first word of English they'd spoken since we met them. We drove around town for what seemed like hours. They were playing some music on the radio that I never heard before, but I liked it. I asked Rod what it was.

"You couldn't pronounce it if I told you. Do you like it?"

I told him I did.

"So just enjoy."

There was a joint that hadn't stopped since we started driving. I had never been that stoned before. They all started laughing when I tried to talk back to them in what I thought was Mexican. Then they started to laugh even harder. "Lopez, what's so fucking funny."

"They want to know if you ever heard of a loco gringo."

"No, and I don't care as long as they keep passing that joint back here."

"The next thing I know we were at someone's house and it was getting dark. There was a party going on. We all got out of the van. I think I fell out of it. I got up and it dawned on me: *Hell, I was the only white person there.*

For awhile it seemed like my head was clearing up. I asked Rod if I was going to die.

"What the fuck are you talking about?"

197

"I asked him if he realized that I was the only white one there."

"Are you?" and he laughed. "Look, don't worry, you're with us. Just be cool and have a good time."

He gave me a beer and said, "Go sit down. Meet some of my friends, they're good people."

"One of the guys who come over with us in the van sat next to me and said, "Look, my name is Tony. I hope you're having fun and that you're not mad about us giving you shit on the way over."

'No, thanks for getting me high, what the fuck is 'loco gringo'?"

"A crazy stranger."

"That's me."

"Ha, dude, do you want to get high?"

"High? I'm *already* high."

"No, I mean really high." I remembered all I could do was laugh.

"Sure, yeah, why not?"

"You ever try angel dust?"

"No, I don't think so."

"Well, you're in for a treat. Come with me."

Tony and I went into the house and into the bathroom, where he took a small piece of folded paper out of his pocket. He opened it up and dumped some white powder onto a small mirror then with a razor blade he chopped it up, then made four small lines. He said, "Two for me and two for you."

Then he passed me a short straw.

"You go first."

I snorted the first line and it felt like the top of my head was going to explode. I like that, so I did the other one after that, and it gave me the feeling like all I could do was laugh at everyone and everything. Then things started to slow down; it was like everything was in slow-motion.

Rod came over to me and asked if I was having a good time, and all I could hear was 'time, time, time...' I just sat there. The next thing I knew, I was waking up in my rack in the barracks with all my clothes on, with a splitting headache. That was the first time I ever blacked out. It took me some time to start feeling like a human being again.

Rod came over to see if I was up.

"Rod, what the fuck happened? One minute I was sitting there laughing, and the next I'm waking up here."

"You passed out and we brought you back."

"Well, did I do anything fucked up?"

"No, you were cool."

"I'm never doing that stuff again."

"Famous last words. Do you want to go over to the chow with me at four?"

"What time is it?"

"Now? A little after one."

"Sure, I'll probably throw up, but I'll try."

The day went by slowly, and my head was starting to clear. Rod was right; the food and shower helped. We didn't do much that night, just watched TV in some kind of depressed silence. We were all thinking about the next day and our orders."

"You know, Dr. Brown, they teach you to face your fears, but they don't tell you how."

"What do you mean by that?"

"It's hard to explain."

"They teach all the mechanics except how it will affect you later?"

"I think that's what I mean."

"So, you're not sure what to expect?"

"Yeah, I guess."

"I was going over to get some smokes at the club and I asked Rod if he'd like to walk over with me. I wanted to ask him if he was as scared as I was."

"Did you?"

"Yeah, but it wasn't easy. All that young male testosterone macho shit floating around us; it was hard, but I asked anyways. Do you know what he said, Doc? He told me that if we weren't scared that we probably didn't belong there. Then I thought that I would shit myself when we did our first jump."

"No shit!"

We both started laughing.

"Did you know that Lopez pissed himself?"

"So did I!"

"Yeah, the few, the proud, the Marines, in pissy pants, and olive greens."

"Rod said, "While we're in here, we might as well have a beer," and we did. We closed the place. When we got to the club I got my cigarettes and the walk back to the barracks we had to hold each other up. I remember Rod started to sing 'the few, the proud, the Marines, is pissy pants and olive greens', then I started to sing too. The ten minute walk back probably took an hour. A couple of trained scouts lost in our own backyard. We did finally get there, and made sure that everyone heard our new song. Finally the O.D. told us that if we didn't go to bed he'd put us on report. Rod looked at me and started to laugh.

"Davies, do you want to be on report? I don't."

He saluted the O.D. and puked all over his shoes. At that point we knew that we'd better hit the racks. The O.D. told me if I didn't get him to bed, it was going to be my ass. He was not happy. I finally got Rod to bed and passed out in the chair in his room.

"Six o'clock reveille came too soon, and too loud. I woke Rod up and said, "We'd better hurry or we'll miss muster. Another day, another hangover. We got to muster on time."

"You could tell the minute that Walker came in the barracks, he was pissed.

"I don't know who it was and I don't care but someone puked all over the O.D.'s shoes last night. All I can say is that you'd better make it right with him today. You are all leaving here today or tomorrow. It has been a pleasure trying to train you. I don't want to blow smoke up your skirts, but most of you will be heading for a combat unit soon, and some of you might make it, but always remember that you have been trained by the best, and I will tell you the same thing that the gunny who taught me told me: remember your training, keep moving forward and cover your asses, and you'll be alright."

"Then he hollered, 'Ten hut. Semper fi and we all answered back, "Semper fi, do or die, hoo rah," and he left.

Rod and I headed over to the chow hall to get breakfast. After that we headed over to personnel to see if our orders were in. Lopez met us on the steps, "They're in, and I'm headed for Ton Sen Nhut and then the First Marines.

Remember what we were talking about last night on the way over to the club?"

I said, "Yeah, well, we all know that they weren't training us for White House duty."

There was a lot going on in the personnel that morning. We waited for about ten minutes before we got a chance to ask the sergeant at the desk if our orders were in.

"Name?"

"Rodriguez."

"First?"

"Robert."

"Service Number?"

"245345."

"Yeah, here."

"You're next. Name?"

"Davies."

"First?"

"Peter."

"Service number?"

"150503."

"You need to see the major."

"Yeah?"

"I only know that you need to see him. He'll fill you in. Go sit and I'll tell you when he can see you. So, stick around."

"Rod, what is that all about?"

"I don't know, you didn't fuck up?"

"No, Gunny Walker would have told me anything like that."

"What did you get?"

"The same as Lopez. Look, I've got to go over to transportation to see how I'm getting out of here. I'll come back when I get that done and see if you're still around, or I'll see you back at the barracks later."

"Yeah, sounds good. See you then."

"You know, Doc, I sat there all morning and at noon the desk sergeant told me to go to eat and to be back by one, the major would see me then. I headed over to the barracks to see what was going on with Rod and Lopez. When I got there I saw Gunny Walker coming out, and I asked if Rod was inside.

"No, they left about twenty minutes ago."

"Where did they go?"

"Over to catch a plane."

"Ha. Shit."

"What about you? Oh, yeah, you're headed back to the Navy."

"What?"

"Yeah, they didn't tell you yet?"

"No, I don't' see the major until one."

Well, Davies, good luck, and you didn't hear about your orders from me."

"Yeah, thanks, Gunny."

I walked into the barracks and looked around; it seemed empty. Most of the room doors were open and mattress rolled up on the beds; no laughter, no swearing, no music, nobody. It was like no one was ever there. I really wished that I could have said good bye to them. We'd been through a lot of shit together, especially Rod. Back at Quantico he all but did half my things until I could get the knack of doing the Corps way.

"Did you ever see either of them again?"

"No. Rod got killed the first month he was over there, and Lopez just fell off the face of the Earth. Oh, did I ever tell you that out of the twelve us that went to Quantico together, me and Lopez are the only ones left? And no one knows where he went after he got out."

"How do you feel about that?"

"How do I feel about it? Let's see: life in and out of nut wards, broken marriages, drug addiction, failed businesses, nightmares that never end, not knowing what is real and what is not. Yeah, I feel real good about that." Peter sneered.

In a hollow voice he said, "Hell, Doc, I don't know if I'm sitting, or if this is just a dream. Who knows? Maybe I never got out of the elephant grass, either."

"Can we continue now?"

"Yes, go ahead."

"At one I went back over to see the major. This time I didn't have to wait. I went right in. I entered his office and snapped to attention. He told me to relax: "Airman, I have your orders here, and would like to talk to you about them. You're going back to the Navy."

"Sir?"

"Yes, Airman?"

"Why?"

"I have no idea."

"Sir, may I speak freely? I want to go with my team. I've been with them since Quantico. This doesn't make any sense."

"Airman, there's a reason why this is happening, and I don't know what it is. You'll be going to Pax River this afternoon. It's rare that we get a recruit from the Navy like yourself, and I want you to know that your Gunny gave you high marks in all areas of your training. Good luck, Airman, that is all. Dismissed."

I left his office and headed over to Transportation to find out about getting back to Pax. I'm not going to tell you about going back because it was the same as coming over: San Diego to O'Hare then to Baltimore, then a bus to Pax."

"How did your time there go?"

"I felt totally out of place. I forgot half of the things they taught me in school about being an aviation electrician and part of me didn't care."

"Did you make any friends?"

"A few. More like people to get fucked up with; there was always something going on. It was very different from being with the Corps, nowhere near as strict. There was only one inspection a week, if that's what you could call it. The O.D. would come into your room an if everything looked OK he was done. I remember that I was only going to be there six weeks. I only got off the base twice, and that was to go to some parties. I had met this girl, who lived nearby, at the club, and she always knew where the parties were on the weekend. She had a car, so I hung with her a lot, when I could."

"It was never a romance?"

"I have no idea. We were just friends."

"Do you remember her name?"

"Yeah, Liz."

"Were you doing a lot of drinking and drugs at that time?"

"No more than anybody else was. You know, Doc, it seems to me that you and I are about the same age. You would have been a junior or senior in grad school at the time. Was there any of that going on where you were?"

Dr. Brown just answered, "Too shy, too shy. OK, let's call it a day on that. I'll see you tomorrow at the same time."

The doctor and Peter both got up at the same time.

"So, do I have to wait for Travis to go back upstairs?"

"Only if you want to. Peter, you can go anywhere. We talked about that: as long as you follow the rules.

"Yeah, yeah, that's right. Thank you, Doctor."

"Have a good night."

"You, too."

As Prescott started to open the door he turned to Peter. "You know where this is all going, don't you?"

Peter smiled and said, "Have a good night, Doctor Brown."

Travis was just coming out of the monitoring room when Dr. Brown stepped into the hallway.

"Well, how do you think it went today?"

"I wish I knew."

"How so?"

"I think he's leading up to something very traumatic, or he's the best story teller I've ever heard."

"Oh, did I tell you that I'm not coming tomorrow?"

"Good, I'll give him the day off, then."

"We'll get back to it the day after tomorrow."

"I hope you enjoy your time off. See you on Friday."

Travis closed his door and went in to see if Peter was ready to go back upstairs.

"Pilgrim, are you ready?"

"Yeah, I guess."

"Would you like to have a smoke with me before you go back up?"

"Yeah, I'd like that. Is it back to the morgue?"

"No, we'll go down to the smoking room."

"Have you been there yet?"

"No, I've only been to the canteen for real coffee."

"Come on with me. There's two in the building. I'll show you the one closest to the ward that you're on."

As they walked, Travis asked how Peter thought the sessions were going.

"OK, I guess. Time will tell."

When they got there, it was a small cube about eight by eight with chairs all around and ash trays on the wall. A vet asked if one of them had a smoke he could have, so Travis gave him a smoke, and gave Peter one too. Peter couldn't help but notice one guy there was having a conversation with no one. That wasn't unusual in a place like that, there are lots of tormented souls.

"Pilgrim, do you know if there's anybody that could verify your story?"

"Out of the twelve that trained together, I only know of one guy who was not on my team that might. I tried to get a hold of him about ten years ago, when I was going through the same shit as I am now."

"Well, did you?"

"I did."

"Well, what did he say?"

"He said, 'Orc', oh, 'Orc' was my nickname. "If you were smart, you'd not open that Pandora's box," and hung up. I tried calling back a few days later, but his phone number was changed and it was unlisted."

207

"If you give me his name and his last address I'll look into it. Maybe he'll talk to me."

"Yeah, right."

"Pilgrim, give me a shot at it."

"OK. He was living in New York City in Westchester County. His name was Morris Zimmerman."

"I've got to go back. I'll see you later, Pilgrim."

"Here have a smoke for later."

"Travis could you get me a pack of smokes when you go home? I've got the money up stairs."

"Sure what's your brand? Oh yeah, Marlboro lights. Yeah I'll hook you up"

Travis left and Peter decided to have the cigarette that Travis had given him. He got a light from another vet and sat down. His thoughts when back to Zimmy and the PI, and he wondered how close Brown and Travis might be getting to the truth. He knew that all he needed was time to tell his story. For someone, anyone, to believe him. When he came out of his thoughts he and the guy who was talking to himself were all that was left in the smoking room. Peter got up to leave and told the vet to have a good day.

"I know about Orcs. They're everywhere."

"What?"

"Orcs, Orcs." He laughed. "They only come out at night. They say they're your friends, but they try to take you life, in the end, ha ha. In the end. You know, you know."

Peter couldn't get out of there fast enough. His head was spinning and he couldn't get back to the ward fast enough. He made his way back as fast as he could. When past the Nurses station Nurse Webster asked if he was alright.

"Why do I look like there's something wrong?"

"I asked first" she said. "Look, I'm not playing your games tonight."

"I said I'm all right, and I'm all right. Yes, I'm all right."

She followed him into his room. "You look like you've seen a ghost."

"Maybe I have."

"Are you seeing things Peter?"

"Ah, here we go. NO, I'm not seeing things."

"Well, there's something wrong with you, your face is red and you're panting, so your heart rate must be up."

"Okay, you've got me. I saw a young intern walking down the hall and I wanted to get back so I could beat off. Is that good enough for you?"

"Okay Davies, have it your way. I'll put the exchange in your records and let Doctor Brown deal with you."

"All right you do that. Now, do you mind if I look out the window now? I might be missing something good out there."

She left. A while later Beth Anne came in and told him that the dinner trays were here.

"Is it that time already? How time does fly when you're having fun." He leaned over to Beth Anne and said "It's okay to laugh, I won't tell Nurse Ratchet." She broke out laughing as they walked out of his room. Webster just gave them a look and Peter just said. "Uh-oh." And got his tray and sat down to eat. After he was done eating he took the tray back to the cart and went back to his room. Back to the window.

He could see Travis getting in his car to leave. He looked up and Peter bowed. Travis just shook his head and got in his car and left.

Travis was leaving early enough so that traffic would be light. He hoped that Brandon had sent directions so that they could meet the next day. It would be good to see him again and catch up on old times. And maybe, just maybe, get some information on this thing with Peter. When he got home his wife had supper ready.

"You're home on time for a change." She said.

When supper was done, Travis helped her clean up the kitchen. She asked if he had heard from Brandon about them getting together.

"I hope tomorrow, if he sent me an email. I think I'll go find out."

Travis logged on, and there it was. The time and place:

National Mall by the Vietnam memorial, ten o' clock. Be there, your friend, Brandon.

Travis watched some TV and went to bed.

Chapter Five

The next morning came too soon, as usual. But he didn't have to run out until nine that morning. That would give him enough time to get to town, and the mall. He wondered how he should ask Brandon about Peter's records. Life was good for Travis that day. He found a parking space not far from where they would meet. As he walked toward the Wall, he wondered why Brandon would pick this spot. Like most vets, he had mixed feelings about it. He had never looked up names of fallen friends, and probably never would. That was his way of keeping them in his memory, as young and alive. Standing there with his back to the wall, a voice came from out of nowhere.

"Still can't bear to look at it after all these years huh, Travis?"

Travis looked to his right. "Brandon, is that you?"

"No other."

"How long have you had that beard?"

"About five years."

"Christ you look like an old biker."

"Well I am. I had a Harley built for me a few years ago and been loving it ever since."

"Brandon, why here?"

"Why not here, and why haven't you called me in years? And out of the blue all of a sudden you want to talk to me?"

"Okay, I get your point. Let's go get some hot dogs and we'll talk."

"My treat." Brandon said.

"No Brandon, my treat."

"Okay, your treat." He said with a soft chuckle.

"Brandon, you always do that to me."

"After all these years, Travis, you still fall for it. Let's just call it payback for what you're going to ask me about."

"First, Brandon, why did you get done at Langley?"

"Not here. Wait 'til we go sit down alone."

They got their food and drinks and sat as far away from anyone as they could.

"Okay, Travis, it started about a month before nine eleven. Do you remember they promoted me to Major and had given me a higher clearance? Hell, there were only two more steps above I could go anyways. I had this full bird Colonel above me that must have been about fifteen years old. Young academy ring knocker, you know the type. I was deciphering messages from all over the world. More shit than I'd ever seen before. Terrorists from the Middle East. At first it was all directed at Israel and, get this, *Norfolk*, Norfolk Virginia. I would turn the deciphered messages over to the Colonel and he would not only black out what he didn't want anyone to see, he started to rewrite them himself. In twenty two year of deciphering messages I'd never seen a Colonel do that, a *general* maybe, once or twice, but this guy was doing it *daily*."

"What'd you do about that?"

"I went to the general in charge of the whole division and get this, he told me to just do my job. I asked him how I could do my job if the Colonel was changing everything that I decoded. The general set back in his chair and said "How many years do you have now McKenny?" I told him twenty six. "Maybe you ought to put in for your retirement.

Things are going to be different around here. It's a new game now, with new rules. And besides, all of our allies are working together, it's not the same as the cold war."

"Sir, I'm not talking about the cold war, I'm talking about vital messages about terrorist activities being changed."

"Brandon, what were you trying to say to the general?" Travis asked.

"I was simply trying to tell him that something big was going to happen in the first two weeks of September, but they just didn't look close enough. Israel had been on high alert for the last two weeks of August and the first two weeks of September. And that's where we concentrated all of our movements, all of our Intel."

"What else could you do?"

"This is what I did, Travis: I went over the general's head to the two chiefs. Two days before Nine Eleven and they did nothing but send me down for a psych eval. When it came back a week later, I said I was having severe guilt about not being able to catch nine eleven. It was the biggest crock of shit I'd ever heard. So here's what they do. They give me a big party and a send me off with my pension, a hundred percent disability for my post traumatic stress and that's that. So my wife and I opened up a rib joint and I ride my Harley as much as I can and life's good now. And what can I do for you, my old friend?"

"I've got this patient."

"I knew you'd be getting to that sooner or later."

"Vietnam era. He came to us after standing in front of the wall over there for over twenty four hours. When the Metro boys finally approached him, he got into a scuffle with them and tore up one of their cars, so they brought him to us. We doped him up for a couple of days until Dr. Brown could see him."

"Are you still working with that quack?"

"He's not a quack."

"OK, witch doctor then. Does he still play with rocks and stones?"

"Come on Brandon, I'm being serious now. Do you know anything about all the black ops that were going on in Vietnam?"

Brandon just laughed. "What do you want to know? When I first got into Intelligence most of the guys were Nam vets. They used to say that the last five years of the war was nothing but clean up missions. 'Cause it had gotten so dirty that, if it had ever gotten out to the public, half the Pentagon would have been court martialed and most of the White House impeached."

"What do you mean, dirty?"

"One night I was having boiler makers with a full bird Colonel. He was getting pretty drunk, and asked me if I had ever played chess by myself. I said no, I hadn't. He told me that's what they were doing in Vietnam after '68. Fifty cents of every US dollar was going to the North and everyone, from privates to generals, was lining their pockets with black market profits. After a few more drinks he started talking more. It was like he wanted to tell someone. He told me the Pentagon knew it was out of control and they had to do something about it, so they started recruiting from all branches of the service. Draftees, those who had enlisted. It didn't matter where they came from as long as they had a talent that could be used for the cause."

"Why didn't they use what they already had?"

"Well, that's what I asked him. He said it wasn't that simple. For it to work they would have to be either eliminated or discredited."

"How could they hide a unit like that? They weren't all volunteers were they?"

"Yeah, they were all volunteers. They would leave their regular units and train with other active units. Here's what the Pentagon was looking for in them. These were guys with raw shooting talent, language skills. Guys who could adapt to the environment and who didn't have much of a station in society. Some trained at Quantico. Some trained with the Seals, some at Bragg, they were all *over* the place, but when they were done with their training they returned to their regular units until they were needed. None of these guys were Rhodes scholars or Harvard grads like your Doctor Brown."

"You're not telling me they were recruiting kids with low IQ's."

"No, just the opposite. If your boy is one of them, and it's not likely that he is, he would be high functioning and with a high IQ."

"What makes you think it's unlikely that he's one?"

"You know that Colonel I've been talking about? He was part of that program the Pentagon put together. He hung himself in at home in Alexandria, in a house that was way above his pay grade. Travis, the whole thing was put together to eliminate evidence and make sure the assassins were silenced, one way or the other. OK, let me ask you something. What is Brown trying to do with this guy?"

"We're just trying to help him."

"Did you ask him what he wants?"

"He just wants to tell his story."

"Then let him tell his story. What do his service records say?"

"Not much, three quarters blacked out. Times and dates don't fit."

"That Colonel told me two weeks before he died that there were two hundred of them when it started. And by 1989, twelve were left. Most died of mysterious causes or suicide. Quite a few from alcoholism, destroyed lives. Well Travis I've got to get going. I hope I was some help to you."

They shook hands and Brandon said "Make sure it's not this long until next time we meet. Oh yeah, and I remember, the names of the operation was Dante's Inferno."

Travis snapped back "Dante's Inferno? Our boy asked Doc Brown one day if he had read it, and if he liked it."

"Who knows Travis, you might just have one. But be careful what you're delving into, there may be more there than you and Brown are ready for." Brandon stopped. "Travis, did he ever mention training in the PI?"

"Yeah, he did."

"Good luck." Brandon pointed toward the Wall and said, "You know, Travis you're gonna have to deal with that sooner or later," and walked away.

Travis sat and thought about what Brandon had said about dealing with his ghost on that wall, but it would have to be another day. It would have to wait. Although it did seem like Brandon was having a good time with life. Maybe it *was* time to retire. At fifty nine, he had enough time to leave. He'd always wanted to get a motor home and to travel cross country after dealing with vets and broken lives. He knew that he was lucky to have a good home and a good life.

Maybe it was time to slow down and appreciate what was important. On the drive home he stopped at a motor home dealership and picked up some brochures on different types of models they had. He spent the rest of the day looking over them. When his wife got home she saw what he was reading. It was hard to miss, they were all over the kitchen table.

"Are you thinking about that again Travis?" she asked.

"Yeah, I think so."

"Well if that's what you're ready to do, let's do it."

"Have I told you lately how lucky I am to have you in my life? I know it wasn't easy early on with the drinking and the post traumatic stress disorder."

"Yeah, it was rough but we got through it." She said with a reassuring smile. "Remember Travis, I'm Irish and we don't leave our own behind."

"Thank you for always being there."

"Where else could I have been? It's what we promised to each other when we got married."

"What do you say we go out to eat, some place nice with candles and music?"

"I'm curious to hear what Brandon had to say to you. Whatever it was, I like it."

"I'll tell you all about it over dinner."

He told her about the conversation that he had with Brandon. It dawned on him that he was working with a vet, a vet just like himself, whose life was probably destroyed just for doing his duty.

It could just as well be me, and we might not be sitting there today. Travis said to his wife. "I think if we can help this guy that I've been working with that I'm going to put my papers in and call it a day."

"If that's what you need to do, Travis, do it."

Travis made love to his wife that night, and it seemed like it had been a very long time since he had. And it was good. The next morning he was up before the alarm went off. He showered, got a cup of coffee had some breakfast and headed off to work.

He pulled into the parking lot just in time to catch Doctor Brown coming in. "I would like to meet with you this morning about the information I got from my friend. I think it might be helpful." Travis told the doctor.

"I'll see you in my office around ten." Prescott said with a slight nod.

With that Travis went about his normal routine. He had made his decision not to put his talk with Brandon into a report. He would fill Doctor Brown in on the conversation and see what he thought about putting it down into Peter's records. Doctor Brown was already in his office when Travis got there.

"I made some fresh coffee. Would you like a cup?"

"No, thank you." Travis said.

"Well, how did your day off go?"

"Enlightening to say the least. Brandon McKenny is an old friend of mine who worked at Langley for years. He told me about a Colonel he made friends with when he first got there. One night when they were drinking the Colonel opened up to him about a group that the Pentagon had put together after 1968 to deal with all the black market problems going on in Viet Nam. And are you ready for this one? The name of the project was 'Dante's Inferno'."

"Go on. Tell me more. What else did he have to say?" the doctor pressed.

"The Colonel told him that they had recruited about two hundred volunteers. He never told Brandon exactly what their mission was. All he said was that they were very well trained and worked when they were needed."

"You mean like CIA?"

"No, no, no. The Colonel told him they were chosen the way they were because later on they could be either eliminated or discredited. But Brandon doubts if that's what Peter is. Another thing the Colonel told him was that by 1989 there were only twelve of the original two hundred left."

"OK, then, let's get ahold of this Colonel, sit him down and talk with him."

"That's going to be hard to do. He hung himself a few years later."

"Did your friend tell you what happened with the ones that were gone by '89? What's the story with them?"

"Mostly suicides, mysterious deaths, drugs, alcoholism, you name it."

"I'm not liking what this is insinuating Travis."

"Yeah, I don't think I am, either, Doctor Brown."

"Well, I think I'm going to go with what we have."

"How so?"

"I'm going to confront Peter with this, and see where it goes. He's coming down with us at one today, and we're going to try to keep him here as long as we can. I want to try a long, long session to see if maybe, with this Dante's Inferno thing, it might trigger another one of the episodes he had a few days ago."

"Sounds good to me, doctor."

Travis left and went back to his work while the doctor went on his rounds.

Beth Anne walked into Peter's room and, as usual, he was staring out the window. She knew she was going to ask him what he continued looking at out the window.

"Peter, what are you looking at?"

Peter slowly turned his head toward her and said, "The world my generation left you."

"Well, maybe you'll have to tell me more about that some time."

"Maybe I will."

"You'll be seeing Doctor Brown after lunch."

"Hey, is Nurse Ratchet still pissed at me, Beth Anne?"

"No, I don't think so. You'll probably have to do something new today to piss her off again," she said, and they both laughed.

Just then Travis stuck his head in Peter's room. "Did she tell you that the Doc was going to see you after lunch, Pilgrim?"

"Yes, she did."

"Do you want to have a smoke before? I got you these yesterday." He said, while throwing a carton of Marlboro Lights at him.

"Hang on Travis, let me get you some money."

"Nah, don't worry about it. They're on me."

"You sure?" Peter asked. "What, you and Brown getting ready to try some new experiment on me and you're trying to soften the blow?"

"Pilgrim, it's a gift. Stop being so paranoid, for god's sake."

"Well Travis that's funny. I'm in a nut ward. What else would you want from me? Rational behavior?"

"Good point Peter."

Peter put the cigarettes in his locker after he took out a pack.

"Pilgrim, I'll see you after you're done eating. Later." Travis said as he left.

Peter got his lunch tray and sat down. Looking at his food he thought about how institutional food should come with warning labels. He ate it anyway, though. When he was finished he put the tray back and waited for Travis. Peter was hoping they'd have time to get a real cup of coffee before seeing Brown. Just as Peter finished that thought Travis came through the door. Peter signed out on the checkout sheet and headed toward Travis, and asked if they'd have time for a real cup of coffee and a smoke before seeing Brown.

"Yeah, I think so as long as we make it fast."

They lucked out. There was nobody else in the canteen for the coffee, and they could slip out the side door for a smoke.

"So, tell me, Travis, when are you going to retire from here and go have some fun with your family? Aren't you tired of working with nut jobs like me?"

It took Travis by surprise.

"Let's see, I don't see you as the motorcycle type...let's see...Maybe...yes. A motor home. Set out across America, see the grand canyon and Yellow Stone National Park." Travis got a chill down his spine. "So," Peter continued, "which is it?"

"Oh, Pilgrim, I'm not ready to retire yet."

"You ought to think about it. I hear the open road puts a lot of lead back in the old pencil if you know what I mean," Peter snorted with laughter.

"Come on, Pilgrim, let's go."

"We certainly don't want to keep the good doctor waiting now, do we? Who knows, this could be a big, big day. One never knows, now, do we."

For the very first time Travis had a strange feeling that Peter knew everything that was going on. But Travis knew that rationally there was no way he could, it just had to be a coincidence. Or was it…

When they got to Doctor Brown's office he was waiting for them.

"Peter how are we doing today?"

"OK" Peter said. "How about you? And by the way, why do doctors and nurses always ask how 'we' are doing and not how are 'you' doing? I'm confused."

"Okay Peter, go in and make yourself comfortable."

Peter went in and sat down, the Doctor came right in behind him.

"I would like to have a long session today, are you up to it?"

"Don't you mean, *Are we up to it?*"

"Touché, touché."

"Yeah, a long session will be fine with me. It's not like I have anywhere else to go."

The Doctor sat down, leaned forward and said "Peter, what does Dante's Inferno mean to you?"

Peter sat back and started clapping and laughing. "You know, doc, you and Travis are all right. You've gotten further than anyone else. Okay then. Where do we go from here?"

"Well Peter, that depends on you."

"I made a deal with you and Travis that if you would let me tell my story I would stop resisting the help. Seeing as you've gotten this far, I'll be right up front with everything. Let me ask you something. What do you know about Dante's Inferno?"

"Very little."

"That's good. Because you don't need to be digging too much around that. I'll tell you the whole story, but I'll tell it to you my way. It's been a long time coming, and if I don't tell it the way I need to I'll never get the rest I do so need. Is that okay with you?"

"It's good with me. Okay, get comfortable. Where do you want to start?"

"I had just barely gotten through Pax River, but it was finally over. And I was going on to...who knows where. I was hoping to go back to where I thought I belonged, but that didn't happen. You see, when you're done at one duty station they list your next one on a bulletin board in the barracks. *And,* are you ready for this? My next duty station was six miles from where I grew up. I was beginning to think I was losing my mind. A VP squadron in Brunswick Maine. So, I called my folks. They were very happy that I was coming home. By then I had been gone for 18 months with only one leave, after boot camp. And a couple of weeks I had managed to get home when I was close by enough. So, the next day I picked up my orders at personnel and my travel pay. One thing was different. There was only one set of orders this time. All I could think about was how nuts this was. I left that afternoon and landed in Portland, Maine at about five that evening. I met a chief on the flight from Boston to Portland who offered to give me a ride from Portland to my folk's house. Seeing as it was Friday and I didn't have to check in until Monday, I had the weekend to myself. It was hard being home. I wanted to tell my family all about what I had been doing but like everything else in my life, because I was the youngest my brothers would have thought I was bragging or lying. To most of them, I was just there. Everybody was better than I was and I couldn't do anything right."

"Someone must have been on your side."

"What a good way of doing it. My side. Like a battle… yeah, my sister Louise was. She looked out for me and, in later years, my kids, too. Just a good woman, that one. She worked hard and was fair. I was lucky enough to eulogize her at her funeral when she passed away. I could always count on her. She died too young….just too young."

"How old was she?"

"Fifty two. Too young. My oldest brother, he's a good man, but he never showed his feelings. I have great respect for him, he's worked hard all his life. His wife always treated me more like a son. Just good people."

"How about the rest of your siblings."

"I have a sister in Wisconsin I really don't know that well, and the rest of them I wouldn't give you ten cents for. All self centered. Put a knife in your back in a heartbeat. You wanna see the scars?"

"Your mother and father?"

"My father was forty when I was born. He drank a lot, only on weekends. He wasn't abusive."

"Your mother?"

"Oh for god's sake doc, we went through all this when I first got here. I'm not going through it again. I'm here to talk about Dante's Inferno, and this mess that I had gotten myself into. Like I said before, I got home on Friday and I had the weekend off, before I had to check in on Monday. My folks asked all kinds of questions about what I had been doing while I was gone. I managed to avoid anything real. I knew my mother would have a heart attack if she knew what I had been doing. I remember watching the evening news with her one night and when a report about Viet Nam came on she said *I'm glad that you aren't going there. And you know the president said last week that that was almost over anyways.* I told her that I had heard that too. I told them that I had been up since four thirty and that I was tired and that I was going to go to bed and that I'd see them both in the morning. I must have been real tired. I didn't get up until eleven the next day. I got myself a cup of coffee and went and sat on the porch to drink it. My father was already sitting out there. That was his favorite place to sit in the morning. Even though it was Saturday and he'd been retired for a couple of years, that was what he did. Sat on the porch. A couple of kids came over and asked if I would play softball with them that afternoon, I told them 'maybe', but they insisted. They were about seven or eight years old, little street urchins. I tried to get out of it but they wouldn't take no for an answer so I gave in and said, "what time?"

"We'll come and get you when we're ready. We'll go to the field then."

There was a baseball diamond behind my sister's house. She lived in the same neighborhood as my folks. I knew her boys would be coming along as well. One o' clock came around and sure enough, there they were. One little guy with a very loud voice screamed, "my team gets the big boy!" and off we went.

It was a lot of fun watching those kids try so hard to hit the ball and run the bases."

"Did it remind you of doing that when you were a child?"

"Hell, no. I was always the last to be picked. Besides doc, I sucked at sports. I was watching the kids play when, out of nowhere, Russell, the kid that wanted me on his team, started screaming again.

"Ice cream man! Ice cream man!" At first I didn't know what the kid was screaming at, then I heard it: a jingle, I think it was 'Pop goes the Weasel'. Then I knew it was. The ice cream truck. One kid told me that Russell could smell the ice cream truck all the way downtown.

When we got to the truck it seemed like I was the only one who had any money. Then it dawned on me why they wanted me to play. It cost me twenty dollars, and it was worth every dime to see their faces, when I told them they could have anything they wanted.

The game was over, so on the way back from the field Russell and that voice of his informed everyone that the next time we played, I could pitch, and they all agreed.

My father was still sitting on the porch when I got back. He asked me how much they'd gotten me for. "Twenty," I told him. My father just shook his head and said, "that Russell is a piece of work. He'll either get somewhere in life or he'll do time."

Peter leaned forward, and with a very serious look on his face continued "I'm going to tell you about Russell, doc. Russell was shot to death trying to rip off a drug dealer. He was twenty two years old, and he was dead. The neighborhood that I grew up in was a half step above being a ghetto. Lots of broken homes. More neglect than you can imagine and abuse that kept the emergency rooms busy. You see, Russell was just trying to find a better way of life, but no one ever told him there were other ways of getting there." With that Peter sat back. "By that time it was about five o' clock. I asked my father if I could use his car to go for the night. He wanted to know what time I thought I would be back. Of course I didn't really know, so I told him, "Look, I'll be careful."

And he said, "Remember, no drinking in my car OK?"

"I don't intend on drinking", I told him.

"Where are you going?"

"I'd like to see some friends I haven't seen in a while, ok?"

"I guess. But remember, you'll have to put gas in it."

"How about if I fill it up for you when I bring it back?"

"For god's sake, don't be out to late and make your mother worry. Or I'll be up all night."

"Okay, I'll try not to."

With that I showered, got changed and headed out. I wanted to see Larry, my old band mate, so I headed to his house. When I got there his mother told me he was living on the beach with some friends. Knowing Larry that could mean a lot of things. She gave me directions and I headed down. It was easy to find. I spent most of my summers in high school down on Popham. Well, I found Larry's house and knocked on the door. Someone hollered, "Come in!" Larry was standing in the living room, and he said, "Peter, wanna get stoned?" Just then, a half-dressed girl shotgunned me. When I got my breathe back, Larry welcomed me to the House of Drool. That would have new meaning as the night went on. Larry was the kind of guy who could find money under rocks. He always knew how to make it. Not always on the right side of the law, but always smart. I asked him who was living there with him.

"There are three guys including me," he said, "two girls and whomever comes around."

It was Saturday night and people were coming in and out of the house. The fucking house was filled with so much smoke that you didn't have to take a toke to get high. I had a good buzz going and only had a couple of beers when Cindy, the girl I met when I was home on leave from boot camp, stopped by to get some pot for a friend of hers who was too shy to get it for herself. She asked if I was home for long. I told her I didn't know exactly how long, but I was stationed in Brunswick. I told her, "I haven't checked in yet, I don't do that until Monday. As far as I know we might be going on deployment soon."

I asked if she'd like to go sit on the beach and have a beer. "I don't drink," she told me, "and if you think you're going to get lucky you're better off here with one of these hippie chicks."

"Well, I guess that's about as direct as you can get. Now that we're past that would you like to go sit on the beach?"

"That'd be okay."

"Do you get stoned"

"Sometimes."

"Well, how about tonight?"

"The night's young. Let's just go sit on the beach and see what happens."

I was getting frustrated with her. She had a come back line for everything I said.

You know, Peter, I kind of like you," she said with a laugh.

So we went and sat on the beach and talked about how much we both loved the ocean. I told her I thought she was lucky for having been born and brought up on the water. She just nodded her head.

"I love how powerful it is. And the sound the waves make when they crash on the shore and how small it always makes me feel," I said to her. Again, she just nodded. Then she started talking about getting out of there and living somewhere else, but never far from the ocean. The time went by fast and said she'd have to be heading home before her brother did. She lived with him and his wife. She told me that her folks had died in a car accident a few years ago. I told her I was really sorry to hear that and asked if I could give her a ride home.

"No, I don't live that far from here," she said, "and it's better if my sister in law doesn't see me come in a car she doesn't know."

I asked her what that was all about and she said, "Maybe I'll tell you another time, but not tonight."

Before Cindy and I had gone to sit on the beach Larry had given me two joints. Seeing as we hadn't smoked them I figured I would.

"It was really good pot," Peter said with a chuckle. "I smoked both joints and the next thing I knew it was morning and people were already coming to the beach for the day. I hurried up and got back to the car and headed home, knowing what would be waiting for me there. When I got there, sure enough, there it was. My welcoming committee. My oldest brother, my sister and my mother and father all waiting to give me shit."

"About what?" Prescott asked.

"Well, it's like this. At about eleven o' clock on the night before my mother had started calling everybody up to find out if they had seen me, or if they had heard of any accidents."

"But, you told your father you were going out."

"Look, you're not getting it. The woman would make life miserable for everyone if she didn't get her way. And I always seemed to be in the middle."

"What did they say to you when you went in?"

"The same shit as always. Why did I make them worry and keep them up all night?"

"What did you do?"

"I just went upstairs and went to bed."

"It all seems strange to me. You're in the service, but they don't trust you to be out all night after you've been out for 18 months on your own."

"It may be strange to you, but that was my life at home. I decided to sleep through half the day until things calmed down. By the time I got up I was looking forward to playing softball with my new friends. Probably the only ones who acted like adults around me, at that time. Russell held true to his word, and I was the pitcher. They got me again, though, and again it was worth the twenty. The beauty of kids, Doc, is that they aren't as consumed by all the shit we adults are. When I got back from playing with the kids my folks asked if I was going to stay with them or live on the base. I was going to stay on the base. It was easier than dealing with them. Don't get me wrong doc, I love my folks, but I had too much to deal with, with Dante's Inferno, and at that point I had no idea what was going on, either. I had been training to do a job that didn't seem to have a mission.

I went to bed early that night. I had to be at the base at eight the next day. My father said he would give me a ride in the morning so I could check in. That would take most of the day. The first thing I had to do was go to the squadron personnel office. Then to pay master's, then to medical, and after that, to division, to see where I'd be working. When I got to the personnel office there was a tall, thin guy with blonde hair leaning over the counter. He looked at me and said, "Are you new?"

"Yeah."

"Hi, I'm Terry, and you are?"

"I'm Peter."

He told me, "I can help you with anything you need around here."

Some second class sitting behind the desk spoke up and said, "He's the biggest pain in the ass in the fleet. Terry, will you get the hell out of here? And go over to the b.o.q. and pick up those guys."

Terry looked at me and said, "I don't think he had his Metamucil this morning. I think he's feeling all bound up."

The second class said, "Terry get the hell out of here."

Terry looked at me and said, "I think he's constipated."

I couldn't believe what I was hearing. The second class just took my orders and immediately told me to stop Terry before he leaves. "Tell him to wait a minute."

The second class took some papers out of an envelope and handed them to me saying, "Go with him, he'll take you where you need to go."

I told him thanks.

As I was opening the door the second class said, "Hey Sailor, I wouldn't take much stock in what Terry says," and he pointed his finger to his head and made a circle, insinuating that Terry might be a little crazy. I just nodded and went out the door.

Terry was waiting in the duty truck, radio blaring. "I'll drop you off at pay masters and pick you up after I get rid of the Zeros."

"Zeros?"

"Yeah. That's what I call the officers around here." All I could do was laugh and shake my head. "Do you mind if I call you Pete?"

"Yes. It's Peter."

"Okay, Pete." He dropped me off and I went into pay masters. I was there about twenty minutes when Terry showed up.

"Are you ready Pete?"

"No, Terry it's Peter."

"Okay, I'll take you over to the hospital now. Do you want to get stoned? I've got some really good dope."

"For Chrissakes, it's only nine o'clock in the morning."

"Is that too late?"

"No, no, I'll pass. Maybe later."

"Okay, but if you change your mind all you have to do is ask."

Then he pulled a joint out of his pocket and started to light it. I grabbed his arm and said, "No no, not with me in the truck."

"Oh man, I'm sorry. You don't get stoned?"

"Not when I'm on duty, Terry."

Terry looked over at me and smiled like he knew something I didn't, and he did. As fucked up as that kid was, he got me to everywhere I had to go that day. When I was done running all over the base checking in, I went back to the hanger and to personnel. Terry dropped me off in front of the personnel office. Although I thought it was the last thing I had to do, the second class I gave my orders to told me I'd have to see the XO before the end of the day. I asked if he knew why.

"I don't get paid to know anything other than he wants to see you when he gets back."

"Do you know when that will be?"

"Again, I don't get paid to know these things. Just hang around, get a cup of coffee and wait."

I had a bad feeling in my stomach that I knew what it was about. After a half hour had gone by, the second class asked if I really lived five miles from the base.

I said, "yep".

"You know, I've been in the navy twelve years and the closest I've been stationed to home was a thousand miles away. You're either lucky or you know somebody high up."

I told him my uncle was the president.

"That's bullshit."

"Well, then, how about just lucky?"

"That's better."

I just laughed and got up to get another cup of coffee. The phone rang as I was getting it, the second class told whomever was on the line, "yes, Davies is here, I'll send him right up."

"The XO will see you now. He's two decks up on the right, all the way down at the end of the passage way."

I put my cup of coffee in the trash and the second class gave me back my orders. "You'll need these." I must have had a confused look on my face as I was leaving. I stopped and asked him how I got up stairs from the office.

"You go out that door, turn right and then turn right again. That'll take you to where you wanna go." I thought to myself then, 'what if I don't want to go?'

I found the XO's office and knocked on the door and heard *"come in."* He was sitting behind his desk. I snapped to attention.

"At ease, Airman Davies. I have your orders here, and they're much different than normal to say the least. The Navy asked us to give you some latitude so you can work with the Marines we have here on base. And that information is not to go beyond myself and the CO. It doesn't say much about what you're doing with them, either. Only that it's a pilot program that you've been chosen for. Airmen, could you fill me in on some more details?"

"No sir, I'm sorry. I was told when I volunteered for this program that only the superiors in charge of it could do that."

"I see."

He gave me back my orders.

"Also, there's a set in there for Captain Leeman over in the Marine barracks. You'll have to see him today. Okay then. What will you need from us?"

"Not a lot sir. The Marines will take care of most of the things that I need. If I could get a ride to and from, from time to time, it would help, seeing I don't have a vehicle of my own at this time. That's about it, Sir. Sir, I want to let you know, that I will not let my duties with the Corp get in the way of my duties here."

"Very good airmen. Well then, welcome aboard."

I had a bad feeling that that went way too easy, but I was going to find out that the whole outfit was pretty lax. When I went back down the stairs to personnel, Terry was again leaning over the counter, giving the second class a hard time about something.

"Where are you going now?" Terry asked me.

The second class said "Davies, get him out of here and lose him somewhere."

All I said was "Yeah, sure."

"I got in the truck with Terry and headed over to the marine barracks."

"Why are you going there?" Terry asked.

"Do you have to ask so many questions?"

"Yes. It's my job to know everything that goes on around here. That's how I stay out of trouble."

"Well, I'm not telling you why."

"Okay. I'll find out from the corporal. He'll tell me if he wants any speed this weekend."

"Terry, you're unbelievable."

"Pete, I believe you're beginning to like me."

"Don't be so sure. And it's Peter!"

Terry just laughed. "I know you don't want me getting stoned while you're in the truck, but would you like a beer?"

"A beer? What, are you fucking nuts?!"

"Some people think so."

"No, I don't want a beer."

"Then do you mind if I have one?"

"Terry, if that's what you need to do go ahead."

I couldn't believe what was going on. He was driving the duty truck on the base on the main road with a beer in his hand, and to him it was totally normal. He dropped me off at the Marine barracks and told me to have Andy call him when I was done. He'd come back and pick me up.

I went into Captain Leeman's office and handed the envelope to the corporal and told him I was there to see the captain.

"Wait a minute I'll see if he'll see you now."

He stuck his head in the captain's door and said there was someone to see him. When the corporal came back he told me to sit down, the captain would see me in a few minutes. About ten minutes went by before the Captain's door opened and he called me in. He went behind his desk and I snapped to attention.

"Airman, at ease." So, you're part of Dante's Inferno."

I didn't know what to say, it was the first time I'd heard it called that here.

"You're here to work with us on keeping your shooting skills up. We aren't sure what this pilot mission is about, but the Corp doesn't question orders, it follows them. While you're here I expect you to hold to these standards. Do you understand?

"Yes, sir."

"When you leave here you will report to Gunnery Sergeant Holmes' office. He will get you set up with what you need. You will treat him with respect and listen to his advice. The corporal will take you to his office now. Dismissed."

I told the corporal that I need to see Gunnery Sergeant Holmes, and all he said was, "Lucky you."

We walked to the other side of the building to his office.

"I'll tell the Gunny you're here to see him. Sit there and wait," he said, pointing to a chair in the hall. After he told Holmes I was there, he left. The Gunny opened the door and just looked at me, and closed the door again. I think I sat there for well over an hour. When the door opened again he motioned for me to come in. He stood by the door as I walked past him and then slammed the door behind me. I snapped to attention.

"Don't bother with that, you're wasting your time. So what are you doing here?"

"Captain Leeman sent me to see you."

"I know that."

I was going to ask him why he asked me that but I knew better. I could see by the looks of his office he was hardcore, the room was filled with more Marine memorabilia than I had ever seen in my entire life. I didn't want to piss him off for any reason. I don't know why, this guy just intimidated the piss out of me. In the last ten months I had dealt with lots of guys like him, but he was different. He walked behind his desk, and sat down. Just staring at me.

"Okay Airmen, relax. Captain Leeman tells me that you're here to work with us. I personally think it's a fucking joke. But that's what the orders are and that's what we're gonna do. The Marine Corps and the Navy department want you to continue shooting and honing you skills as a marksmen. The Captain tells me that this is some new program they've started, I don't know anything about it and I don't want to. I'm assigning Corporal Williams to help you get situated. He'll assign you a locker and take you out to the range to show you what we have for equipment. In our armory we have three oh eights and seven hundred Remingtons. Which do you prefer? You use an eight power scope or a ten power scope?"

"I was trained on a seven hundred Remington with a ten power anti-roll scope."

He picked his phone up and made a call. A few minutes later a Corporal came in and he introduced him to me as Williams.

"Davies came from the Navy and is going to be working with us for a period of time."

"I only expect one thing of you Davies, while you're here with us you will act accordingly to our rules and regulations. I will not tolerate the bullshit that goes on in your squadron across the way, or there will be hell to pay, do you understand me?"

"Yes gunny, I understand you."

"Okay, corporal, get him hooked up tomorrow morning with what he needs. Bring his daily shooting scores to me."

I left the office with the Corporal. Williams told me to meet him back there at oh seven hundred. I ask him if there was a phone so I could ask a duty driver for a ride back to the hanger.

"There's no need. Terry's been waiting outside for you for about fifteen minutes."

"So you know Terry?"

"Everyone on this base knows Terry."

"He's quite a guy."

At that the Corporal just laughed.

I left the barracks and found Terry waiting for me. I got in the truck and just as sure as shit Terry was drinking a beer. Terry asked, "You staying here on the base or you going home seeing as you live so close?"

"I'm gonna keep a room at the barracks but I'll go home occasionally."

"Well if you need a ride home let me know."

I told him that, after I checked in at the barracks, I could use a ride home if he didn't mind.

"Hell yeah, no problem I'll give you a lift home. Besides, I like the long ride."

"Long ride, what the hell are you talking about it's only five miles," I protested.

"That should be good for at least an hour and a half."

"Terry, even the longest way is only fifteen minutes."

"Man, are you *new*. You have so much to learn about how it works around here. But I got faith in you. You'll be alright Pete."

"Terry, it's Peter, not Pete."

"Okay I'm sorry, I'm sorry."

He got me over to the barracks, and it took me about fifteen minutes to get a room. I didn't even bother looking at it, I knew they were all the same anyway. I got back into the truck and told Terry I was done for the day, but I needed to stop at personnel for a few minutes before we left base.

"Oh, okay, no problem."

In personnel I asked the second class if he had my work assignment for the next day. He told me to muster the first lieutenant division at oh eight hundred. I knew it was cutting it close having to be at the marine barracks at oh seven hundred but I knew I could make it. I got back in the truck and asked Terry, "Is this a stock radio you've got in here? It's so loud it's making me deaf."

"No, I customized it. You all done for the day? Ready to go home now?"

I nodded and we left the parking lot, and headed toward the main gate. All of a sudden he's makes a U turn on the main drag.

"What the hell are you doing?"

"I forgot something," he said.

He swung into a convenience store parking lot and asked if I needed something to drink. I figured I'd go in and get myself a soda. Terry bought a six pack of 16 ounce Budweisers, and I bought a coke. As we were walking out the door he shows me the six pack.

"I told you it was gonna be a long ride."

We managed to get through the gate without getting busted. I just knew that having an open beer in a duty truck had to be some kind of violation. It *had* to be. I gave him directions to get me home, and he asked me "Is this the long way or the short way?"

I told him it was the short way.

"Oh no, I don't want that. I want the long way."

So I told him where to turn to take the long way. It was a nice day, and I like driving back roads anyways.

"Well, we're off the base now, you sure you don't want a beer?"

I didn't even think about it before I took one. By the time we got to my house the six pack was gone.

When we pulled in the driveway of my folk's house my mother was standing in the door. Terry waved to her and said "*Hi!*" She waved back. I asked Terry to wait a few minutes before he left. I had a strange feeling. He agreed to wait.

Walking past my mother, she asked me if I had been drinking. I told her I'd had a couple beers. She said, "I hope you aren't gonna start that stuff like your brothers." I made a decision at that moment to go back to the base and stay in the barracks. That way I'd be there at oh seven hundred, I wouldn't be late, and I'd avoid the shit I figured I'd get at home tonight. My father was sitting in the living room and asked me what I was doing. I told him I had come home to grab a couple bags, because I'd being staying at the barracks for a while to do some duties. He wanted to know when I'd be getting back, I told him probably not until the weekend, and that was only if I didn't have weekend duty. If I did I probably wouldn't be around until next week.

I could tell that it bothered him that I wasn't going to be staying home. He was a man of few words and even fewer emotions. I ran upstairs and grabbed my two bags and headed back out to the truck. I told my mother, still waiting on the porch that I'd see her that weekend.

I threw the bags in the back of the pickup and jumped into the cab.

"You headed back to the base, Pete?" Terry asked.

"Yeah I'm headed back."

"Is there a longer way to get back?" he asked with a sly grin.

"No, Terry, there isn't."

"Then I'll just have to drive slower."

I shook my head and said, "You do that."

"On the way out of the neighborhood my folks lived in was a small store. Guess what Doc. He stopped and bought another six pack."

"Was this guy, Terry, getting a little drunk by this time?" Prescott asked.

"Nope, not at all."

"So you made it back to the base alright yeah? Did you have any more to drink?"

"I had a couple more with but I stopped at that point cause of the shit I had to do the next day. I didn't want to start off on the wrong foot. Then Terry dropped me off at the barracks, and I went to my room. I got everything set up and then decided to go over to the club and grab something to eat, since I hadn't eaten all day. After I got supper I headed back to the barracks, set my alarm for five and went to bed.

When I got to the Marine barracks the next morning at seven, Corporal Williams was waiting for me and we headed over to the armory. He got me set up with a rifle, and the right scope. I needed a little adjustment on the back of the rifle to suit my needs. He then assigned me a locker so I stashed my things and headed over to the hanger to muster at eight. Before I left Corporal Williams had given me a schedule of when the rifle range was open so I could figure out when to go and work around my schedule at the hanger. Scheduling was going to be awkward, it seemed like I would have to do my shooting on the weekends. I'd have to check with the gunny to see if that'd go with him.

Talk about being in two places at once right Doc?" Then Peter chuckled to himself. "After the eight oh clock muster I went into the first Lieutenant's office and got introduced to Lieutenant JG Wilkins. This guy was a ring knocker to end all ring knockers."

"I've heard the term ring knockers before, but give me your description," prompted Dr. Brown.

"We called them ring knockers cause they graduated from the naval academy and they all wore this great big academy rings on their right hands. For some reason they all like to tap their rings on tables and shit. That's where it comes from." Peter explained before continuing. "Anyway, I introduced myself to him, and he immediately told me that I would be working with Rodriquez and Miller, and that they would be there in a few to tell me what I would be doing. And he left. I got a cup of coffee and sat down and waited. And waited. And waited. A guy walked through the door eventually, looked in Wilkinson's office and said to me:

"Good, we got rid of that asshole for the day." Sitting down in the maintenance room he asked, "Who the fuck are you?"

"The question is, who the fuck are you?"

"I'm Rodriquez."

"Well in that case I'm Davies."

"Well, it's good to have you with us."

"Well, the introduction was a little rough don't you think Rodriquez?"

He laughed a little and said, "That was just my Latin temperament, we're hot blooded you know."

"You don't say. What are we going to be doing today Rodriquez?"

"Today you get educated."

"About what?"

"In this division you do as little as possible, we all cover for each other, nobody sees anything, and the standard answer for any question coming from a zero about any of us is I just saw him, or he'll be right back."

"Rodriquez, what do we do for jobs in this division?"

"You're gonna stand two four hour watches a week, those are line watches. Wilkins will post the schedule on this bulletin board right here, and other than that our job is to find ways to get out of doing any jobs."

"I don't know if I like the rules you're giving me, Mr. Rodriquez."

"Well, you can do it your way if you want. But you'll be sorry. You really don't want to make the rest of us look bad, do you?"

Peter leaned forward from his chair in the doctor's office. "I want you to get this picture, doc. For almost a year I had been trained with the most uptight, gung-ho, squared away mother fuckers on the planet and after all that training they stick me in an outfit that makes the guys from McHale's Navy look like Patton's first army. I made a decision at that point that I wasn't going to buck it. I was going to go along with it and see what happened. So I looked at my new friend Rodriquez and told him that he wouldn't get any trouble out of me, and that I'd go with the system. His reply was *"Cool. Would you like to burn one?"* You know what I told him Doc? *"Sure, why not?"*

So we went outside, behind this little shack on the back side of the hanger and got stoned. For the rest of the day all we did was nothing. There were six of us in the first Lieutenant Division, let me rephrase that, there were seven.

Terry was included. At sixteen hundred, or four oh clock Lieutenant JG Wilkins came back and said that everything looked ship shape, and mustered us out for the day. And that was it. Everybody left and headed for the barracks or home if they lived off base. I was walking over to the marine barracks to see Gunny Holmes about my schedule and how we could work around it. I wasn't looking forward to that. I didn't know how he would react. Just then Terry drove by and stopped. He asked if I needed a ride, and I told him that I wanted to walk.

"That's cool. When you're done with the grunts, call. I'll pick you up if you want."

I just stopped and looked at him. "How do you know where I'm going?"

He laughed and said "Remember, I know everything. Later Pete."

I hollered at him, "It's Peter you fucking idiot!"

I was just getting to the marine barracks and the gunny was coming out. I met him at the bottom of the stairs and asked if I could talk to him. "You'll have to do it while we walk. It's happy hour at the club and I'm running late."

"Gunny, with my work schedule at the hanger I won't be able to go to the range every day, but I can do Saturdays and Sundays."

He stopped. "That'll work but you can only do Saturdays. The range is closed on Sundays. Besides that'll work even better, I'll be able to keep an eye on you. I go there every Saturday to shoot myself."

"Again, thanks Gunny. I won't let you down."

"I don't care if you let me down but you better not let the Corps down."

"Okay. I'll see you on Saturday. Thanks."

"Hey squid, would you like to have a drink?"

I just stopped and said, "You want me to have a drink with you?"

"Yeah."

"But is that ok?"

"If I say it is it is. Come on."

As we walked over to the club he asked how long I'd lived in this area.

"All my life." I told him.

He told me he was going to retire there and buy a house in Harpswell so he could go fishing every day. Then he asked, "Do you like to go fishing?"

"No, not really."

"You should take it up, it's relaxing."

"Eh, maybe after I get out."

"Tell me something squid. How'd you like Quantico just coming from the Navy?"

"Gunny, I didn't know what to think."

"Well, you must have adapted. You're here."

"Gunny, I wish I knew where I was."

"Well, I've been in the Corps over twenty six years. You'll know when it's time."

"I wanted to ask him if he had any idea what I was getting ready for, but I hadn't known him long enough and I still didn't trust any of it. It didn't hit me until we got there that I was going into an NCO club and I was only an airmen. I told him, "Gunny, I can't go in there I'm just an airmen."

"You're with me, it's okay let's have a drink."

"You're the boss."

"Yes, you're right about that."

So we go in, and no one said anything. We went up to the bar and the bartender already had the Gunny's drinks sitting there waiting for him. The bartender asked me what my poison was and the Gunny spoke up and said, "He'll have the same as I'm having." And he was drinking boilermakers. A shot of Irish whiskey and a Bud chaser.

"With a name like yours you can't be Irish."

"No, Gunny, I'm French and English."

"Well, I won't hold that against you as long as you can hold your whiskey. Irish whiskey, that is."

He lifted his shot and looked at me. I lifted mine. And he said, "To the Corps, Semper Fi."

I didn't repeat it. He set down his glass and said, "We're going to do this once more, are you ready?" I nodded that I had got the message. We did it again this time together. We drank the shots, slammed the glasses down on the bar and drank the beers. You know doc, that was my introduction to one of the best men I've ever known. He ordered another round. By the third round I had enough nerve and a buzz to ask him why he was treating me so well. I had a really good buzz on and it didn't seem to be affecting him at all.

"Gunny, can I ask you a question? Every place I've been with the Corps I've been treated like shit until I proved myself. I haven't known you for two days and you're buying me boilermakers."

"Davies, I got a chance to look at your folder that we got from the Navy folder, not what was in your orders that Captain Leeman and I had. Your training folders. We've had those for two weeks. I know as much about you as you do."

I must have looked like I was getting nervous because he said, "Oh, relax you've made the grade." He told me he wished that half the grunts working under him were as good as I was. And then he continued, "Besides, I've got a soft spot for you Navy boys." Then he got real serious. "When I was in Korea I was just one on patrol with a rifle company. I was on point when all hell broke loose. I got hit three times and I thought I was going to die. My whole patrol was pinned down and I was screaming. I didn't think anyone could get to me. When I felt someone pulling on my leg I looked up and it was our Corpsmen. He shouted at me to keep my head down and that was the last thing I remember before I woke up in a hospital. My wounds didn't send me home but I was laid up for three months. Our Corpsman Billy Lakeland wasn't so lucky. Pulling me out got him sent home in a box. So, I don't give you Navy boys any shit. But the English I'm not so good with." He shook his head and quietly laughed. "Besides, if I don't give you some shit how could I collect my pay with any pride?"

"Gunny, you know I don't have a clue what this is all about."

"Well, the one thing that stuck out to both Leeman and I was a security check they did on you. When they go that far back they're looking for your weaknesses."

"I don't think I like that idea that much."

"Don't worry about it, it could be a good thing later. Davies, my guess is they're putting a clean up team together."

"What do you mean, clean up team?"

"Look, I'm going to give you some very strong advice. This feels like spooks shit to me."

"Spooks?"

"Yeah, scum CIA black ops stuff. Those guys do just about whatever they want so here's my advice, always remember your training, cover your ass and keep moving forward and you'll make it out ok."

"Gunny, thanks for the drinks I'll see you this weekend."

"Yep, be there bright and early. I want to see if everything they're saying about you is true."

I told him that I'd try to live up to my reputation and he just laughed and waved me off. I walked back over to the barracks and went into the lounge to see if anything was going on. Terry was drinking a beer and asked if I wanted one. I nodded yes. He handed me a cold bud and I already had good buzz on from the drinks I'd had with the gunny, so I figured 'what the hell I might as well tie one on with Terry.' So Terry and I sat there and talked and got drunk. Or, should I say I got drunk and he just kept up with no effect. He said it was because he was from Wisconsin, and people from Wisconsin were born drunk. He had joined the Navy because he'd gotten into some trouble with the law and the judge had given him the choice of joining the service or doing some time in youth hall. I asked him what youth hall was.

A place for little pricks like me. He said.

Terry was right. I was beginning to like him. You know, sitting there talking to him you'd realize there was a lot going on in his head, and at the same time he seemed to be totally out of control. As time went on I was going to find out that he had dirty on just about everyone in our outfit. And having him for a friend was a good thing.

"Pete, tell me how the fuck you got to go into the NCO club with that general after work?"

"Terry, he wasn't a general. He's a gunny sergeant."

"I know that, he's Gunny Holmes."

"Then why the fuck did you ask me?"

"To see how honest you'll be about the next question."

I thought to myself 'here we go.'

"Seeing you're from around here you must know lots of girls that I could get to work for me."

"Doing what?"

"You know Peter."

"Terry, what are you talking about?"

"Look, the hours are good, two days a month, they don't have to be all pretty or smart."

At that point I grabbed another beer and started to laugh. "I think I got it. You want me to help you set up a pimp service."

"Yeah, that's it."

"Terry, you need your head looked at."

"Okay, what if I give you ten percent of every girl you find for me and you can have all the pussy you want for free."

"Terry you need years of good psychiatric help. I'm going to bed."

As I was leaving he yelled, "Okay, thirty percent."

"Terry, go to bed."

The last thing I heard as his voice faded was, "Okay, forty." I didn't answer back. I got to my room and got ready for bed. I set my alarm clock for five and went to sleep.

Chapter Six

Five o' clock came early. After I'd had a shower I went to the galley for breakfast. When I got to the galley the whole first lieutenant division was sitting at the same table. A part of me didn't want to sit with them. I was hoping that they didn't notice me. But then I heard Terry holler

"Pete, over here, over here."

So over I went. Rodriquez, who I was beginning to think might be running the whole thing, asked if I wanted to go with him and Terry, to put things in cold storage in Topsham, for when we went on deployment. I asked when we were going on deployment and Terry spoke up. "In about four months."

"Then why are we taking things to storage now?"

The whole table broke out laughing. I asked what was so funny. Rodriquez spoke up: "You know that asshole we work for?"

"You mean Lieutenant JG Wilkins?"

"Yes, that asshole. Listen here new guy, we'll move that stuff a dozen times."

"Who sets up the schedules anyways?"

"I do," Rodriquez said.

I was starting to not like Rodriquez, and I had a feeling that he and I were going to get into it. I just knew it.

"Well, Rod, if you do the scheduling what does Wilkins do?"

"He kisses the asses of other officers so he can climb the big ladder to the Pentagon and make a name for himself.

Don't worry, Davies, you'll have your day with him. We all have, except Terry. Terry's been banging his old lady and she protects him from our illustrious leader. You think we're shitting you, you'll see. Just keep your eyes open and you'll get the education they didn't give you in A school."

After we were done eating we all headed to the hanger for muster. When muster was over with we all went into the first lieutenant's office to get the daily orders, and just like Rodriquez said, Wilkins said, "You and Terry take the body truck over to Topsham with the boxes that are in the cages on the hanger floor." Then Rod said they'd need more help. Wilkins said, "Fine, pick someone and get it done. The rest of you sweep all three decks, clean the heads and I'll be back later. Dismissed."

"You know, doc, I don't think I ever felt more trapped, and the one thing I did know is that the longer I was with this band of misfits the more I was becoming one. I don't think it was their fault. They had no supervision and I knowing that having talked to the Gunny had made matters worse in a way. I had no doubt that I had a mission that was coming and I needed to be ready. You know, Doc, all I wanted was to ask someone….anyone what the fuck was going on and what it was all about and I couldn't. No one knew."

"Would you like to stop for the day?" Prescott asked.

"No I'd like to go on."

"All right, go on then."

"I had gotten to the point where I didn't want to stay on base and going home didn't seem like a good option either. I spent a lot of time with Gunny Holmes on the range and talking to him in his office. Because of my having to work five days a week in the hanger and one day a week on the range it didn't leave much time for a life outside of the base, but I managed. I would leave Saturday afternoon when the range was closed at two and have Terry give me a ride home. Then I would hook up with Larry and hang out at his place on the beach. I was hanging out with the girl that I told you about that I met at Larry's house, a lot. We were going out regularly and it seemed to be getting pretty serious. I was thinking that maybe when I got back from deployment I might ask her to marry me. I knew that I would have made third class by then or so I thought. You see things in my life seemed to turn around fast. Maybe too fast."

"How so?"

"Well, one night Cindy called the barracks and Terry answered the phone. I was sitting in the lounge having a beer, he came to get me and said,

"Davies it's for you."

I asked him who it was.

"I don't know. Some girl. She sounds like she's pretty upset. What the hell did you do now?"

I told him I hadn't done anything. I took the phone and said hello, the voice on the other end was Cindy. She couldn't stop crying.

"What's going on? Come on. Can you please tell me what's going on."

"No, not on the phone. I need to see you."

"You know I don't have any way to get there."

"I don't care. I've got to see you right now." And then she hung up.

Terry was always hovering over everyone and everything asked what was going on. It was the first time he called me Peter.

"What's going on, how can I help?"

"Are you going to drive me down to Popham beach in the duty truck?"

"Hell no, but wait a minute. Get ready. We'll be leaving in a few minutes."

He went and borrowed a friend's car and when he came back he said, "Come on Peter, lets go, come on. Is there something wrong with your girlfriend?"

"I don't know."

"I thought you told me you and her were hitting it off really good. You told me the other day it was serious."

I'm sitting next to this guy in a car that I've known for two months, that most times seems like he's completely out of his mind. Now there's a guy driving me to see my girlfriend that I had never seen before.

"Look Peter; if you need any money or any help just let me know."

"All I could do was look at him. Even then I thought I might be going crazy at times."

"What would make you say that?" the doctor asked.

"Doc, did you hear me? One day he wants me to help him set up a prostitution service, and the next he's willing to help me with my problems."

"Just because he was a little out there didn't mean he didn't care about you."

"I came to know that he did."

"How so?"

"I'll tell you about that soon. Well, we finally got there and when we did Cindy was outside sitting on the porch. I asked her what this was all about.

"I think I'm pregnant."

"What?" Was all I could say.

"You told me that you used a condom."

"I did."

"Are you sure?"

"Yes I'm sure."

"Well, my period is over twenty days late, and it's never late."

"How could this have happened?"

"How the hell do you think it happens?"

It was becoming an argument and it was getting hot and heavy between us. When Terry got out of the car he said, "What the hell are you two doing? You should be happy. Weren't you planning on getting married anyways?"

"Not this soon. Besides, she never said yes."

"I don't even know you. But I know him, and he's a really good man. You could be hooked up with a fuck up like me, and no one deserves that. Now either tell him yes, so we can celebrate, or no, so we can drown our sorrows."

"Who the fuck are you anyways?" Cindy asked.

"Oh, I'm Terry." He said, sticking out his hand. She just pushed it out of the way. "Okay, have it your way lady. I'm just trying to help."

"Look Cindy. Don't get pissed at him. This is our problem."

"When my brother finds out it's going to be a problem alright. Have you noticed that you haven't met my brother yet? When he finds out he'll probably beat the shit out of me and probably find out and shoot you. He's going to be home soon. I would get out of here and let me deal with him."

"I can't do that."

"Well, you don't have any choice now do you?"

"Look, you're having my child. I do have the right. Do you want to get married or don't you."

"Yes, but how is that going to change anything?"

"Maybe we could live with my folks until we get a place of our own."

"Your folks? I haven't even met them yet."

"They're good people. They'll understand." At least, I had hoped they would I thought then. I made sure that I didn't tell her that I wasn't sure."

"Look, get out of here. My brother is coming home soon, I'll call you later. I need time to think."

I started to walk off and she cried out my name and ran to me. She threw her arms around me and said, "I do love you. And I want to be with you, but I'm scared this is all going so fast. I don't know what to do."

"Look, we'll figure it out. As long as we stick together and have each other we'll figure it out. And it'll be all right, okay? I love you too, and I want to be with you forever."

"The baby too?"

I shook my head. "Yeah, the baby too. Call me in about an hour."

"Okay."

With that I got in the car and Terry said,

"Peter, this is all fucked up but we're going to get through it. Just tell me what you need, first things first."

"You were listening, weren't you, Terry."

"Of course I was."

"What the fuck am I going to do with you?"

"Let me help you, that's what. Okay?"

"Alright, do you have any ideas then?"

"I think better with a beer."

"Well, you're out of luck. There are no stores until you get to Bath."

"I always come prepared." With that he stopped the car, got out and pulled out a cold rack of Bud from the trunk. It was ice cold.

"How do you do this?"

"Well, Dad, it's all done with mirrors. Here, drink, this will calm you down. Okay Peter, how much money do you have saved up?"

"About seven hundred dollars."

"That's not even enough to give that girl a good ring."

"Well, I'm sorry if I'm not as enterprising as you are."

"And that's exactly why you're going to let me help. Am I getting through your thick skull yet Davies?"

"Look, help all you want. I don't know when I can pay you back."

"Who said anything about paying me back? I'll just boost my dope prices, let the zero's pay and still make money."

We got back to the base and waited for Cindy to call. While we sat there Terry told me that he had all the money that I needed for a good ring and wedding and a down payment on a small apartment that you could afford.

"How about furniture?"

"We'll find everything we need, just take care of your girl friend."

An hour went by and she hadn't called. I was beginning to worry about her. I remember what my friend told me about Cindy's brother. Apparently he was nuts and drank like a fish. Two hours went by and still no call. Terry asked why I didn't call her.

"They don't have a phone. She goes over to the old ladies house across the street and uses hers."

Terry asked me if I knew her number, I didn't.

"You know Davies, do you know anything other than how to get poor defenseless girls knocked up?"

"Apparently not, you asshole."

"Peter, you need a lot of work but I'll get you through it if it kills me. Besides if she doesn't call back in the next half hour we're going back there and we're taking the crazy Cajun on the third deck with us for back up. He'd rather fight than fuck anyways. Besides, that's about all he's good for. That and sniffing jet fuel fumes."

When I looked at the clock again it was getting close to eleven thirty and I was really starting to worry. My thoughts were all over the place. *Did her brother have a fit? Did he somehow find out what was going on? Did she decide not to marry me?* My head just wouldn't slow down o I got another beer from Terry.

"Man, you have got to calm down. It'll work out," Terry said.

I opened the beer just as the phone rang. Terry answered it. I went to take it from his hands and he pushed me away. All he said was, "We'll be right there, and yes I understand. Alright thank you."

"Terry, what the fuck is going on?"

"Look, there's been a car accident and your girlfriend is in the hospital. She's banged up a bit but she's going to be okay. So, let's go to Bath and see what's going on."

I didn't know what to do so I went and sat down. Terry came over and said, "Look asshole they called because she wants to see you, now."

"I need a beer before we go."

"No, you don't. You can have all the beer you want when we get back. Now let's go."

So I got up and head out with Terry. We got in the car and started out toward Bath Memorial hospital. Terry decided to bring the crazy Cajun just in case. He sat in the back seat and didn't say anything the whole way. When we got there Terry told the Cajun to just sit in the car and if there was any trouble we'd let him know. He just said, "*Got it.*" And that was the only thing he said the entire time.

Terry and I walked into the emergency waiting room. There was a woman sitting there who I had never seen before. She stood up and said, "Which one of you assholes is Peter?"

Terry and I looked at each other and then I said, "That would be me."

"Do you know what you put that girl through tonight?"

Terry with all his couth and class said, "Before you give my friend a hard time who are you anyways?"

"I'm Cindy's sister. And who are you?"

"I'm Peter's friend."

So I asked her, "So what happened, I was talking to her at her house less than three hours ago."

"My brother's wife, the bitch Sandy heard the whole conversation between you and Cindy. See, Cindy thought she was asleep but that nosey tramp was listening. And she told my brother the whole story."

"Can I go in and see her?"

"Go on."

Terry motioned for me to go in and stayed with Cindy's sister in the waiting room. Cindy was on a gurney and looked pretty banged up. I walked over and leaned down and gave her a kiss on the forehead. She started to cry so I held her hand and told her that it would be all right.

"You know doc, I've been telling people that I love that my whole life and I still end up fucking up their lives."

"How was she? Was she okay?" The doctor asked.

"Yeah, she was going to be okay. Her sister was right. Cindy's brother's wife told him about the conversation that her and I had and that she might be pregnant. He flipped out. He slapped her around and threw her out of the house with her things and into his car. He was taking her to her sister's house in Bath but he was half drunk like usual and missed a corner and went off the road into a ditch."

"Did he get hurt?"

"No, not a scratch. Cindy broke her arm and had to have some stitches on her head. And we found out for sure that she was pregnant, because she lost the baby. The doctor told her she was about seven weeks, and that would be the first life I was responsible for."

Doctor Brown leaned forward. "How can you think that you were at fault for her brother's actions?"

"From the day I volunteered for Dante's Inferno my life has been a whirlwind of pain for anyone that comes in its path or mine."

"You can't know that, Peter."

"Look doc, I told you I would work with you to work on this but how the fuck could you have any idea about what someone's life is like other than what they tell you? How about this doc. All my life I've always wanted to ride in an AC cobra, and never got a chance to. You have one in your stable, that's what rich people call it right? And you don't drive it, that's a fucking waste. Oh yeah, I went to the library and looked up your name and your background. I know you're here because you want to be, not because you have to. You could be making three times as much as you make in this system on the outside. But you choose to work here, why?" Peter sat there waiting for an answer. "Well, why?" he pushed when none came.

"Because I thought it was the right thing to do."

"I made my decisions based on the same reasons. Do you still believe the bullshit you learned in school? About equality and justice for all? That was Exeter day school, right? You don't have to answer that. I know that's where you went."

"Peter, I'm your doctor, I'm not suppose to get involved on a personal level."

"Maybe you ought to try it. When I'm done telling you about how I thought I was doing the right thing, and how it got me here with you I hope that you will not only know my path but will see it for what it really is."

"Peter, would you like to stop for the day?

"No, I would like to go on a little longer."

"Ok, what happened with your girlfriend?"

"We got married. It wasn't the best situation. The Navy didn't want me to, but I told them she was pregnant so they reluctantly let me anyways. Here's how it went. My

261

family didn't like hers, her family didn't like mine, the only sane one at the wedding was Terry. As nuts as he was. He did just what he said he would. He helped. Because I was going on deployment in a couple months we decided to move in with my folks. It wasn't the best thing but we had to make it work until I got back from wherever. The thing I liked most about being married was that I wasn't thinking about what was ahead as much as before. I still worked on the range on Saturdays. Terry made sure that Cindy and I had what we needed. Doc, do you know how much money I was making at that time, being an E3 with a wife? It worked out to just about 363 dollars a month. Lots of money, huh?" Doctor Brown didn't say anything to that. "Now, by this time I was getting very close to Gunny Holmes. Being with him on Saturdays. One thing though, he thought that getting married was a bad idea, but gave us fifty dollars and a card anyways. Although, he didn't show up at the reception. We always used to go back to his office after we were done on the range. We'd have a beer and a shot of Irish whiskey of course. That man taught me more about surviving what was ahead of me than all the training I'd been given combined. One Saturday he didn't show up on the range and I was wondering where he was, so I asked another grunt where he was and he told me that he was in his office doing something. It was strange that he wasn't there. He had a routine for everything. So, I decided to cut the day short and went to see what was going on with the guy. I got a ride back to the marine barracks with one of the guys that was going that way. When I got there his office door was open. I knocked and asked if I could come in. He motioned for me to enter so I did saying, "Hey, Gunny, I missed you on the range today."

"The day's not over yet. How come you're here and not out there shooting?"

"I just wanted to see what was up with you."

"Look Davies, your job is to be the best shooter you can be. What the fuck do you think this is all about. The Navy and the Corps didn't spend all that money on you so you could drink boiler makers with me all day."

"Look, Gunny, I'm sorry I bothered you. I'll see you next week."

"Davies, get your ass back in here. I won't be here next week, I'm going on leave."

"Good for you, you deserve it."

"I wish it was R&R."

"Gunny, what the hell is going on with you, if I could ask?"

"Sure, why not. Want a drink?"

"Yeah, I'd like that."

He made us drinks and told me he was meeting his only son in Boston. And I said, "Well, that's good."

"My son and I haven't spoken a word to each other in over ten years. You see, he thinks I'm a warmonger and a baby killer. He's one of those west coast hippies. He and I have to get together and settle his mother's estate. She passed away from cancer last year."

'I'm sorry to hear that. Were you married long?"

"No, just long enough to see me leave, come back and leave again. Somewhere in between coming and going we had Eric. Oh I can't put all the blame on him for us not getting along. I was off fighting some war some place and he was growing up. Not the greatest father figure would you say?"

"Gunny, it's not my place to say."

"I know I gave you a hard time when you first got here Peter, but I'm going to tell you what I think is going on with you and all the training you've had. I think you're going to be right in the middle of some shit that no one knows is going on. So you listen, and you listen good. When you get over to where ever you are going it will become apparent what is going on. I want you to take this with you and study it through and through." Then he handed me a manual on the fighting tactics of the French foreign legion. And all he said was, "They are the best, bar none. Remember that. Have one more drink with me, then get the hell out of here and go home to your wife."

We did the shot ritual, drank down the beer and I started to leave. "Peter, you would have made a great marine." I said thanks, and left. That was the last time I saw him alive. On the way to Boston a drunk driver on 128 drove him into the side of a semi. He was killed instantly."

"Well, these things happen." The doctor said.

"Did you ever have three people that you were very close to die on you before you were twenty one? First Rod in the delta, then Cindy losing our baby and then the Gunny, and it wasn't going to stop there."

"Well, Peter, we need to call it a day."

"Yeah, I think you're right." Peter got up and stretched. "Doc, what are you going to do this weekend for fun?"

"Well, I don't really know. Play some golf, read. No real plans."

"Well, I've got something for you. Get that big Ford and take it out on the highway and open it up until you're so scared that all you can think about is dying. You'll want to back off but don't. Push a little more until you feel the adrenaline flow through you like a freight train going through your head. Then on Monday you can tell me how good it feels to be alive."

Doctor Brown was speechless. All he did was nod his head, and left. A few seconds later Travis came in. "Pilgrim, have a good weekend. I hear they're having movies in the theater that the American legion is showing."

"Oh, I can't wait. Hey Travis, do you think he'll do it?"

"Do what?"

"You know, the thing with his Cobra."

"Pilgrim, what are you talking about?"

"Travis, stop it, I know that you listen to every word in here. I thought we were friends. You don't have to lie to me."

"Okay, you got me. And, not a chance in hell."

"I got twenty bucks says he does it."

"I'm not betting with you on that."

"Okay. Could be dollars for that motor home. Remember that old lead pencil."

"Okay Peter I gotta ask you something."

"Ask away."

"I sometimes get the feeling that you know about things going on around here and there's no possible way that you could know."

"Oh, you mean the thing about the motor home? Oh hell Travis, that was just a lucky guess."

"Time to go." Travis said after a moment.

"Or maybe it wasn't a lucky guess at all" Peter said, laughing while he pointed to his head.

As he was walking away from Travis he started to whistle. Travis headed back to his office and got ready for home. He met Doctor Brown in the parking lot as they were leaving. Walking together they both stopped and turned to look up at Peter's window, but he wasn't there. They got into their cars and straight ahead in the canteen windows there he was. He held up his coffee to them and they turned on his lights and he was gone.

Chapter Seven

"Why does he do that?" Doctor Brown asked himself. Then he picked up his cell phone and called Travis. "Would you like to have a drink with me at Perry's hang out?" he asked.

"You know I don't drink Doc, but I'll have a soda water with you." Travis said. Then he hung up and Travis thought to himself about how strange it was for Doctor Brown to ask him to have a drink, after all the years they'd worked together. He had never done it before. Travis pulled in first. A few minutes later Doctor Brown pulled up, and they walked in together. When they got up to the bar Gary, Travis's old friend, held out his hand.

"Two times in a few weeks? What's the occasion?" he asked.

"The doctor wanted to have a drink with him." Travis explained.

Gary just lifted his left eyebrow "drink? Soda water with a twist of lime right?"

"Right, Gary."

"And what can I get for you?" Gary asked the doctor.

"A double shot of Jack Daniels, no ice."

"What brings you good people here tonight? Remember, it's Friday. And this place is going to turn into a zoo soon."

Doctor Brown asked Gary where Perry was.

"Well, he's not coming in tonight he's working. No one to watch the kids, so to speak," explained Gary.

"Does it really get that bad?"

"Sometimes, if you don't believe me, ask Travis. He used to be one of my best customers. Or should I say worst. It's been so long now I can't remember."

"Come on, Gary, I wasn't that bad."

"No you weren't. You weren't that bad at all." Gary winked at Doctor Brown as he said this and then walked off to help another customer.

"Travis, tell me what's your real opinion of Peter?"

"Is this the right place to talk about a patient doc?"

"Travis you've never called me by my first name."

"I don't think it would be proper."

"Says who?"

Prescott downed his shot and motioned to Gary for another. "Oh, come on, Travis, tell me he doesn't give you the willies every now and again. Do you ever think that maybe he can read your thoughts, or what's going on with you, what you're going to say before you say it?"

"Yeah, I do. But what does that have to do with what we're trying to do with him?"

Gary brought Prescott his drink and he downed that one as well. "You know, Travis, maybe it's what he's trying to do with us."

"You know Prescott, maybe you're too involved with him to help."

"Maybe but I will see this thing play itself out, if it's the last thing I do. I'll see you on Monday Travis. Have a good weekend."

"You, too, doctor."

"It's Prescott when we're outside the hospital."

Prescott sat in his car thinking about what Peter said about the Cobra, and being afraid of it. He always had been scared to open it up. Trying real hard to leave those thoughts behind he realized he had to get home. After two double shots and through the zero tolerance in the DC area, being caught with a DWI would not be a good thing. The traffic was heavy and it took some time to get home and the whole way his thoughts were with Peter and about how maybe life really was about facing your fears.

When he finally got to his house is started to rain. He hit the garage door opener and stopped. For some reason he heard the sound of rain on the roof of his car, but it had been years since he'd stopped to just listen to it fall. It brought back fond memories of his youth. It was like time just stopped and he could visualize Dan Jenson's '62 Corvair and how it made that awful noise. Thinking about that turned his thoughts to Abby and how much he did love her, even after forty years his heart still pained for her touch and the way she laughed and how she made him feel alive. Coming out of his thoughts he hit the steering wheel with his fist he screamed, "Fuck you, Peter." Calming himself he opened the garage door and pulled in. Before getting out of his car he looked to his left, and the cars he had in that garage. It could easily hold ten cars, and for some reason it didn't seem right. He grabbed his brief case and got out. But before going inside he walked all the way to the end, looking at every one of them. With their covers on you really couldn't see them anyways. It felt somehow like a gift you could never unwrap. But one by one he took their covers off. First the Bentley, then the 1958 Mercedes 300 SL, then the 69 Shelby GT 500, and then his favorite the 65 427 Cobra, then the last a 1963 split window coop Corvette. It was the first time he could remember seeing all six cars with the covers off at the same time, and as far as he was concerned they were going to stay that way. With all the covers in a pile in the middle of the garage he went into the house. He met Lauren in the kitchen still working. "Lauren, what are you still doing here? It's so late."

"There was a big gathering this afternoon and it went late."

"Look, leave that until tomorrow."

"The misses won't like it."

"Well, she'll just have to do it herself if she's not satisfied."

Lauren thought to herself '*This should be good tomorrow.*' She was glad that she had the next day off. "Doctor Brown, I've got you supper for you. Do you want me to heat it up?"

"Not tonight, I'll get it when I'm ready. Lauren, how long have we known each other now?"

"All our lives."

"It's time that you called me by my first name, you always did when we were kids. What's different now?"

"The misses wouldn't like it."

"Lauren, are you tired of her rules? I know I am." Lauren didn't say a word. "Ah hell, I know you are."

"Doctor, I think I'm going to go now." Prescott gave her a look. She knew him well enough to know what it meant. "Alright, Prescott."

"See, that's better. What are you doing this weekend?"

"I've got things in town to do."

"How are you getting there?"

"A friend is coming to get me."

"Tell her not to bother. You can take the rover."

"I don't know if that's a good idea. The misses said your daughter would be using it."

"Not tomorrow. You are. She can take the metro." Lauren thought he was losing his mind.

"I'll see you later Prescott." As she went to leave through the garage she saw all the cars with their covers off and knew something was up. She had grown up with him and had always known him to be very reserved. This behavior was not like him. There was something going on with her old friend, but she didn't know if it would be right to ask. His wife had made sure that their friendship was on a professional level and that's where she worked to keep it. Prescott waited until he was forty four until he got married. Before that he was married to his work. Being a wealthy bachelor he had a long string of women in his life but nothing serious. Then his mother introduced him to Patsy. She was just what his mother wanted for him and it seemed to work. She spent the family money on pet projects and got her name and photo in the paper's social section. It never seemed that those things meant anything to him. He would just attend and write checks. Lauren thought that something might be changing, and she thought it might be for the good. Patsy might not like it but oh, well, that's life. Then Lauren chuckled to herself as she went to her apartment and closed the door.

Prescott grabbed a bag of potato chips out of the kitchen cupboard and headed to his office. The first thing he did was open his desk drawer and get out his bottle of Jack Daniels. Then he sat down and filled a glass that he'd brought with him from the kitchen. He filled it to the top, ripped open the bag of chips and drank down his glass of whiskey. Sitting there looking at the mail he heard someone walking through the house. Then his wife came through the door.

"Prescott, what are you doing?"

"Well, it looks like I'm eating chips and getting drunk."

"Why?"

"Why not?"

"Prescott this is not like you. And what are you drinking?" She went to grab the bottle and he pulled it back. "I thought I asked you not to drink that stuff."

"Patsy my dear, I happen to like it, and I will drink it any time I want and where I want."

"Why are you being this way?" He just sighed.

"Patsy, have you ever looked at what we have. We have eight bedrooms and eight full baths for three people. And if that's not enough we have a two bedroom apartment on the back side of the house for Lauren. Did you know there are people out there that were brought up with eight or ten people in two rooms? And may have grown up just as happy as we think we are."

"Prescott, are you all right?"

"I'll tell you when this Jack Daniels is gone."

"I told you I would never live with someone who didn't want the same things I do." Patsy said.

Prescott laughed and said "Are you threatening to leave, again, if I don't do what you want?"

"I didn't say that."

"That's good. Because my dear old mama might think your family has the same background as we do, but we both know better don't we? Patsy, the Allen's may have been worth something two or three generations ago but now all you have is the name. And there's always the prenuptial you signed, you do remember that don't you? So my dear we've come to an impasse. Either sit here and have a drink with me of this low bottom booze, or go to bed while I finish off this bottle."

She stormed out of the office and the doctor poured himself another glass full. By now he was getting a good buzz on and his thoughts of Abby came back. He remembered that in his prep school senior year book he kept a picture of them, the summers in Maine. When he got up to get it off the book self he almost stumbled, catching himself. He laughed, he hadn't been that drunk in years. When he sat down with the book he drank about half his glass before he even opened the book. There was an envelope in back with pictures in it. He finished that glass and poured another as he pulled the pictures out. There it was, him and Abby sitting on some rocks by the ocean. He started to weep. *All my life it was always do the right thing, no matter what I wanted. Then again* He looked down at the images. So young, so happy, so alive. So alive.

After the next glass of Jack Daniels and his tears Prescott drifted off to sleep in his chair. The sun coming through his windows in the office woke him up. He had a splitting head ache and his back hurt from sleeping sitting up. The pictures were still sitting there. He just looked down and rubbed his thumb over Abby's face and put them away. Then he set the book back where it was before. Then he picked up the empty bottle and shook it and shook his head realizing that that was probably the wrong thing to do. It just made his head hurt worse. He made his way into the kitchen. Lauren was standing there with a glass full of orange juice and four aspirin.

"I thought you had today off."

"I do but when I saw the car covers in a pile I had a feeling you might need these."

"Uh, another mind reader."

"No, Prescott, I've just known you for a very long time. You should take a shower and get outside, it's a beautiful day. Try and enjoy it."

Then he passed her the keys to the rover. "Not today, not today."

"Do you need anything while I'm in town?"

"I can't think of anything."

"Maybe a new bottle for your office?"

"Ah yes."

"That's what I thought. Have a good day. See you later."

"You too, Lauren." His head hurt so bad he decided to give himself a shot of vitamin B. It's what they would do in med school for bad hangovers.

After the shot and a cup of coffee he went up stairs to take a shower. Patsy was still sleeping, and he hoped she stayed asleep until he felt better so he could deal with her about last night. The shower helped. It had been years since he'd gotten that drunk and for some reason he didn't care. Besides, his life had become a series of work, writing checks for charites he'd never heard of and dealing with his step daughter's latest problems. The thought came to him, and he wondered if anyone in Peter's family ever had an eating disorder and speaking out loud he said "not likely." After he was done with showering and was getting dressed Patsy started to wake up. She rolled over and asked him what time it was.

He looked at the watch on his bed stand told her it was a quarter of nine. "Where are you going?" she asked sitting up. "I thought you were playing golf with some people from the botanical garden today?"

"They're going to have one less doctor to bore on the greens with their philanthropic adventures."

"Well then don't you think we should talk about last night?"

"What's to talk about? I got drunk, you got pissed, I passed out. All very simple don't you think?

"Prescott, what has gotten into you?"

"I'm not sure. But when I find out you'll be the first to know."

"Where are you going?" she asked again.

"I want to drive the hell out of one of my cars."

"For what reason?"

"No reason. And that's the beauty of it."

"I don't understand."

"I didn't think you would." He leaned over and kissed her on the cheek and said "I'll see you later."

"Before you go, did you remember that Anna needs to use the rover today? So her and her friends can go to the mall."

"I did, and she can't, not today. Have her take the bus like most kids have to. And don't give her any of my credit cards any more. When she starts doing things around here then we'll talk about it. Until then she's cut off."

"You can't do that."

"Oh, yes, I can, and I just did." With that he left on the way through the kitchen he got another cup of coffee and then headed into the garage. Using his keys he opened a small locker where all the car keys were kept that only he and TJ had access to. He grabbed the cobra's key and put the rover's keys in the box and locked it again. *If Anna needs to use a car she can use her mother's BMW.* He then went over to a closet that had jackets on it for each car and picked up the one with the Shelby insignia on the back of it, but that's not the one he wanted. He wanted the one behind it. It was an old RAF fighter pilots jacket that his uncle had given him years ago when he was still a teenager. It was all weather beaten with a real fur collar. He loved that old coat but his mother never wanted him to wear it because she thought it made him look trashy. *What bullshit* he thought as he pulled the jacket on. He then walked over and hit the button that opened the garage door. As he walked back toward 'the big ford' Prescott couldn't help but admire it. A thing of beauty, raw power. At one time it was the fastest production car in the world at one time and there weren't many of the original ones left. He opened the car door and remembered how small the car was. Even though he was only five eight and 160 pounds it was like putting on a fine leather glove. But once you were in you became part of the car. He pushed in the clutch, put the transmission in neutral and turned the key. It never ceased to amaze him when the engine came to life. Nothing but raw Detroit iron. 427 cubic inches with 675 horses, you could feel the cars torque all the way through your body. Again he pushed the clutch in and put the snake into first gear, eased it out of the garage, onto the driveway and then onto the street.

Then into second gear. The highway was about three miles from his house but today it seemed like an eternity. His head was somewhere between going for a ride, or trying out Peter's idea. Prescott was not prone to impulsive behavior, but this was all new. Taking Travis out for a drink.

Setting some rules with his wife, the conversation he had with Lauren, the cars, and now thinking of opening this beast up for the first time. The thought came to him that maybe it was him that needed some therapy. Turning onto the high way it occurred to him that for this to work Peter would have to witness it with his own eyes, and that would be the biggest risk of all. Take a patient out of the hospital, then endanger his life by taking him for a ride in a car that will do well over 180 miles an hour, with every intention to do just that. By the time he snapped it into fourth gear he was headed to the hospital. He had made up his mind, he was going to see how all this played out.

When he pulled into the hospital parking lot Peter was standing in the window of the canteen like he had been the night before. He made eye contact with Prescott. Peter just smiled and nodded his head. Prescott felt like the son of a bitch knew what was going on. He turned off the car and got out anyway, and went in. He went past the canteen. And Peter held up his cup of coffee.

"Now this is good coffee. Want one?" Peter asked.

"No, what I want you to do is get dressed and come with me. We're going for a ride."

Peter pointed to the car. "In that?"

"Yes, in that."

Prescott got right in Peters face. "I've played your games since you got here and now you're playing mine. If you tell anyone about this I will drive you to metro myself. Is that clear?"

All Peter said was, "Completely."

"Okay. Now we'll go upstairs and check you out and I don't want you to say anything." Peter just nodded his head.

Doctor Brown told the head nurse on the ward that Peter had a meeting with some people at metro, that he was taking him and he didn't know when they'd be back.

"Well, you'll have to sign him out." The nurse said, "because he's restricted to the hospital pending legal issues."

"Yes, I know all this, I'm his doctor." With all the paper work done they left and headed toward the parking lot. Walking toward the big Ford Peter smiled. It was black with white stripes and that all familiar snake on the hood.

Again Peter asked, "You're taking me for a ride in this?"

"Yes. Now get in before I change my mind."

Peter, being about six one and 240, had to squeeze but he got in. Prescott looked at him and said "I could get arrested for this so buckle up."

"Don't worry, no one will bother you."

"And how do you know that?"

"Just trust me."

Prescott thought to himself, "Now I'm trusting a psychiatric patient. I belong in there with him." He started up the Cobra and headed out onto the highway.

DC's beltway was heavy with traffic as he eased the big Ford into the fast lane. It was hard to hear with no top on the car. Peter asked if they were going for a ride, or was he going to try out his thoughts on being alive?

Prescott answered back, "How can I open this thing up with all this traffic?"

"If you really want to, the road will be clear for you."

"You really think so, huh?"

Peter shook his head.

"And I suppose you have an answer for the police, too?"

"They won't bother you, either."

"The hell with this, I'm taking you back. This is a bad idea."

Peter started to laugh. "So, you *are* afraid."

"No, I'm not."

"Yes, you are."

"I've *had it* with you. Who the hell do you think you are?"

"I'm Abby Westrum's friend, that's who I am. And I have been since you broke her heart, rich boy."

Prescott cut across three lanes of traffic and pulled off into the breakdown lane. He turned the engine off.

Peter got out of the car and lit up a cigarette.

"Did you and your family spend your summers in Maine on Southport Island?"

"And Nowegan Inn, right?"

"Yeah, so?"

"I had a girlfriend who worked there, who was best friends with Abby. They roomed together when they weren't kissing your rich asses for tips."

"This can't be…"

"Oh, yes it can. It was 1969. It's too bad you weren't more like your buddy, Dan…" Peter thought, 'Dan', 'Dan'… "Jenson, right?"

"Yes."

"We liked Dan, he paid top dollar for the dope you boys used to smoke. Oh, and while we're on the subject, she was so brokenhearted when your Mommy made you break up with her, she miscarried your child."

"She would have told me that."

"How could she? You were already gone. Or, did you forget you didn't even have the nerve to tell her to her face?

You left a letter in her mailbox in the servant's rec room. Smooth move, rich boy. You know something? We're not all that different after all, are we, except for one thing: I've been forced to face my fears, and you run from yours."

"You have no goddamned right to talk to me like this, no right at all."

"What are you gonna do, call the cops? And just what are you going to tell them, when they ask what you're doing with a psychiatric patient, that's -oh- not supposed to be off hospital grounds? I guess you could tell them it was a new kind of therapy."

"Look, you fucking asshole, get in the car. You *want* a ride? I'll *give* you a ride."

Peter got in, and Prescott turned the key, and the big Ford came to life, rumbling.

"Prescott, I do believe you're pissed."

"Fuck you."

"Now that's not very professional, is it now?"

Just then, Peter's head snapped back as Prescott side-stepped the clutch. Tires started to screech, and when he hit second Peter's head snapped back, again. Then into third gear; the ass end swerved a little until Prescott pushed the pedal to the floor. About that time, the broken lines in the road started to become solid. Prescott slammed it into fourth; again, Peter's head snapped.

Peter glanced over at the speedometer; 120, and they were still accelerating. Both of Prescott's hands were glued to the steering wheel, and his eyes were on the road. It seemed as if they were all alone, that there was no one on the road, except them.

Prescott glanced at the speedometer: 140, 150, still climbing. At 160 everything seemed to slow down, and the blood pounding in his ears was deafening. It felt like his heart was going to explode in his chest.

Just then, he thought he heard Peter whisper, "Now, a little more, and you're home."

The last time he looked down at the speedometer, it was pinned at 180. He let off the gas, and the Ford began to slow down: 170, 160, 140, 120, 90. Back down to third. 70, then back into fourth.

Prescott took a deep, deep breath. Somehow, his head seemed clear.

"OK, Peter, we went for your ride. What more do you know about Abby Westrum?"

"The last time I saw her was in 1969, then she headed back to Colorado."

"Did you ever hear from her again?"

"No."

"Then why did you tell me you'd been friends with her for a long time?"

"I think part of me wanted to piss you off, or get back at you, for some reason."

"Why?"

"For having so much, when people like me have so little. It may not be a sane reason, but let's not forget where I am. I really want to thank you for making a man's dream come true. I've always wanted to ride in one of these, and it was all I ever thought it would be."

Prescott glanced over at him. "You know, you were right about the fear."

"Yeah. No big deal. Call it payback for the adventure you just took me on. Whaddaya say you take me back now? I'd like to have a cup of coffee."

Prescott found an exit ramp and got off the highway. He drove around until they found a Starbuck's. They whipped through the drive-up window, and he asked what Peter wanted.

He told him, "Just a plain coffee would be fine."

Prescott ordered two, and parked the car. He told Peter it was his turn to ask some questions.

Peter replied, "Go ahead. What do you mean, the link between you and Abby Westrum?"

"At first, your name sounded very familiar. As my head started to clear up, I thought it was you, but I wasn't sure. Then the day when you were in my room, talking to me about my options with you and the Metro, I noticed your shoes. How Abby used to laugh about how your mother used to make you wear those shoes on Sundays. Everybody else wore sneakers and sandals, you wore imported loafers. That's when it hit me."

"You should have told me then, so I could have had another doctor take your case."

"No, that wouldn't have worked."

"Why is that?"

"It just wouldn't have. Besides, I like what you and Travis are doing. You've gotten more information than anyone else."

"I don't think I can work with you anymore, after today."

"That's not gonna work. You're the only one who might be able to do something about what I have to tell you. And, besides, we made a deal that you would help me through this, so I can finally rest. You have to let me tell you about Dante's Inferno. It desperately needs to be told. That's why I chose you."

"What?"

"I mean, that's why I need you, to help me with this. And, because I think that you may be able to make a difference."

"Peter, what brought you down here, anyway?"

"I think I told you I have two kids in North Carolina, and it had been a while since I'd seen them, and I wanted to go down and look over them. Besides, I got divorced recently from my fourth wife."

"Well, how did that go?'

"Just about as bad as the other three, doc."

"Was it your choice?"

"I don't know whose choice it was, really, doc. All I know is this: I'm no day at the beach to live with. One thing is, I always seem to marry well-educated women. My fourth wife came from your neck of the woods, in Boston."

"Look, Doc, I've gotten to the point where I don't even blame any of them, anymore. In and out of hospitals like this, it's just part of the whole thing, that's all. I'm sure I'm not the first Viet Nam vet with post traumatic stress with multiple wives, am I, doc?"

"No, you're not."

"Is it OK if I ask you a few questions, now, doc? Ever been married before?"

"Nope."

"Have any children?"

Prescott just sighed. "I have a step-daughter."

"Well, I looked over your bio on the Internet. Only child, huh? That must have been rough, in a way, wasn't it? Lot of similarities between an only child and the youngest."

"How so?"

"Well, I told you about how crazy and domineering my mother was. Did you experience any of that?"

All Prescott said was, "A bit."

They finished their coffee and headed back towards the hospital.

Prescott turned to Peter and said, "Not even Travis should know about this, you know that, don't you? Are you good with that?"

"I am. You know, Doctor Brown, I am a man of honor. I believe in it, and I have tried to live it. It will not go beyond you and I."

About that time, they pulled into the parking lot. Prescott came to a stop, and turned the car off.

"Can I trust you to go back in without me?"

"Remember I told you about honor?"

Prescott just nodded his head.

Peter got out of the Ford and began to walk off. Then he turned around and came back.

"The hangover is gone, isn't it? That JD will do it to you every time." He grinned, then turned and headed into the hospital.

Prescott just shook his head, again. *How the hell does he know that? Well, this is turning out to be a hell of a day. Wow.*

Chapter Eight

When he got back to the ward, Peter decided to take a nap. Saturday afternoons were always boring in a VA hospital, but having gone for a ride in an AC Cobra made all the boredom worth it.

Peter signed himself back in with Nurse Webster. She asked him how things were with Metro.

He told her, "I think it's going to be OK now."

"There's movies this evening, if you're interested."

"I think for right now I'm just going to take a nap. I'll see how I feel when I wake up."

Prescott headed for home. It dawned on him, for once, that things didn't always have to be black and white. He was having a very difficult time processing all that had gone on since the night before. Would it be right to try to get in touch with Abby after all these years? Would he be opening up old wounds? Maybe he should call his friend Dan Jenson, and talk to him about it. But, the first thing he had to do was talk to Patsy about changing a few things in the Brown household. And that could blow up. That wouldn't be the first time, but this was something he wasn't going to back down on. Things were about to change, and he felt good about it. When he got home, TJ was working on the cars. Prescott pulled the Cobra into the garage. TJ asked if he'd had a nice ride.

"The best. You were right, TJ, it needs to breathe now and then."

TJ was a short, stocky man with a beer belly, in his sixties, who used to work for *Maclarrion* racing when he was younger. He knew more about fast cars than just about anybody in the D.C. area. He could tell by the tires that the car had been driven hard and fast. He took off his ball cap and scratched his head.

What got into him?

He wasn't going to ask. Besides, it was good for the cars the doctor had, except of course for the Bentley. They needed to be driven hard once in a while. It was what they were made for; like thoroughbred horses, they had to run or they would grow old and die too young.

TJ asked Prescott if he wanted him to put the covers back on.

"No, just on the Bentley."

Then he went into the house. As he opened the door to the kitchen, Lauren was standing there.

"How did your day go?" she asked.

"It had to be one of the best days I've had in a very long time."

"Well, the day is still young," and she pointed up stairs. He just looked up and shook his head. Lauren told him that she pick him a bottle of J.D. for his study.

"How much do I owe you?"

"It's a gift, Prescott, from an old friend," and then she left.

He knew he would have to talk to Patsy about what was going before the day was done. Part of him didn't think that she would understand, but he knew that he had to try.

He grabbed a soda out of the fridge and headed up to see what she was doing. When he arrived, she wasn't there, but he could hear her in the work-out room. It seemed the only time she worked out was when she was pissed.

Here we go.

The door was open and she was on the treadmill. She had her head phones on. He knew that she saw him, but wouldn't make eye contact.

He stood there sipping his Coke for a while, then walked over to toss the can in the waste basket. That got her attention. She stopped the treadmill.

"You know, those go in the recycle bin."

"Is that the only way I can get your attention, if I do something you don't approve of?"

"Of *course* not."

"Well, that's not how I see it. Look, I've been standing here for fifteen minutes and not once did you take note of me standing there."

"Well, I've had a *terrible* day."

"And why is that?"

"I don't think you'd understand."

"Let me try."

"Anna had a fit because she couldn't have her own way; you know how sensitive she is."

"She's not sensitive, she's *fucking spoiled.*"

"Prescott, why are you swearing at me? You *know* how that upsets me."

"Well, then, why don't you call your therapist? I'll pay him three hundred dollars so he can tell you that your brother got all the attention growing up and you're overly sensitive because older brother got to go to Switzerland skiing before you did. Then you come home, have two or three glasses of wine and write out a check to your favorite charity with lots of zeros for some instant gratification. You'll feel better when you're done, and you won't have to look at the three thousand pound elephant in the living room, whose *name* is *Anna*."

"What are you talking about?"

"Oh, hell, where do I start? When was the last time you saw her eat a real meal?"

"She *has* to watch her weight. You *know* she wants to go to modeling school."

"For god's sake, she's *sixteen* and she can't weight *eighty pounds.*

"She's *small boned.*"

"Patsy, she's almost *six feet tall. When* are you going to open your eyes? She's in *trouble.*"

"I don't think she's the one in trouble. I think it's *you*, and what about last night?"

"I can see where all this is going. If you don't want talk about the real problem that's going in this house, then I have nothing more to say."

As he started to walk off, she started to scream, "You come back here! This is *not* over, you *will* talk to me!"

Prescott stopped. "I can see where your daughter gets it, now."

"If you don't come back here right now I'm going to my mother's in Wellesley."

He shouted, "You can use my credit cards for that." He didn't say anything else, but he could still hear her from downstairs, so he went into his study and closed the door. The bottle that had gotten him drunk was on the table, so he decided to have a drink. There was a clean glass Lauren had put with the bottle. He poured himself a small drink to sip on. Looking through his Blackberry, he tried to find Dan's home phone number. He needed to talk to him about the conversation he'd had with Peter that morning.

I think I have it somewhere.

He looked everywhere, then gave up. Maybe it was on the e-mail that Dan had sent him.

Just as he turned on the computer the door to his office slammed opened and Patsy was standing there. "One last time! Are we going to *talk* about this or *what?*"

"Patsy, we're either going to talk about your spending and Anna's anorexic problem or were not talking."

"Anna is *not anorexic!*"

"So now you're a doctor? This conversation is *over.*"

"Then I'm going up north to Boston."

"Patsy, if you think that I'm going to beg you to stay like all the other times, you're wrong."

"Well, then, *Anna* and I are *leaving tonight.*" "Have a safe trip, and close the door behind you when you leave."

He had gone through the same thing with her many times before; she would go to her mother for a while, and after a few days she would call, crying about how she would change. I'd let her come back and within a month it was same thing. But not this time; if she was going to change, it would have to be in Boston and not here. After that episode he drained his drink instead of sipping it.

Hell, maybe the next one.

Getting back to his computer, he found the e-mail that Dan had sent, and it had his home phone number on it. He poured another drink and sat there before calling. How would he tell Dan about having the conversation with Peter, a patient?

Prescott had to use the bathroom, just in time to see Patsy and Anna putting things into Patsy's car. He wondered how long it would last this time.

He finished in the bathroom and headed back to his study. By the time he passed the window again, they were already gone, so he went back to his study. He sat down and sipped his drink, picked up the phone and called Dan. The phone rang three or four times. Prescott was beginning to think no one was home, then a voice said, "Hello, Jenson residence."

"Is Dr. Jenson in?"

"Yeah, he's in the garage. I'll tell him to pick up the phone in there."

Prescott told the girl on the other end, "thank you".

"You're welcome."

"Hello, Dr. Jenson here."

"Dan, it's Prescott."

"Prescott! How the hell are you?"

"Dan, I'm all fucked up."

"Is that really you, using that kind of language?"

"Yeah, it is."

"What's going on, buddy? Has the VA finally driven you over the edge?"

"Maybe. Look, I'm in the garage. Let me go into my study, pour myself a good drink. I've got a feeling I'm going to need it."

"Hang on, I'll be right back."

Prescott waited a few minutes.

"Prescott, are you still there?"

"Yeah."

"What's going on?"

"Remember the e-mail you sent about seeing Abby out in Colorado?"

"Yeah, I've got a patient that knows her."

"What? How?"

"From when we used to summer in Maine."

"You mean on Southport Island? So what's the big deal? Heh, heh. Hey, how did this guy link you two together?"

"He says that he used to go out with Abby's friend that worked for Nowegan."

"That's possible. Lots of the girls that worked there went out with the locals."

"Hell, he even knows *you*."

"How?"

"He said that his buddy used to sell pot to you."

"Ha, ha. Wait a minute, is his name Larry?"

"No, it's Peter."

"Peter?"

"Peter."

"Is this guy about six one, six two, one-ninety, two hundred, very sarcastic wit?"

"That's him, only now I think he's heavier.'

"Well, we're all heavier, now that we're older. Man, that friend of his had some good weed."

"Dan, he also told me that she was pregnant, and had a miscarriage when we broke up."

"Prescott, breaking up with someone you've been banging all summer by leaving a note the day you leave was a little screwed up."

"If you remember, I told you that I'm looking at my computer right now. I can catch a flight out of Manchester at seven, straight through to Dulles. I'll be in at ten thirty.

Pick me up. We need to talk about this. Is the missus going to be home, or is she out tonight giving your family's money away?"

"No, she's headed for Boston."

"Hell, things really *are* falling apart for you. Don't worry your therapist is on the way. Do you still keep a bottle of JD in the house?"

"Yeah, you'd better get another one. I've got a feeling it's going be a long night, I think."

Prescott hung up the phone and sat there.

What was so important that Dan would fly down here tonight just to talk?

Prescott was starting to wonder whether it wasn't all getting to him, with everything going on. Having another psychiatrist to talk to couldn't hurt, especially after the stunt he pulled with Peter that morning.

It was four o'clock and he thought he'd take a nap before it was time to pick up Dan at ten. He went upstairs, set the alarm clock for nine then laid down. He fell right off to sleep; before he knew it, the alarm was going off. It took him a few minutes to wake up from sleep and the JD. When he finally came around, sitting on the edge of the bed, he turned off the alarm. Then he bent over to put on his shoes. He picked up his loafers and threw them across the room. Then went into his closet and got a pair of sneakers. After putting them on he went into the bathroom and splashed some water on his face. When he looked in the mirror, he wondered how the years had treated Abby. His hair was getting thin and it was harder to hide the gray. If it wasn't for contacts he'd have to wear glasses all the time, but all he could see of Abby was her on the beach, the wind blowing through her long brown curls, and laughing. Coming out of his reverie, he knew it was time to get Dan. He headed down the stairs and through the kitchen into the garage. Putting on his jacket, the same one he wore when he and Peter were out, he started to get into the Rover. He stopped and got out.

Let's do this right.

He got in to the Shelby, started it up, opened the garage and headed out. He was like a kid with a new toy, banging every gear, burning the tires and going way over the speed limit. He was weaving in and out of traffic and loving every minute of it. It didn't take him long to get to Dulles. He parked it and went into the terminal. Dan's plane had just landed, so he stood by the gate and waited. A few minutes later Dan came strolling out. All he had with him was a back pack slung over his shoulder. Walking up to his old friend, he crowed, "Christ, Prescott, you look like *shit*! What the *hell* have you been doing to yourself?"

"Is that any way to greet an old friend?"

"It is when it's true. What is going on with you?"

"I've got a patient that I think is driving me crazy, literally."

"It's always a patient with you, or is it that money pit you married?"

"Well, you won't have to deal with her. She's gone."

"Yeah, you told me on the phone."

Walking to the car, Prescott asked, "How was Abby when you saw her? How does she look?"

"Good."

"Is she doing OK?"

"Hold on. You and I have a lot of things to talk about before we get to that. Let's get something to eat and head for your house and that bottle."

"Where are you parked?"

Prescott pointed to the Shelby. Dan just stopped.

"You must be sick. You left *that* in a parking lot?"

"Well, let's go find some food. Is there any good take out where you live?"

"Yeah, there's a good Chinese place by where I live that delivers."

"That works. Do you have a menu?"

"No, but I can stop and pick one up."

"That's good, because I like to see a place before I eat there."

"The food's sensational Chinese."

They got the menu and headed for Prescott's house. Dan asked if Lauren was still with him.

"Oh, yeah."

"I always liked that girl. I hope I get to see her before I leave on Monday."

"You will."

After the garage was closed up they went into the house. They decided what they wanted to order, and Prescott called the order in. Prescott told Dan it would be about forty five minutes before it got there.

"OK, where's that bottle of Jack?"

"It's in my study."

"Well, let's go."

Prescott grabbed two glasses and they headed into the study. The bottle of whiskey was still on the table. Dan poured them both a glass.

"I don't need that much," Prescott replied.

"With what I have to tell you, believe you me, you will," Dan answered. "Now, sit down. Abby didn't have a miscarriage."

"What are you talking about?"

"You mean that Peter, my patient, was lying?"

"No, as far as he knew, she had lost it."

"Dan, what are you saying?"

"Remember, it was the end of summer and we were headed back to school to finish our senior year?"

"Yes."

"Well, everyone else was leaving, as well. Abby went home to Boulder and had your daughter."

"Why didn't she let me know?"

"She tried, but your mother intervened. Seeing you were both under age, Abby's folks got a hold of your folks, but, *listen* now, it took Abby's folks a long time to get your name from her. Finally she told them it was you."

"How come I never found out?"

"Your mother buried the thing. Hell, she even tricked you into giving a blood sample to find out if the child was yours or not."

"How the hell did she do that?"

"Remember when we got back to school and on spring break we decided to go to Egypt to see the pyramids? We had to get all those shots; remember the doctor calling you back for more blood? It was your mother who engineered that for a paternity test." Prescott drank down his drink and poured another. "This is all bullshit."

"Oh, yeah, why don't you ask Lauren? She knows the whole story, and has from the very beginning."

"How could my mother do that?"

"How could your mother do half the shit she pulled with people's lives?"

"You never did like her."

"It's not that I didn't like her, it's that I didn't trust her."

About that time Lauren came in through the kitchen and into study. She opened the door.

"Well, I'll be damned, as I live and breathe, it's not *Dan Jenson.*"

"Lauren, my lovely Irish beauty."

They hugged.

"It's been too long, way too long."

Prescott asked, "What brings you out this late?"

"There's two bags of food in the kitchen. The delivery boy couldn't get you to answer the door so he came around the back. You're lucky I was up reading or you wouldn't have your food."

Dan asked her to stay and have something to eat with them.

"No, I think I'm going back home and to bed."

"No, Lauren, I think you need to stay. I'm telling Prescott about Abby."

She just shook her head. I'll get another glass. I'll need a drink for this."

"Why did the two of you keep this from me?"

Lauren, we've been together all these years. Why, why?"

Dan spoke up first.

"It wasn't her fault. When the paternity test proved she was your child, your mother had her people look into anyone that knew anything about it, that was close to it, and made sure they wouldn't say anything to you."

"How could she do that?"

"It was all very simple: if Lauren said anything she and her mother would be out of a job, and would never work in the Boston area again. Lauren's mother's retirement would disappear."

"What about *you*?"

"It was not that I didn't want to tell you. When one of her henchmen approached me I told him to fuck off. Then he told me if I wanted your child to have good up-bringing and a good education with a nice but conservative trust, I should think twice about it. The last thing I wanted was to see your child grow up without all she deserved."

"My god, Dan, I have a daughter, I should get a hold of her. How can I get in touch with her?"

"Prescott, you'd better have another drink."

"Why?"

"Just have another drink. She died two years ago."

"How?"

"Of breast cancer."

He put his down his glass.

"Dear God, what have I done?" and started to cry.

Lauren went over and put her arms around him. "It's going to be all right."

By then he was sobbing and saying, "Why didn't I do something?"

Dan answered, "What could you do? You didn't know until today, and if you did know, we know that you would have tried, but your mother would have won. You know that, don't you?"

Prescott just shook his head.

Dan asked Lauren if she thought finishing off that bottle was a good idea.

"I do," she answered. She poured Prescott another drink and one for herself.

Dan lifted his glass: "A toast to old friends and times gone by. Lauren and Prescott raised their glasses:

"To old friends and times gone by."

Not much was said the rest of the night. After the second bottle was gone, Dan and Prescott were asleep in their chairs. Before Lauren went home she took one last look at them.

Damned English just can't hold their whiskey. Then she closed the door behind her and headed for bed.

Chapter Nine

The next morning she got up and cooked them a breakfast. When it was ready she went to the study with two cooking pans and started beating them together. The noise was so loud Dan fell out his chair onto the floor. Prescott just opened his eyes slowly.

"Lauren, what the *hell* are you doing?"

"Well, boys, if you're going to drink like Irishmen you'd better eat like them, as well. Breakfast is ready."

Dan said from the floor, "You know, you're still beautiful."

"Listen here, Dan Jenson, that talk might have worked when we were children but it don't work now."

"Lauren, did I hear a bit of your brogue just then?"

"When I only get three hours' sleep, it comes out."

"Do you remember how that brogue got us into trouble when we went to Ireland that summer?"

"Yes, and it's just as well to forget all about it." Lauren stood in the doorway, shaking her fist at him. "And, Dan Jenson, if my mother would have found out she would have castrated you."

Prescott just pointed his finger back and forth at them. "You two?"

"Do you know how dense you can be? Do you pay any attention to the things going on around you?"

"Come on, before your food gets cold."

The three of them sat, eating.

Prescott asked her name. Dan answered, "What name?"

"Abby's daughter."

"Phoenix."

"Like in Arizona?"

"No, as in the mythical bird."

"Why?"

"Because she rose out of the pain and bullshit your mother and her cronies put Abby through, while she was carrying the Phoenix."

After they got done eating, they all cleaned up. "We'll talk some more."

Dan asked Lauren, "Do you remember going to the merry barn when we were at Nowegan? They had live bands and a bunch of us kids would go on Saturday night. Prescott, did you ever go?"

"No, Saturday night was when mother had guests over to our cottage for drinks and bridge. She wouldn't play unless I was her partner. Lauren, do you remember the night that guy that Abby's friend was going out with was there, and he gave us a ride back in his SS Chevelle convertible?"

"Oh, yes, didn't he tear up the culvert spinning his tires over it, bringing us back?"

"Yeah, we were all laughing, and when the security cop asked who did it, we all blamed some guy that was leaving?"

"When we got to the rec room I sat in the car with him, talking, and we started to make out 'til somebody came running past and said that security was coming back for him. I got out and he took off. Too bad, he was a good kisser."

"Well, Lauren, Prescott's patient is your guy."

"Are you kidding me?"

"Nope."

When breakfast was done they went upstairs and got showered. Dan was done first and had cups of coffee for him and Prescott. They went out back on the deck. It was a nice day; the sun was shining. After sitting down, Prescott said, "Dan, tell me about how Abby is doing."

"She's been happily married to the same guy for almost thirty years. They have two other children, all grown up and on their own."

"What does her husband do?"

"He's a plumber."

"A *plumber*?"

"You know, for a second you sounded like your mother. Yes, he's a plumber, and no matter what you may have been taught, you don't need all this to be happy. I mean, for chrissakes, Prescott, I live in Vermont, with two teenaged daughters, from different mothers, who have no social skills other than texting and talking on their cell phones. I live in a three bedroom house, I only have enough patients to keep me going. I volunteer most of the time I have for free, at the local alcohol rehab. I don't need anything else. I'm happy with what I have."

"Yeah, I'm beginning to see that. And Phoenix?" "She used the trust that was set up for her and became a school teacher."

"Do I have any grandchildren?"

"Biological? You do. She has two boys, eighteen and twelve." Dan looked up to the sun then over at Prescott.

"I've been your friend since we were four. Any ideas you have of getting a hold of them would be *wrong*, so get that right out of your head. I know you to be a man of honor; that means you live with your mistakes."

"Do you think that's what Abby would want?"

"Yes, because that's what she told me, and before we put this thing to bed, she *also* told me, if and when I saw you, to tell that you were her first love. There would always be a place in her heart for you, and she hoped you felt the same."

Dan got up and threw out the rest of his coffee. "Come on, Prescott, we're going for a ride, and I'm driving. I always wanted to drive that Cobra, and today's the day."

Prescott asked, "Where are we going?"

"To see this patient of yours, and you're going to fill me in on the way about what's going with our old friend."

"He's not *my* old friend."

"That's right, your mother made sure of that."

"What does that mean?"

"Look, get honest with yourself. She sheltered you from anything she didn't agree with. Now, give me the keys to the damned car, and let's go."

Prescott got in and looked over at Dan.

"Prescott, I hope I don't blow the transmission. It's been a long time since I've driven a stick, so hang on. Hey, is your insurance paid up?" and then laughed.

He slammed it into first gear, burned rubber out of the garage and onto the street.

"Oh, *boy*, I could get used to this! OK, tell me about your boy."

"Well, he came to us from the Metro."

"The police?"

"Yeah he had been standing catatonic in front of the Viet Nam veterans' memorial for twenty four hours when they approached him. He got violent, so they brought him in to us."

"Look, I don't need his whole history. How is your therapy going with him?"

"Well, it's not."

"What do you mean?"

"I can't put him under. He won't take to it."

"What *are* you doing with him?"

"I took him for a ride in this car yesterday."

"Is that a new type of therapy you're using?"

"Look, Dan, all he wants is to tell his story."

"And what's *that* all about?"

"The best we can figure out, he was with some secret group called Dante's Inferno in Viet Nam."

"That sounds very familiar. I don't know - let me think about it."

As he down shifted into third gear, he crowed, "Oh, do *I* have to get me one of *these*!"

"Easy with the car, Dan."

Dan banged the car into fourth and gave it more gas.

"Slow *down*. Your exit is coming up."

When they finally got to the hospital it was Sunday and the parking lot was almost empty. Prescott showed Dan where to park. When he turned off the engine, he said, "We need to do this more often."

"What's that?"

"Get drunk, *all* of it. Now let's meet this guy." They went in through the back door. When they went past the canteen, Dan said, "Let's get a cup of coffee and talk. I remember; I know why that sounded so familiar. I was working with a girl whose father had committed suicide. He shot himself in front of her one night."

"How?"

"With a shotgun. Blew his head almost off."

"And how old was she?"

"Twelve. The kid had a lot of problems, but we got her through it. The thing I remember was, she had blocked the whole thing out. The only memory of him she had was them sliding in their back yard one winter. I had to put her under hypnosis to draw out the rest.

"She told me that when he got drunk he would say that 'Dante's Inferno was waiting for him for killing his brothers in arms', over and over until he passed out. And, get this, the night he shot himself he wasn't drunk. He and his wife and the girl were watching the news. They were showing the Viet Nam memorial being unveiled. When the cameras did a close-up of the names, all he said was, "Which ones?" then pulled his twelve gauge from behind his chair, put it in his mouth and pulled the trigger. Neither the wife or the girl had time to stop him."

"When the Metro brought him in they said that he was repeating the same thing over and over."

"And what was that?"

'Which ones?'

Dan threw his empty cup in the trash.

"Let's go see him."

When they got to the ward, Nurse Webster asked "You're finally here. Peter's been asking when you were coming all morning. I told him you weren't coming in today, and all he said was, 'He'll be here', and then right back to his room.

Dan rolled his eyes at Prescott as they headed for his room. When they got there Peter was standing by the window.

"Peter, I brought an old friend of mine to see you. He's a doctor like me, and we'd like to talk with you."

Peter broke out laughing. "Well, if it's not Dan, Dan, the marijuana man. I saw you getting out of the big Ford when you were coming in. I'm sorry, my friend Larry doesn't do that sort of thing anymore. Now he sells real estate; in some circles, that's just as bad."

"Dan had a patient whose father might have been in Dante's Inferno."

"Oh, yeah, where's he now?"

"He's dead."

"How?"

"He shot himself."

"That's a shocker. So, tell me, Dan, how are you going to help?"

"Dr. Brown tells me that you have blackouts, or grayouts, and you don't remember anything afterwards."

"That's right."

"And that all you want is to tell your story about Dante's Inferno?"

"That and the aftermath of being involved."

"I've got a couple of ideas. Dr. Brown and I are going to talk about it, and we'll be back to fill you in about it, and see what you think."

Before Dan and Prescott left, Dan told Peter, "We'll be back in a while, so keep an eye that big Ford, OK?"

Peter nodded, and they left.

Walking down the hall Dan stopped and told Prescott, "Wait a second, I'll be right back."

He went back into Peter's room and asked him if he had any sleep deprivation training while he was in the service. Peter nodded.

"This is good, good. I'll be back."

Dan went back to where Prescott was waiting. Prescott asked, "What was that all about, lack of sleep?"

"We're going to keep him up and let him tell his story for however long it takes, 'til he goes into one of his gray-outs."

"Are you crazy?"

"How long had he been standing in front of the wall?"

"Over twenty-fours."

"And where did he come from before that?"

"He drove from Maine."

"That's about thirty, thirty-five hours without sleep. My guess is he's got a secret that's so deep, every time he tries to bring it up, he goes gray and it goes back into his subconscious."

"He's not going to go for it."

"Yes, he will, because he's had the desperation of trying; he doesn't know he's in a gray out"

"Where did you come up with all this?"

"Theories. A doctor in England has been helping patient with PTSD this way for about ten years."

"But has it been cleared for this country?"

"Not any more then taking young men and fucking up their lives over *idealistic bullshit.*"

"OK, we're going to have to get your PA involved with this, too. Who are you working these days?"

"His name is Travis Gonzales."

"Could we get him in here today?"

"If I call, he should be home."

"OK, you do that, and I'm going to talk to your boy."

"Don't you think you ought to slow down? Remember, he's still my patient."

"Prescott, I'm going to tell you something. All the time we were growing up, I always envied you. You were a good athlete, and me, I sucked at every sport I ever tried. If it hadn't been for you, I would have flunked out of school a dozen times. It all came so easy to you, while I struggled, and all the time I would make fun of you, and how perfect you were. Remember, you went right into college and I went on the road with the Grateful Dead, and it was you who convinced me to try to get into med school. I thought you were nuts, but you helped me with the entrance exams, and all the times I wanted to quit, you told me that I could do it. That made me try a little harder and, now here was the turning point of my life: a book you gave me on my birthday my last year in med school. Do you remember that book?"

"Of course."

'The Thought and Reflections of Dr. Carl Jung.' I couldn't put it down and that's why I went into psychiatry. All because you did the right thing. All that happened with Abby, *that* was your mother's doing, not yours. The Prescott Brown *I* know never would have done that, so don't blame yourself. I knew your mother and I don't think anyone could have gone toe to toe with her especially a boy of seventeen who had lived under her thumb all his life. Somehow, all this with Peter is linked to our youth and we owe it to him and ourselves to see this thing through. Prescott, let me help, OK?"

Dan stuck his hand out. "Let me help, Prescott."

"Yeah, let's do this."

They shook hands and hugged.

"I'll call Travis."

"And I'll see Peter."

Dan walked into Peter's room. He was sitting there almost like he was waiting.

Peter spoke. "It's time to put the fire out in Dante's Inferno, isn't it?"

Dan just nodded his head. "Is that what you want?"

"Yes, more then anything."

"OK, well, let's do it."

Dan said, "In about an hour we're going start a session and we're not going to stop until you tell your whole story. Are you up for it?"

"Of course. One time in training I was up for six days with no sleep and very little food."

"Good, you'll need to draw on that. I'll be back to get you in a few."

As Dan was walking out the door he turned back to Peter.

"You know, man, back in Maine you sure did have some good pot."

Peter replied, "Nothing but the best."

Dan left, and went to Prescott's office. He was sitting there, waiting.

"How's Peter?"

"He's good with it, but I got the feeling he knew what was coming."

"I told you that coming over here."

"Maybe that will help us when the time comes." What about your PA?"

"He's on the way. OK, Dan, how does this all work?"

"The same as any other session, except it doesn't stop until the thing he's holding onto comes out or he becomes psychotic."

"That's absolutely insane."

"And taking a patient for a ride at one hundred eighty miles a hour is sane?"

"Point taken."

"We're going to need a cardiac crash cart, adreneline, haldol and thorazine."

"Would you like me to schedule an operating room, too, just in case?"

"Prescott, you're still having a hard time with new things."

Dan, you're going to stop for just *one minute.* Have you ever done this before yourself?"

"No, I've assisted at Cornell and Belleview."

"OK, Dan if this goes bad, we're out of work, then think of all the time you'll have to drive your cars."

Prescott said, "I can't believe that you're talking me into this."

Just then Travis came through the door.

"What's so important that brings us in on Sunday?"

"Travis, I would like to introduce you to Dr. Dan Jenson, an old friend and colleague from Vermont."

They shook hands. Dan asked Travis if he'd heard of sleep deprivation therapy.

"Yeah, they're using it all over Europe. I've read about it in some of our journals. They seem to be having good luck with it. Hasn't been cleared for the States yet, but they tried it at Cornell and Bellevue."

"Oh, *that's* where I saw your name. You assisted in those sessions. So, what am I doing here?"

"We're going to try it on Peter."

Travis raised his eyebrows and looked at Prescott. "Are you are *joking*?"

"No, we're not."

"If this goes bad, my pension is gone."

"Don't worry, we'll take full responsibility."

"If that's what you're willing to do for me, I'm in."

"Let's do it."

"OK, Travis, you go get him. When he gets here, hook him up with respiratory, heart, blood gas, pulse."

"Prescott, can you get the other things we need down here without too many questions being asked?"

"No problem."

"Prescott, call the kitchen and have some food and coffee sent down - strong coffee. Because you left off with him, you'll go first. We know that all he wants to do is tell his story; we're going let him, but we're also going to ask a lot of questions. Keep him moving on his story. If this works like the ones I've done and the ones I've read about, we're going to get tired a lot sooner then he will. That way we'll do two hour sessions so we can get some sleep.

"How about Travis?"

"He's got alarms that will go off if we need him, so he can nap in there."

"You know, if this works for him, it's a new process, to help us with all the kids coming back from over there, the latest war. God damned wars."

"But its not approved."

310

"Well, you can use some of that money and influence that your family has, and maybe you can change it instead of planting sculpted gardens for the elite."

Travis came walking down the hall with Peter. Peter went into the session room.

Dan turned to Travis.

"Does he smoke?"

"Yeah, get him an ashtray and some cigarettes and a lighter."

"Travis, there's a smoke alarm in there find a way to turn it off or call maintenance, and have them do it. OK, Travis?"

"I've got a guy I know in maintenance. He'll turn off the whole system for me if I ask, but it might cost me a bottle."

"Just do it. We'll get him his bottle. Just ask him what he drinks."

After Peter was all hooked up, Travis gave him his smokes. Peter asked, "What's this all about?"

"Well, the doctor told me to tell you to smoke all you want because its going to be a long night."

Peter laughed. "It's their lungs," and lit one up. Travis, Prescott and Dan all stood outside in the hallway. Dan asked, "Do we have everything in place?"

Prescott nodded. "Yes, everything that you asked for is here. Travis, is he all set?"

"Yeah, good to go."

Dan grinned. "Well, Prescott you're on."

"Dan, is this a psychiatric session, or a Broadway show?"

"Oh, Prescott, you have such little faith."

"Dan, this had better work, or it's your ass, or should I say, *our* ass."

Dan put a hand on each of his shoulders, looked him in the eyes and said, "Prescott, this is *going to work*."

As Prescott walked in and sat down, Peter blew a smoke ring in the air and said sardonically, "Thanks for the smokes."

"You're welcome. Let's get started where we left off on Friday."

"When I got the news about my old friend the Gunny I felt like I lost the only one that understood what was going on with me. At that point I felt that I was alone and couldn't tell anybody about our connection. I was in the hanger hiding from work. Terry found me and asked if I was all right. I asked him "Why?"

"Well, I heard about your friend over at the Marine's barracks. Terry never ceased to amaze me with his ability for competition and ruthlessness at any given time, but if I could trust anyone among the bunch of bandits I was with in First Lieutenant, it was Terry. He asked me if they were going to have some kind of service for the Gunny. I told him I didn't know, but I was going over to the Marine's barracks after work to find out.

"I'll be around, so if you need a ride come see me and I'll give you a ride home. Besides, I'd like to see Cindy. It's been a while."

"Have you got that girl with child yet?"

"No, not all this shit is over."

"Oh, all that secret shit you don't want anyone to know about?"

"Yeah, that's right Terry. Secret shit."

All Terry said was, "Cool."

After work he gave me ride over like he said he would. I saw Captain Leeman coming out of the barracks as I was going in. I saluted him and asked if there would be a services for the Gunny.

"No, not here."

"Where?"

"Arlington. The Corp is handling everything." "Captain, would it be all right if I went into his office one last time?"

"You know the Gunny thought a lot of you Davies, and not just because you stood up to every thing the Corp dished out to you. It was your shooting. He was left handed, too, and one hell of a shot. Yes, you can go in his office. Just remember his ritual before you leave, and lock the door when you do."

I didn't know he was a left handed shooter when he was on the range he only shot pistols, and always right handed. When I got to his office the door was partly opened; I half expected him to tell me to come in. He would ask me the same question every time: "Where are your score sheets?" I'd pass them over to him and on the days I told him I didn't think I did so well, he'd just laugh.

"Compared to what?" he'd just say.

When I came out of my thoughts I started to look around his office, at all the pictures and memorabilia. There were pictures of him in Korea, Viet Nam and other assignments that he'd been on. His office was like a museum to the Corp, but there wasn't one medal to be seen anywhere. Then again, it wasn't like him to brag, anyway.

I opened the little fridge that that he kept in the corner. There was one Bud. I got a chill because I knew it was for me, and that the gunny somehow knew that I would be there for it. I looked for his bottle of Irish whiskey next. The first draw I tried was locked. The next one opened; the whiskey was there. He kept shot glasses on his desk next to a pitcher of water. I took one glass and filled it up, cracked opened the beer. It was the first time I had sat in his chair and it felt strange, like I didn't deserve to be in it. My thoughts kept going back to that locked drawer, and how I wanted to see what was in it, but that would be wrong so I stood and toasted the Corp, like he had taught me on the first day we met. I fell back in the chair and started to cry. Another friend gone. I drank the beer and wondered what was in that drawer, and I finally opened the middle drawer. Everything in his life seemed to be in order except for the relationship with his son. Every pen, paper, paper clip, stamp, all in their place, even the eraser. Suddenly I spotted two keys. I got them out and tried the first one; it wouldn't fit, so I tried the other one. It worked, so I opened the drawer and found two bottles of Irish whiskey and a shadow box with all the gunny's medals in it. I was looking at a man's life and commitment to his country and it humbled me: good conduct, sharp shooter, expert shooter, four purple hearts, a Navy Cross, two Silver Stars, two Bronze Stars, the Legion of France for an expeditionary tour in IndoChina with the French Foreign Legion, and last of all the Congressional Medal of Honor. I could see why he was being buried in Arlington. That was another reason I came down here; I've never been to his grave. Well, I didn't get to it before the Metro boys brought me in."

"Well, maybe when you leave."

"Oh, yeah, I'll see him when I leave."

"Well, after that you must not have had much time before you left on deployment."

"A month or so."

"How was your new wife dealing with you leaving so soon after being married?"

"She was doing really good. We were planning on getting a place of our own when I got back."

"How long were deployments there?"

"About nine months."

"Well, that would have given you time to save up a pretty good sum of money."

"Look, the unit I'm in is going on deployment. I'm going to the fucking Philippines. Have you even been listening to me? Do you think that they spent all that money on me to keep me with burn-outs and fuck-offs? Just fucking listen!"

"All right Peter. Are you getting agitated?"

"Yes! Travis got you all that info on Dante's Inferno, that's where I'm going! Can I *continue* now?"

"We had two weeks left before we left. I'm sitting home one night when the phone rings. My mother picks it up and says that its for me; some officer from the base needed to talk to me. I take the phone it's the XO of our squadron, telling me that I have four hours to get my things and report to the flight line at one hundred hours. I started to ask something and he said, "Four hours", and hung up. My wife wanted to know what was going on. I told her that I didn't know anything other than I had four hours to be on the flight line, so we started to scramble. My dear old mother wanted me to call him back and ask him what was going on. I told her it didn't work that way, but she wouldn't listen. Cindy and I got all my things together in short time, in spite of my mother's ranting. I called the barracks and got a hold of Terry to pick me up. My father said he would give me a ride over, but I knew that I had to stop at the Marines' barracks for the rest of my things. Terry pretty much had most of it figured out anyway, so I didn't much care any more."

"How did your wife take it?"

"Like a trooper; she was crying. I told her I would be all right and send her money. All she said was "Please be careful, and come home to me.""

I told her, "I promise."

"You kept your promise."

Peter sat up, lit a cigarette and started to laugh. "Look, Peter, Dr. Jenson will be coming in soon."

"That's good, because I don't think your getting it."

"I'll be back in a while."

Prescott left and Dan met him in the hallway.

"How do you think it's going?"

"He's getting pissed more and more."

"Good, it's working."

"Dan, it's only been two hours."

"That's right, but he know what's coming and, here's the best part, he *wants* it. Chances are, he's been living with this thing, whatever it is, for over thirty years, and it's time for him to dump it. That's why we're here, Prescott.

"Is there any coffee?"

"All kinds." Dan pointed to a table that Travis set up for them, with food and coffee. Dan got a cup of coffee and headed in.

"Peter, do you need a cup of coffee before we continue?"

"Yeah, that would be good."

"What do you want in it?"

"Just black is fine."

"OK, I'll be right back."

As Dan came back into the room he asked, "Peter, what did you mean when you told Dr. Brown that he didn't get it? You know, about the promise to your wife?"

"I was a naive boy with the training of a well- oiled killing machine, and I was about ready to use those skills. I may have come back physically, but I left that boy who promised to come back in a country that I barely knew existed, a few years before. Hell, I didn't have a clue of what I had become. How could the people who loved me know? What were they suppose to think, or do? And *that*, Dan, is what he doesn't get."

"Give him time, he will."

"Maybe."

"Let's get back to you leaving."

"My buddy Terry came and got me. It was a scene at my house: my mother was screaming "Don't go!" my sister just told me to be careful and to write. "How about your wife?"

"She kissed me and said "Be safe," and that she loved me. I told her, "so do I", then got in the truck and didn't look back. That was the last time they ever saw the Peter they knew; that Peter was never coming back. Could we get back to me getting to the base now?"

"Yeah, if that's what you want, go ahead."

"I had a hour to go before I had to be on the flight line. Terry said I should go to personnel to see if I had a orders or an itinerary. I told him I had no idea what was going on. He said, "OK, then let's try there first, before we go on the line.""

He was right; the XO was there and I went into an office with him.

"I've got travel orders for you. You're taking a P-3 to Pax and then a C-140 to Hickam in Hawaii. There you'll get picked up, and from there I have no idea. Good luck, Airman."

I thanked him and got Terry to drive me to the flight. It was easy to know which plane it was; the only one getting ready to leave. Everything on the line was shut down for the night. I asked the ground support guys if that was the ride to Pax. They said, "Yeah", and that it was leaving in half an hour. I told them that I had some things to take on board. They pointed to the flight mec and called him over.

He asked, "Are you riding with us to Pax?"

I said I was, and where could I put my things. He motioned me to come with him. Terry grabbed what I couldn't carry and we put my stuff on board. The flight mec showed me where I would be sitting, gave me a few emergency instructions, and that was it. Terry and I climbed back out, sat in the truck and had a smoke. We sat there for what seemed like a long time, and out of nowhere we both said to same thing: "I'm going miss you," then we both started laughing. "Terry, look after Cindy for me."

"I'll do that. You be careful, and remember what Holmes taught you."

I started to say, "How do you know what he taught me," then I repeated it with him.

"Now, it's my job to know what goes on around here."

We shook hands and said, "Later."

I headed into the plane got ready to leave. Someone closed the door and we started moving. As the plane taxied out, Terry was still sitting there in the truck. I made eye contact and the fucking whack job saluted me.

"What was whacked out about that?"

"Terry didn't even salute officers. Come to think of it, I never saw him salute anybody, other than that one time."

"The flight was OK. I slept most of the way. Someone woke me up when it was getting light out and we were about to land. The orders the XO gave were good. I knew right where to go for my next flight. It helped that I had been at Pax before. I would be on a AC-140 Air Force transport. Good plane, but strange seating."

"How so?"

"You sit on the sides of the plane in cargo nets. They're comfortable, but you can feel all the plane's vibration on your back."

"Is that bad?"

"No, not really. After awhile it puts you to sleep."

"How did that flight go?"

"Long. I thought we were going straight through to Hawaii. We landed three times, two times on bases that I didn't know, then in San Diego. We kept picking up more service men and women, all branches. The plane was almost full when we left San Diego. By the time I got to Hickam I had been flying for more then eighteen hours, and I was beginning to feel it. I was hoping I would stay the night and head to wherever I was going the next day. That wasn't going to happen. After unloading I went into the terminal and got a cup of coffee. The XO didn't have any idea where I would go from there, so I sat down and enjoyed my coffee. Then a voice over the intercom said, "Would Airman Peter Davies please come to the Information Desk. I got up, threw out my coffee, grabbed my four bags and headed for the Information Desk. When I finally got there I was met by a full bird Colonel. Not Marines; Army and Green Beret. He asked if I was Davies; I told him I was. He asked for ID. I showed him my Navy ID card.

"You're due for a hair cut, Airman."

"All I said was, 'If you say so'.

He immediately got in my face.

"Yeah, I say so, and so it is."

"All I said then was, "Yes, Sir." He called two other soldiers that were with him over to help me with my things. The Colonel got into a jeep and left. I got into the other jeep with one of the soldiers. He shook my hand.

"My name is Morris Zimmerman, but my friends call me Zimmy."

I asked, "Where are we going, to Paradise? I thought Hawaii was Paradise."

"No, we're going to the Philippines, where the most beautiful woman in the world are half Spanish and half Japanese. Look, I've got a wife at home, I'll pass."

All he said was, "We'll see about that."

In time we came to an air field far off from Hickam. I asked Zimmy if this was part of the main field.

"No, this is ours."

"And who is "ours"?

"That's a good question. I don't really know. All I know is, we use it to come and go, pick up and drop off, and that's about all I know. I see you're a five. "What's your job with this outfit?"

"I'm a supplier."

"Oh, like a quarter master?"

"No, I can supply you with anything you want, anything at all."

All I could think of was Terry; not another fucking Terry. I just laughed. It might not be a bad thing; Terry was a good friend, but the verdict was still out on this guy. We sat on the tarmac.

"What are we waiting for?"

Just then he pointed up. A C-130 was about land.

"That's our ride home. Have you ever been on one of those?"

"Yeah, that's how I got to Hickam from the States."

"You're in for a treat. They shake like hell, but they're tough."

The C-130 made a pass and roll-dropped four pallets of cargo next to the landing strip, circled back around and landed. About the time it stopped, a deuce and half pulled up; when the cargo door in the back opened, about twenty guys came out, got in the deuce, and it left. The colonel that I had dealt with when I first landed here was nowhere to be seen; it was just me and Zimmy. The loading chief came out of the plane and motioned to us to come on, so I started to get out of the jeep. Zimmy grabbed my arm.

"That's not what he means. Watch." Zimmy started up the jeep and drove into the back of the plane.

"OK, now get out. He has to tie it down. I'll show where your going to sit or sleep. You're probably ready to sleep by now. You were at NAS Brunswick eighteen, twenty hour ago."

"Yeah, I'll get you hooked up. Come with me." Three quarters into the plane was a cabin. He opened it; there were bunks and a fridge. It was all insulated and there was plenty of flight food in the fridge.

"Get something to eat and sleep. It's a long flight from here and we've got some stops, so get something to eat."

It had been well over twenty four hours since I'd eaten anything. The food was OK. There was beer in the fridge, San Miguel; it was bad, but very cold. I went to lie down. Zimmy came back.

"You'll have to sit up 'til we take off, then you can go to bed."

The cabin had two jump seats. We put on our harnesses and in no time we were in the air. A green light came on.

"We're good now," he told me. "Take off your harness and get some sleep."

He went to leave. "Oh, here, take these, they'll help you get some rest."

I took the two red pills he gave me and it knocked me out 'til we got to where we were going. I later found I was out for twenty one hours, and I don't remember any of it.

Zimmy woke me up. "Welcome to Paradise."

I asked, "What time is it?"

"Three in the afternoon."

"What day?"

"You left home four days ago, so it would be Wednesday. Come on, I'll hook you up with a room and you can get a shower; after that, some real food. The Colonel will want to see you after you're done, but don't hurry, he's here 'til eight tonight."

The compound where we were not only had its own landing field, but it was completely self contained. This place had the best of everything. Zimmy brought me to the barracks were I would be staying. I not only had a room of my own but it had its own shower in it. I had to ask Zimmy, "Is this all for real?"

"Looks real to me. Look, Davies, you'll get used to it, we all did. There's lots of other perks, if you know what I mean. Just look in the fridge."

He opened it and it was full of beer.

"How about food?"

"Get showered, I'll show you that next. There's new utilities for you in the closet. We all wear the same uniforms around here, no branch insignia, no rank, no medals. The only time you wear your official uniform is when the Colonel tells you."

So I showered and changed my clothes. Zimmy said he'd be back to show me where to eat. I was ready when he got back.

"Come on, let's go."

"We got into the jeep and drove over to this building that looked like a restaurant you'd find in a mall parking lot, today, without the awnings. We parked the jeep and went in. It wasn't like any galley I had ever seen. All I can say, Dan, is that it was a fucking restaurant: menus, waiters, the whole deal, and all staffed by Philippine nationals. So we go in and some young girl walks us to a table. The thing that went through my mind was, I wondered if the grunts in the shit got that kind of treatment."

"Look, Peter, I need another cup of coffee. Could you use one?"

"Yeah."

"Hold on, I'll be right back. Same black?"

He just nodded his head and blew out a smoke ring.

Dan got the coffee and asked Travis, "Are you seeing any difference in his pulse?"

"No."

"You let me know when you do?"

"Yeah, you got it."

Dan went back in, gave Peter his coffee and sat down. "Do you want finish your smoke before we continue?"

"No, let's do it."

"I had a steak, a baked potato, a salad and apple pie for dessert; a glass of cold milk, too. While we ate, I looked around the room. There were probably thirty or forty guys eating, all in the same utilities. It all seemed very strange.

Zimmy said, "The Colonel will see you now." "Does the Colonel have a last name?"

"We don't like to use last names around here."

"And why is that?"

"You'll find out when you see the Colonel."

Zimmy drove me over to the Colonel's office. It was a large building with three stories; the outside was done in white stucco, and the only windows were in the front, where you entered. It was getting to be evening and I was hoping it would cool down. The heat and humidity were brutal. I asked Zimmy if it was always that hot.

"No, it gets hotter."

I answered back, "You're all kinds of help."

"You'll get used to it, we all did." He dropped me off at the Colonel's building. I asked, "Where do I go?"

"Go through those doors and ask for the Colonel. He's probably waiting for you, anyways." I walked in and there was a receptionist sitting there. I told him I was there to see the Colonel.

"Oh, you must be Davies."

I told him I was.

"Good, the Colonel will see you now." Pointing to his right, he said, "Take the elevator to the third floor."

The door opened into the Colonel's office. The receptionist, who apparently had no name, had called the Colonel to tell him I was on my way up.

The Colonel stood up. "It's good to meet you, Davies, come in and sit down."

I snapped to attention.

"There's no need of that type of formality here, now that you're part of Dante's Inferno. I can imagine you must have many questions to ask. Well, now's the time, ask away."

"What the hell is this all about?"

"First of all you were selected for your shooting abilities and the fact you understand bastard French. You have a very high IQ, and you have the ability to see in three dimensions and you have a photographic memory."

"What kind of bullshit are you giving me? I'm a tenth grade drop out, I don't have photographic memory, and the part about speaking? I can't. My folks spoke to me in French and let me answer them back in English, and that's it. I'll give you being a good shooter, and that was an accident. If the gunner's mate in boot camp wouldn't have let me shoot left handed I wouldn't be sitting here with you. I'd be scraping paint off the side of some old tin can somewhere. OK, so what I'm doing here?"

"In a nutshell, you're going to help your country clean up the mess some of our countrymen have made."

"How?"

"You're going hunting."

"Hunting? For what?"

"Those very countrymen that made a mess of this war, so when it's over, they're not an embarrassment to have to explain."

"You can't be serious. I think I get it now. You want me to go out and kill our own people, because they made a mess of this war?"

"That's right."

"Well, don't you think you ought to start in Washington? That's where I'd start every mission." "You'll have the best support and backup you need."

"Here's what I need: when I volunteered for this, they told me I could quit anytime I wanted, and that time is now."

"Well, Davies, I'm sorry to hear that, but when the government gives its word, it sticks by it."

"When can I get out of here."

"It will take a few days to make all the arrangements, so until we can get you out, have a good time. Let Zimmy show you some hot spots. No need of being here and not getting something out of it, right?"

He stood up and shook my hand.

"Good luck in the fleet." I thanked him and left. Zimmy was waiting outside for me.

"Well, how did it go?"

"What do you mean, how did it go?"

"Are you coming or going?"

"I'm going."

"Ah, don't let it bother you. About fifty percent leave. Seeing you'll be leaving, would you like to see some hot spots tonight?"

"Nah, I've only got about ten bucks to last me 'til pay day."

"Don't worry about it. When someone leaves like you, the Colonel always makes sure they have a good time before they go."

"I think it's his way of giving you something for all the bullshit you went through to get here."

I told him after what I heard from the Colonel I could use a good time."

Zimmy said, "Forget about it, it's all behind you now. Let's party."

We drove back to the barracks and went inside. Zimmy stopped a Philippino who was working and started talking to him. After a few minutes he told me we were all set, get ready, and we'd head back in about an hour.

"Oh, Davies, wear civvies."

As I was getting dressed I thought how odd it was, a kid with a New York accent could speak this language so fluently, but there was nothing normal about that place. I was glad that I brought some light clothes with me, because it was getting towards nighttime and it was still hot as hell. The humidity was brutal. I sat on the bed waiting for Zimmy to get back and grabbed a beer from the fridge. Get this, Dan - the place had a.c. I had never lived anywhere with a.c., ever.

I finished that beer and grabbed another. It felt good to know that all that shit was almost behind me and I would be going home, back to the squadron, even if they were a bunch of fuck-offs. It was better than getting involved with this. I would do my four years, get out, go back to my old job, buy a house and maybe build a hot rod, have some kids and play some music.

About that time a knock came on the door.

I said, "Come in." It was Zimmy. I had to laugh.

He was dressed up like a pimp.

"What's so funny?"

I asked if he always dressed like that.

"Only when I want to impress the local ladies."

Just then he reached into his pocket and pulled out a wad of cash and passed it to me.

I asked, "What's that for?"

"A good time."

"Look, I can't take this from you."

"First of all it's not from me."

"Well, then, who's it from?"

"The Colonel."

"And why is he giving me money?"

"I told you that he does this for everybody that decides not to stay."

I looked at the money. "I don't know this money, how much is here?"

"Three hundred in U.S. dollars."

Dan interjected, "Didn't it seem *strange* to you that this guy was going to give you money to go out and party after you turned him down?"

Peter sat up straight. "Dan, Dan, *Dan.* Now *you're* the one not getting it. I was basically a poster child for stupidity. I was naïve, I had no idea. I was just happy to be *going home.*"

"Sorry, Peter, I had to ask."

Peter chucked sardonically. "It's all right. Where was I?"

"So I asked him if that was a lot. He responded,

"We'll I'll tell you this; you're going to have a night you'll never forget, I'll tell you that. Come *on*. Look, you seem uptight. Grab a beer for the road and we'll get going."

"How are we getting to town?"

"In the jeep."

I asked, "Is your name Terry?"

"No, it's Zimmy, why?"

"Oh, it's just a joke, I'll tell you later."

After we got off the compound he asked if I wanted to smoke a joint.

"Not now, maybe later. Before we left I asked if your name was Terry. Terry was I friend I had at my last base, that used to use the duty truck to go anywhere he wanted. So, when you said we were taking the jeep to town, it reminded me of him.

"Oh, I get it now."

It took us about an hour to get to town. It was more like a city then a town. To this day, I don't even know the name of it. I was in and out of the compound only five times over the next nine months when I was in that part of the world."

"What? I thought you told the Colonel that you were not going through with the assignment."

"Hang on, that's coming. So, I only went to that town with Zimmy that one time."

"So you didn't have a good time?"

"That's the problem I had too good a time. Goddamnit, Dan I'll *get* to that, *give* me a fucking minute."

"OK, OK, Peter."

"I was only there *three weeks* before I left. Is it *OK* if I get back to being in town with Zimmy now?" "Sorry, Peter."

"So, by now it's nine, nine thirty, and the whole place is lit up, kind of like Las Vegas, but sleazy and dirty. The street we were parked on was your typical strip: half dressed girls, pimps trying to push their girls on you. I asked Zimmy, were we going to a classy place? I told him I hope so, there's not enough penicillin in the world to get me to fuck any of these girls. So Zimmy stops this guy and starts talking to him, in what sounds a lot different than the guy in the barracks. It sounded like a completely different dialect. After he got done talking with the guy, he said, "It's only about four blocks from here."

"What's four blocks from here?"

"OK, let me try to explain this to you. All the shit you see on the street, that's for the locals. Where we're going is a club that only caters to high end business men, international bankers."

"Have you been there before?"

"Many times."

"Then why did you have to ask that guy back there where it was?"

"Because the locals don't like it. They move it about every couple of months."

"Oh, that must be a really classy joint."

"Davies, with the money the Colonel gave you, to you could have maid services for six months, with all the bennies, if you know what I mean."

"I get it."

"When we finally got to the place, our jeep was sitting there.

"How did that get there?"

Zimmy rubbed his fingers together as though he was counting money.

"Davies, everything has a price, everything, and in the PI it's not high."

The place was in a warehouse with entrances and an awning and a door man. The door man was definitely not Philipino. He seemed to know Zimmy, shook his hand and asked who I was. Zimmy introduced me; by his accent, he sounded Australian. He asked where I was from. "I figured you mates were from the states."

"Maine."

"Never heard of it."

I thought to myself, 'Then why did you ask,' but it was his turf, and besides, I didn't know what I was getting myself into. The door man asked if I was a cherry to the place. Zimmy just nodded.

"Well, mate, you'll never be the same after tonight. Have a good time, and good luck."

The minute we walked in the music started a girl wearing nothing but a scarf around her waist showed us to a table that was on the third level. It was hard to believe that they could move a place that elaborate every two months. The sound was good, the lighting good and the girls were *very* good. No sooner than we sat down, another girl brought us two drinks. I pulled some money out to pay.

Zimmy said, "The first drinks are on the house."

I took a sip of my drink. It was very sweet and had hardly any trace of alcohol in it. Man, was I wrong. After I put the drink down, I told Zimmy I had some questions for him.

"Look, by your accent I would guess that you're from New York. Being able to speak this language so well.

"You're right, I'm from Brooklyn. I'm Jewish, and I'm a linguist, and my specialty is Asian languages."

"Then what are you doing here?"

"That's a good question, a question that I cannot answer. Look, Davies, you're leaving here in a couple of days, and you'll never have to look back, so for tonight why don't you have a good time and forget about the Colonel and the compound? Just focus on what's right here. Have a few more drinks." Zimmy told me he'd be right back, and left. I finished my drink and called the waitress over for another. I was surprised how good her English was. I asked if they had any Jack Daniels; they did. I told her I'd have a double and a Budweiser. She said she'd be right back with them. I sat listening to the music. It was amazing how good the band was; they were playing all the hits from that time. They almost sounded like a stereo and records. Zimmy had been gone for quite a while. I had time to get my second drink and I was working on the beer. Coming up over the stairs I saw Zimmy. When he got to me he sat down.

"How about smoking a joint with me now?"

After the drinks I didn't care. I asked, "Where are we going to go?"

He laughed. Zimmy held his hand up and waved it. A few minutes later, another girl brought a water pipe and set it on the table. Zimmy looked over at me.

"It's not really a joint, it's better. Have you ever done it like this before?"

I just shook my head, no.

"Well, let me show you how."

So he did, and I got the knack of it right off. He was right. It was better, a lot better. I was getting really high. All of a sudden there were three or four girls sitting with us; the one sitting near me was dressed like all the others in the place, a scarf around her waist, heels and that was it. She snuggled up as close as she could without sitting on me, but that was coming. You know, Dan, she was absolutely beautiful; hair was jet black and all the way down her back, and eyes black as night with the fire of an Arabian stallion. You know, the one that won't be bridled. I think maybe she had more Spanish than Philipino. I was becoming total infatuated with her every move; the way she smelled, the roundness of her breasts the way she leaned against me, so warm, so wanting, so, so tempting. Even though the hookah had six or eight pipes coming off it, plenty for everyone at the table, she had to share mine, and at that point, with the hash and the drinks, everything I believed in was beginning to fade.

Before I knew it I was kissing her and fondling her breasts and she was rubbing my crotch. It was getting out of hand, when Zimmy leaned over and said, "Hold on, stud, there's back rooms for that, why don't you two go there so you can be alone." She hardly spoke any English, so Zimmy said something to her, and when he was done she took my hand and we headed to a room somewhere on the third floor. All I remember was making love to that that raven haired beauty all night without any thought of my wife at home or the promises I had made to her.

Chapter Ten

The next morning when I woke up my head hurt like hell and I was alone. I sat on the edge of the bed wondering were Zimmy might be. Next to the bed was a long silk cord, and on the night stand was a note that said, 'pull for services.' I thought, 'what the hell', so I pulled it. While I was getting dressed, Zimmy came through the door. "Would you like some coffee?"

I asked what time it was.

"Three o'clock."

"In the morning or in the afternoon?"

So I started to hurry to get my clothes on, so we could go back to the compound. I told Zimmy I'd be right with him.

"Don't hurry."

"But we need to get back."

"We'll get there when we get there."

Zimmy, how did I get so fucked up?"

"Do you remember that drink they gave us on the house when we first got here last night? It has coca in it."

"'Coca' as in 'cocaine', and after you started getting friendly with the girl you ordered four more. That and the hash."

"Oh, yeah, the Jack Daniels. Did I do anything stupid?"

"No, nothing any other GI would do in that circumstance."

"And what would that be?"

"You got laid, and if you asked me it was a fine choice."

"Can we get back to base?"

"You mean compound?"

"What the fuck ever you call it. Can we go?"

"Sure. Do you want some coffee?"

"No, I just want to get the fuck out of here."

"OK."

"Let's go."

As we were leaving I asked Zimmy to find me something to drink. He pulled into a small store. He said, "I'll go in." I told him no thanks, I'd go in myself. I found a cooler and got a couple bottles of water when I looked in my pockets I had only two or three bills left from what Zimmy had given me the night before, and the water took two of them. When I got back to the jeep I had I one dollar in my hand.

I showed it to him. "This is all I have from last night."

Zimmy said, "Cool, cool."

"Are you fucking nuts? You didn't tell me those girls were pros."

Zimmy started laughing. "Look, you backwoods hillbilly from where ever you come from. In New York, a girl like that would cost you five hundred and she wouldn't be staying. You got it for three hundred and she stayed all night, so stop whining. Besides, it wasn't even your money. I'll get you back to the compound. Get some sleep. The Colonel will want to see you tomorrow."

"How do you know that?"

"He sees everybody after they go to town."

"Why?"

"To see if you may have changed your mind about staying."

"I haven't changed mine."

"Good for you. Tell me, Davies, is everyone from Maine as big of an asshole as you are?"

"No, some are bigger."

"Good, I'll make sure to eliminate it from my vacation plans."

"We didn't say anything to each other the rest of the trip back to the base. He dropped me off at the barracks and I went to my room, took a shower and went to bed. I figured if anyone needed me they knew where I was. I slept through the night.

The next morning came a knock on the door. I asked, "Who is it?"

"It's Zimmy. The Colonel wants to see you in an hour. Do you want to get something to eat before?"

"No, I just want to get this over with and out of here."

"If you're going to continue talking to me, at least open the door. There are people who are trying to sleep, and you're being loud."

So I opened the door and let him in.

"You know we should try to play nice, like big kids."

"What, more New York humor?"

There was part of me that liked him and part of me that wanted to rip his head off. He was only about five with thick glasses and he couldn't weigh one thirty. I asked again, "What are you doing here? With your skills you could write your own ticket."

"If you were staying you might find out, but seeing your leaving it's all moot."

"No, it isn't."

"At least let's get a coffee before you see the Colonel."

"OK."

We left and headed over to the galley. I got a coffee and Zimmy got a bagel. He dropped me off and said, "I'll be back later to get you." I asked how many times a day flights came in.

"It's hard to tell. Some days it's like Kennedy and other days, nothing."

I went in and informed the GI at the desk I was there to see the Colonel.

"He's waiting for you. Do you know how to get there?"

"Yes, I know." Then I pointed up with my finger. The doors to the elevator opened up in his office. "Davies, did you enjoy your time on the town with Zimmy?"

"He sure does know the hot spots."

"He sure does. Did that sway your mind about staying with us?"

I just shook my head.

The Colonel just sighed. "That's too bad. You would be a helpful part of our mission."

"Mission? Killing our people is not my idea of a mission, it's more like murder."

"You know, Davies, I think we can work together in spite of our ideological differences. Well, so much for that. I have some good news for you."

"And what's that?"

"Your wife is with child."

"All I could do was start laughing. "Do you remember that I was home less then a week ago and she wasn't?"

"But you're wrong. The day after you left or should I say, the night you left, the next day she went to see the family doctor, Jimmy Smith, and when he examined her he found she is not only pregnant, she's three months pregnant."

"That's not possible. She had her period last month."

"My wife had her period half way through her pregnancy with our first child."

"OK, OK, what does that have to do with any of this?'

"We'll get down to it, shall we? I have something to show you, I hope you like them. I certainly did."

"He pulled a manila envelope out of his desk and passed it to me. "Why don't you sit down and enjoy this."

I opened it up and pulled out pictures of me and the girl from the night before.

"What kind of pictures?"

"What kind do think? Dan, you're a big boy, you know."

"No, I don't."

"They were of us fucking and anything you can think of, do you get the fucking picture? The asshole was blackmailing me into working for him."

I threw them at him and went after him. Four guys came out of nowhere and stopped me, set me down in a chair.

"Now, you can make this easy on yourself or hard, it's up to you. Your flight plans and the pictures are right here, but I'll tell you the pictures will get there three days before you do. Or, you can come to work for me, and these will stay in my desk tell you leave, at which time you can burn both the prints and the negatives. I'm giving you five minutes to decide, starting now."

He turned around and made himself a drink, looked at his watch and held up three fingers as if to say, "three minutes". He finished his drink, set the glass down and held up one finger.

At that point I told him, "You win, you son of a bitch, and you can bust me for that if you want."

"Hell, no, I've been called a lot worse. Besides, Davies, I like you. You're the first to ever come after me. That showed balls."

"Peter, how are you doing? You and I have been at this four hours."

"I'm doing great. Getting tired, Dan?"

"A little. I'll send in Prescott. Let's see how he holds up through the gore I've got to tell him.""

Peter started to laugh, lit up a smoke and continued to laugh.

"OK, Peter, I'll see you in a while. Prescott will be in in a few. Do you need a coffee?"

"Yeah."

"OK, I'll get Travis to get you one."

"That's cool."

Dan went out in to the hall and into Travis' monitoring room.

"How's it going? Did you see any changes this time?"

"The first time he spoke with the Colonel his heart rate spiked a little. Then when he was talking *this* time, it slowed down."

"Isn't that odd?"

"Now get this one: the last time he spoke about being with the Colonel everything went right off the chart. Everything. But there was one noticeable difference in him. I've been doing this with Dr. Brown for at least ten years, and this breaks all the rules."

"Well, before this session is over we may have a better idea of what's going on with him. Keep up the good work, Travis."

Thanks, Doc."

"It's Dan."

"OK, Dan, thanks."

As Dan was leaving he asked if Travis would get Peter a cup of coffee and make it half decaf and half regular. "We're going get him off the caffeine within the next four hours." Where's Prescott?"

"In his office."

Dan walked into Prescott's office. He was sitting there.

"Dan, do you believe all that you've been listening to?"

"Of course I do."

"He's my patient and I will see him through this."

"I asked you if you think it's true."

"It doesn't matter what I think. What I see is a man who has had experiences, something very traumatic, bad enough to fuck up his whole life. That's what I care about. And do I think that the government is capable of doing things like he's telling us? Hell, yes. Just look back in time; we've been around the shit that went down, from the Bay of Pigs to the Iran-Contra hearings, and those are the ones we've heard about. You know, old friend, I'm beginning to think your boy in there might have as much help for you as you do for him."

"Dan you've always got a theory, don't you."

Dan just laughed. Prescott left and walked into the room where Peter was sitting.

"How are you doing, Peter?"

"Fine, and you? Prescott. I'm well."

"What happened after you decided to work for the Colonel? You got blackmailed into working for him?"

"If that's what you want call it. Do you have another word for it?"

"No, I guess not."

"I got the shit kicked out of me."

"By who, Zimmy?"

"Oh, hell it was probably my fault. I started it anyway."

"What happened?"

"After I left the Colonel's office, Zimmy was waiting for me outside, so I pulled him out of the jeep and he proceeded to kick my ass. He hit me so many times I thought I was in the ring with Ali."

"Who stopped it?"

"He did. I was on the ground with my hands over my head. My face was all bloodied and it felt like my ribs were cracked. Zimmy helped me up.

"I'll get you over to the dispensary."

I was still pissed. "Don't bother. Look, you moose-fucker, if you think I had anything to do with him setting you up, you're wrong. I found about it yesterday. I make it my job to know as much about this place as I can. Look, I'm sorry about hitting you."

"*Hitting* me? More like beating the shit out of me."

"Look, let me get you patched up and I'll fill you in on what's going on. It might make all this easier to understand."

"OK."

"What happened then?"

"After I got patched up and found out that my ribs weren't broken, Zimmy and I went to his room and had a beer. He told me his story.

341

"My family was Orthodox Jews, and wanted me to go to Israel and serve in their military. I wanted to go to study Asian languages at Berkeley, but they would have no part of that. So I had to go to college in New York."

"Is that were you learned how to speak?"

"Not really. When I was a kid living in the city, one of my uncles owned a pharmacy on the edge of China Town. I would deliver scripts. I just had a knack for it. Then, when some of the old people saw that I was interested in their language they would teach me more, and that's how I got here."

"Zimmy, I don't think it was all that easy."

"It wasn't. I did end up in Israel and in the service. Did you know that everyone in Israel serves for two years? After the first year the Moussad approached me about me language skills. They recruited me to see how many other languages I could master. They were very interested in different Arab dialects. The problem is that I'm only good at Asian dialects."

"So how *did* you get here, and where did you learn to fight?"

"Well, you can thank the Moussad for that. I was sent here to learn your tactics and to be of any kind of help I could."

"Well, then, how much do you know about how this place runs?

"Not so much, but here's what I do know: the Colonel. The Moussad is far more open about it's missions than we are. I'm not saying publicly. Why we're training, in a nut shell, is this: this is a black ops camp. There are men here

from about six or seven countries, and even some mercs."
"How do you keep all this together without it leaking?"

"I'm not sure. Probably like the Colonel did with you: he finds your Achilles' heel and exploits you with it. So, tell me, Davies, what's your specialty?"

"What do you mean by that?"

"Everybody here has something there very good at, or should I say 'exceptional'."

"It's shooting."

"Oh, sniper. Anything else?"

"I speak some French."

"I would guess that you're headed for Nam, Laos or Thailand, maybe even Cambodia."

'And why is that?"

"There's still a lot of French in the languages there. Remember, the French were there for a long time. Even a group of mountain people, the Montes, speak a dialectic very similar to Canadian French."

"Well, that would be me."

"Davies, you're in luck. You'll have me for a teacher for at least two weeks."

"What happens after that?"

"Well, the Colonel will assign you to our leader. Here, there are no companies or units. Our leader gives you orders for the day, and you do them. What do you say we go get something to eat?"

I told him I was getting hungry.

"You might as well take advantage of the perks," he told me, so we went to eat the food in that galley. It was very good. I had fish and shrimp with vegetables.

We were almost done eating when some guy came over and sat down with us. He told Zimmy to leave. I said, "Hold on."

Zimmy said to me, "It doesn't work that way around here. I'll see you later," and left.

The guy told me his name was John, and he was going to be my leader for my time there.

"The first thing is, I'll have your dog tags."

I gave them to him. He gave me back a set with numbers on them.

I started to ask him a question, but he cut me off. "No questions yet. We go by first names only, and you do not discuss anything that I tell you unless I say it's OK, do you understand?'

"I do."

"You have the rest of the day off. Tomorrow you will go to class for three hours to learn about local dialects."

Zimmy already has…"

"Hey, I'm talking. I told you, no questions yet."

This guy was a complete asshole.

"After class, you'll go to the rifle range to see if you're as good as some Command think. I'll be there, and I'll be your spotter. I'll have instructions for you while you're here. You will follow, them to the letter. Do you understand?"

"I do."

"And your first mission is in two weeks. You'd better be ready."

He passed me a handbook and left. I picked up the book and headed back over to the barracks when Zimmy drove by.

"Do you want a ride?"

"Yeah, why not?"

I asked Zimmy why he left when John was so rude to him. Zimmy told me that because he was not a field combatant, some of the regulars treated him that way. He told me that, this time, he was almost done, but he didn't want to go home. I asked him why.

"I love these people. They're so different from were I'm from. They take time to look at life and to appreciate what they have, not always wanting more."

"Well, so much for that."

"Did your leader give you the book read? Read it and follow it, and you'll be OK, you hear?"

Zimmy and I had a few beers that night, and he told one joke after another, and they were all about Jewish people. I had never heard half the things he was telling me, so he had to explain a lot of them.

I didn't see much of him after that night other than in his class, and in there he was all business. My leader kept me busy for the two weeks before my first assignment, but I ran into Zimmy in Hawaii coming home a year later. It was good to see him.

He was happy to introduce me to his new wife. He was getting ready to catch a plane, and he quickly wrote his address on a pieces of paper and handed it to me.

"Get ahold of me if you're in the city. Good luck."

That was the last time I saw him. I called a few years ago to see if he knew more about the shit that was going on, and he pretty much hung up. You know, Prescott, I always got the feeling that Zimmy knew a lot more then he was saying."

"It sounds to me like the whole thing was shrouded in deception."

"That's a hell of a way to put it. The only thing I know for sure when I left the compound was my name, and I was going to do whatever I had to do to get home in one piece.

"Fuck this, I need to take a piss. And I need a minute to get a coffee."

"All right."

"Let's take ten."

"I'll get a coffee, too."

When Peter pulled the leads off and went out the door, Prescott was behind him. Travis was standing there. He motioned with his hand to Prescott, 'Come in.' Peter was in the bathroom. Travis showed the doctor the readings showing that, at the moment Peter said he would do whatever it took to get home in one piece, everything in there went dead.

"Is it the same as before?"

"The same. I think this is going to be a very interesting night."

"Yeah, I think you're right."

After we get him hooked up again, show this to Dan."

Prescott craned his neck to look into the hallway. Peter was making his coffee. When Dan came out of Prescott's office, Prescott said casually, "Dan, come here. Travis has something to show you."

Travis explained the episodes to Dan.

Dan asked, "Do you have him on brain scan? How are you setting it?"

Travis replied, "On alpha."

"Is this one good for REM mode, for checking for sleep apnea?"

Travis nodded.

"Can you use both at the same time?"

"I can, but why?"

"I've got a hunch that we'll see something if he goes into another one of those 'things', and I believe he will. I've bet Prescott cars on it."

"That's big of you," Prescott retorted.

Dan said, "You're welcome, Prescott."

"OK, let's get him hooked back up," Prescott told Travis.

Peter was already sitting in the chair when Travis came to hook him up. "Pilgrim, the next time you have to take a leak, let me know. I can just unhook the probes from the chair."

"OK, I'll try."

"How do you like the coffee? I had them make it just the way you like it."

"Travis you should have been a used car salesman, you're so full of shit."

"Why thank you, Pilgrim."

Prescott came in, sat down, held up his cup and remarked, "It's good coffee isn't it?"

"What is this, a nut word or a fuckin' commercial for Starbuck's?"

Prescott laughed. "Peter, you have one hell of a sense of humor. OK, where were we when we left off?"

"The reason I had class with Zimmy was so I could listen to translators to confirm that the info they were giving us was exactly what the person that was being interrogated was saying."

"And what if it wasn't?"

"Then I was to kill him."

"How?"

"Shoot him in the head, whatever, as long as he was dead. I picked up on the broken French that the mountain people spoke with very little trouble. Hell, half the people at home spoke broken French anyways. I just substituted the words from the mountain people's language. I read the book that my leader gave me, but also I was reading the one Gunny Holmes gave me. He knew more then he was telling, too, and that's good. He knew I had to learn it on my own, it was the only way I was going to survive."

"The two weeks went by fast and the leader kept me moving from 06:00 to 06:00, six days, for both weeks. Lots of time on the range, just more of the same. The day before the weeks were up I had a meeting with the Colonel and my leader at 08:00. The Colonel had pictures of a south Viet Namese Colonel and a American army warrant officer.

"Here are your targets."

He picked up his phone and called someone to join us. A tall man about thirty came through the door on one side of the Colonel's office and introduced himself as 'Robert'."

"Robert will be your spotter and Intel coordinator. This mission is in and out."

"The Colonel told John and Robert they could leave and that I was to stay when they left. I just stood there.

"Davies, this whole thing will be over before you know it. If your having any second thoughts, remember, I have the picture and I have no problem using them, if I have to. Our missions are far more important then any one individual, so go do your duty to your country and be proud that you have the skill to do so."

"I just stood until he told me to leave I knew then that I was dealing with a fucking psycho.

"John and Robert will fill you in on any particulars that you will need to know. Dismissed."

I left. I took the elevator from his office. When I got off Robert was waiting.

"You'll need further briefings, so be at Building 16 at 11:00 hours."

"I went back to my barracks and sat down on the bed. I wondered what the hell I had got myself into. I know I was fucked. There was no question that he'd send those pictures home if I didn't do the missions. In my ear I could hear Gunny Holmes: 'Cover your ass.' The only way I was going to get through this was to make them believe I was one of them. I didn't know if I could pull it off, but I had Cindy and my unborn son to think about, and how much I wanted to see them, so I stood up, raised an imaginary glass in air and toasted to the Gunny.

"Semper Fi, do or die."

"You know, doc, before I get into some of the shit, I want to tell you just how this whole thing worked - Dante's Inferno, that is. It's something that the American public needs to know, that these things can happen. The Colonel tried to tell us that the missions were about all the black marketing that was going on, but I think it was really about drugs, and I think the drug was opium."

"How did you come to that conclusion?"

"I'll get to that in a minute. At eleven I headed over to Building 16. Robert and John were both there. It was like a small hanger with people working everywhere, mostly Philipino nationals. John led Robert and I over to this table draped with uniforms." He turned to face us both. "For this mission you'll be with the hundred and first."

I asked if we were being assigned to them.

"No, you're just using their uniforms. Robert, you're WO3 Williams, Davies, you're Spec 4 Howard. You'll go in as observers. Find your targets, complete your mission, and come back. Robert has all the Intel you'll need. Gentlemen, we leave at 04:00 by C-130, tomorrow. You have the rest of the day and night to prepare."

The Intel was right on. The C-130 got to Tan Son Nhut Air Force base. We got a jeep that we signed out under our new names, drove to a small town where, the Intel said, the Viet Namese Colonel would all ready be, because he owned it. The warrant would be in around three in the afternoon. We got a beer and waited. Even though I had made up my mind to go through with this thing, my stomach was doing cart wheels. I knew that a couple shots of Jack would do the trick. I told Robert I was going to get a shot to calms my nerves.

He said, "First time. Yeah, you do that, but make it a double."

It was a well stocked bar. It had all the best top shelf stuff. The bartender gave me my shot.

In through the door walked the first man I would ever kill. I downed the shot and went back to sit with Robert. The Intel told us that the warrant officer and Colonel would drive to a small field about six clicks away. We were to leave before them and ambush them in the field, because that was where they exchanged money for goods. The Intel also said that there would be a deuce and a half in the field, and to leave it, someone would get it later we were only there to eliminate and return the money to the compound.

We got to the field in plenty of time. The truck wasn't there yet. We wondered if something had gone wrong. At the edge of the road was an old abandoned building. The grass was two or three feet high. It was perfect.

I got my Remington out, set up the bipod. It was a no-brainer shot, no more then seventy to one hundred yards. Robert drove our jeep into a gully so it couldn't be seen. He covered it with grass. When he came back he got his range finder out.

"You won't need that. You just cover my back in case they're not alone."

About that time we heard a large truck coming. It was the deuce.

My mind started: *What if the driver stays? I'll have to do him, too. God, this insane.*

My hands started to shake, and I begin to sweat even worse than I was from the ninety degree heat.

I could see the truck through my scope. There was a jeep behind it. The deuce stopped by the old building. The driver got out, and left in a jeep.

I was relieved. Again, we waited. The Intel said wait until they exchanged the money before we did our job.

About a hour went by. Then we heard a car coming down the road, but it wasn't a jeep like the Intel said it would be. There was only one driver, the colonel.

He pulled up, got out, and started to look all around. When he thought it was safe, he lit up a cigar and leaned on the side of his car. It was beginning to feel like time had stopped. The blood was pounding in my ears. I had to keep wiping the sweat from my eyes.

I heard vaguely, over and over in my head, *let's get this over with.*

I kept hearing somebody in training say, '*The only one that counts is the first one, the first one..*' a sound brought me out of my head. It was a jeep coming toward the car. It was the warrant officer.

He walked over to the deuce and looked inside, then rubbed his hands like he was proud of his work or happy about what he was doing. That would be short lived.

He walked up to the colonel and stood there for a while, talking. The colonel looked very nervous, for some reason. Maybe he could sense that we were there. By now we hadn't moved in what seemed like days. The warrant started to wave his hands in the air and pointed at the truck, shaking his head. Then the colonel walked over to the trunk of the car and opened it. He pulled out a small suitcase, closed the trunk and opened the case. The warrant reached in and took out some bills that were American then threw them back in and closed the case. He started to walk off. When he got to his jeep he threw the case in, grabbed his M-16 and shot the colonel. I got off one round. It hit him in the chest, he went down and that was it."

"I think the fact that he killed the colonel somehow made it easer. Robert got the suitcase from the jeep. I stayed in position, in case anyone came back while he got our jeep from the gully.

"When he pulled up with the jeep I jumped in. We started driving, and I told him to stop when we passed the deuce again. I jumped out. I had to see what was inside I looked in and was shocked: it was empty. I got back in the jeep and told Robert to get the hell out of there. I told him that the truck was fucking empty two people are dead. "For what?"

"We don't question we just do our job."

"Yeah, you're right."

"Tell, me, Peter how did it feel to kill that man?"

"I would try to explain it, but I don't think you would understand."

"Try me."

"OK, remember the day you pushed the big Ford to the edge? Was your heart pounding?"

"It was"

'Did it feel like you might piss yourself?'

"It did."

"Now, wrap up the power of the first time you had an orgasm with a partner then multiply that by five. That's the best I can do."

"That's one hell of a description, but I think I get it. OK, where did you go from there?"

"To Saigon, to the best hotel in town. There we got to meet a guy that was in civilian clothes and who had a French accent. He told us our next mission would be coming in a few days, and that we should take advantage of the local color. The Colonel from the compound had sent us a gift, so we could enjoy our stay: money to spend while we were there."

"The French man had new uniforms for us with rank. I stayed the same as before and Robert became a captain. We kept our weapons. He said he'd be back later to show us the best spots to have a good time in, and left. Robert went to his room and I to mine. I was surprised at just how big the room was. I wasn't much for going out right then. We'd been traveling for two days, or was it three? It was hard to remember, with all that had gone on, so I decided to take a long bath. The tub was big enough for four people. I had never seen one like it before. I would soon find out why it was so big.

I filled it with hot water and got ready to get in when I realized that there weren't any towels other then wash cloths. I got my clothes back on and called the desk. The guy who was on the desk spoke good English. I asked why there weren't any towels. he asked if I was ready to bathe? I told him yes, that's why I needed the towels.

"They'll be right up."

A few minutes later someone knocked on the door. I opened it, and two young Viet Namese girls came in. One had towels, the other a tray with what look like soap and shaving gear. I told them 'just the towels'. They didn't understand a word of English, or that's what they wanted me to think. I kept going "towels, towels". I picked up the phone. The one with the tray went into the bath room. When the desk man answered, I asked, what the two girls were doing?

I was told they were there to bathe me.

"No, no, you don't understand, that's not what I wanted."

The desk clerk said, "Excuse me, I'm so sorry, I'll send two boys up."

"I didn't know. No one told me about things like that. Man, was I dumb."

So, I told the clerk the girls were fine and did the hotel have any American whiskey? He said they didn't have any Jack Daniels, but they had Jameson. *The gunny's drink.*

"Send me up a bottle with the seal still unbroken on it."

"Doc, I need something cold to drink, do you think Travis could get me a Pepsi?"

"I think we can do that."

Dan asked Travis if there was a soda machine around here.

"There's two down the hall to right. Cans or bottles?"

"Both."

"OK, I'll go."

Dan went down and bought one caffeinated and one decaf. He poured the caffeinated out and substituted it with the decaf. When he got back he told Travis, "When you bring this to him, open it then pass him the bottle and cap."

Travis just looked at him.

"He's not drinking the real, its decaf."

Travis did what Dan asked and went back to the his post at the desk. Peter took a long drink from the bottle and thanked Prescott for it.

"Back to hotel. By the time the whiskey got there I was in the tub and being washed by two young girls that couldn't have been fifteen years old. When the whiskey got there, one of the girls set a tray next to the tub and poured me a drink. She pointed to the ice that was in the bucket that came with the tray. I shook my head, 'no.'

She passed me the glass and I shot it down. I passed it back to her and motioned for another. After the forth drink my head was spinning. I started to think about the man I had killed the day before: *Did he have a family? What dreams did he have for them when this was all over?*

With a few grams of lead and a good eye I took that all away in a heartbeat, and for what?

I took the bottle and drank from it then by then the bottle was three-quarters gone. I know why the girls were sent up: it was either the thought in my head or those young beauties. I don't need to fill you in with the rest of the night. After a second bottle was brought up, I passed out, so I never did get to see the hot spots that night.

Chapter Eleven

"I woke the next morning with Robert knocking on my door."

"Peter, get up. We have to meet with the Frenchman at noon." I picked my watch up off the bed stand. It was only nine fifteen. I went to door and opened it. He asked if I had a good night.

'Yeah good enough that at home I'd be in jail this morning."

"What do you mean?"

"Never mind. Just be careful if you decide to take a bath around here."

"You must have met the bath girls."

"But I did have options."

"Peter, this is very different culture then ours. You'll get used to it."

"Why? And in the process I'll become an alcoholic and pervert."

"I asked if there was anywhere to get any real American food.

"You're in luck. We're headed over to our embassy, that's where we're meeting the Frenchmen."

"I got dressed and ready to leave. He passed me an embassy pass.

"Put this on your right side pocket."

"Saigon was a beautiful city. The part we were in was the French colonial part. The embassy wasn't far from there. Driving through the city, I couldn't help but think how all this would end: the Tet offensives in '68 really shot our chances of winning, or that's what Cronkite told us on the evening news. The war was not winnable for me; it was like being on another planet. I had never been anywhere away from Maine 'til I joined the Navy, and most of that was training, or in bars."

"Well, we finally got to the embassy. We showed them our passes and they flagged us right through. The place looked like a fortress. The amount of fire power guarding that place was mind boggling. Robert parked the jeep and we went in. Robert had the suitcase from the mission a few days before we checked in and waited for a Marine to take us to meet with the Frenchmen, or so we thought.

We walked into the room: all marble floors and banquet tables that had to be fifty feet long, and at the other end stood the Colonel.

"How are you boys doing?'

Robert said, "Fine, Sir."

"All I said was, "I'm OK."

"I want you both to come down here and look at something with me."

Robert got there first and passed the suitcase to the Colonel.

"I hope you boys like the accommodations I made for you."

I almost asked if he had pictures of that, too, but I bit my tongue.

"Do you see all the pictures I have here? Your next mission is going put you in the field for at least a month to a month and a half. Robert, you're out of this. I'm sending Dennis."

About that time a very tall black man came out. We all shook hands.

"Dennis is going because of his experience calling in air strikes. Peter I heard great thing about your first shot on your first mission."

"Thank you," is all I said.

"Dennis can also spot for you, if need be. He's as well trained as you are. Over the next two days I want the two of you to study all this Intel. Know it by heart."

"I asked where our travel information was."

"I'm just about to get to that. There's a third man going with you on this mission. In through the doors walked Captain John William Jacobs, the ring knocker from hell."

"Peter, why do you call him the ring knocker from hell?"

"I didn't say that."

"Yes, you did."

"No, I didn't."

"Yes, you did."

"Well then, if I did it's because I've been talking to the both of you for hours and I'm getting loopy. The coffee sucks."

"OK, sit there for a minute and I'll get you a coffee. Hang on, I'll be right back."

"And the soda isn't working either. Look, I need some caffeine."

Prescott went out into the hall. Dan was standing there. "Get him a cup of real coffee."

Travis asked Prescott to put an ear piece in.

"Why?"

When he mentioned Jacobs' name, everything went nuts. I'll feed you his reactions so you can probe him."

"What, are you working for me or this one?" and he gestured to Dan.

"We're working for him," Travis said quietly, and pointed into the room were Peter sat.

Prescott brought Peter's coffee into him.

"The next pot will be stronger, you have my word."

"OK, lets get back to where we left off. The Colonel told me and Dennis that Jacobs had all the particulars set up for getting to our destination, and all we had to do was follow his orders to the letter."

"Is that clear?"

Dennis and I both answered, "Yes, Sir."

Jacobs asked only one question: "Have you both been cleared for low altitude night jumps?"

Again, we both answered 'yes'. He gave us both a list of extra thing we would need for the mission. The Colonel told Jacobs he was dismissed. He left.

"Robert will give you a ride back over to hotel and any place you need to go. You're leaving from here with Captain Jacobs the day after tomorrow at 05:00, is that clear?"

I asked Dennis if he was hungry as I was.

"You got that right."

"Roberts said that the embassy had a good cafeteria and we should try it."

The food was great and you could have all you wanted. While we sat there, Dennis looked over our orders. Jacobs gave us extra clothes, three times the match ammo for my sniper rifle and two hundred rounds of forty ammo. I was to carry an M-16 with as many clips as I could carry."

Prescott heard Dan in his ear, "Ask him, how come he knows Jacobs whole name, but doesn't know any of the others' from the compound?"

"Peter, I'm curious about something. How is it you don't know any other full names of the people you associated with the compound, but you know Jacobs?"

Peter came almost out of the chair. "Because he's a *fucking kid killer* and he *like*, he *like*, he *like*..." then silence.

He just sat there.

Peter was in some sort of trance.

Dan came running in. "Everything in the booth is out. Travis is getting help," he shouted as he headed for Peter.

Dan grabbed Peter's wrist. "He's got a good pulse."

Prescott got his stethoscope. "Good heart rate."

Dan shone a light in Peter's eyes. His pupils were not responding. Suddenly he inhaled so deeply you could almost feel the air being sucked out of the room into his lungs. Dan was standing right in front of him.

"What the hell are you doing, Dan? What is going on?"

"We thought you were in trouble."

"About what?"

"Do you remember what we were talking about?"

"Yeah, we were talking about the extra things Jacobs wanted us to take on that mission. So after we ate, we went back over to the hotel where Roberts and I had stayed. Roberts' old room was next to mine. We spent the afternoon studying the Intel the Colonel had given us. What we didn't know was that it wasn't going to be as easy as the one before. We didn't really know where we were going, only that a group of our people had stockpiled enough supplies to start their own war. Our job was to get in close enough to pick off

361

the major players: an army lieutenant, a colonel, two majors, a warrant and two sergeants, and as many North or South Vietnamese as we could.

It appeared from the Intel we had that they had set up a distribution center and we were going find it and do our thing, then call in an air strike on it. The part that neither of us liked about the whole thing was that we didn't know where we were going. Jacobs was the only one who knew.

Dennis and I worked well together. It didn't take long to figure out that he might be in the same boat with the Colonel as me, but I didn't dare ask.

I had gotten to the point where trusting anyone was a liability, no matter how much I liked them. Robert got us to where we had to go and everything was ready. We met Jacobs at 05:00. We traveled for four days with him by jeep, chopper and boat. Dennis asked Jacobs if he could see the maps.

"All you need to know is your mission. Where we're going has nothing to with that mission. Do you understand?" Dennis just shook his head.

"Coming back to me, I was sitting on the back of a gun boat headed up some river. Dennis asked me "Where do you think we are?" I told him, "Hell."

He said, "No really. I don't I think were headed into Laos or Cambodia."

I looked at him. "I don't care where we are going, I just want to get this over with and go home, so stop asking questions and get ready for this mission. Just think about that, just that. "Now leave me alone."

He sat down next to me and didn't say anything for a long time. Then he said, "You're right."

I just nodded my head. After the boat ride we caught a chopper to a small air strip on the edge of a mountains range. When I saw them, I knew we weren't in country any more. I wasn't sure where we were, but I didn't think we were suppose to be there. I had learned to keep my thoughts to myself, and I was going keep it that way."

"When we landed at that air strip, Jacobs told us to follow him into our quarters, that's where we would be staying for a few days, and not to have any interaction with anyone unless he told us to.

I made a mental note of what I saw there: three C-130s being loaded with pallets of what I didn't know. All the planes and choppers were without markings. No one wore any insignia and all the air craft were black.

All the talks I had with Gunny were paying off. I hoped I was not on a spook base. It was becoming clear that the Colonel and compound were all connected. The thing I couldn't figured out is, where did grunts like Dennis and I come in? Then it came to me: we were disposable. My whole body shook with the thought I might never see home again, or Popham, or Cindy or even the child I might never see. I had to pull my self together. I had to focus on the mission and cover my back.

I was sitting on my cot in our tent when Jacobs came. He asked where Dennis was.

I said that I didn't know where he was.

"When he comes back the both of you meet me in the command tent," and then he left.

A few minutes later Dennis came back and we headed over to see Jacobs. He told us that we were making a night jump into a remote area close to the mission site, and at that point we would pick up four other grunts for support. He asked if we had all the Intel down; we both said 'yes'.

"Get you gear and be ready by 23:00 hours. Steven here will get you set up with your jump gear. That's all."

We had six hours to think about it.

Peter leaned forward. "Did I ever tell you how much I hate jumping?"

"I think you did."

"And did I tell you, the first time I pissed myself?"

"I remembered you saying that."

"Do you still feel safe, having a guy like me protecting you?"

"Yes, Peter, I do."

Peter just looked at him. "Do you really mean that?"

"Yes, I do."

"Thank you, Doctor Brown."

"Peter, what happened then?"

We did the mission. We did all the killing Jacobs wanted and then some. We picked off our targets, then all hell broke loose. Dennis called in for an air strike when we were on the side of a mountain and our target was in the valley below us. When we heard the screaming of the jets coming in, I thought we were out of the shit. I couldn't have been more wrong.

After Dennis called in the strike we backed out, but it wasn't far enough, or the coordinates were off. They not only slammed the valley, they slammed us. We didn't have time to dig in, all we could do was pray that the rock, boulders and ordnance flames wouldn't hit us. It went on for what seemed like hours. The noise was deafening. You could feel the heat.

When it was over, there wasn't much left. They had blown half the mountain into the valley along with Dennis and two other grunts that we had picked up for support. There wasn't a trace of them. Gone. it was like they never existed. All that was left was me, Jacobs and two of the four we picked up. We were all pretty banged up, but nothing we couldn't field dress. Then the long trip back to who knows where."

"OK, doc, how long have we been at this today?" "No, yesterday, since yesterday."

Peter started laughing and laughing.

"Hey, Dan, did you hear that Prescott is answering my sarcasm with sarcasm? I think he's coming around. And Dan, would you bring a *real* cup of coffee, not one from the decaf pot? Travis, have you made up your mind about the motor home yet?"

In Prescott's ear Dan said, "It's starting. Don't tell him how long he's been up."

Travis called downstairs and found out what time he got up yesterday.

"He's going on thirty six hours. Let's switch so you can take a break. You've been at it for six hours."

"Peter, Dan's going to come in for awhile. He'll bring your coffee. Do you need to use the rest room?"

"Yeah."

"OK, let Travis unhook you. Go take five and will get started again."

After that, Prescott walked out and went into his office. Dan went in with him.

"Dan, how do you think this is all going?"

"Within the next eight hours he's going to tell us everything that has to do with Jacobs."

"Dan, I didn't realize he's attached to this one until now. For this one, he has a name. I mean, that could be you or me setting in there, by the luck of birth we were born to money and privilege, but that's all that separates us from him; nothing more, nothing less. All these years I always I thought by working I was doing my part, giving back. Now, maybe, I think all I was doing was relieving my guilt."

"Dan, do you remember anyone who came from where we came from that fought in that war?'

"No, not really, not unless they had some cushy job. You know, Prescott, you haven't had much sleep in the last 48 hours yourself, and a lot of things have gone on in your world: the thing with Abby, your daughter, your wife. Are you up to going through with the rest of this?"

"I started it and I will finish it. He deserves it. No, I take that back, *we* deserve it.

"OK, Dan, you're on?"

When Dan walked in, Peter was already hooked up, drinking his coffee.

"Dan, you don't mind if I call you Dan, do you?"

"That's my name."

"Doesn't your friend Prescott have one big set of balls?"

"Yeah, what makes you say that?"

"Last week when he gave me a ride in the big ford, did you know he pinned it? I like going fast, but I don't know if could have done that. He's good for a rich boy."

It was like Peter was acting almost drunk. That sometimes happens with lack of sleep.

"Peter do you remember how many missions you went on?"

"Too many. Well, that's not really an answer, is it?"

"I guess not. Did I tell you I got a bronze star? Do you ever get back to Maine?"

"What did you get the bronze star for?"

"Letting my spotter die."

"What do mean by that?"

"The Colonel set me up with a guy named Mark Hill."

"I thought you only knew their first names."

"Of course; there was John William Jacobs."

"Stop fucking interrupting me when I'm talking to you. Dan didn't your nanny teach you any manners at all?"

"Sorry, go on."

"Mark and I went on three missions together. We were in the field, the first time, for three weeks. One night he asked how I got involved with Dante's Inferno. I told him that I had good luck and guilt by association, and he started to tell me about being at West Point, and a close classmate of his got caught giving a lower classman a blow job. He told me that he thought his friend might be a homosexual, but wasn't sure. They court martialed his friend and gave him two options: testify against his friend, or come here. He graduated, got married, and the next thing he knew, he was here, wherever that was."

Then on our third mission, we had completed the task and were headed for an LZ."

"What's an LZ?"

"Ho, ho, it's a fucking landing zone. It's where you get picked up, if you're lucky. Oh, that's right. They don't teach things like that at Harvard, do they?"

"No, they don't. Peter how did you get the medal?"

"Mark and I was headed for the LZ through an area that was traveled by the enemy, whoever that was. He would take point for me, and then I would. The trails were known to be full of booby traps. About ten minutes after Mark took the lead he missed one and it got him. It punctured his back and I couldn't stop the bleeding. I stripped us of everything except our 45s some ammo and I carried him to the zone."

"Well, isn't that what you're supposed to do?" "You and Brown are so blind. I got him to the zone and the chopper was there, but he was dead. You *fucking assholes.*

"Peter, Peter, listen, its Dan. Could you have done any better? You tried, that's all anyone can ever do."

"Dan, did you ever follow the Dead like you told Larry? You want to remember it was Larry that got you your ticket to see then in Bangor, in sixty nine." "Peter, I did, but now I really want you to tell me and Prescott about John William Jacobs. You and I both know it's time. We're all very tired, and you have been holding onto what ever happened for so long that it's consumed most of your life. It's time."

"I never expected the bronze star. I told the Colonel to send it to Mark's family after that mission. I got back to the compound. Zimmy was gone. I had been in and out of the shit for almost seven months, so the Colonel gave my ten days R&R, all expenses paid. I went to Australia. Dan have you ever been there?"

"No, maybe some day."

"They love to drink, they love Americans."

"Peter, I want you to tell me about John William Jacobs."

"Dan, I need a coffee."

"No, tell me about John William Jacobs, and you can have all the coffee you want and I'll have one with you, but not until you tell me."

"Why?"

"Because you want to, you have to."

"Why?"

"Because it's killing you, Peter."

Peter starting laugh hysterically for what seemed to be a very long time. He finally calmed down,.

"So, you want to know about John? OK, I'll tell you, but not before I get a fucking cup of coffee."

"Is that a promise?"

"What are we, school kids now? Yes, it's a fucking promise."

"I'll be right back." Dan stepped out. Travis was standing there with Prescott.

"Travis, get him a coffee."

Travis told Dan that after Peter stopped laughing, all the readings on the equipment in there had gone flat.

"It's got be the equipment. He's almost there. We have to go with it.

"Now what do you want me to do?" Travis asked.

"Take notes in case anything changes."

Travis got the coffee and Dan went back in.

"Well, here it is."

Dan sat down.

"Where is Prescott? I want him in here."

Dan asked if he wanted him to leave.

"No, I want the both of you in here for the last thirty. No one has ever taken the time to listen to me or cared enough to try to find out about what was going on with me and so many others like me, but Prescott does. I'm only sitting here because of him. Not drugged on Thorazine or Haldol or whatever the VA would feed me to make me comfortably numb."

Peter called Prescott to come in. Peter sat up and pulled all the sensors off. Dan asked why he pulled them off.

"They won't work now anyway."

"Why is that?" Dan asked.

Peter just ignored him and instead thanked him for the coffee. Prescott got a chair and sat down. Dan was a bit confused since Peter had stopped laughing. He didn't look like someone that had been up for over forty hours talking. He was clear, much clearer than Dan and Prescott or Travis.

"It was the last mission that I went on-thirteen in all. Quite a number. Wouldn't twelve kills, three assists I didn't know it would be my last. We left from the compound, me and John William Jacobs, who was going to be my spotter and handle all the Intel, like always. We had been out for four days, traveling all over the countryside. I had become familiar enough with the country by then to know that Jacobs liked to go in circles for some reason. We were not in Viet Nam; we hardly ever were. On the fourth day around noon, we heard someone coming up the road ahead of us. We went in to the bushes until they passed or that's what I thought. I was the first to see who it was: a young man, his age was hard to guess, maybe seventeen or eighteen. I gave the signal to Jacob that it was OK, and to wait. I guess he saw him too, so he jumped out of the bushes and grabbed the boy and started to interrogate him. Thanks to what Zimmy had taught me about the dialects, I knew we were in Cambodia.

You could hear the fear in the boy's voice. Jacob's voice was getting louder and louder; the boy was crying. I couldn't understand what was being said. I was too busy watching to see if anyone was coming. I knew he was begging for his life; then the yelling stopped.

I turned to see what had happened. Jacobs was wiping the blood off his knife on the boy's shirt. He had cut his throat back to the spine. I will always remember the gurgling sound he made as he bled out. I looked at him. I asked, "Why?"

All he said was, "The only good gook is a dead one. Now take care of that," pointing to the body.

All I could at that point was remember what the Gunny had thought me: it was like a mantra, over and over in my head.

"Two days later I got to our objective it was a village of about thirty or forty. Some North, some Cambodian. We found a small cave that was perfect for observation. This was where, supposedly, the South Viet Namese were selling goods to the North, and there was an American major that was with them, setting it all up. We sat on a ridge about two hundred feet from the cave. There was some activity going on; I really don't know what happened. One minute I'm looking through my scope, the next all hell is breaking loose, so Jacobs and I scrambled to get to the cave. It's like we were in a cross fire. Whoever was shooting at each other didn't even know that we were there. We managed to get to the opening of the cave. He took a round in the shoulder; it deflected and grazed my temple. I dragged him into the cave, and inside, as far back as we could go. Jacobs was hit bad and I didn't think he would make it. I was OK, as long as the firing continued, but when it stopped his screaming could have given our position away. I hoped that the firing would continue until he bled out. I didn't even try to stop the bleeding. I wanted him to die, and die soon.

Then the shooting stopped. I held my hand over his mouth to stop him from screaming but the tough son of a bitch bit me, so without even thinking I pulled out my K-bar and drove it into his heart and twisted it. There was enough light in the cave to see the life leave his eyes, and it didn't bother me.

"When his body finally went limp I pulled my knife out and wiped it off on his shirt. That, gentleman, is what Dante's Inferno was all about. I stayed in that cave with his dead body for the next two days. I would crawl out to ridge to see if there was any movement. On the second day, late in the afternoon, I looked down into the village, which was deserted. I got all of Jacobs' Intel that he had. I decided to leave any of his personal things, like his ID tags and tell the Colonel, if I ever got back, that we got split up and I never saw him again."

"I traveled mostly at night. If the Intel was right, I could get to our LZ in six days and I was already two days behind. I had to make up for lost time. I don't know how I did it. I got to the LZ, put out a landing flare and a beacon. Four hours later I could hear a Huey in the distance. I lit off another flare and twenty minutes later I was in the air. Two chopper rides later I was at the same air strip that Dennis and I had landed at a month ago."

It had been days since I had any real food or sleep. When we landed I went to the command tent and told whoever was in charge what unit I was from. All he said was, "Man, you look like shit."

He told one of his men to get me some food, a shower, and for me to get some sleep. He would inform the Colonel that I had made it back.

I don't know how long I slept, but I caught a C-130 back to the PI. When I got back I reported in to the Colonels office. He wouldn't see me until the next day, so I got a room at the barracks and decided to get drunk. I had saved up some cash from R&R. I told the new guy driving the jeep if he would find me a fifth of Jack Daniels, I would give him a big tip. He found me that bottle and it did the job. I counted on it to do the job for a lot of years, 'til it stopped working, and that's why we're here.

The next morning I caught a ride over to the Colonel's office hoping I could get in to see him, so I could get the whole thing over with at that point. I didn't care if he sent the pictures home to Cindy. I had had enough. I wanted to go home.

When I did get in to see him, he asked how the mission went. All I said was, "It went like all the others."

"Good. And where's Jacobs?"

"We got split up and I haven't seen him since. Maybe the son of a bitch finally got what was coming to him. I don't what happened. All hell broke loose and we got split up. That's all I know. I made it back to the LZ and here I am."

"Well, are you ready for another mission?"

"No, I'm going home."

"OK."

"Are you going to send the pictures to my wife?"

"I never was going to in the first place."

"Well, then, maybe I'll get a hold of the New York Times and tell them about all the shit I've been doing for the last nine months."

He just started laughing. "Davies, do you know how many times I've been threatened with the same thing? Hell, some fool even tried it. By the time we're done discrediting you as a nut, a drunk, a mental case, you won't even be sure of the truth yourself. So, go home to your pathetic little job, get drunk on the weekends, beat up the old lady just for the hell of it every now and then, and forget you were ever here. Because we sure as hell will."

"I'll get you out of here on the next flight this afternoon. Dismissed."

That was it. I left his office and went back to the barracks and just sat there. I still had the same clothes they gave me at the air strip. I finished off all the beer in the fridge."

"I heard a knock on the door. It was the kid who drove the jeep. He handed me my orders and told me my flight was leaving in an hour.

"I looked at the orders. I was going back to my squadron. They were just getting back from deployment. I told the driver I would go with him immediately."

"When the plane lifted off, I was glad and sad at the same time. I left so much of my soul on those killing fields. I was never going to be the same again, never."

"You know, in retrospect it might have been better to have ended up like Dennis, or Mark, or even Jacobs."

Prescott asked, "Why?"

At that point, Peter no longer seemed to be looking at them, but *through* them, as if across a great distance.

"Why? *Why?* Because…because…*this* is why. I've spent the better part of the last thirty years looking over my shoulders, not being able to sit in a room without having my back to a wall. Not trusting anyone, not even my family. Hearing a car back-firing and jumping four feet in the air. Using the booze, the drugs to sleep, anything to stop the dreams, *anything*. That's the legacy that thousands of men and women have to live with, and for *what?* A small piece of land, an ideology, oil. Is any of it worth the price? No. The price is too high, and it always will be."

"And that, Dan, Travis and Prescott, is what my government gave me for my part in Dante's Inferno. It's ironic they called it that, isn't it? An ascension into Hell."

"Thanks for finally listening. It's OK if you think I'm crazy, I don't care anymore. Could I go back to my room? I'm very tired and need some sleep now."

He got up and left the room. Travis met Dan and Prescott in the hall as Peter was slowly walking away.

Travis said to Prescott, "Everything came back on about fifteen minutes ago."

"Did you record it?"

"I did."

"Good, that's all that matters. We heard him."

They all headed home for some much needed sleep. Peter slept for over twenty-four hours. When he got up, he took a shower and had breakfast. Then he got his meds and went back to his room.

When Travis finally got up he called his wife at work and asked her to take the afternoon off so they could go look at motor homes together.

All she asked was, "Is it time?" He replied, "It's time."

"OK, I'll be there," and hung up.

When Dan and Prescott got up, Lauren asked if they had time for breakfast. Dan said, no, he had to catch a flight home, he'd get something at Dulles. He and Prescott both got a cup of coffee and headed out. Before he left, Dan gave Lauren a big hug and told her, "Talk to him," pointing to Prescott.

"You do the same, Dan. You stay in touch with us, too, OK?"

He smiled. "OK."

That morning they used the Rover. As the Rover pulled out of the garage, Dan looked over at the cobra.

"That's one hell of a car, the big Ford," and chuckled.

"Well, Dan, what do you think we learned from all that?"

"I think this could be a new breakthrough for resistant patients like Peter."

"*No*, Dan, what do you think about his *story*?" "Well, he's one of two things: the world's best storyteller, with special effects included, or he's telling the truth."

"Do you think he's for real?"

"Only he knows that for sure. But do I think our government is capable of such things? No question." Prescott pulled up to let Dan off.

"I've got to get to the hospital."

"Look, wrap this one and take a couple of weeks' vacation. Come up to see me, bring Lauren with you. The mountains will be good for the both of you."

They shook hands. Prescott said, "Be safe," and to call when he got home. Dan said, "Yes, Mom," as he was slamming the car door. Then he was gone.

Prescott pulled into the stream of traffic leaving Dulles. There was a guy in the median with a sign that read, "Gulf War vet, will work for food." He wanted to help the vet with some money but the light changed and traffic was moving so fast he couldn't get alongside him. He turned at the next intersection and went back, but the vet was gone.

When he reached the hospital parking lot he looked up to see if Peter was standing where he had been so many times since he got there, and he was. He looked different somehow. As we made eye contact he just nodded his head. Prescott nodded back and went in. He had four days' worth of paperwork to do. Travis wasn't coming in, so the paperwork could wait.

Prescott got some coffee out of one of the vending machines, sat down with his mail. It was mostly junk. One caught his eye; it was from the Metro Police, and it was about Peter's pending charges. The letter requested Prescott to call the District Attorney's office at his convenience. He immediately dialed the number listed in the letter. The phone rang two or three times. Then a voice on the other end said "DA's office." Prescott asked to speak to Alice West.

"Just one moment, I'll transfer you."

"Thank you."

Again, the phone rang. He didn't want to leave a message, he wanted to speak to an attorney.

A voice said, "Alice West, can I help you?"

"Yes, this is Doctor Prescott Brown from the VA hospital. I'm calling in reference to my patient, Peter Davies. He was brought in by the Metro approximately nine weeks ago."

"Hold on a minute, I'll get the file."

Prescott waited less than a minute.

"I have his file right here, doctor. It appears a friend of his from Maine, a professor named Gene Riddell paid for all the damages."

Prescott asked about the disorderly conduct charge that was pending.

"Is he doing well?" DA West asked crisply.

"Very well. His therapy is going far better then we anticipated, given where he was when he arrived."

"Look, I'll leave this open, and if he stays out of trouble for six months, I'll drop the charges."

"I'm sure he'll be happy to hear that. Thank you for your time."

"Thank you, doctor. Have a good day."

After that, Prescott did his rounds in good spirits. Things were quiet. Peter would be his last patient. When he got to Peter's room, he knocked. Peter was still standing by the window. He turned toward Prescott, with a calm look on his face.

"Good morning, doc."

"Good morning, Peter. How did you sleep after all that?"

Peter ran his hands his through his hair. "Last night, or should I say in the last twenty four hours, I had some of the best sleep I've had in years. I had dreams of old loves, my children, and in the dreams was the hope of being able to dream again."

"There was an old man in AA that used to say the secret to a happy life was looking at life's glass being half full instead of half empty. Don't get me wrong, I'm not saying my glass is half full, but today I think that it *is* possible. It's a good place to start. What do you think, Doctor Brown?"

"I think it's a good place to start, too, Peter. I have some good news for you. Metro called; a friend from Maine paid for your property damages."

"Who was that?"

"A professor named 'Riddell'?

"That would be Gene," Peter sighed. Prescott asked Who is Gene?"

"An old friend that taught me many things about myself; he was my mentor."

"Do you see him anymore?"

"Hopefully soon."

"It's good have friends like that."

"There's more. The DA's office is willing to leave the case open for six months, provided that you don't get into any trouble in that time. She'll close the whole thing out."

"You know, doctor, it's time for me to go."

"Where will you go when you leave here?"

"I'll go to see my children, but before I leave DC I have to go Arlington, to see were Gunny Holmes is buried."

"Peter, there's still the situation with the black-outs."

"No there isn't. They're gone."

"We can't be sure of that."

"Doctor Brown, trust me, they're gone. We both know they are. I've almost finished my mission here and time to go So, why don't you sign all the papers to get me out of here while I get dressed? I've got a good idea...why don't you come with me?"

"Where?"

"To the Gunny's grave, and you can come to the wall wile I finish what I came for."

"I really can't do that today."

"Why not?"

"There are rules."

Peter chuckled. "Rules? When the administration finds out about that voodoo you and Dan pulled, you might be standing on some median someplace with a sign that says, "Will work for food."

"What?"

"You heard me. And besides, you know they'll find out, they always do."

"I really don't think I can."

"Look, Prescott, I'm asking you to see me through this. It wouldn't have been possible without you."

"OK. I'll go. I'll get your discharge papers ready. That will take about half an hour. In the meantime, get your things together."

Peter had bought some new clothes from the PX. Nurse Webster came and got Peter to sign some papers. He thanked her for all her help.

All she said was, "That's what I'm here for."

Beth Anne told him 'good luck'. He patted her hand and winked at her. She smiled back.

As Peter and Prescott drove out of the hospital, parking lot Peter started to laugh. Prescott asked what was so funny. "Having you as a doctor is quite an adventure. One day we're driving a half million dollar car at god knows what speed, the next day your trying to drive me crazy from lack of sleep. And *today* I get to ride in a car that was built and designed for the Serengeti, on the streets of DC. Who could ask for more?"

"Does your sarcasm ever end?"

"Probably not, but I think you're going miss it.

A little, maybe."

Prescott smiled back. "Maybe."

He grew quiet for a minute. "Doctor Brown, did I ever tell you about my son?'

"A little."

"He was nine months old when I first saw him. He has piercing blue eyes, and every time I looked at him, it reminded me of how close I came to never seeing him at all. His life and his sister's have not been easy, having me for a father. They're both very intelligent and have good work ethics. And how I do miss them, just being able to hold then when they're in pain or sad."

"You know, it's never too late to start over with them."

"I think looking over them is the best I can do."

They finally got to Arlington. They found the Gunny's grave. Peter stood there for a few minutes, looking down at the markers with the Gunny's name on it. Then he heard the sound of bagpipes in the distance playing 'Amazing Grace'. As peter looked across the field of white crosses that Arlington is so famous for, 'Amazing Grace' was the Gunny's favorite song. But now he wondered, *If their voices could be heard, what would they say?*

Prescott said, "What? What did you just say, Peter?"

"Was I thinking out loud again?"

"I think so."

As they turned to walk away, he asked Prescott, "What do you think they might say? That's what I was thinking."

"I think if we knew that, it might be a saner world."

Peter asked Prescott if he'd ever been there before; Prescott just shook his head. Peter answered he hadn't, either.

As they drove off Prescott asked Peter, "Where to next? Do you want to get your van?"

"No, let's go to the Wall where I started. That's what I'd like for us to do."

"Are you sure you're ready for that?"

"The question is, are you? And besides, maybe this time, before they arrest me, you can tell them I'm cured."

"They'd probably arrest both of us, then."

"Yeah, the Metro doesn't have much of a sense of humor."

"Would you if you were a cop in this town?"

"Good point."

They had good luck finding a parking space on the Mall that day. It was only a short walk to the Wall.

Prescott asked Peter if he thought it ironic that a Viet Namese artist designed it. Peter remarked that he'd heard a lot of vets complaining about it. Personally, he thought it was the best one because to him it looked like a bunker. When they found a parking lot they had to walk half way across the Mall. It was a beautiful day and there were people with children. You could hear music everwhere.

All of a sudden Peter stopped. "Can you hear that?"

Prescott asked, "What was it?"

"The song."

"What song?"

Listen, that's an old Jimmy Clift tune, 'I Can See Clearly Now'. Well, can I?"

"I think maybe we both can."

Prescott nodded his head. As they got closer to the Wall, they were about halfway down the walkway. Peter stopped and stood looking at it. Prescott stood doing the same.

It was a beautiful spring day. The sun was shining and the cherry blossoms were starting to bloom on the Mall. Peter reached into his jean jacket's inside pocket, and pulled out some folded papers. He turned to Prescott, and said quietly, "Doctor Brown, here are the names of two hundred men who did time in Dante's Inferno. I'm asking you to use your money and influence to do right by them and their families."

"I never asked you whose names you were looking for when the Metro hauled you onto our doorstep."

"Do you remember? I was looking for the names on this list. But they're not there, *yet.*"

Prescott unfolded the list; the first name he saw was Peter Davies. He turned to ask Peter where he had gotten the list; the reflection from the sun bounced off the Wall's polished marble. It blinded him for a moment; as his eyes adjusted to the light, Prescott looked over where Peter was just standing. He was gone. He looked frantically to see where he had gone, but there was no sign of him anywhere. He looked at the papers again, and he put them in his pocket and jogged back and forth to find were Peter had gone. The hair on Prescott's neck stood up and out loud he hollered, "Where did you go, you son of a bitch?"

A woman and her child walked past and shook her head about his language. Prescott ignored her. Out of breath and frustrated, he stopped where he and Peter had been standing earlier. He noticed something. On the ground where Peter had been standing was a bronze star, broken in half. Prescott picked it up, looked at it, then looked at the Wall. He put the medal in his pocket with the papers and looked once more to see if he could see Peter, but that wasn't going to happen. Prescott somehow knew that and with that thought he headed home. He looked at the Wall once more. For a moment, he could see the cracks.